ALSO BY JUDITH A. BARRETT

GRID DOWN SURVIVAL SERIES

MAGGIE SLOAN THRILLER SERIES

RILEY MALLOY MYSTERY SERIES

DONUT LADY COZY MYSTERY SERIES

DANGER AT THE FARM

Grid Down Survival

Book 5

Judith A. Barrett

DANGER AT THE FARM

GRID DOWN SURVIVAL, BOOK 5

Published in the United States of America by Wobbly Creek, LLC

2022 Georgia

wobblycreek.com

DANGER AT THE FARM is a work of fiction. Names, characters, businesses, places, events, locales, and incidents either are the products of the author's imagination or used in a fictitious manner. Any resemblance to actual persons, living or dead, or actual events is purely coincidental.

Edited by Judith Euen Davis

Cover by Wobbly Creek, LLC

ISBN 978-1-953-87021-6

DEDICATION

DANGER AT THE FARM is dedicated to the brightness of the sun and to readers who love a good story with great people.

PREVIOUSLY...

STUART

Angel, Red, and I left Major's farm and traveled to Dad's farm in Georgia to help after Dad was injured. We stayed when the attacks on nearby farms became more frequent, so we could help the neighbor families set up roadblocks. Angel and I believed attacks from other gangs would only escalate, and we were right. What I didn't realize was that the attacks weren't random; one of our own was the target of a vendetta. Angel knew, and she and I stopped the obsessed criminal.

I've known since the first day I saw her blue eyes that I would marry Angel; she is the smartest and the most talented girl I've ever known. I was happy to wait until she finally came around to my way of thinking. Angel and I and her best friend, Red, and Andy, the nephew of Dad's neighbors, were married at my folks' farm.

We still need to decide whether we're going to stay in Georgia or return to Major's farm in Florida. Angel doesn't want to leave without Red, and Andy doesn't want to leave his aunt and uncle. I don't see how we can make everyone happy. What do you think, Angel? Do you have anything to add?

AIMEE LOUISE aka ANGEL

I'm good.

ROSALIE aka RED

We have a bunch of people living at the two Georgia farms that are close together. I keep a list of who is where because I like lists, but I realize not everyone else does.

If you are the type, like me, who likes to keep track of names, then I have a list for you. If you'd rather skip my section and jump straight to the story, my feelings won't be hurt. I like non-list people too. I included Pops' farm in Florida because we are a large, extended family, and besides, the list didn't feel complete without them.

<u>Newton Farm</u>

- Sandra and Scott Newton
- Aimee Louise and Stuart Newton, and Henry, who is six years old: he's practically a Newton; I can't leave out Henry's puppy, Brody.
- Rosalie and Andy Webster
- Peyton, David, and Brandon Griffin; Brandon is eight years old, and his puppy is Tracker.
- Cal and Blanche Henderson
- Doc Larkin, and his dog, Ethel

Webster Farm

- Jennie and Leo Webster, my Andy is their nephew; Leo's dogs, Holly and three farm dogs. Nate named one Fire Dog; Leo says the other two are named Farm Dog. They also have three cows, but no one has named them yet.
- Nate, Charo, and Dolly Cabello; Dolly is five years old, and she named her puppy Pixie.
- Judge Rodney Cabello, Nate's dad
- Tom and Lela Mitchell and their twin granddaughters, Sam and Cami Sue, who are six years old. Currently the twins don't have any puppies, but maybe the girls will claim the Farm Dogs or the cows.

Pops' Farm in Florida

- Major and Vanessa Elliott, and Pops' German shepherd, Shadow. Angel and I call him Pops, and so do all the kids.
- Jack, former county sheriff, and Molly Starr and their four children: Annie, who is fourteen, Josh, who is twelve, and the twins Brett and Sara, who are ten.
  - Mr. Young, widower and nearby neighbor who moved to join Pops' farm after the grid went down.

Thanks for sticking with me. You don't have to remember everyone's names or how they're related to each other, but at least you know where a handy reference is. Don't be surprised, though, if we have to shift around to adjust to changes. It all depends on whether Angel and Stuart decide to stay in Georgia or leave for Florida.

CHAPTER ONE

Major shielded his eyes from the rising sun as he peered at the two men carrying rifles who strode down the dirt road from the deputies' house to his. When Shadow trotted toward the gate, one of the men waved and called out, "Hello, the farm. It's Brad and Wally."

Major hurried to open the gate then shook hands with the two deputies. "Molly's got coffee on the stove. Let's go inside."

Wally's face was tight as he shook his head. "We need to talk with you and the sheriff in private."

"I'll tell him, then we'll meet you at the barn."

When Major rounded the corner of the farmhouse, the sheriff, Vanessa, and Mr. Young were drinking their morning coffee on the back porch.

"Need a little help at the barn, Sheriff," Major said.

"What's going on?" Sheriff asked as they strode away from the porch.

"I'm not sure; Brad and Wally are waiting for us there. Wally said they needed to talk to us privately."

After Major and the sheriff reached the barn, Wally said, "Kris's uncle stopped by our place on his way to Tampa to check on his daughter and her husband and family. He was worried because he hasn't heard from them in months. He told Kris he was sorry to bring sad news, but her dad died a month or so ago, and her mother and her sister are alone on their large farm in Alabama. We decided to leave right away and stayed up most of the night to pack; we're ready to go."

"That's a shock; our condolences to Kris," Sheriff said.

"We've been worried about the gangs south of us that are attacking homes and have considered going to Alabama for a while, but this sealed the decision for us; Jim's going too," Brad said. "He's looking forward to seeing Kris's sister again. They're friends from way back."

Wally nodded. "We'll pull out as soon as we get back. We just wanted you to know we're leaving. We packed as much as we could then slept a few hours. Russell had a lot of equipment in the attic that might interest you, and you may want to check before the scavengers realize we're gone."

"We left two boxes of books in the living room for you that Heather and I thought would interest you. Heather's box has mostly medical and nursing reference books, and I loaded up a box with paperbacks that I think the boys will enjoy," Brad said.

"What can we do? Do you need more gas? We have a little extra," Major said.

"We've got plenty of gas to get there, and it's getting old, so we might as well use it up. Jim went into town to see if he could find any radios; we'll leave as soon as he gets back. We'll get in touch when we can."

"God speed," Sheriff said as the men shook hands.

Major and Sheriff continued to watch the deputies until they were no longer in sight.

Major exhaled. "Sure hate to see them go. Pastor John and Chuck have been talking about leaving too because their father is ill."

"I didn't know that; we'll have to check on them," Sheriff said.

When they went into the kitchen, Molly tossed her curly dark-blond hair and put her hands on her ample hips. "Where are Brad and Wally? Didn't you invite them to stay for breakfast?"

"They had to get back; we can talk after everyone's at the table," Sheriff said.

While everyone ate, Major said, "The deputies and their families are on their way to Alabama. They're going to help Kris's family on their farm."

"Will they be coming back soon?" Sara asked.

"No, they are moving there to stay," Sheriff said. "Major and I will go to their house after breakfast; Wally said there is a lot of equipment in the attic that they didn't have time or room to pack, and there might be some things we can use."

"Let me know if you need me to drive a trailer there for you; otherwise, I need to stay. Molly and I hoped to get most of the canning done before it gets too hot." Vanessa pushed her brown hair with its silvery streaks away from her face with the back of her hand.

Sheriff coughed, and Major nodded as he sipped his coffee.

When everyone rose to clear their dishes, Mr. Young said, "If you adults could hold up just a minute, Annie has our morning ham radio report."

After Josh, Brett, and Sara cleared their plates and headed to the door, Josh stopped before they left. "We're excused, right?"

Molly nodded, and the three youngsters bolted out the door.

Annie said, "The hams have been talking about the gangs. No one thinks they're organized, but there are a lot of them swarming the countryside and looting."

Mr. Young added, "A big part of the problem is the city water and sewer systems have finally failed from lack of electricity. Most of the people who had relatives in small towns left the cities last year, but more people are on the road now with whatever they can carry. One ham said his cousin and family were headed north on foot from Miami to come to his place outside of Orlando."

Molly frowned. "That's a long journey, but what about our water? Is it safe?"

"We have a really deep well, Molly; our water is fine, and our septic isn't dependent on electricity to pump away the waste from our toilets. We've been careful about washing hands and staying clean because we have a reliable source of water," Major said.

Mr. Young nodded. "We use our gray water to flush the toilets."

"Is that a camping term?" Vanessa asked.

Mr. Young chuckled. "Sure enough: it's water that was used to rinse or wash dishes, clothes, or hands; water that flushes waste from the toilet is black water."

"So, that's why we pour bathwater and water from the kitchen sink into the toilet," Molly said. "I thought we were just being efficient by not hauling up extra water from the well."

"It's been a few years since we've heard of anything even remotely like cholera; we'll be fine, won't we?" Vanessa asked.

"Yes and no," Mr. Young said. "Our water is safe, but the gangs are a real threat to travelers and to vulnerable homes."

"Are we a vulnerable home now that the deputies have left?" asked Molly.

Mr. Young furrowed his brow. "They were a good buffer for us, and we were a good backup for them. So far, it sounds like there have been only a few home invasions near us, but our information is skimpy. Some of the hams are going to contact relatives in other places to see how they are faring."

After breakfast, Sheriff asked, "Would you like to go along, Annie?"

"Can I learn to hitch the trailer to the truck?" Annie asked.

"I think that's a good idea," Major said. "Sheriff?"

"Go ahead; it'll be nice to have another driver who can manage a trailer."

Annie quickened her pace to keep up with Major's long stride.

Major smiled. "We'll walk around the truck first, then you can hop into the driver's seat, and I'll guide you with hand signals. After you've hooked up the trailer, you can drive the truck to your old house."

"Really?" Annie beamed.

"I'm going to run on ahead; see you there." The sheriff jogged to the end of the driveway then picked up his pace when he reached the road.

"Dad wants to stay in practice in case Red and Aimee Louise come back," Annie said.

Major smiled. *Good luck, Sheriff.*

Annie hopped into the driver's seat and grumbled as she moved the seat forward, "Everybody's taller than me except the twins, and Brett's catching up."

"Don't let Dead Eye Red hear you say that," Major chuckled. "Your dad left the gate open for us, so after we're on the road, stop, and I'll close it."

After Annie backed the trailer to the truck hitch, she joined Major at the back of the truck; he taught her how to secure the hitch, then they climbed into the truck.

"I'm nervous about going through the gate then making the turn onto the road." Annie bit her lip. "What if I hit the gate with the trailer or drive into the ditch?"

"You'll do great; we'll take it slow, and I'll talk you through it."

Annie held her breath as she cleared the gate and completed the turn. When she parked at the deputies' house, she exhaled.

Major chuckled. "Were you holding your breath the entire time?"

"Not quite, but close." Annie's cheeks reddened as she smiled.

Sheriff waited for them on the porch; after he and Major went inside, Sheriff pulled down the attic stairs and climbed up. Major listened to the footsteps as the sheriff stepped carefully around the attic.

Sheriff returned to the stair opening. "Russell stored his solar panels up here, and I see two deep cycle solar batteries."

"We could certainly use them. Mr. Young brought some batteries with him, but we never got around to picking up any solar panels when they were available."

"I'll hand the panels down first. I'll have to bring down the batteries one at a time; they aren't boxed up. Knowing Russell, I suspect there are some inverters somewhere too. I'll look."

Sheriff handed down each panel from the attic to Major, who carried them to the living room.

After all the panels and batteries were loaded onto the trailer, Sheriff said, "I brought down the two inverters I found and raised the attic stairs back into place. There were some rolls of insulation in the attic, but I couldn't see where we'd have any use for them."

"I don't either," Major said. "Annie loaded the two boxes of books while I loaded panels. Are you ready to go?"

Sheriff locked the door behind them. "I'm not sure I'm ready to run back. I need to run more regularly."

"Do you want me to drive, Annie?" Major glanced at her tear-stained face.

Annie cleared her throat. "I'm fine; it was sad to see Mom and Dad's house so empty, and…" She brushed away a stray tear, "they weren't there, but I need to be able to drive no matter what, right?" Annie sniffled as she climbed into the driver's seat.

When Major glanced his way, Sheriff nodded.

She's as strong as Aimee Louise and Rosalie. "You're probably right," Major said. "You want to ride up front, Sheriff? I'll ride in back."

"Thanks, Major. Are you sure?"

"I'm positive; I need the time to think, and I know Annie will be happy to show you how well she's doing."

Sheriff nodded. "We'll talk when we get back."

After Annie parked the truck at Major's farm, Sheriff said, "Very well done. Thanks for all your help."

Annie beamed. "I'll check in with Mom. If she doesn't need me, I have some work to do in my greenhouse."

Mr. Young and Josh joined them at the barn.

"Reporting in," Mr. Young said. "All was quiet."

"Thanks, you're relieved of guard duty," Major said.

Mr. Young smiled before he left for the house. "We were excused from canning duty while you were gone."

Josh nodded. "Guard duty was more fun."

While Major, Sheriff, and Josh unloaded the truck into the barn, Sheriff said, "Josh and I can run to check on Pastor John and his family after lunch. Molly's been asking me how they're doing, but a visit hasn't been a priority."

Major nodded. "I'd like to go too, but I don't want to wear out Mr. Young; he'll take his usual nap if I'm here."

Sheriff nodded. "He's slowing down, but his afternoon nap always recharges him."

After they unloaded the truck, Sheriff and Josh carried the two boxes of books to the house while Major parked his truck in its usual spot.

* * *

When Sheriff and Josh reached the back porch, Molly and Vanessa had the large portable propane stove fired up and ready to can the next batch of jars. Mr. Young rocked in his chair and sipped a glass of water. "Molly told me I'm in charge of watching the burner. Best job I've ever had."

"I need to be your trainee," Josh said.

Mr. Young chuckled. "We'll have to put that on our list."

Sheriff inhaled as he and Josh carried the boxes inside. "Chicken soup. Yum."

Molly continued to stir the large pot on the stove. "What's in the boxes?"

"Heather left some medical and nursing books, and Brad packed some paperbacks for the boys."

"Sara and I might like to look at the nursing books." Vanessa filled canning jars then put lids and bands on them.

After the sheriff and Josh set down the boxes near the great room window, Josh hurried out to help with the chickens and goats.

"I hate that they're gone." Molly sighed. "I'm sorry they have such a long trip ahead of them. Did they say when they expect to get there?"

"I don't think they know. They should be able to make it in a day if they don't run into any trouble. Jim went into town early this morning to get any radios that might still be in the sheriff's office; they'll try to get word to us after they're settled."

"While Vanessa cans the last batch of venison, I'll get lunch started. Would you let everyone know we'll be eating soon?"

"Sure will. After lunch, maybe Josh and I will check on Pastor John and Chuck," Sheriff said.

"I'd appreciate it; take a couple of jars of venison with you."

Sheriff nodded as he left to spread the word about lunch. He found Josh, Brett, and Sara weeding the garden. "Lunch will be ready soon; Josh would you run to the barn and tell Major while I look for Annie in the greenhouse?"

When the sheriff went into the greenhouse, Annie was adjusting her watering system.

"My rain barrel has plenty of water, but the flow has slowed. I need to see if something is partially blocking the tubing somewhere." She brushed her hands on her jeans. "Brett said he'd help me check the system this afternoon."

After lunch, Sheriff and Josh grabbed their backpacks and rifles before they left for Pastor John's. Major and Shadow waited for them in front of the barn.

"We're ready to go, Major," Sheriff said. "You can set the pace, Josh. If it's too fast for me, I'll tell you."

Shadow trotted to Josh, and Major chuckled. "I guess Shadow's going with you."

Josh started off slow to warm up, just like Aimee Louise had taught him then increased his speed with Shadow at his side and his dad keeping the pace behind them. When they reached the state road, they stopped in the shade of the trees alongside the road.

Aimee Louise's rule about no talking while running serves us well. I'm out of breath. Sheriff scanned the road in both directions then nodded, and Josh and Shadow darted across the road. Sheriff waited a moment then followed them.

When Sheriff, Josh, and Shadow neared Pastor John's house, they stopped in the brush. Josh and Shadow stayed low while Sheriff crept to the edge of the trees for a better look. Sheriff whistled the cardinal call, and Josh and Shadow joined him.

Sheriff scanned the house while a mockingbird trilled a repertoire of songs, and a hawk swooped down then flew away with a snake in its talons.

Sheriff whispered, "No vehicles; no goats."

Josh nodded.

Sheriff waited a few more minutes. "If there's shooting, or I'm in trouble, run tell Major."

Josh bit his lip then nodded.

Sheriff motioned for Shadow to follow him as he quietly walked into the open then toward the house. When he reached the front porch, he saw a weathered slip of paper taped to the door: "Sheriff, be back soon."

He stuffed the note into his pocket then tried the door; it was unlocked. When he went inside, Shadow stayed on the porch.

Furniture is intact; bookshelves are picked over. He went into the kitchen. *Pantry is empty; cupboards and drawers are mostly empty.*

He checked the bedrooms downstairs and upstairs. *Beds are gone; house even feels empty.*

He found a note on the dining room table: "Dad is not well; we're going to move Mom and Dad to the old farmstead where it's safer. Take what you can use. Blessings, John & Chuck. p.s. Will avoid Atlanta. Not safe."

Sheriff folded the note and stuck it into his pocket before he stepped to the front door and whistled for Josh.

When Josh joined him, Sheriff said, "They left, but I don't know when. I don't think there's anything in the house that we could use, but we should check the barn."

Before they left the porch, Sheriff locked the house door.

"Wow," Josh said as they walked into the barn, "There's a lot of stuff here."

"Here's a utility wagon; let's load it with things we know we can use."

"This looks like the wire on the antenna." Josh picked up a large coil of wire and dropped it into the wagon. He opened a drawer. "These are brand new boxes of screws and nails. Annie would love these."

"I found two rolls of field fencing still wrapped in plastic," Sheriff said.

After they put more items into the cart, Sheriff said, "It's not full, but it would be too heavy if we put much of anything else in it. I'll pull the cart; stay out of sight and cover me."

When they neared the state road, they drank water from their canteens then gave some to Shadow.

Sheriff scanned the road then said quietly, "Go."

Josh and Shadow raced across the road, then Josh knelt on the other side in the trees. Sheriff examined the road again before he pulled the large cart to the trees.

"Whew, sure am glad we didn't put anything else in our cart." Sheriff wiped his damp forehead with his shirtsleeve. "I'll lead again; cover me."

When they neared the farmhouse, Sheriff said, "Find Major, and I'll meet you in the barn."

When Major joined him in the barn, Sheriff handed the note to Major. "Pastor John and Chuck left."

Major read the note and shook his head. "If I remember right, Pastor John's family is in South Carolina." Major turned the note over. "No date."

"This note was on the front door." Sheriff pulled the crumpled note out of his pocket.

Major smoothed out the paper and read the note then turned it over and raised his eyebrows. "It's dated. This is over six weeks ago." He exhaled. "Show me what you brought back."

After they went through the contents, Sheriff asked, "Do we want to ask Mr. Young what else might be there that we could use?"

"We can ask him, but it would have to be something that would make it worth the risk of another trip."

As they strolled to the farmhouse, Sheriff said, "That's true. We can't afford anyone getting hurt or worse."

"We're down to four shooters: you, me, Annie, and Josh with no backup close to us at all. Plainview's a ghost town since the water system failed; at least people got out early before disease could set in like the cities. Mr. Young can wave a shotgun, but he'd be the first to admit his eyesight's become almost as bad as his hearing," Major said.

"So, what do we do?"

"Let's call a porch meeting and talk about it this evening after supper."

"Kids too?" Sheriff asked.

Major nodded. "I think so; we don't want them to worry about what might be wrong if we try to leave them out."

As the sheriff headed toward the door, Major added, "If Annie's available, I'd like to empty the wagon and could use her help organizing it."

Sheriff stopped by the greenhouse.

"Hey, Dad. Brett helped me find some debris in the line from the cistern to my watering system, and we cleared it out. I'm just checking a few connections, then I'll be done."

"That's good news; you've done a great job with your greenhouse."

"Thanks, Dad." Annie's cheeks reddened.

"When you're finished, Major and Josh brought back supplies from Pastor John's house. He's emptying the wagon and would like for you to help him organize the items."

"I have two more connections to check, then I'll go help him."

After Major and Annie finished organizing the barn, Major said, "I thought we'd just put those few things away, but the barn was really a mess, wasn't it?"

When they strolled into the kitchen, Vanessa put her hands on her hips. "Where have you been all day?"

He shook his head. "It's Annie's fault. I wanted to put away a few things, but we ended up organizing the entire barn, and now I don't have any excuse for spending an uninterrupted, peaceful morning trying to find the right bolt."

"Two days," Vanessa said. "I give you two days to get it back to your normal chaos."

Mr. Young asked, "Is that a bet? I'll take one day."

Annie snickered.

"No betting," Molly said, "but if we were, I'd take a half day, and everybody needs to wash for supper."

"I'll take two hours." The sheriff came into the kitchen. "What are we betting on?"

"Nothing. Find the two boys and Sara to wash for supper," Molly said.

"I will." Annie and Shadow dashed out the back door then returned with the three younger children.

CHAPTER TWO

While everyone ate, Major said, "After the dishes are done, and Annie and Mr. Young have given us their radio report, we'll have a meeting on the back porch."

"Everybody?" Sara asked.

Sheriff nodded. "Everybody."

Brett elbowed Josh. "Must be important."

After everyone gathered on the back porch, Mr. Young asked, "Is it okay if we give our radio report first?"

When Major nodded, Annie said, "The hams have more reports of attacks on homes in small towns and out in the country."

"The Miami, Tampa, and now Orlando areas have been hit hard in Florida, and the same news is coming in about Atlanta and Savannah in Georgia," Mr. Young said. "We suspect the same is probably true nationwide."

"Do we know how the rest of the world is faring?" Vanessa asked.

"No one has heard anything yet," Annie said.

"Our educated guess is that it's world-wide," Mr. Young said.

"Is there something we need to do?" Molly asked.

"Our water is fine, but we don't have anyone nearby," Major said.

"Which brings us to our next problem," Sheriff said. "The deputies and their families left this morning for Alabama; Josh and I went to Pastor John's today to check on them, and they left about six weeks ago."

Molly narrowed her eyes. "That means we don't have anyone we can call on for help."

"The attacks have stopped, and we're not too close to the interstate, so we'll be fine, right?" Vanessa asked.

"We haven't seen any attacks lately, but we have to be ready," Major said. "We don't have enough people to set up a twenty-four-hour watch or enough sharpshooters to defend the farmhouse."

"We have plenty of people who can shoot," Vanessa said as she counted on her fingers. "Major, Sheriff, Mr. Young, Annie, and me."

Josh cleared his throat.

"Sorry, Josh," Vanessa said, "and Josh makes six."

"No offense, Vanessa, but Mr. Young is a good backup with his shotgun, but his eyesight isn't what it used to be, and I've never seen you shoot a gun," Sheriff said.

Vanessa scowled. "I'm sure I could. All I have to do is pull the trigger."

"You're more like me," Molly said. "Sheriff taught me to shoot years ago, but I don't care to relearn in a stressful situation where the family's survival depends on me."

"We actually have three shooters who can protect the family; Josh is good with his bolt action rifle and would be willing to help," Mr. Young said.

"That's not good enough." Vanessa raised her voice.

"You're exactly right," Major said, "and that's why we're having this hard conversation."

"You could teach me to shoot," Vanessa said. "You've taught Rosalie, Annie, Josh, Brett, and Sara."

"You're right, but we took our time; their training began over a year ago," Major said. "We don't have that kind of time."

"Do we need to build some barriers, so we're more of a fortress or a castle? Annie can build anything," Sara said.

Sheriff raised his eyebrows. "That's definitely something we should consider, Sara. We need to look at where we should beef up our perimeter, and how we could do it."

"We could get more people who can shoot," Brett said. "I think Aimee Louise, Stuart, Red, and Red's new husband, Andy, should come here."

Major smiled at Brett. "Very good."

"We may not be close to the interstate, but the highway from Tampa north is almost a straight shot because it isn't that far from us. We need to go somewhere safer," Molly said.

"Right," Mr. Young said.

"All the good ideas are taken," Vanessa grumbled, then her eyes twinkled. "Whatever we do, we need to remember pizza, right, Josh?"

Josh grinned, and Brett and Mr. Young cheered and fist-bumped.

Major chuckled. "You have a great point: we don't have a source for cheese anymore since Vicki left with her milk goats."

"If Aimee Louise were here, she'd say, 'Everything,'" Molly said.

"Exactly," the sheriff said. "Now we just need to put the pieces together."

"I think we ask Aimee Louise how to put the pieces together," Annie said.

Mr. Young nodded. "First thing in the morning, we can ask."

"What do we need to do in the meantime?" Molly asked.

"I have tomatoes that are ready to be picked. They could be canned," Annie said.

"If we go off Heather's basic list she gave us a while ago, we start with clothes, food, medical supplies, hand tools, guns, and ammo," Major said.

"Thinking about clothes, we've got a stack of dirty laundry. Could we spare enough gasoline to run the generator for washing clothes? We don't have to dry them because we can hang them on the clothesline to dry," Molly said. "I think we have four loads or five, which would take about three hours to wash."

"We could do that," Major said.

"Annie and I could go out early tomorrow morning to see if we can harvest a deer," Sheriff said.

Major nodded. "I'll fill in on the radio with Mr. Young in the morning."

"Brett and I could go through the storage closet upstairs to find medical supplies," Sara said.

"I'll take care of the chickens and goats while you do that," Josh said.

"Let's reconvene at lunch tomorrow for updates," Major said.

After everyone had gone to bed, Major and Vanessa rocked together on the back porch. She scooted her chair closer to his, and he reached for her hand.

"Have you ever heard the whole is greater than the sum of the parts? This family proved it again tonight," he said.

"Ooo, you're quoting Aristotle? I didn't know you had any philosophical thoughts in you." Vanessa snickered. "Just kidding; it was amazing to hear all the ideas that attacked the problem in different directions. Which idea was your favorite?"

Major chuckled. "Hands-down, yours. It was the most offbeat thing I've ever heard you say, and it was brilliant. We can have food, clothes, safety, medical supplies, guns, and ammo, but if we don't have fun, we're done."

Vanessa giggled as she rose and pulled him to his feet. "Let's go to bed, old man, and I'll show you my fun side."

* * *

The next morning, Major quietly dressed in the dark then carried his boots to the kitchen. He stepped into his boots then poured himself a cup of coffee before he joined Molly and Mr. Young on the back porch. "Good morning, early birds."

"Good morning, Major," Mr. Young said.

"We were too slow to be the early birds this morning. The hunters slipped out of here at least two hours ago," Molly said. "I offered to make coffee, but my man said he didn't want any doe to smell his coffee breath. I didn't know whether to be worried or jealous."

"We were just talking about the deputies, Major," Mr. Young said. "When Kris got that scare a while ago when someone tried to snatch the babies, her first reaction was to leave the house. Do you know what happened? Why didn't they move to Pastor John's after all?"

"Wally was smart," Major said. "He took her to visit Pastor John, and Vickie was so excited to have company that she gave Kris a tour of the house."

"Smart man." Mr. Young nodded. "My old house was perfect for Pastor John, Chuck, and their families. I couldn't see how two more families with babies could fit in."

"I didn't know Wally had arranged a visit. If they had no other choice, they'd have made it work, but both groups were settled in and comfortable in their own homes," Molly said. "How did you adjust from living alone for years to this unruly mob in your house, Major?"

Major chuckled then downed his coffee. "I have no idea how I survived so long without the commotion and all these people to tell me what to do."

He peered into his cup. "I'll be right back with the coffee pot."

When Major came out with the hot coffee, Molly cleared her throat, and Mr. Young sighed. "Not for me."

While Major refilled his and Molly's cups, Molly said, "I don't know what we'll do when we run out of coffee. What we've been drinking this past year is two years out of date. I don't think we'll last another year, and I'm totally clueless on a substitute. We'll have to switch to tea."

"Make it weaker each week," Mr. Young said. "We'll never know."

"I can't do that." Molly smirked.

"Understood," Mr. Young said.

"Is this what y'all do every morning? Plot against the rest of us?" Major asked when he returned from putting back the coffee pot on the stove.

"You're one of us, now, Major," Mr. Young chuckled. "After you finish that cup, let's—"

Mr. Young was interrupted by a rifle shot.

"That was Annie's rifle," Major said. "Dang it. We need to get on the radio. Molly, keep us posted. They may be tracking the deer for a while because sometimes the animals run into the brush a few yards before they drop."

"I'm excited for her," Molly said. "That makes two this season. Mr. Young, I want to help process the deer; it's something I can do for her."

"She'll love it." Mr. Young's knees creaked as he rose from his chair then headed to the door.

When Major and Mr. Young sat at the radio, Mr. Young said, "Annie and I leave the radio on these settings; if you prefer different settings, feel free to change them."

"Will you take the driver's seat? I'm rusty," Major said.

Mr. Young nodded then signed on. When he reached the contact he'd been calling, Major grabbed Annie's notebook and jotted down the ham's call sign.

Mr. Young said, "I need to chat with Angel. Anybody got her ear?"

Major smiled. *The old timers are sticklers for call signs, but everybody knows Angel.*

A ham said, "I'll get back to you in five."

Mr. Young smiled. "She'll be on in five minutes."

"Care for more coffee?" Major asked.

"Not for me; Molly has cut me off at one cup a day, and it doesn't do me any good to argue with her."

Major came back to the radio room with his full cup and took his seat as Aimee Louise came on the radio.

"Mr. Angel there too?" Mr. Young asked.

"He said Archangel is here," Aimee Louise said.

Mr. Young snickered and offered the microphone to Major.

"We need your ideas to help us find a good resolution for a problem," Major said. "The deputies and Pastor John's family have left. We have only two experienced shooters and need to rebuild our community quickly."

"We have a solid community of shooters and are not near any primary highways. Your community is here," Aimee Louise said.

Major frowned. "We should come there?"

"How many drivers do you have who can pull a trailer in tow?" Aimee Louise asked.

"Two." Major glanced at Mr. Young, who nodded.

"You and Sheriff; your drivers are also your shooters," Aimee Louise said. "We will come get you. We can bring two of the large transport trucks, and you can pull one trailer with a driver and a shooter."

"Can we talk tonight?" Major asked.

"Yes, unless the skip is bad, then we'll talk in the morning. We'll be prepared to leave before first light tomorrow."

After Major signed off, Mr. Young removed his glasses and rubbed his face. "That certainly took a turn I didn't expect."

"I guess we'll have a meeting after Sheriff and Annie return," Major said.

"I'll be in the kitchen in a minute; I need to catch up on the regular news. I may skip the meeting, so I can clean and strip the deer for canning," Mr. Young said. "I'll go along with whatever you and Sheriff decide, but Aimee Louise's logic makes sense to me."

"I'm not sure I'm ready to leave the farm," Major said. "There has to be another way."

"I suggest you and the sheriff hash this out before you present any options to the rest of the family. Let me know how I can help."

Major stood in the doorway. "After the sheriff and I talk, I'll help you with Annie's deer."

"I could use the help." Mr. Young turned back to the radio.

Major strode to the barn for the utility wagon then headed toward the woods where Annie and the sheriff had gone to hunt.

When he reached the edge of the woods, he shouted, "Sheriff! Annie!"

Annie shouted excitedly, "Pops, I got a buck!"

"I'm bringing a wagon," he called out.

Sheriff came to meet him. "Major, she got a huge, nine-point buck. She's sitting with him; we dragged then rested. I should have thought of the cart, but both of us were excited. We'll have to save the antlers for her."

Sheriff led the way; Major smiled at Annie's beaming face. "I got a buck, Pops."

"I see that; he's a beauty."

Annie nodded. "I thanked him for helping me to feed the family." A tear slid down her cheek.

"He dropped right where she shot him," Sheriff said.

Sheriff and Major half-lifted and half-dragged the buck into the cart. Sheriff pulled the cart, and after Annie gave her rifle to Major, she pushed.

When they reached the house, Major said, "Hear the hum of the generator? Molly's already at work."

Molly ran out to meet them, and Mr. Young waited on the porch.

"Annie, that is an awesome animal. He'll feed the family for months. Mr. Young said he and Major will help you strip the meat while Vanessa and I prepare for canning." Molly hugged Annie. "Congratulations, sweetheart. I'm so proud of you."

After Annie went inside, Molly cocked her head as she peered at the sheriff. "You didn't even take your deer rifle."

Sheriff smiled. "It was her hunt. I took a rifle that was more defensive."

"You're a good dad." Molly's eyes welled up; she abruptly turned to go inside, but the sheriff stopped her with a hug.

"Thanks, sweetheart." He kissed her lightly, and her face reddened.

"Let's get the deer hung up," Major said.

Sheriff pulled and Major pushed the cart to the back of the barn, and Mr. Young followed them.

While Major and Sheriff raised the deer for cleaning, Mr. Young said, "I came along to tell you what the hams said this morning after you left, Major. I didn't want to say anything earlier because I knew Molly would panic. There are more than just desperate people headed our way. A ham from Ft. Lauderdale said that an organized group, almost like an army, was sweeping towns for food, fuel, ammunition, and guns. He said they are murdering whoever is in their way, stripping houses bare, and in many cases, burning neighborhoods behind them. He's south of Orlando and said he got away just ahead of them. According to him, this army seemed to be using the interstate as a base as they invade the countryside. He thought they started in Miami and are headed north. This was just one report, but I thought it was worth following because if it's true, we need to know how fast they are traveling."

Sheriff furrowed his brow. "Thank you for not saying anything until we have confirmation. I'd rather not scare Molly needlessly; she's been under a lot of strain."

Mr. Young nodded then trudged back to the house.

Sheriff shook his head. "A man Mr. Young's age should be enjoying his retirement. He carries more than his share of burdens."

Major explained what Aimee Louise said and talked about his reluctance to leave.

Sheriff exhaled. "Whatever we decide, both of us need to be behind it one hundred percent, right?"

Major nodded. "Tell me what your gut says."

"My initial reaction is that it is logical, but it would be, wouldn't it, coming from Aimee Louise?"

"I agree it's logical. Do you see any alternatives?" Major asked.

"Everyone who lived in the county knows we have resources, and if everyone knows, the whole world knows. Even if the deputies and Pastor John had stuck around, we'd still be a target."

"You're right; I've been around here for a long time, so everyone knows where I live; you're the sheriff, and everyone knows you moved here with your family: more targets," Major said.

Sheriff nodded and gazed at the deer. "I'm not the sheriff anymore; I need to leave the sheriff thing behind."

Major raised his eyebrows. "I hadn't thought of that: just the name alone makes you a target. We'll have to work on calling you Jack."

Sheriff grinned. "Or Mr. Molly."

Major guffawed. "I dare you to tell her that."

"Ha." Sheriff snorted. "I'd be afraid she'd like it, and I'd be stuck."

"So, Jack, do we tell Aimee Louise and her band to stay in Georgia or go when they roar up to our gate?" Major asked.

"What do you think?"

Major sighed. "I wish I could think of a way we could stay here, but it's best for the family to go, and the only way to do it quickly is with the transport trucks. I guess I'm ready for a new adventure with my old friend, Jack."

As they strode to the house, Jack said, "Do me a favor and call me Jack every time you think of it. It will help everyone else get used to it."

"Will do, Jack. Let's grab some breakfast, then after we tell the family what's going on, we have the perfect excuse to escape: Mr. Young needs our help butchering the venison."

When they went into the house, Mr. Young sat at the table with Annie, whose eyes twinkled as she ate her breakfast.

"Thought you got lost. Wash your hands, and your breakfast will be on the table," Molly said.

When they returned, Major said, "Molly, we'll need another quick family meeting after we eat, right, Jack?"

Molly's eyes widened. "Is that part of the meeting?"

"Yes, ma'am." Jack poured honey on his pancakes.

"I'll alert the troops," Mr. Young said. "We'll meet you on the back porch."

After they ate and cleared their dishes, Major and Jack strode to the back porch.

"I'm on washer duty," Vanessa said, "so if I need to run inside to empty the washer and reload it, you're not allowed to say anything until I get back."

"I'll catch you up," Molly said. "Would that work?"

Vanessa nodded.

Jack said, "When we talked last night about our options, do you remember that after everyone presented great ideas, Annie said Aimee Louise could put the pieces together?"

"Of course, we do," Vanessa said.

"Annie was right," Major said. "I talked to Aimee Louise this morning; after she listened to me, she put all the pieces together."

"She came up with something logical and obvious," Annie said.

Major smiled. "Right again, Annie. We need barriers, more people, to be not so close to the highways, and we need pizza."

Sara nodded. "When do we leave for Georgia?"

Everyone stared at Sara. "What?" she asked. "It's logical. Do they have goats and chickens?"

"They have cows and chickens," Major said.

"Hey, if we take our goats, and they have cows, we can have pizza and ice cream in Georgia; we're in, right, Brett?" Josh elbowed Brett, who nodded.

"That's not logical," Sara said. "How are you going to make ice cream in Georgia?"

"It's north of here, right? So, it must be colder there," Brett said. "Mr. Young will figure it out."

Molly rolled her eyes, and Mr. Young said, "Maybe slushy ice cream."

"To answer Sara's question about when, Aimee Louise, Stuart, Rosalie, and Andy will leave tomorrow morning to come help us move to Georgia," Jack said. "They'll drive two large transport trucks."

"Wow, that's awesome," Brett said.

"I've really got to get busy now," Vanessa said. "The laundry needs to be drying on the line."

"I'll have everything ready to can the venison as soon as you get the meat to me." Molly rose.

"There's one more thing before everyone runs off. The sheriff is a target for bad guys because we call him sheriff," Major said.

"Then let's quit. Are you okay if we call you Jack, honey?" Molly asked.

"We can still call you Dad, though, right?" Sara asked.

"Yes, please call me Jack or Dad." Jack smiled.

"Okay, Dad. I gotta go." Vanessa dashed into the house, and Molly followed her.

"We've got the chickens, goats, and garden," Josh said.

"I'll get you started with the deer, then if you don't need me, I'll help Molly," Mr. Young said.

"I'll help Mom too," Annie said.

The children scattered as Jack and Major walked along with Mr. Young to the barn at Mr. Young's pace.

After the men carved out three good-sized roasts and the smaller tenderloins, Major carried the large roasts, and Mr. Young carried the smaller pieces to the kitchen.

On their way, Mr. Young said, "I'd like to go to my old farm. Now that I've been thinking about what we could use, I'm wondering if John and Chuck left my old horse trailer. It would give us a trailer that's enclosed that we could start packing today. I've also been thinking about the extra propane tanks I had. That might be something else they didn't take that we could use. I'd feel comfortable using my old truck to pull that trailer. I've done it for years We could take my truck; it's already camouflaged with rust and peeling paint. I wouldn't mind checking the house again; I've still got my truck and house keys on my keyring."

Major chuckled. "We'll go as soon as we get all the meat stripped and to our canning experts."

After an hour, Major and Jack had the deer stripped. Major said, "I'd like to take the innards to the west pasture where Carl can find them. He's the coyote with a notched ear that Rosalie watched on the game camera."

Jack chuckled. "I'll take the bones inside for Molly to roast for our spoiled dogs."

"You mean our spoiled oven guard dogs," Major said as he loaded the offal into his gut bucket then put the bucket into the wagon.

"If anyone is free inside, I'll send them out to go along. The kids will get a kick out of taking a treat to Carl," Jack said.

As Major pulled the wagon to the west pasture, Josh and Brett caught up with him.

"Can we pull the wagon, Pops?" Josh asked. "We didn't know Dead Eye Red had a coyote named Carl. We'd like to help leave Carl his treat."

Major smiled. *I'll bet they'll brag about feeding Carl when they see Rosalie.*

When they reached the west pasture fence, Major said, "This is where Red always saw Carl."

Josh frowned. "Do we dump out the bucket or spread it around?"

Brett added, "We want to do it right."

"Just dump it right out. It'll be gone by morning."

On the way back, Josh said, "We want to study coyotes. Do we have any books we can read?"

"I'm not sure, but I'll bet Mr. Young will know."

Brett nodded. "Mr. Young knows everything. You just have to get his attention, so he can hear you."

Before they reached the farm, Josh said, "Me and Brett were wondering when we'd get our shooting practice this week. We're kind of worried that we might have to skip it."

"We're not skipping it; it's important to stay sharp. After we get back, find Sara and bring your rifles to the barn, then we'll go to our shooting range."

As soon as they were at the farm, Josh and Brett ran to the house, and Major took the bones to Molly.

"I'm taking Josh, Brett, and Sara out for our weekly shooting practice. We'll be back in a bit," he said.

Molly turned on the oven and placed as many bones as she could on two cookie sheets then popped them into the oven.

"That's fine, and you won't have to worry about where the dogs are because I have a feeling that Shadow and Penny are going to be my best friends for the rest of the day," she chuckled.

Josh, Brett, and Sara joined Major as he headed to the back door. As the four of them walked to the shooting range, Major smiled. *They're carrying their rifles just like Jack and I taught them. I'll bet Jack is as proud as I am.*

After they set up their targets, Brett and Sara watched while Josh shot his new deer rifle.

When they checked his target, Josh beamed. "I'm improving, Pops."

"You certainly are. You want to take your target back to show your dad?"

"Heck, yeah." Josh removed his paper target from the board then they all walked back.

"It's my turn to go second," Sara said, and Major nodded.

She took her time and carefully aimed her .22 with each shot. "That felt better, and I didn't close my eyes once," she said.

"I think you'll be pleased with your shots," Major said as they all walked to her target.

"That's my best ever. I can take mine too, can't it?"

"Sure can; it's great to celebrate every success and let others celebrate with you," Major said.

Sara beamed as she removed her target.

"You're up, Brett," Major said. "I like how y'all rotate positions when we shoot."

"It was Mr. Young's idea," Sara said. "He's very smart."

Brett stepped to the line and took his shooting position then whispered, "Relax," as he exhaled. He aimed then shot his .22.

When he finished, he lowered his rifle, and Major said, "Let's check."

They all walked to check his target, and Brett beamed then glanced at Major, who nodded.

Brett removed his target. "I can't wait to show Dad too."

"Can you clean your guns without me after we get back?" Major asked.

Josh nodded, and Sara said, "Of course, we can; it's your rule."

Major raised his eyebrows. *I didn't know that, but I think Sara might be right.*

"Remember it's important to carry your rifles when you go anywhere," Major said on the way back to the house.

After shooting practice, Major found Jack stacking boxes of ammunition in the hallway. "I thought I had more, but this is it, Major," Jack said. "Molly already told me she'll organize the food we'll take. I'll attack the tool shed next."

"I have ammo, and I'm certain Mr. Young does too, so we'll add ours. Mr. Young and I are going to his old house. If his horse trailer is there, we'll bring it back. It would be nice to have an enclosed trailer to transport our supplies. We're hoping two old men in an old truck won't draw all that much attention."

"I'll let everyone else know and put Annie and Josh on watch duty until you get back," Jack said.

When Major reached Mr. Young's truck, Mr. Young was in the driver's seat. "I figured you could be my driver trainer and let me know if I'm safe to drive any long distances. I'm comfortable with my old truck, so we'll see how my sight does driving. If I go into a ditch, I'll turn over the wheel to you to get us out." Mr. Young grinned.

Major chuckled as he hopped into the passenger's seat. "Let's go. I kind of like the idea of two old guys out on an adventure in an old truck."

After Mr. Young eased the truck through the gate, he asked, "Should we be considering taking my camping trailer too?"

"Maybe so; it gives us another covered trailer," Major said. "I'll discuss possible arrangements with Jack after I get back."

As they rolled through town, Major shook his head at the neglected streets and buildings. "Jack said the town had been abandoned; it's shocking how quickly it's deteriorated to a ghost town."

Mr. Young slowed when he came to the edge of town, and a man who held a shotgun stepped onto the road across from Pete's Diner.

"It's one of the old timers," Mr. Young said.

Major nodded and narrowed his eyes. "I'll watch Pete's Diner in case there's an ambush."

Mr. Young stopped and lowered his window when the old man approached his truck.

"I recognized your truck, Mr. Young." The man peered at Major. "You got yourself a passenger." The man raised his shotgun. "You okay?"

Mr. Young chuckled. "My nephew showed up on his way to Tallahassee; he don't talk much. We're going to my old farm to see if we can pick up a few things for him. You doing okay?"

"Your nephew made me nervous. A man came through a couple of weeks ago on his way north. He said some guys roughed him up and asked him if he knew a major. When he asked them what kind of major, they turned him loose. He tole me to be careful, so I been staying scarce. I ain't seen Major in a while; he must have left like everybody else. I been scavenging food and supplies from the houses in town and taking them to that old abandoned shed back in the woods that Pete planned to be a hunting cabin twenty years ago before the town built up; I'm too old to travel and don't have any family. I'm getting by just fine."

Mr. Young nodded. "Take care of yourself."

As he sped up, Mr. Young said, "What do you think about the men south of here asking about a major?"

"I'm not sure what to think. Do you think word's getting around that we have food at our farm?"

"I'm worried it was more personal. Did you notice he didn't recognize you? When you quit shaving last week, was that on purpose?"

Major chuckled. "No, I lost a bet with Jack; didn't think of it as a disguise."

"I wouldn't mind not shaving, but I'm not ready to give up my regular haircuts," Mr. Young said.

"Why did you tell him I was your nephew?" Major asked.

"So when I tell the story later to Josh, I can claim we were incognito. It makes a better story."

Major shook his head. "I should have known."

When Mr. Young pulled his truck into his driveway, he asked, "How did I do?"

"Like a pro."

Major scanned the barn. "Is your trailer inside the barn?"

"No, I've got a pole barn in the back field. Ready for a bumpy ride?"

CHAPTER THREE

"Major sounded skeptical. Do you think he'll agree with us?" Stuart asked after Angel handed over the radio to Leo, and they strolled to the shortcut to the Smith farm.

"Yes, he'll discuss it with the sheriff, but they'll agree," Angel said.

"I don't see what else could have worked. If they don't come here, do we talk to Red and Andy about going there?"

"It would be a mistake. Pops' farm would still be underpowered because the four of us can't make up for eight people, and we'd leave the folks here underpowered by four. As far as other resources, Mom's garden is far superior to Pops' in Florida because of the soil and the rainfall, and Jennie has cows."

"Do you think Josh will mention pizza?" Stuart grinned.

"Of course, he will," Angel said. "Ready to run?"

Stuart nodded, and Angel raced away. *You'd think I'd learn to just run.* He shook his head and took off after her.

When he reached the Smith barn, Angel waited for him. "Do you think the old barn could be fixed up enough to become habitable?" she asked.

"That would be a good David question," Stuart said. "I wouldn't even guess what materials a project like that would need."

She scanned the building. "Not that we'll need it; we have a logical solution to housing when Major and everyone else gets here, but it would still be nice to have a contingency. Do you think Mr. Young will bring his trailer?"

"I don't know; he was having eyesight problems when we were there. If it's deteriorated, he might not feel comfortable driving."

"True." Angel raced out of the barn to the shortcut to the Newtons' farm.

Stuart snorted. *My fault. I forgot to ask her not to leave me behind.* He ran along the shortcut at his normal pace.

When Stuart reached the house, Andy rose from the front porch steps. "Red and Angel raced up the driveway to the road; Angel said they'd meet us at the barn, so we could talk to your dad. They invited me to run with them, but I used you as my excuse. Do you know what we're going to be talking about?"

"Yep, but I'd rather go through the details with everyone at one time. It's Angel's idea, but I'll explain when we get everyone together."

"I wanted to talk to you, anyway. Aunt Jennie's been really irritable lately. She tries to hide it, but I've noticed she's snapping at Uncle Leo, and that's something she's never done."

"Do you think all the extra people in the house is more than she can handle?" Stuart asked.

"Might be; she was always particular when we visited. Mom told me she dreaded going to visit Aunt Jennie because she felt sorry for her. I never really put together why, but I think I get it now. There were only three of us, and I'd forgotten the longer we stayed, the more irritable Aunt Jennie became. I was thinking she might be sick or something. If the Cabellos eventually move back to their house, it might help her."

"The Mitchells will still be there," Stuart said.

Andy shrugged. "I know, and I can't see Lela being crazy about splitting up the girls, even though Cami Sue and Sam have been avoiding Dolly. Dolly's resilient like her mom; she doesn't care. We'll just have to see how that works out. I had thought about talking to Doc Larkin, but now I think Aunt Jennie's anxious, not sick."

"Mom would take in the Mitchells; actually, Mom would take in the whole crowd, and we'd be sleeping in the attic until we get the barn fixed up." Stuart smiled. "She's energized by having people around, and Dad's completely different from how he was when Angel, Red, and I came here to help out. He seems to be thriving on the chaos too."

Andy shook his head. "I think Aunt Jennie's competitive streak took over, and she forgot she isn't like your mom."

"If you're still worrying after the Cabellos leave, we can turn it over to the experts."

Andy nodded. "Red and Angel amaze me too."

When they reached the barn, Andy said, "That's odd; I expected them to be here."

"So did I." Stuart turned to find them to see what was wrong when they whizzed past him and into the barn.

Red grinned. "We found a huge box turtle crossing the driveway and stayed to watch it until it crawled into the trees."

Stuart shook his head as he hurried to catch up with them.

Stuart strolled to the barn. "Angel and I talked to Major this morning. All their neighbors have left, so they have lost their backups. Angel suggested they come here, and Major is considering the idea. We think the safest way for them to travel here is for us to take two transport trucks and bring them back. All they have are two drivers who are also their two shooters, so they aren't prepared to travel here without help."

"How many people again?" Andy asked.

"Five adults, and four children," Red said.

"Where will they stay, Angel?" Scott asked.

Stuart smiled. *Dad knew she'd have it figured out.*

"We need to look at the Mitchell and Cabello houses and estimate what it would take for them to be habitable, including what furniture would be required, at a minimum," Angel said.

"When will we know whether they are coming here?" Scott asked.

"It depends on our radio reception: either tonight or tomorrow morning. We should be ready to leave before light tomorrow," Angel said.

"But that's before we'd be able to talk to them." Andy furrowed his brow.

"True, but what other choice do they have?" Red asked.

Scott nodded. "I see your point. They can't stay, and they can't come in one vehicle or take the chance with two vehicles."

"We'll ask David to go with us to check the Cabello and Mitchell houses," Angel said, then she and Red left to find David.

"I assume Angel will drive one truck, and I'll drive the other," Andy said. "What else do we need to take?"

"Extra diesel to get us back, sleeping bags, our backpacks, and extra ammo," Stuart said.

"I know you want to leave enough room for what they'll need to bring, but it sounds awfully barebones to me; what about chainsaws?" Scott asked.

"I'll add chainsaws to our list," Andy said.

Scott nodded. "Depending on what you find when you check the houses, I think they'll need to bring beds and all their other basics."

Scott stayed in the barn, and Stuart and Andy headed toward the house, Andy said, "We won't have to run with Red and Angel because David runs at our speed."

"Good point. I'll leave now to check the road and wait at the end of the driveway," Stuart said. "Maybe I can talk them into running with me the rest of the way to make sure the two houses are safe."

"Better yet, let's both go; they'll figure it out," Andy said.

Stuart and Andy ran at their fast pace then slowed as they neared the road.

"I'll look," Stuart whispered. "Back me up."

Andy nodded as Stuart dropped low to crawl past the cover of the branches across the road and into the field of tall grass.

When Stuart came close to the ditch, he stopped and listened to the chirps and songs of birds establishing their territory and the chatter of a squirrel in a tree across the road. He glanced at the hawk that silently glided above the field and trees. After he moved to the clearing, he quickly scanned the road to be sure it was clear before he returned to Andy.

"Looked clear. I'll check across the road from the Mitchell and Cabello driveways."

Stuart strode through the tall grass near the road until he reached the point to cross the road to the driveways. He froze at the occasional faint sounds from the distant state highway. *Cars? Trucks?*

He stepped to the clearing and carefully scanned the road before he returned to Andy.

"Whew," Andy whispered, "I think I hear Red, Angel, and David coming. I'm always ready to cover for you, but I don't know if I can take on the two of them by myself."

Stuart nodded. "I know the feeling."

When Angel, Red, and David arrived, David puffed as he caught his breath.

"Sorry we took so long; Holly showed up at the house and was determined to come with me. Sandra enticed her into the house with a treat." David exhaled then slowed his breathing. "Red told me she and Angel would run at my pace; I didn't know I ran that fast."

Angel gazed over Stuart's head, and he turned his head. *Too late; she knows I checked the driveway.*

"Who's leading?" David asked.

"Angel and I will," Stuart said as he followed Angel who had already slipped into the brush toward the two driveways.

Stuart kept Angel in sight as they moved quietly from the brush to the field. Angel waited for him at the edge of the brush, then the two of them crawled to the road. When they reached the ditch, Angel pointed to her eyes, and Stuart nodded. Angel slowly rose then stepped to the ditch as Stuart assumed a kneeling shooting position with his rifle. He watched her hands for any signal as she stepped to the roadside then slowly scanned the roadway from east to west. He held his breath when she continued to the middle of the road and repeated her careful examination of the road. She crossed to the other side of the road and examined the shoulder, ditch, and driveways then slowly returned as she repeatedly scanned her surroundings. When she reached him, she knelt next to him, and he exhaled.

"I heard some traffic on the state road, but there are no signs of foot traffic or tire tracks on either side of our road. We can go up the driveways," she whispered.

Stuart nodded; after he whistled his cardinal call, Red, Andy, and David joined them.

"Angel, David, and I will take the Mitchells' driveway; Red, you and Andy go up the Cabello driveway, take your time, and watch for any signs of trespassing. After you clear the house, join us at the Mitchell house, and David can give us his assessment."

As they walked up the driveway, Angel stepped into the trees on their left side. When she returned, she motioned for them to follow her. As they made their way through the brush, she pointed to a dirty, torn piece of gray cloth that was half-buried in the leaves, and Stuart frowned.

She led them through the brush and small trees for six more feet then, they broke through into a small clearing that was surrounded by larger trees. David scanned the area, and Stuart moved closer to the circle of ashes with remnants of burned chunks of wood. He picked up a small branch, stirred through the ashes, and found several burned cans with ragged edges.

David strode to Stuart's side and picked up a chunk of wood. "It's cold: that's good." He scrutinized the campsite then slowly walked the perimeter as he inspected the surrounding area. "I don't see any signs of someone being here recently. We can keep going."

On the way back to the driveway, David asked, "How did you find it, Angel?"

"I smelled the charred wood and the old woodsmoke that lingered on the bushes," she said.

David glanced at Stuart; Stuart shrugged.

When they reached the house, Angel and David waited in the trees while Stuart went to the back of the house. After he opened the front door and waved them inside, Angel and David hurried to the door.

David sniffed as he walked in. "Smells musty, but that's all. I'd like to find the attic stairs and check for any water damage." He glanced around the living room. "Nice fireplace."

While David was in the attic, Angel waited in the living room while Stuart checked the kitchen.

Red called out, "Anybody home?"

Angel went to greet them, and Red and Andy came inside with her.

"What's the verdict?" Red asked.

"David started in the attic; he hasn't come down yet," Angel said. "Stuart's in the kitchen."

Andy raised his eyebrows at the sound of banging in the kitchen. "Sounds like he's wrecking it. I'll check on him."

Red snorted. "He went to help."

David sneezed as he climbed down to the main floor. After he raised the attic stairs back into place, he strode into the living room, and Stuart and Andy joined him from the kitchen.

"No signs of water damage or leaks." David brushed cobwebs off his arms. "I haven't seen any broken windows yet; so far, the house is habitable."

As David examined the interior of the rest of the house, Stuart and Red accompanied him while Andy and Angel straightened the kitchen.

When the group reconvened in the living room, David said, "It's a single story, but this old house has four bedrooms, three baths, a utility with a washer and dryer, and a dining room that looks like it was used as an office. A family could move in here, set up the beds then clean the next day. We'll have to replace the mattresses in the bedrooms. Someone ripped them up; they must have been looking for something. I only saw an old shed; is that it for out buildings?"

"Mr. Mitchell has an old barn too; it's not close to the house, but it's in relatively good shape," Stuart said. "How's our list for this house, Red?"

"Thankfully, not much: mattresses and cleaning but no repairs. Ready to go to the other house?"

Red led the way through the shortcut to the newer house.

After they were inside, David scanned the great room. "This is really nice. Where's the access to the attic?"

Andy led David to the hallway, and the springs creaked as they pulled down the folding stairs.

After David was in the attic, he called down, "I like this house; the attic has roughed-in floors. If I thought I'd have a chance at separating Peyton and Sandra, I'd say I'll take this house." He chuckled as he climbed down the stairs.

David raised the staircase, then he and Red checked the rest of the house. When they returned, David said, "Same as the other house, just a decade or so newer. Four bedrooms, three baths, a utility room, and an office. Kitchen and living room are bigger. The fireplace is nice here too. How's our list?"

"No repairs, but we'll need beds. One of the bedrooms must have been a sewing room: it didn't have a bed, and two of the bedrooms had only one twin bed in each of them," Red said.

"Mr. Young will want to bring his camper," Angel said.

Stuart nodded. "He's probably campaigning for that right now. Let's take a walk to see where it could be parked at the older house. That's where Major and the farm family will go, right?"

"Yes."

"We'll close up the house then be right there," Red said.

After Angel and Stuart headed toward the older house, David caught up with them before they reached the shortcut.

"If you can wait a second, I'd like to check the stove here to be sure the connection to the gas is safe," David said. "I'll check the connection at the older house too. I inspected the fireplace flues at both houses, and they are clear. If we can't find a good place to park Mr. Young's trailer, Tom's tractor is still here, so we might be able to clear a spot close to the house before they get here."

While they waited for David, Angel said, "I wasn't surprised you and Andy checked down the road before we got there."

Stuart kissed her lightly. "I know, but we thought we were being sneaky."

"Yes."

David hurried out of the house. "The stove is good to go. One more thing: I want to check the propane tank's level. I suspect it's fine here, but it might be low at the other house."

After David returned, he said, "The propane level is fine. I'm ready."

After they were outside, David asked, "Do you know if Tom and Lela ever had a camper or a motor home? Most people with some property want to park their motor home near the front or back door, so it will be easier to load and unload. I'll start searching at the back door."

As Stuart searched for spots close to the front door, he smiled when David whistled a cardinal song. Angel raced to the back of the house, and Stuart followed her at a trot.

David grinned when Stuart rounded the corner while Angel stood next to David and bounced on her toes.

"I found a concrete pad that is the perfect size for a trailer or a motor home," David said. "It would take me ten minutes to clear a path for Mr. Young's trailer to get to the pad if I can get the tractor going. I'd like to see if the tractor will start and clear around the pad while we're here. I found a chicken coop that needs repairs, but Annie can take care of the repairs, and it wouldn't take long for the two of us to salvage that old shed to build a goat shelter. She'll want a greenhouse, so we'll need to clear an area for her. We have the electric chainsaws and the small solar system to recharge the batteries, so at least we won't have to chop down trees with an ax. I'll check the stove and propane tank, then I'd like to clear that area."

As David strode toward the house, he stopped and pointed to the side of the house near the fireplace chimney. "I was so focused on inspecting the inside then looking for a site for Mr. Young's camper that I completely missed the antenna. It must have been for the TV. I guess that's why Tom didn't mention it, but couldn't that be repurposed for the ham radio?"

"Is that a possibility, Angel?" Stuart asked.

"Not the antenna, but Mr. Young might want to use the mast for his antenna rather than put up another one. If we had a transceiver at the Newton farm, I could build a decent antenna for it."

While Stuart, Angel, and David headed to the driveway, Angel twisted her fingers around her sweatshirt's neckline.

"What's wrong, Angel?" Stuart asked.

"More traffic on the state road; we need to check it now."

After Stuart whistled, Red and Andy raced to join them.

"Go," he said as Angel sped down the driveway with Red at her side. "I'll try to catch up with them."

"We've got your back," Andy said.

Stuart raced down the driveway; when he arrived at the road, Angel and Red were across the road. Angel held up three fingers then pointed at the state road.

Stuart peered down the road. *Nothing there.*

His eyes widened, his heart raced, and his breathing was ragged. *They went to the highway.*

He swallowed hard as he checked the road then raced across to Angel and grabbed her into a tight hug. He bit his lip to keep from screaming at her. "You scared me," he whispered.

"Why? You know I'm not reckless," she said.

He sighed then murmured, "That's a matter of interpretation."

Angel continued, "Three cars are parked in a line on the shoulder about a mile from here and are pointed east; we think they are staging, but we don't know why."

Stuart peered down the empty road. "They could be scout vehicles for a convoy."

Stuart glanced toward the Mitchells' house. "David's anxious to check Tom's tractor and clear the spot for Mr. Young's trailer. I'll tell him to go ahead and send Andy down to wait with you. Come get us if we need to get out of here, and we can leave through the woods."

When Stuart met Andy and David, he said, "Three cars are staged east of us, but they're pointed toward the highway. Andy, if you'll stay with Red and Angel, David and I can see if we can get the tractor going. Send Angel if we need to shut down the tractor."

After Andy headed down the driveway, Stuart and David jogged to the old tractor. Before he attempted to start it, David said, "I'll check the battery first. Tom may have disconnected it."

"I'll check for the key."

David peered at the battery then connected the cables before he checked the fuel.

"I found the key," Stuart said. "It was in the cupholder under an old rag. Dad always did that."

"We've got fuel. I'll crank her up."

Stuart watched as David fiddled with the throttle then finally coaxed the old tractor to keep running.

"How can I help?" Stuart asked in a loud voice.

"Check for any tools or equipment I might have missed seeing around the old pad; it wouldn't hurt to see if there are any shovels or anything in the old shed, and let me know if I need to kill the engine right away," David shouted over the noisy engine.

Stuart saluted with two fingers then trotted to the pad. He carefully scouted the area but found only a shovel. After he set it by the back door of the house, he hurried to the shed while David made his way to the concrete pad with the tractor. Stuart pulled out a garden rake, a spade, and a rusty bowsaw from the shed. After he put them next to the shovel, Stuart turned to watch David and raised his eyebrows. *He's almost finished.*

A few minutes later, David drove the tractor back to where it was parked and turned off the engine. He exhaled then grinned. "We need to add hearing protection to our backpacks."

After he put the key back into the cupholder and covered it, he disconnected the battery cables.

"Ready," he said.

As they headed toward the road, David said, "The house is ready for Major's family; I'm glad we don't have to make another trip back."

"It made sense to do it while we were here."

After the group returned to the Newton driveway, Stuart said, "We'll check the trucks after lunch."

"I'll grab Brandon if he doesn't have a lesson this afternoon, and I'd like to see Tom to talk about a spot for Annie's greenhouse," David said.

"Teacher Blanche might be interested too," Andy said.

"Sounds like a barn meeting to me." Stuart chuckled.

After they reached the house, Cal and Doc were on their way outside, and Holly bounded out to greet David.

"Everything okay?" Cal asked.

David knelt to snuggle Holly. "Everything's ready for Major's family, and the Cabellos can move when Major and his crowd occupy the Mitchell house, so they'll have nearby backup to help Nate protect his family."

When they went into the house, Blanche, Brandon, and Henry were clearing the table, and Scott was washing dishes as the group went inside.

"Better wash for lunch before these hungry rustlers think it's time for second lunch," Blanche said.

"Rancher Blanche is right," Sandra said. "Your lunch is ready."

After Henry hugged Angel and Stuart, and Brandon hugged his dad, Blanche, the boys, and the two puppies hurried outside.

"Are the boys studying cattle this week?" David asked as he sat next to Peyton; Holly flopped onto the floor on the other side of David.

"Best I can tell, this week's topic is nutrition," Sandra said. "We had chicken noodle soup, and our lunch topic of the day was who had the most chicken in his bowl."

"Doc claimed he won, but Blanche told him it didn't count because he cut a few pieces of chicken in half with his spoon. Cal stepped in and declared it a tie." Scott chuckled.

"Sorry I missed that," David said as he dipped his roll into the chicken broth.

"It's pretty much how it goes around here at lunch time," Sandra said. "Blanche announces a competition, and it goes downhill from there. Peyton and I told the boys the point of the lunchtime competitions was to learn skillful negotiations."

"Cal's getting pretty good at it too," Peyton said. "I'd have given them all a time out, starting with Doc."

"Will we be able to get the Mitchells' house ready in time for Major and the Florida family?" Scott asked.

"Thanks to David, we're ready. He checked the houses, and the Mitchell house will need a little cleaning, but David found a concrete pad in back and cleared away the weeds with Tom's old tractor, so if they bring Mr. Young's camper, they will have a good place to park it. They'll need to bring a few beds, but I suspect Molly's already planning on that," Stuart said.

"I'll get with Blanche to talk to her about Annie's greenhouse," David said. "I'm sure she'll want one. Blanche and the boys can research the trees we'll have to clear for optimal sunlight in the winter. If I can pull Brandon away for a bit, I'd like to take him with me to talk to Tom about the best location to clear for Annie's greenhouse."

"I wouldn't mind going along too, and maybe we could take Henry and give Rancher Blanche a break," Scott said.

"She'll probably think you're trying to fire her. She'll want to go along too," Peyton said.

"We'll just take the troops and all the dogs then," David said.

"As long as Jennie doesn't get any ideas that you all are planning to stay with her," Sandra grumbled.

Stuart coughed then took a big gulp of water. "Sorry. Got a little something caught in my throat."

He glanced at Andy, who shook his head.

CHAPTER FOUR

"What are the rest of you going to do this afternoon?" Peyton asked.

"We want to check the trucks and see what we need to do to have them ready to move first thing in the morning," Stuart said.

"Angel wants to leave long before daylight, so we can be there and loaded up before lunch. Our goal would be to have lunch on the road and arrive here in the early afternoon," Red said.

"Should I come with you to help?" Peyton asked. "I'm available."

"I'd rather you stayed here," Stuart said. "I don't want to leave the house undefended. Mom can shoot, but she has too many other responsibilities that require her attention. Blanche can shoot too, but it would be nice if she had some down time to herself."

Peyton snickered. "I can't imagine Blanche even knowing what to do with down time, but I understand your point."

Stuart smirked. "Didn't make any sense to me either as soon as I said it."

"We'll work on packing you something for lunch tomorrow. Are you going to eat breakfast before you leave, or do you want something to take on the road?" Sandra asked.

"On the road," Angel said.

Sandra nodded. "If you talk to Major this evening, tell him I'll pack enough lunch for them too, so they can focus on packing for the trip."

"Speaking of shooters," Peyton said, "Sandra, you and I need to start wearing our pistols even around the house. We're not good about stopping to strap them on before we go outside. I'll talk to Blanche, Cal, and Doc Larkin too, because sometimes Cal and Doc, in particular, forget just like we do."

"You're right, Peyton. Everyone should be wearing their holsters all the time, and we're the ones who are around the house most of the time; that makes the children easy targets, doesn't it?"

Peyton shuddered. "I'm afraid it does."

"Thanks, Peyton," Stuart said as he followed Angel, Red, and Andy to the front door. Stuart, Angel, Red, and Andy turned toward the shortcut to the Smith barn. When they reached the trees, Red asked, "Ready?"

"Go on ahead, honey. We'll see you there," Andy said.

Angel and Red raced into the woods; Stuart said, "You catch on quick."

Angel and Red met them when they stepped into the clearing at the Smith barn.

"We were surprised when we checked the three trucks. We'd forgotten how much fuel we had," Red said. "We'd like for you to pick the best two of the three trucks for us to take tomorrow. We won't need all the fuel, so we think we should take a little more than we need and move the rest into the truck we don't take."

"We need to clear the driveway to the road, so we can leave as early as possible," Angel said.

"We'll take care of it," Stuart said.

"In that case, we'll start pulling together what we want to take tomorrow," Red said.

After Angel and Red raced to the path to the Newton farm, Stuart and Andy checked the tires, engines, and brakes of the three trucks.

"All three are in good shape. We could take the two that are closest to the road." Andy shrugged.

"Good enough; after we move the excess fuel cans to the third truck, why don't we see if Nate's available to help clear the driveway?" Stuart asked.

"I like the way you think; it's a great excuse for you to check the house dynamics."

When they reached the Webster farm, Nate, Fire Dog, and the judge were standing near the barn door; Dolly and Pixie were running in a wide circle, and the two farm dogs stood guard at the garden fence while Cami Sue and Sam pulled weeds with their grandmother.

Nate and Fire Dog strode to Stuart and Andy. "Dad and I are hiding out here under the guise of helping Lela watch the children. Charo is determined to move to our house immediately, and I've got the feeling Jennie is ready to volunteer to carry everything singlehandedly. I told Charo she could move after Major and the rest of the family were here, but she told me that she could do everything herself and didn't need my help. She's on a total tear."

"If I go inside, I don't suppose you'd tie a rope around my waist and pull me out if I get into trouble." Stuart chuckled.

"On your own, bud." Nate smiled.

"I'll stay out here," Andy said.

"Nope; you have to go in with me; we can't violate the two-person rule, and we're about to enter a danger zone," Stuart said.

As they reached the house, Judge called out, "Good luck."

"Oh, boy," Andy said after they went inside the house. Charo's angry voice carried down the hallway from her room in the back of the house as she rattled off a tirade in Spanish.

"Do you know what she's saying?" Andy asked.

"She's speaking so fast that I can't understand all of it, but from her tone and the few words I am catching, a wise man would run," Stuart said.

"We're going back there, aren't we?" Andy rolled his eyes as Stuart headed toward the hallway.

When Charo saw Stuart in the doorway, she stopped midsentence and glared. "Did Nate send you?"

"Nate's outside with Dolly and Pixie. What's going on?"

Charo wiped her brow with her shirtsleeve then plopped down on her bed and burst into tears. "I miss my beautiful home. I need to be there now, so Nate can rearrange the furniture for me, and I can cook in my kitchen and feed my family."

"That makes sense to me. We're going to Florida early in the morning to pick up Major and the rest of the family; they'll be moving into the Mitchell house. After we unload their things, we can move you back to your house. Could you have everything ready to move the day after tomorrow?"

Charo's tears slowed. "Having a goal helps me to focus. It doesn't make sense for me to throw everything into a random box; Dolly will need clean clothes tomorrow. What can I do to help you get ready for tomorrow?"

"We put up barriers at the end of the Smith driveway, so no one would come on the property. We need to clear it now and could use some help."

"Well, that's certainly something Nate could do. What's he doing that is keeping him from helping you?"

"He and the judge are keeping an eye on Dolly, Lela, and the twins. I didn't want to pull him away."

"I can be the watchdog. I can't get my belt around my waist anymore, but I can sit outside with my rifle."

"That would be great," Stuart said. "We could carry out a chair for you, so you could sit in the shade."

"Bring two, so Judge can sit with me." Charo brushed away her tears and grabbed her rifle. "Let's go."

Charo hurried out the back door while Andy and Stuart picked up two kitchen chairs. Before they reached the door, Jennie came downstairs. "Where do you think you're going with those chairs?"

"Charo and the Judge are going to sit in the shade and watch over the girls," Stuart said.

"I don't see why they have to sit in the shade. Sunshine's good for people; it's Vitamin D," Jennie said.

"Do we have some camping chairs we could take for them?" Andy asked.

"What do I look like? A store?" Jennie flounced out of the room and stomped up the stairs.

After they carried out the chairs, Stuart said, "As my grandmother used to say, somebody done trampled on her last nerve."

Andy snorted. "Probably us."

"When we take in the chairs, we'll have to be sure they're clean. I know Mom would throw a fit if we brought in chairs with muddy legs and put them on her clean kitchen floor," Stuart said.

As Stuart and Andy carried the chairs across the yard to the shade, Nate asked, "How'd it go? I was shocked when Charo came outside and told me I was released."

"Stuart said a wise man would run. We didn't, if that tells you anything," Andy said; Nate smiled.

After Charo and the judge were situated in the shade and in a good place to watch the children and the surrounding area, Stuart, Andy, Nate, and Fire Dog headed to the Smith farm.

"Let's see what we can do about moving brush and branches. I seem to remember we looked for the heaviest branches we could find," Andy said.

"We may not have to clear the driveway completely; we just need to be able to get out. When we return, we could leave one truck with Major, at least for a while, so they don't have to unpack everything as soon as they arrive. We'll use one truck for people to ride in back, and there may be enough room for any beds they bring; the other truck can transport boxes of food, supplies, tools, and clothes. I'm sure they'll want to bring their chickens and goats too, but they're probably figuring all that out," Stuart said.

When the three men reached the Smith barn, they pushed through the brush that had overgrown the meandering driveway, and Fire Dog darted into the brush.

"I'd forgotten about all the loops this driveway had," Andy said. "Do we want to clear away the brush before we try to leave in the morning?"

"We wouldn't want to clear it all the way to the road, but if we don't clear it at least part way, we'll lose our whole advantage of leaving early," Stuart said.

When they reached the barrier of old logs and brush they had put across the driveway, Fire Dog was waiting for them.

Stuart checked the road. "Road's clear both ways."

"If we clear most of the driveway with a tractor, we could use the tractor to move the heavy logs before we leave, then after we get back, we can use the tractor to put our barrier back in place," Andy said.

Stuart nodded. "We'll bring one truck back here and leave the other one with Major."

"I was thinking we could start loading the third truck with the items to go to our house while you're gone," Nate said.

"We loaded that third truck with our excess fuel, but it wouldn't take you long to put it into the barn. You could load it, but it wouldn't be safe to take the truck on the road to go to your house until we're back, so we can make sure it's clear for you and to watch your back."

Nate ran his fingers through his hair, and Fire Dog leaned against his leg. "I don't ever remember life being so complicated before the grid went down. We have to think of every step and examine every threat along the way. Sometimes it's overwhelming."

Stuart nodded. "That's why there is such strength in our group. No one person has to take on the entire burden. We're good at sharing."

"What are you worried about, Nate?" Andy asked.

Nate furrowed his brow in thought as he leaned to rub Fire Dog's ears. "I'm worried about everything, but we all are; I see that now. My real worry is Charo because she's..." Nate chuckled. "I was going to say delicate, but she's far from it. I know we'll figure out the rest because we're a good team. I think I've gone into protective mode because Charo is pregnant. When she was pregnant with Dolly, I never worried about her because all I thought about was work, and that may be adding to my drive to be over-protective because I feel guilty."

Stuart nodded. "Angel is remarkably brilliant and talented, but I worry about her all the time."

Andy rolled his eyes. "I'm in worse shape. Red is fearless; if she knew how much I worry about her, I'd be in big trouble."

Nate chuckled. "I feel better: you two have it much worse than I do."

As they headed back on the meandering driveway to the Smith barn, Stuart said, "I'd like to talk to Leo to see if we can bring the smaller tractor to the Smith farm to clear away the driveway."

"We'll have to take it on the road from Leo's driveway to the driveway here," Andy said.

Nate said, "I'll talk to Leo. You'll need a tractor operator and a guard; Fire Dog and I can be the guards."

"Andy, I'll see if Dad or David can do the tractor work; they're the most skilled, if you'll go inside with Nate. We'll head your way, so meet us on the shortcut somewhere after you talk to Leo; if Leo prefers that we don't use the tractor, we'll talk to Dad and David about getting Dad's to the road. We're all going to have a busy afternoon," Stuart said.

"I'd like to come out with you in the morning and close up the temporary gate after you leave, so you won't be idling on the road," Nate said.

"Maybe we can come up with a way to alert you without waking up the whole household," Andy said.

"I'll ask Charo; she'll have a good idea, and I'll get points for remembering to include her in a decision." Nate grinned.

As Nate, Fire Dog, and Andy headed toward the Webster house, Stuart ran to talk to his dad and David.

CHAPTER FIVE

Major smiled as Mr. Young skillfully maneuvered his old truck across the yard and around the barn then parked near his horse trailer as he beamed.

"Sure felt good to be behind the wheel." Mr. Young climbed out of the truck.

Major stepped out and scanned the trailer. "Yours is quite a bit larger than mine and newer. We'll be able to load more into it."

Major strolled around the trailer and inspected it. "Tires look good. Do you have a spare?"

"I think I have one spare, maybe two. We can check the barn," Mr. Young said.

"I'll hitch it up and pull it around to the front of the barn," Major said.

Mr. Young nodded as he guided Major to the hitch. After the trailer was connected and ready to roll, Mr. Young went to the barn to look for the spares while Major drove to the barn.

"Two spare tires," Mr. Young said. "Not much of anything else here. My small utility trailer is still in there, but we don't have any use for it."

Major loaded the tires into the pickup truck bed.

"Before we leave, let's check the house to see if there's anything we could use," Mr. Young said.

As they neared the house, Major asked, "Is that Chuck's truck parked alongside the house beyond the stand of trees?"

They strolled to the side of the house, and Mr. Young nodded. "Sure is. They must have taken Diane's van because it had more room for all the children."

Major opened the driver's door then lifted the mat. "Keys were under the mat." He stuck them into his pocket and checked the console and pulled out a small bottle of hand sanitizer and a pair of men's leather work gloves.

Mr. Young checked the glove box and pulled out a flashlight; when he clicked it, the light came on. Mr. Young smiled. "We found treasure."

After they returned to the front of the house, Major tried the front door, and it was unlocked; he narrowed his eyes. *Sheriff told me he locked the door before he and Josh left.*

Wait out here," Major whispered as he unholstered his gun and went inside. The musty smell tickled his nose, and he stifled his instinct to sneeze. After he quickly checked all the rooms, he returned to the front door. "No damage that I can see to the door, but the kitchen's been stripped. Sheriff said there were a few things left in the kitchen."

Mr. Young frowned. "I need to check something." He hurried down a hallway and returned with four rifles.

"I locked these in a small closet in the back bedroom. Someone tried to force the door open, but there was a deadbolt in the floor that they missed. The key was still on the ledge. There's ammunition in the closet too."

"I'll load it into the truck." Major took the rifles from Mr. Young.

"I'll look around and see what else I can find," Mr. Young said.

After Major loaded the guns, ammo, and the box of canned goods, he found Mr. Young in one of the upstairs bedrooms.

Mr. Young's eyes had welled up; he nodded toward three stuffed animals on a twin bed. "I may be a sentimental old fool, but we need to take these; I think they must have been left by mistake. We can't abandon them."

Major swooped up the toys. "I agree. Have you found anything else?"

Mr. Young shook his head. "That's it. I'm glad we came."

"So am I. It's certainly a reminder to do one last check before we leave."

Before they reached the truck, Mr. Young said, "I'd like to drive back to the farm. I want to be confident and ready to roll with my camper trailer tomorrow."

Major nodded and climbed into the passenger's seat.

On the way back, Major asked, "Speaking of ready to roll, should we hook up your camping trailer and bring it around to the front of the house to load?"

"That wouldn't be a bad idea. I looked in the barn because I thought I had a spare tire for the camper too, but I couldn't find one. I know there's one on the back of the trailer, but I'd hoped I had another one. Of course, after we get it to Georgia, we'll just plan on staying put." Mr. Young smiled.

"I think you're right." Major sighed as he gazed out his side window. "Is the idea of leaving your farm permanently weighing on you? I'm struggling a bit over leaving mine."

"In a way, but I wouldn't want y'all to go anywhere without me, and we have to keep the young'uns safe."

When they reached Major's farm, Mr. Young slowed the truck then eased through the gate. "I'll tell you, Major, that gate terrorizes me. Only one more time, then I'll be happy to leave it behind."

Major chuckled. "After we pull out your camper, we better check with Molly to see if she needs us to do anything, then let's get with Jack and Annie to see if we can come up with a list of what we absolutely have to take."

Mr. Young nodded as he made a wide turn then backed the trailer close to the barn and parked. "Yes! I still got it." He swaggered to the back of his truck.

While Major unhooked the trailer, Mr. Young asked, "Should we check with Molly before we pull out my camper?"

Major glanced at him. "To quote Josh, 'heck, no.'"

Mr. Young chuckled. "I'll secure everything inside my camper."

Major nodded. "I'll bring your truck around in a few minutes."

Mr. Young walked around the front of the house to his camper. After Major backed the old truck close to the camper, he strode to the door, and Mr. Young called out, "Almost done."

"We'll need to pull away the deck," Major said.

Mr. Young came out of the camper onto the deck. "Didn't think about that. Good news is that we didn't attach it to the camper. The bad news is that it is well-built."

Major frowned. "Could it fit into the back of a pickup?"

"Not intact." Mr. Young narrowed his eyes. "We built it in sections. Maybe we should consult with Annie, but I think we can remove the stairs and railing from the deck then remove the deck from the four ground posts. I seem to remember we put it together with screws; if we did, we've kept the batteries for the electric drill charged with our solar charger. The easiest way to salvage the posts is to cut them close to the ground. All the pieces will be flat enough to store, except the steps."

"I'll find Annie." Major jogged toward the greenhouse.

When Major reached the greenhouse, his eyes widened.

"Hi, Pops," Sara said. "We're helping Annie salvage all the irrigation tubing, so we can take it to Georgia. There probably isn't a greenhouse at our new place, but Mr. David will help us build a new one."

"Almost done," Brett said. "Mom said we could help."

"I hate wasting water, but we'll have to dump the rain barrels and take down the gutters and pipes," Annie said.

"I'll help you with that," Major said. "After we've finished, Mr. Young and I could use some help at the camper."

"If you dump the barrels, Brett, Sara, and I can finish rolling up and packing the tubing because there isn't much left to do," Annie said. "We can pack the gutters and pipes too."

"You want me and Sara to come to the camper after we're finished?" Brett asked.

"That would be helpful because we're not quite sure what we're going to be doing next," Major said.

After Major and Annie tipped over the barrels, they left them upside down to dry then took down the gutters and pipes that collected the rainwater.

On the way to the camper, Annie asked, "What's up?"

"If it's feasible, we'd like to take apart the deck, so we can take it with us to Georgia," Major said.

"Let's check. I think we put it together with screws; if we did, it will be simple. If we used nails, we should knock it over with a tractor," Annie said.

"Sounds like we won't have to have a big discussion. I'll be optimistic; I'll grab the drill and extra battery." Major hurried to the barn while Annie rushed to the camper.

When Major arrived, Annie grinned. "All screws. I can take this apart in thirty minutes."

"How do we help?" Major asked.

"I'll start with the railings, and you can remove them, then I'll attack the deck and stairs."

"Ready? Go," Mr. Young said.

Annie giggled. "You timing me?"

"Certainly, I'm watching my sundial."

Major held onto the railing while Annie removed the screws and put them into her pocket. When it was free, Major stepped down while Annie held onto it then lifted it away from the camper.

"I think I see where the steps are attached to the deck." Annie quickly removed the screws, and Major confirmed the steps were no longer attached.

Annie and Major inspected the deck again, and Major furrowed his brow. "Looks like all we need to do is to remove the cross pieces then remove the deck from each leg. We need more help to hold up the deck until we can move it away from the camper."

Annie nodded. "To be safe, we'll need Dad, Mom, and Aunt Vanessa."

"I'll get them," Mr. Young said.

After Mr. Young left, Major asked, "You know we're going to be in trouble, right?"

Annie shrugged. "At least I'll be in good company."

Major chuckled. "I'll run grab some lumber from the barn to help prop up the deck."

After Major returned, Annie said, "Perfect."

Mr. Young followed Jack, Molly, and Vanessa to the camper.

"We're here to help," Jack said. "Molly and Vanessa are not allowed to yell at you until next week."

"I made them pinky-swear." Mr. Young beamed.

Major cleared his throat. "While Annie removes the screws supporting the deck, we'll hold up the deck, so it doesn't fall on her."

"We have lumber to help hold the deck," Major said.

"I'll put them in place, if you'll tell me when and where," Mr. Young said.

Annie glanced at Major. "I plan to start with the brace."

He nodded, and she quickly removed the screws then handed the braces to Mr. Young who set the short board with the railings.

"Now for the posts." As the deck loosened on the side Jack was holding, he braced to hold it up.

"Ready for the support," Annie said. "Mr. Young, place the board near the post."

Annie quickly removed the screws then moved to the opposite side where Molly stood.

Major frowned. "Annie, do the stair side first. If you do it last, you won't have an escape route."

Annie nodded.

"Vanessa, stand on the end of the stairs close to Jack. I'll take the other side. After the stairs are loose, Molly and I will switch, and you can hold the stair side together, then I'll move to the last side."

After all of the deck was free, Jack said, "Walk my way slowly and don't anybody fall, especially me."

"I've got your back." Mr. Young put his hand on Jack's back and walked slowly away from the camper. After Major cleared the camper, and everyone was on level ground, Mr. Young said, "Prepare to lower slowly; watch your fingers and toes."

When the deck was on the ground, everyone audibly exhaled.

"Major and I can move the stairs around front with the tractor when we're ready to load it. Thanks for your help," Jack said.

Molly and Vanessa hurried to the house.

"That was scary, honey." Jack hugged Annie.

"I was fine; you were here," Annie said. "If you need me, I'll be at the greenhouse."

"What's our next step?" Jack asked.

"I was thinking about loading the deck into the camper, but I'd forgotten how big it is. It might fit into the horse trailer. It would be a good barrier."

"Let's load what we can into the camper, then I'll take the deck around to the front with the tractor later," Jack said.

"I think we have a gate that we can use to contain the goats in the horse trailer. What do you think about putting the deck flat inside the supply truck for the generators to ride on?" Major asked.

"Much simpler, and we won't have to worry about the heavy deck falling on the goats," Sheriff said.

"How can I help?" Mr. Young asked.

Major peered at the camper. "Hold the door while we carry in what we can."

Major and Jack put the railing and braces inside the camper.

Major leaned against a post. "I don't have the energy to attack these right now. If we cut them off later, we can carry them with the tractor or load them into a wagon, and the boys could haul them around to the front for us."

"Best plan I've heard all day. Josh might like to take a chainsaw to them. It would be great training. So, what are we going to do?" Jack asked.

"I'm going to hook up the trailer to Mr. Young's truck then pull it around front," Major said. "I wouldn't mind if you walked behind the trailer and whistled if I need to stop."

"Makes sense to me. It's been two years since this old camper has rolled," Jack said.

Major backed Mr. Young's truck to the camper, then he and Jack hooked it up to the hitch. Major hopped into the driver's seat and muttered, "Here goes nothing."

The camper groaned as Major pulled it straight out; when he made the turn to go around the house, the camper creaked and moaned like a ghost-inhabited, abandoned mansion. Major glanced from one side mirror to the other. *So far, so good.*

Major stopped before he reached the driveway and climbed out of the truck.

"We've got a low tire," Jack said. "No surprise. Let's get some air in it then let it sit for a bit to see how it does."

Major walked to the rear of the camper. "Spare tire looks good."

Brett ran around the corner from the back. "Mom said to come inside for lunch and to cool off."

The three men strolled to the back of the house at a much slower pace than Brett who sped ahead of them.

"We brought Mr. Young's horse trailer back from his farm," Major said. "It's in good shape. He's planning to drive his camper to Georgia tomorrow. I think he'll be fine, but I could ride with him while you drive my truck with the horse trailer."

"We'll need a shooter with me if I'm driving the horse trailer," Jack said. "Who did you have in mind?"

"We'll most likely be in the middle of the convoy. I'm thinking Annie or Molly could be the shooter with you," Major said.

"Annie will be my shooter," Jack said.

"Don't blame you; can't say anything more because we're almost at the house."

Mr. Young chuckled.

While they ate lunch, Major said, "The plan so far is that Aimee Louise, Stuart, Rosalie, and Andy will be bringing two large transports here tomorrow. I'm not sure when they'll be here, but we should have everything we want to load into the transport trucks no later than mid-morning. Mr. Young will drive his old truck and pull his camper, and I'll be his shooter. We can switch off drivers if he gets tired. Jack will drive my truck and pull Mr. Young's horse trailer, and Annie will be his shooter."

"I don't like that at all," Molly said. "Annie's not..." Molly pursed her lips when Annie glared at her. "Sorry, my mistake; Annie's the best one to ride with her dad."

"Where will the rest of us ride?" Vanessa asked.

"I suspect we'll have one transport truck for supplies and one for people," Major said. "We have five that can ride in the back of one of the trucks."

"We won't fill the truck, though," Vanessa said. "Maybe they should bring only one transport truck."

"We'd like to take everything we'll need," Jack said. "With two extra trailers, we won't have to leave anything important behind."

"I thought we could easily put two or even three mattresses and our food for the trip and even extra food in the people truck," Major said. "We expect our travel to be in one day, but we need to plan for an additional day, just in case. It'll be nice to have a comfortable place for people to rest while we're traveling."

"We should put the chickens and goats in the horse trailer, and the irrigation supplies could go into the camper," Mr. Young said.

"We could put pillows and blankets in the rain barrels if we make sure they're dry first," Molly said.

"We should load guns and ammo into both trucks," Jack said.

"Just a minute." Vanessa held up her hand. "I need to grab a pen and paper to get this all down. Red would tell us we need a list."

"I'll get it." Annie rushed to the computer room; after she returned with her notebook, she quickly jotted down their list then handed it to Vanessa.

"Thanks, Annie. We'll keep the list on the table, so we can all add or refer to it."

"How's the canning going?" Major asked.

"We just finished," Molly said. "Vanessa and I will pack food for the transport truck this afternoon."

"What about Number 48?" Josh asked.

Jack raised his eyebrows. "Didn't even think about it; Major?"

"Now was the perfect time to bring up our two-seater utility vehicle that Mr. Young gave us, Josh, because it would have been much more complex later to figure out how to take it along. Let's load it into the back of my pickup before we hitch the horse trailer to the truck. We've got ramps around here somewhere. My truck can take the load, especially since the majority of the space in the horse trailer will be the chickens and goats."

Josh added *Number 48* to the list and grinned. "I want to be the next driver."

"As soon as we eat, you can drive it to the truck, then we'll look for the ramps," Jack said.

Molly grumbled as she and Sara cleared the table, "All these people growing up is getting on my nerves."

"It's okay, honey, I'll never grow up." Jack winked at Sara, and she giggled; Molly glared at Jack.

Jack grinned then turned to Annie. "Annie, what do you think about loading your plants from the greenhouse into the camper? We can put down a tarp then move them in."

"We'll need extra help lifting them into the cart then into the trailer," she said.

"I'll help you," Major said.

"Brett and I can carry the irrigation and gardening supplies," Sara said.

At the end of the afternoon, Major joined Jack and Josh who were putting tools alongside Number 48 that Jack and Major had loaded into the back of Major's truck.

"I've disconnected the generators. I thought they could go into the supplies truck. When you finish what you're doing, come to the back porch; we probably need to regroup to see what else we can do before dark," Major said.

While everyone sat on the porch and drank water, Vanessa said, "We need to take our rocking chairs."

Major groaned, "They're so bulky."

"We need to take the chairs," Vanessa growled.

"We can put them into the back of Mr. Young's truck," Molly said. "They're bulky, not heavy. You and I can take care of it, Vanessa."

"You just spoiled a great fight, Molly." Vanessa winked, and the children giggled.

Molly smirked as she flipped her hair. "I put on my Aimee Louise hat."

Major, Jack, and Mr. Young guffawed, and Vanessa glared. "It wasn't that funny."

"Yes, it was, Aunt Vanessa." Sara hugged her. "You're awesome; we need the rocking chairs."

"Anybody behind in what they planned to do?" Jack asked, and the rest of the family shook their heads.

"I'd like to keep working until supper and radio time, then we can plan what we'll do in the morning, finish up any tasks, and clean up before bed," Molly said. "We won't take the beds apart until morning, but we'll need help getting the mattresses downstairs first thing, so we'll be ready when the trucks show up."

"Annie and I will set up the barriers for the goats in the horse trailer after our break; we plan to put the chickens into the dog crates in the morning, but we'll need the Chicken Gang to help," Major said.

"We are the experts, aren't we, Mr. Young?" Brett asked.

Mr. Young nodded. "Just give us the word, and we'll wrangle the chickens. For now, I may need a power nap before I tackle anything else today."

"I think that's a great idea; sofa's all yours, Mr. Young," Molly said.

"I'll meet you at the barn, Dad," Josh said.

Jack strolled with Major and Annie on the way to the horse trailer. Jack said, "Josh and I put the rototiller inside the horse trailer.

We'd have liked to take the tractor, but the rototiller was second best to get the garden going."

"Sara and Brett put all my small pots of seedlings into the camper. They should be safe there," Annie said.

"Josh and I will load a cart with cans of fuel, then we'll load the cans into the truck with Number 48. We'll include tarps, so we can cover the fuel for travel before we leave."

"After we get the horse trailer set up for the goats, Annie and I are going to pick up all our game cameras. I almost forgot about them, but she reminded me."

When they were inside the horse trailer, Major said, "We got that old gate that should block the goats from getting out; we could push a trunk against the gate to keep them from knocking it down."

"Might work," she said. "I'll get the gate. We could put the chicken crates on top of the trunk and secure the crates to the hooks on the sidewalls of the trailer."

Annie returned with the gate on a cart, and Major lifted it into the trailer.

"Excellent; fits fine." He set the gate against the trailer wall. "Let's check the game cameras. I'll jog, but I can't run."

"It might be better if Dad and Josh run to get them. They're our best runners," Annie said.

"Good idea; let's see if we can swap jobs with them," Major said.

Major stepped wrong when he exited the horse trailer and twisted his left knee. He grabbed onto the trailer door before he fell.

"Dang it." He put a little weight on his knee and winced. "I think I've hurt my knee; I need a stick or something that I can lean on until I've had a chance to walk this off."

"I'll be right back," Annie said.

Shadow stayed close to Major.

Annie raced away, and Major eased himself to sit on the trailer. *Dang fool timing for an injury.* Major seethed as he stared at the sky then slammed his fist on the trailer floor.

Annie returned as quickly as she left; she carried a sturdy branch, and Jack and Josh followed her.

Major used the branch and the trailer door to rise to his feet, and Shadow whimpered in sympathy.

"Are you okay? What happened?" Jack furrowed his brow.

"I stepped wrong and twisted my knee a bit. It'll be okay in just a minute. Could you and Josh run grab all the game cameras? Do you know where they all are?"

"I do," Josh said.

"Did you finish loading the fuel cans?" Major asked.

"Not quite," Jack said. "We'll get the cameras then finish."

"Annie and I can finish up. She can hand the cans to me, and I'll lift them into the bed."

Jack frowned.

"If I can't handle it, Annie will tell on me and find someone else to help." Major's smile was weak.

Jack nodded. "Yes, she will, and she has my full permission to boss you around. It'll be good practice for her."

Annie giggled, and Josh rolled his eyes.

After Jack and Josh left, Annie asked, "What can I do?"

"Let me see if I can walk if I lean on the stick. If I can, we'll finish getting the rest of the fuel cans into the white truck. Are there more at the barn?"

Major leaned on his stick then took a step with his right foot as he tried not to put any weight on his left leg but winced and grunted at the pain as sweat broke out on his forehead.

"This isn't going to work," Major said.

"Put your right hand on my shoulder, and see if that helps; if it does, I'll find another stick," Annie said.

Major put his hand on her shoulder then took a step. "That worked. I'll wait for you."

When Annie returned with a second stick, she said, "If you put the sticks in front of you, could you pick up your right foot and kind of hop forward?"

"I'll give it a try; anything's better than just standing here," Major said.

Major held onto the two sticks as he hopped forward a step. "This is going to be slow, but maybe I'll get a rhythm going."

Major hopped midway across the yard then stopped. Sweat ran down his face from the exertion.

Annie frowned.

"What are you thinking, Annie?" he asked.

"We need to get you to the computer room and prop up your leg. You'll want to be in place for the radio call later. I'll get Mom, and she can fuss over you while I find someone to help me with the fuel cans."

Major nodded. "Take Vanessa."

Annie grinned. "Okay."

Major increased his hopping pace as they went across the yard. When they reached the front steps, he paused before he hopped up the first then second step. After he rested on the porch, he said, "Okay, I'm ready to go inside."

Annie opened the door, and he hopped the short distance from the doorway as quietly as he could, but Molly hurried from the kitchen and caught him before he made it into the radio room.

"What happened?" she glared.

Major exhaled. "I stepped wrong and twisted my knee. I have to give it a chance to rest."

Annie disappeared, and Shadow hovered while Molly helped Major to the chair in front of the radio. "Sure wish we had ice; do you have any shorts? I want to put a cold cloth on that knee."

"Why would I have shorts?" Major asked.

Molly rolled her eyes. "Jack has some gym shorts he can't wear since he's lost weight from running; I'll give them to you, and you can put them on. If you don't have your pants off and the shorts on by the time I return, I'll help you."

Vanessa and Annie hurried to the front door. "I'm going to help Annie with the fuel cans, Molly; I'll be back as soon as we're done," Vanessa called out before she closed the door.

Molly narrowed her eyes. "Is my daughter covering for you?"

"She's doing a good job, isn't she?" Major smiled.

Molly tossed a pair of shorts at Major, and he caught them before they landed on the floor.

"I'll be back; be ready." Molly stormed out of the radio room.

As soon as she left, Major unbuckled his jeans then stood on his right foot as he held onto the desk and dropped his pants to the floor. He had pulled on the shorts and was lowering himself to his rolling office chair when Molly returned.

After she draped his knee with a cold, wet cloth, she asked, "How do we take the washer with us?"

He sighed at the cooling from the wet cloth. "I have a dolly in the barn that we can use, but Aimee Louise will know whether the house still has the Mitchells' washer. We don't know whether the trucks have ramps; they might, but the ramps I planned to use to load the generators will be fine for the washer too, if we need to take ours."

"I didn't think about a washer already being there," Molly said. "Does that coolness help?"

"Yes, thank you."

"I'll put Sara on cold cloth duty; I apologize in advance." Molly cackled as she left the room.

"That's brutal, Molly," Major called out then shook his head. *Oh, man. Nurse Sara is a tyrant.*

He glanced around the radio room, and his eyes widened as he called out, "Molly!"

CHAPTER SIX

Molly ran to the radio room and clutched the door jamb as she tried to catch her breath.

"What's wrong?"

"We forgot we need to take all our electronics. Send in Mr. Young or Annie to box up everything including my computer, the printer, the girls' laptops, and all the wiring."

"Fine. Don't ever scare me again," she fumed as she flounced out of the room.

Sara marched into the computer room, and Penny followed her; Sara carried her medical kit and wore her white handkerchief tied in the style of a motorcycle rider's bandana with her painted pink cross that she had sprinkled with silver and gold glitter. "Do you have a fever, Pops? I have my thermometer if you do. Mom said you need to have a cold cloth on your knee. I brought you a glass of cold water, so you can be cold on the inside too. Mom said your foot needs to be propped up. I'll find a box after I bring in your next cold cloth. I'll take that one; it's probably too warm." Sara whisked the cloth off his knee and hurried out of the radio room; Penny flopped down on the floor and watched the door.

When Sara came back with a cold cloth, she carefully laid it across his knee.

"I appreciate it, Nurse Sara. I think you'll make my knee better before tomorrow. After we get the swelling down a little, maybe we can wrap it later. Do you think you can ask your mom to help with that?"

"Would it be like wrapping a pencil with a ribbon that has glitter on it to make it fancy?" she asked.

"Exactly, except I don't think I need the glitter."

"Glitter will make it heal better, Pops." Sara narrowed her eyes.

Major smiled. "Good point, Nurse Sara; we'll go with glitter too."

Sara nodded then rushed out. When she returned, she carried a small box.

"I thought a bigger one would be better, but Mom said this one was good because it fits under your desk." After Sara placed the box, Major propped his foot on it, and Sara peered under the desk. "Mom was right."

Mr. Young stood in the doorway and saluted Sara as she left with Penny at her side. "Well done, Nurse Sara."

"Are those the boxes for the electronics?" Major asked.

Mr. Young nodded. "Molly and I thought these two would be big enough for the computers and printer. She has another box for the radio hardware and wiring. I'll box up your computer, the laptops, and the printer; Annie can take care of everything else after your morning radio session."

The front door slammed, and Mr. Young met Josh in the hallway. "I'll take the game cameras, Josh," Mr. Young said.

"Thank you. Dad's taking the tractor around back to move the stairs around front while I get the chainsaw. I'm going to cut off the posts for the deck, so we can take them too."

Mr. Young returned with the game cameras. "I'll put these in with the laptops." He chuckled. "Josh is sure excited about the chainsaw."

Mr. Young packed up the computer equipment, then before he left, he pointed to the radio. "Might as well listen in case the Georgia folks make it on earlier than we expected." Major turned on the radio. He listened to reports of spreading disease and plunder then turned off the radio. *I'm depressed enough that I hurt my leg; sounds like the gangs are moving north more quickly now.*

After his third cold cloth, Molly came to the door. "I understand you're getting the magical glitter wrap before supper. I'll help you put your jeans back on after that."

When Major raised his eyebrows, Molly chuckled. "Where do you think my daughters get it from? We'll help you do whatever you need to do."

Major chuckled. "I don't want to slow the family down or cause a big fuss."

"That's exactly what I thought, and it makes sense to me."

After Molly returned to the kitchen, Vanessa came in the back door, and Major cringed. *Here it comes.*

Molly spoke in a voice loud enough for Major to hear. "Major twisted his knee. It's actually nothing, but Nurse Sara is on the job, so he's kind of stuck for the evening."

Vanessa snickered. "I'll bet he's loving that."

Molly chuckled. "He tried to convince her that she'd healed it, but she insisted on a glitter bandage later."

"I'll make it a point to stay out of Nurse Sara's way. I'm caught up on my things; do you need any kitchen help?"

"Sure do. I need the rest of the food in the pantry to go into our canning jar boxes."

Major smiled. *Well played, Molly.*

Major turned on the radio to listen. The hams' conversation had changed to a discussion of the weather. He frowned. *Storms in western Alabama.*

Mr. Young came into the room and sat on the chair next to Major. "Have you heard from Georgia yet?"

"Not yet; it's depressing to hear how many people are dying from diseases that never occurred before the grid failed and the economy collapsed. The gangs seem more organized; of course, some of the hams are convinced we've been invaded by another country, but I think the drug gangs have built small armies to take over resources."

Mr. Young nodded. "Food, clean water, weapons, ammunition, medicine, and turf."

"That's it."

"Do you remember the brother-in-law of the sheriff near Orlando?" Mr. Young asked. "I'm getting old: I can't remember his name or which sheriff, but rumors were that the brother-in-law was the leader of a large drug gang; the accusations that the sheriff shielded him ruined the sheriff's career. I'll think of his name after a while."

Major narrowed his eyes. "Are you talking about Cliff Roybal? There were quite a few of us that went to bat for the sheriff, but the fever pitch and vitriol of public opinion fueled by the media crushed his soul. I arrested Roybal over twenty-five years ago for racketeering; he could have been paroled by now. After I retired, I didn't try to keep up with any of that."

"That's it: Clifford Roybal. He's definitely the type to hold a grudge. My cousin's daughter went to high school with him; she told my cousin there were days that a warning went out to stay home from school. One day she didn't get the message and witnessed something she shouldn't have. My cousin sent her to live with his mother-in-law in South Carolina to finish her schooling." Mr. Young shook his head. "Hadn't thought about that in a long time."

Major frowned. "That was twenty-five years ago; we don't know that Roybal has pulled together his gang."

"Maybe he hasn't, but somebody's looking for you, Major." Mr. Young furrowed his brow. "Not good."

"I'd forgotten about what we'd heard on our way to your farm yesterday." Major shifted his leg and groaned. "Sorry; tactical error."

"We've adjusted to calling the sheriff by his name; should we call you Dave?"

Major shrugged. "You could, but I'd forget to answer; even Trish called me Major."

"Guess we'll take it to our brain trust." Mr. Young chuckled.

Major sighed. "I'd hoped we could ignore it."

Mr. Young pushed himself to his feet. "I did too, Major." He smiled then slowly shuffled out of the room.

Major watched Mr. Young leave and narrowed his eyes. *He's moving so slowly these days.* He smiled as he shook his head. *He's still getting around and doing what he likes; he's happy.*

Annie hurried into the radio room. "Oh, good. I was afraid that you were on the radio, and I missed something. Mom said we can eat by the radio if we haven't heard from Georgia when she has supper ready. She knows we don't want to miss Aimee Louise. Mom and Sara will be here in a few minutes to wrap your knee. Sara painted part of the wrap, and they are waiting for the glitter to dry. It's nice of you to go along with Sara's glitter; she's really proud that she's helping you get better."

Major smiled. "If glitter can't do it, nothing can."

"What can I do for you?" Annie asked.

"Nothing; I'm fine."

Annie crossed her arms and raised her eyebrows. "What would you be doing if you weren't stuck in here?"

Major furrowed his brow. "I'd be checking the barn one last time to be sure I didn't leave any tools behind."

"Perfect. I'll check the barn and the equipment shed; didn't you tell me that tools have a habit of growing feet?"

Major smiled. "I guess I did."

"I'll be thorough but fast; I don't want to miss the radio call with Aimee Louise."

Annie dashed out of the house, and Major put on his headset and listened while hams discussed the weather and frowned. *Couple of tornados in Alabama moving from west to east.*

"Did you hear about all the people trying to leave the cities? I heard Miami and Atlanta are turning into ghost towns," a ham said.

"Not to be morbid, but with all the disease in the cities, ghost towns are literally true with all the deaths," an older man said.

The first ham added, "I don't see how they could get very far because most of them are on foot, not used to walking, and probably don't have what they need to survive on the road."

"I'd heard some of the city folks left in a panic when they realized how bad off they were and planned to buy food after they reached the outskirts. I don't see how that could work because the stores in the small towns were stripped over a year ago and never restocked," a third ham said.

"They would be easy pickings for robbers to take what they do have," the first ham said.

"Those bandits are like locusts," the third ham said. "I wouldn't want to be in their path. I heard they're coming north from Miami and leaving nothing alive behind them."

"A few of the evacuees planned ahead and have the right supplies and a destination. I expect my son and his family to be here in two days," the older man said.

Major smiled. *They'll make it.*

He took off his headset. *We'll make it.*

Molly came into the radio room and closed the door. "Major, see if you can put any weight on your knee."

When Molly held out her hand, Major handed her the damp cloth then held onto the desk while he half-rose, half-pushed himself to stand with his weight on his right leg.

He exhaled. "So far, so good; here goes nothing."

He put a little weight on his left leg and winced in anticipation as he stood then equalized his weight and lifted his hands away from the desk.

"Standing isn't bad," he said, "but I'm not so sure about taking a step."

"Okay, you can sit; easy now," Molly said. "I had to see if you were improving, and you are. Stay off it the rest of the night, and you'll be okay tomorrow if you don't stress your knee. We'll still wrap it later, and I'll rewrap it in the morning."

"Thanks, for pushing me, Molly, I think." Major rolled his eyes. "I wouldn't have been brave enough to try that without your gentle encouragement."

Molly snorted.

Major asked, "Do you think I can make it to the porch for our regular radio meeting?"

"Let's have everyone come in here, so you'll be available for the radio in case there's more news."

Major nodded. "That's actually a good idea. There's a weather system in Alabama that concerns me. I wish Rosalie was here to interpret for me."

"Come on, Shadow; you need a break, and Penny is ready for supper. We're better off with the entire family together, aren't we?" Molly left the door open as she hurried to the kitchen, and Shadow followed her.

"Yes, we are." Major turned back to the radio and put on his headset to listen.

Nurse Sara tapped on his shoulder, and he removed the headset.

"Mom told me you're getting better, and the cold on your knee helped," she said as she draped the damp cloth across his knee. "She said this is your last cold treatment, unless you tell me you need more. Do you need more?"

"No, the cold helped, but I think your mom is right," Major said. *Thank you, Molly.*

"Good. Mom said I can help Aunt Vanessa bring extra quilts and blankets downstairs, so we can take them to Mr. Young's camper. We'll need extra blankets because it's cold in Georgia. Aunt Vanessa will carry them, and I'll tell her to be careful where she steps, so she won't fall."

"That sounds like a lot of work; I'm glad you'll be helping her."

Sara nodded. "After we get them all downstairs, Aunt Vanessa will carry them to the camper. I think it's best to put them on the bed, but Aunt Vanessa said we'd have to see what's already there."

"Sounds like you have it all planned out," Major said.

Before she left, Sara asked, "Mom said I should ask if you want your door opened or closed. We might be noisy."

"Closed is fine." *Molly's a genius.*

Major listened a little longer then frowned as the transmissions faded. He adjusted the dials then removed his headset and sat back as Mr. Young tapped on the door then came in with Shadow on his heels.

"How's it going?" Mr. Young asked as Shadow flopped onto the floor next to Major.

"I lost my signal; before I did, most of the talk was about how unprepared most of the people are when they leave the cities."

"Shall I fiddle with the radio a bit to see if I can find anything?" Mr. Young asked.

Major pushed against the desk to roll away his chair from its position in front of the radio. Mr. Young pulled his chair closer and put on the headset.

Jack came into the radio room. "Heard anything?"

"There's a strong weather system in Alabama and reports of tornados. I miss Rosalie because she'd be able to tell us if we should expect bad weather tomorrow. Besides that, all I've heard was rumors but nothing from Aimee Louise and Leo yet," Major said. "My signal faded out, so Mr. Young's going to see if he can find anything."

"Do you think there's a possibility Stuart and Aimee Louise will postpone coming tomorrow?"

"I didn't get enough information about the storms to know, but I suspect they'll leave to come here; I'm more worried about heading back. Aimee Louise, Rosalie, and I were in one tornado when we were on the road, and that was more than enough for me."

"The good news is that Rosalie will know; otherwise, I'd be tempted to say we plan on postponing a day."

"I don't want to delay too long if we can avoid it, though, because the occasional roadblocks to ambush travelers have been replaced by organized gangs of killers. I'd rather be settled in Georgia with our defenses in place."

Jack nodded. "You're right, and now that I think about it, if Aimee Louise, Stuart, Rosalie, and Andy weren't coming to help us, I'd say we should leave right now."

Major snorted. "We could have done that if we'd left the day before yesterday, but we gave Molly an entire day to prepare. We need the trucks to haul everything."

Jack groaned. "Can you imagine what we'd be loading if she'd had a few more days?"

Major chuckled. "Don't get me thinking about how to strap the tractor onto the top of the horse trailer."

Before he opened the door to leave, Jack grinned. "You and Molly shouldn't talk; I'm not ready to put the sofa on top of Mr. Young's camper, either."

Mr. Young set the headset on the desk. "We're just not getting anything. Annie and I planned to ask Stuart to take down the antenna when they get here, but if there's a solar disturbance of some kind interfering with the radio transmission, we could take it down earlier. Unfortunately, we have no way to know if that's the case, so we'll just have to keep listening until transmissions resume. I'll help Molly with supper. I understand Annie's going to bring you a plate and eat in here with you."

Major put on the headset and closed his eyes. When his head jerked, he was startled. *Didn't know I'd dozed off.* He removed the headset and turned up the speaker volume. *Hope I didn't turn it up too much.*

Annie came in with two glasses of water, and Jack carried two plates of fried ham slices, fried potatoes, and a salad of lettuce, tomatoes, and cucumbers.

"This is a feast," Major said.

Jack set down Major's plate on the desk in front of him then gave Annie her plate after she put the two glasses of water on the desk.

"After we eat, we'll all come in here for the radio and end of day reports," Jack said. "Molly and Vanessa already carried the rocking chairs from the back porch to the truck bed. I guess they wanted to be sure we didn't accidently leave them."

After Major and Annie finished eating, Annie carried their plates and glasses to the kitchen. Major turned off the radio then turned it back on as Molly and Sara came in.

"Would a reset help?" Molly asked.

"No, but it was something to do," Major said.

"We're ready to wrap your knee, but I'd like for you to stand first."

Major held onto the desk as he rose to his feet.

"Better," Molly said. "You can sit when you're ready. Are you going to want your jeans on after we put on your wrap?"

Major eased himself back down onto his chair. "I don't think so. I'm not going to be able to go anywhere tonight, and it would be more comfortable to sleep in my shorts."

"Speaking of sleeping, Mr. Young's going to sleep upstairs in the boys' room, and Vanessa's going to sleep in the girls' room. Vanessa and I decided she'd sleep better if she didn't have to worry about bumping your knee."

"That's not necessary," Major said. "I'd be fine on the sofa."

"No, you wouldn't. I need you to turn toward me because I don't want to wrap your knee when it's bent. Hand the box to Sara, and we can use it to prop your knee for wrapping."

Major leaned back while Molly wrapped his knee; when she was finished, Sara clapped. "Excellent, Mom, you did it just right. You have glitter, Pops."

Major inspected his bandage. "I certainly do. Thank you, Nurse Sara. It's definitely cheerful."

Sara hugged Major then left.

Molly's eyes had misted; Major smiled. "Who knew how healing a little glitter could be? It's certainly reminding me not to take myself too seriously."

Molly cleared her throat. "After we finish up the dishes, we'll come in here for the meeting."

After Molly left, Major plugged in the headset and listened. *Nothing.*

He removed the headset and set it down on the desk as he glared at the transceiver. "Do you need some glitter?"

Annie joined Major first. "Anything on the radio?"

He shook his head.

As Mr. Young came into the room, she picked up the headset, put it on, and grinned. "I've got static, Major. See if you can get anything, Mr. Young."

Major stared at the radio. *I'll get you some glitter.*

Annie held out the headset to Mr. Young as she rose from her seat. Mr. Young sat on the chair and put on the headset. "You're right. It's the beautiful music of static."

He focused on the transceiver as he adjusted the dials. "I've got something."

"Annie, tell your dad we need to have the meeting in the family room. Ask him to come help me, then you stay with Mr. Young, so if he comes up with anything, you can come get me."

Annie dashed from the room, and Jack hurried to the door.

"Jack, I think I can make it to the family room if you can push or pull my rolling office chair," Major said.

"Pull might work out if you don't mind going backward; you can push with your right leg," Jack said.

When they reached the family room, Annie raced to join them. "We got Mr. Leo, but just briefly. He's been trying all evening; Mr. Young told him we'd be ready in the morning, and Mr. Leo said he'd convey the message then signed out. We're a go." Annie grinned then returned to rejoin Mr. Young.

The boys cheered, and everyone else applauded.

"That's certainly a relief to hear from Georgia," Major said. "What's our status?"

"We'll take the beds apart right after breakfast and bring them downstairs, so they'll be ready to load; we'll take the boxes from the kitchen to the porch. We packed clothes into suitcases and put them into Mr. Young's camper. We left everyone two changes of clothes. Backpacks can be packed for a potential two-day trip in the morning, and I have a small box for each person to pack their personal items. Whatever time Aimee Louise and Rosalie show up, we want to be ready to load the two trucks," Molly said.

"We'll load the chickens and goats into the horse trailer tomorrow; we've already loaded their supplies," Jack said.

"Sounds like we have everything lined up. Sara, do you have a piece of that glitter ribbon?"

"Yes, Pops. Do you want some?"

"When you have a chance. Jack, do you mind helping me roll back to the radio room?" Major said.

After Major and Jack reached the radio room, Jack asked, "Are all our handheld radios charged?"

"Yes, and we have more than enough for each vehicle to have one," Major said. "Annie will take apart the ham transceiver; we'd like to take the antenna too, but I hate to wait until tomorrow then spend extra time here while Stuart takes it down."

"Annie, do you know how to take down the antenna?" Jack asked.

"Yes, I do, Dad."

"I'm willing to be the adviser," Mr. Young said.

"Good. Annie and I will do the work, and you can make sure we do it right and are safe," Jack said. "There's still enough daylight to get it done safely if we get moving."

"Here's the glitter ribbon, Pops. Is that enough?" Sara asked.

"This is great. I want to remember that sometimes glitter is important too."

"Yes, it is." Sara beamed.

* * *

Jack strolled into the kitchen. "Mr. Young, Major, and I were talking about the radio, and Major would like to take the antenna with us."

"No, you can't do that," Molly said.

"Do what?" Jack asked.

"I know exactly what you're leading up to; you want to get up on the roof and take down that antenna," Molly said.

"Mom, if we have the radio set up at our new house in Georgia, I could become an extra like Aimee Louise," Annie said.

"We'd like to take it down safely before it starts getting dark," Jack said.

"Well, go ahead," Molly fumed. "I'll argue with Major for bringing it up."

She flounced to the radio room, and Mr. Young, Jack, and Annie hurried outside; Josh, Brett, and Shadow followed them.

"Did we already pack our longest ladder?" Jack asked as he stared up at the antenna.

"It's in the barn," Annie said.

"I'll help you carry it, Annie," Josh said.

"I have the tools we need in my toolbox in the back of my truck," Mr. Young said.

"I can climb into the back of your truck and get it, Mr. Young," Brett said.

"I'll go inside and tell Major we're taking down the antenna," Jack said.

"Not a good idea, Dad. Mom already told him, and she's still talking. Aunt Vanessa and Sara took Penny for a walk to the garden," Josh said.

"Taking one for the team," Jack mumbled as Annie, Josh, and Shadow raced to the barn.

CHAPTER SEVEN

Stuart joined his dad in the barn. "You're a man with a mission; what's up?" Scott asked.

"We need the Smith driveway cleared enough to drive the trucks out in the morning. Nate and Andy will talk to Leo to see if we can borrow his smaller tractor."

Scott nodded. "His larger one would be too unwieldy on those curves. Are you and Andy going to do the work?"

"We have too much to do and need help. Nate offered to be the lookout while someone drives the tractor."

"David would be the natural choice, but David, Brandon, and Henry have a project they're working on. I could do it," Scott said. "If Leo's tractor isn't working, my tractor could do the job."

Stuart nodded. "I thought so too, but I think Andy is trying to help Leo feel more involved."

"He's doing a lot for everyone with his radio, but I know he doesn't see it," Scott said. "What's the plan?"

"Whichever tractor we use, you'll take it to the road with Nate along to make sure the road is safe, then you'll drive to the Smith driveway. The heavy limbs we set across the driveway to block it will need to be moved enough that we can get the trucks out, then you'll take the tractor down the driveway to clear it for the trucks. Nate plans to follow the trucks with the tractor in the morning when we leave and put the limbs back into place; he'll leave the tractor nearby, so we can clear the limbs when we return."

"Very straightforward plan, I like it."

"Andy's going to meet us at the Smith barn or somewhere along the way to let us know which tractor to take. Nate will be ready to go."

"Let's see what Andy has to say." Scott picked up his rifle. "I don't want to leave it in the barn. You can bring it back if I'm driving Leo's tractor."

They met Nate on the path to the Smith barn. "I couldn't get Leo's tractor started. Andy's talking to Leo; he'd like for Leo to help us troubleshoot, but we'll see. I'll look at it tomorrow after the trucks leave. If I can't get it going, I'll ask Blanche to look at it."

Scott nodded. "If Blanche can't start it, we'll use it for parts."

After Scott started his tractor, he headed to the driveway with Nate alongside the tractor, and Fire Dog behind Nate.

Andy joined Stuart.

"Is it strange that I want to run up to the fence and hide in the grass while Dad drives the tractor on the road?" Stuart asked.

"I think it's a sign that you are your father's son and growing some Dad wings. You're getting a taste of what it's going to be like with Henry." Andy smiled.

Stuart shook his head as they strolled to the house. "I'm going to be a terrible dad."

"Probably," Andy said. "You should talk to your dad about that sometime, but include me, because I think I'm going to be worse."

"I already know what Dad will say: we're doomed." Stuart grinned, and Andy chuckled.

When they went inside, Red said, "Good, you're here. We've packed for a two-day trip. Mama Sandra has a small box of emergency food for us, and Ms. Blanche and Doc Larkin pulled together a first aid and trauma box. We gathered extra ammunition and an extra rifle for each one of us, including Angel. Everything's on the kitchen table. We thought we could load everything in a wagon to haul our supplies to the trucks. We don't have the chainsaws. Did you already load them into the trucks?"

"Not exactly," Andy said.

Angel glanced at Andy then said, "We need two. I already talked to Dad; we'll check with Mr. Leo after we load the trucks."

After the two young women dashed upstairs, Stuart whispered, "Angel knows we haven't done anything."

Andy exhaled. "My cloud told her, didn't it? I panicked; rookie mistake."

"Let's carry out the boxes and find a chainsaw." Stuart chuckled. "Unless you want to wait and explain why we forgot to both our wives."

"Your wife sees clouds, and mine breathes fire; let's load up that wagon," Andy said.

As they carried the boxes outside, Andy said, "Sure was a doozie on my part. I'll have to apologize."

"Maybe you should wait and focus on what we need to do for the trip. The wagon's in the barn."

After they loaded the boxes into the wagon, Andy said, "We need to make sure we have sleeping bags. Do we need a tent?"

"I don't think so, but I've been thinking about the old portable stove Dad used to have. It's small but might come in handy if it still works."

"I'll collect the sleeping bags while you search for the stove," Andy said.

"I'll meet you out here," Stuart said.

Stuart put the chainsaw and a spare chain in the wagon then searched the barn and found the old portable stove on a shelf behind a box of screws. *Now to find a propane canister.*

He searched box after box before he found two propane canisters in a box that was marked *roofing*.

He placed the stove and cannisters into a small box then added the box to the wagon.

We're going to need the utility cart too.

He pulled the wagon into the yard then hurried to the garden for the utility cart. After he returned with the cart, he transferred the items from the barn into the cart as Angel, Andy, and Red came out of the house. Angel and Red placed the four backpacks into the wagon; Andy dropped the sleeping bags into the utility cart then hurried back to the house and returned with two small duffel bags.

"What's in the duffel bags?" Stuart asked as Andy added them to the utility cart.

"Extra clothes, rain jackets, and warm coats," Red said.

"Looks like we're ready to load," Stuart said. "We'll pull the wagon and cart."

"We'll meet you at the Smith barn," Angel said.

"We'll get Uncle Leo's chainsaw," Red added.

On their way to the barn, Andy turned to face the utility cart as he pulled it over a section of large tree roots that crossed the path. Stuart dropped the handle on the wagon to help steady the cart before it flipped over and dumped out its contents. After they got the cart past the bumps, Andy helped Stuart move the wagon over the roots.

Andy grunted as he rolled the cart over another large root. "I never noticed before how uneven this path is."

"Sure makes the going slow," Stuart said.

When they reached the Smith barn, Angel and Red had returned from the Websters'. As the four of them loaded the trucks, Nate and Fire Dog joined them, and Scott reached the end of the driveway with the tractor.

"What do you have left to do?" Scott asked.

"Everything's loaded; we'll need to check Red's list to see if we forgot anything, then we can walk the driveway and be done until tomorrow morning," Stuart said.

"Uncle Leo was having radio problems earlier," Red said.

"I'd like to check to see how he's doing," Angel said.

"I'd like to talk to David about the house," Nate said as he and Fire Dog headed to the shortcut to the Newton farm with Scott.

Red pulled out a sheet of paper from her backpack. "Here's my list. The only things missing are what Mama Sandra has planned for us to take with us tomorrow morning."

Stuart and Andy read over the list. "What about handheld radios?" Stuart asked. "I didn't think of them earlier."

"Good catch," Red said. "We'll talk to Leo. If they're charged, we'll be in good shape. If we don't have any, we'll have to rely on flashing headlights and hand signals."

"Dad might have my old one. I've lost track of it," Stuart said.

Angel and Red dashed after Scott.

Stuart shook his head. "I didn't mean for them to ask him immediately."

Andy stared at the path. "I suppose we should have known they would. Did you notice neither one of them said anything; they just darted away?"

"It's like one-foot twitches a signal, and they're gone," Stuart said. "Angel tried to explain to me one time how they do that, but I didn't understand; still don't."

When the two returned, Red said, "He's got it. It might not be charged; he'll check it. He uses a small solar charging system, so it may not have enough time to charge fully today." She kissed Andy. "We'll meet you at the Newtons'."

After Angel hugged Stuart and lifted her face for a kiss, the two women dashed to the shortcut to the Websters' farm.

"Are we walking or running the driveway?" Andy asked.

"Let's walk it; we're less likely to miss anything if we take our time."

* * *

When Angel and Red went into the farmhouse, Jennie met them before they went into Leo's radio room. "Is there any reason the Cabellos can't move tomorrow?"

"It depends on what time we get back from Florida," Red said. "If it's late, they can move early Wednesday morning."

"How late is late?" Jennie rubbed her forehead.

"After three in the afternoon. They would need enough daylight to unpack," Red said as Angel continued to the radio room.

"Three?" Jennie's voice was shrill. "That's not going to happen, is it?"

"We'll have to see; everybody's anxious to get settled."

Jennie pulled away a kitchen chair from the table and sat. "My nerves are shot."

"Can I fix you a cup of hot tea, Jennie?" Lela asked as she came into the kitchen.

"I'll do it," Jennie growled as she rose and went to the stove.

Lela raised an eyebrow then quietly left the room.

"Anything I can do to help you?" Red asked.

"No." Jennie pulled out a cup from a cabinet then slammed the cabinet door.

Red nodded then continued to the radio room.

"How's it going?" she asked.

"Still no signal," Angel said.

Leo removed his headset. "It has to be related to a solar disturbance; it could be down for hours or days. I'll keep trying. Come back closer to dark. If I hear from them before you return, I'll let them know you're leaving in the morning. Before I lost the signal, a ham reported a big storm with tornados hit Alabama yesterday and continued into the night, but no one knew if the storm dissipated or which direction it might be headed. I'll let you know if I get anything more on that."

He pointed to the box on his desk. "Don't forget the radio. It's fully charged, and the solar charging system is in the box with the radio."

They raced to the Smith barn, then while they checked the trucks one more time, Red told Angel how short Jennie was with Lela Mitchell.

"Not good," Angel said.

Red nodded. "Mrs. Mitchell was obviously upset. Looks like we're ready to go."

"When we get back to Dad and Mom's place, we'll have to test the radios," Angel said.

* * *

Stuart and Andy waited on the front porch for Angel and Red. "Were you surprised your dad kept your old radio?" Andy asked.

"I sure was. Dad wasn't doing well for quite a while, and I didn't think he cared about much of anything, but he told me he always kept it charged in case I came home and needed it. We'll check it, but I'll bet it's fully charged." Stuart shook his head. "If Leo has a handheld, we can test them to make sure they work on the same frequency."

"I didn't realize that your dad was ill," Andy said.

"Actually, he was injured and couldn't do the work to take care of the farm; it really dragged him down. I'd almost forgotten about it, but that's why Angel, Red, and I originally came here from Florida: to help out Mom and Dad."

"Sorry to hear that, but I appreciate it. What about the Cabellos and Griffins? Seems like there's some history there," Andy said.

"The short answer is…who am I kidding? It's a long story; ask Red."

"Ask me what?" Red asked as she and Angel sped to the porch.

"I was wondering about the Cabellos and Griffins, and Stuart told me it's a long story," Andy said.

"He's right; I'll tell you on the trip to Florida," Red said.

Angel took Stuart's hand. "We need to spend some time with Henry."

As Stuart rose to his feet, he put his arm around Angel, "Let's find him. You know he's going to lobby for going along with us, and he'll have a great case."

"Yes."

When they rounded the corner, Henry waved from the garden. "Here I am, Mama Angel and Dad." He and Brody raced to them, and Angel knelt to hug him.

When Henry wrapped his arms around her neck, Brody licked Angel's neck and Henry's arm. After Henry stepped back a bit to pet Brody, Brody wiggled between them, and Henry laughed and roughed up Brody's coat with two hands. Stuart chuckled as he helped Angel to her feet before the rambunctious puppy and boy knocked her down.

"We're happy to see you, Mama Angel." Henry grinned. "Farmer Blanche and me and Brandon are planning what we want to grow in our small garden. Brandon and I want to grow jellybeans, but they might all be green."

Stuart and Angel each took one of Henry's hands as the three of them strolled together to the garden.

"Me and Farmer Blanche and Brandon talked about the trip tomorrow. I'd like to go, but we need to study about vegetables before we can decide what we want to plant. Will you be okay if I don't go? Nobody can see as good as me, but Farmer Blanche said you will drive fast, so you'll be okay."

Stuart nodded. "Wise decision; it's important to work on the garden plans."

"Thanks, Dad. Brandon said you wouldn't mind because nobody can do what our team can do, but I wanted to ask first."

Henry and Brody dashed back to the garden as Stuart and Angel turned toward the house.

Stuart put his arm around Angel and whispered, "Farmer Blanche is a genius."

Angel nodded. "I expected a big argument with Henry digging in his heels, not a gentle explanation of why he wasn't going with us."

"I love that the boys see the importance of their team," Stuart said.

When they went into the house, Andy, Red, Scott, Doc Larkin, and Nate sat at the kitchen table while David and Cal stood near the doorway to the dining room, and Sandra and Peyton leaned against the counter near the sink.

Stuart's eyes widened as Angel scanned the room. "What?" he whispered.

"Another team." She continued to gaze over the heads of the people in the room.

Stuart nodded. "What's going on?"

"David and I had a long discussion before we pulled together everyone to talk. We were waiting for you," Nate said. "There's a

lot of tension at the Websters; I'm sure you four have seen it."
Nate nodded toward Andy and Red then Stuart and Angel.

"We have," Andy said. "Aunt Jennie is miserable."

Nate sighed. "We realize we're a big crowd, but we thought
there was plenty of room for everyone. Charo's frustrated because
Jennie wants the household to be quieter; Dad and Tom agree that
Lela is frustrated because she's not allowed to help in the kitchen.
Charo wants Lela to move with them."

"Nate and I discussed whether the Cabello house would be big
enough for the Mitchells and their girls to join the Cabellos. The
house has four bedrooms, and the office could easily be a bedroom
for the judge. They wouldn't be cramped as far as sleeping space at
their new place," David said.

"The three little girls will be together for schooling," Sandra
said.

"Would we be able to move them in one move with the
transport truck?" Scott asked.

"Maybe not," David said, "but we can make two trips, or
better yet, load a trailer then pull the trailer with a pickup truck and
follow the transport truck when it goes to the Cabello house. We
don't have to transport people though, because everyone can walk
unless we decide to transport Charo and the little girls."

"If you're ready to move when we return with the Florida
folks, we can use our defensive team to guard the move from the
Websters' to the Cabellos'," Andy said.

"Is there any way we could move earlier than that?" Nate asked. "I discovered Charo and Lela have been planning this for a while and are almost completely packed."

Scott furrowed his brow. "With the Mitchells going with the Cabellos, Tom gives Nate a third man to help defend the property. Wasn't that the main reason we wanted to wait for Major and his team?"

"We could load everything we can into the truck and move before dark; we'll have enough people for defense. Whatever is left behind can be moved after Major gets here," David said.

"That seems kind of panicky to me," Sandra said. "I don't think we've had enough time to think it through."

"Yes," Angel said.

"A safer idea would be to load after we leave and move after we get back," Red said. "Maybe Lela, Charo, and the girls might like to come here for a sleepover for the next two nights."

"Where will you put all of them?" Nate rubbed his forehead.

"I can always make room," Sandra said.

When Stuart side-glanced his dad, Scott rolled his eyes.

"Good, then we're settled," Peyton said. "We're having a sleepover."

"I'll go tell them right now," Nate said.

"We'll go with you." Andy glanced at Red, and she nodded.

"We'll stay here and help Mom," Angel said.

After Nate, Andy, and Red left, Peyton raised an eyebrow. "Okay, girlfriend, what's our plan?"

Sandra shrugged. "I have no earthly idea. I'm open for suggestions."

Peyton smiled. "David and I could host a big sleepover in the living room with the boys. Charo and Nate could take our room, and the girls could take over the boys' room."

"A sleepover in the living room sounds great; Tom and Lela can have our room," Cal said. "I don't think anybody will be able to talk Blanche out of going to the sleepover."

"What about the judge?" Scott asked.

"Up to him, but if he comes too, he's welcome to bunk with me," Doc Larkin said. "We'll have an old cowpokes' sleepover."

Stuart elbowed his dad and whispered, "Move people not beds; what a concept."

"What can I do for the campers?" Sandra asked.

"Come help me change the linens on the bed for Charo and Nate," Peyton said.

As the two of them headed out of the kitchen, Peyton said, "We'll ask the camp counselor what she wants for our campout."

"I'm not used to having so many planners around," Sandra said, "but I'm working on it."

"Not much choice, is there? We're lucky Red wasn't here; she'd have made a list." Peyton snickered.

After Cal and David left to tell Blanche and the boys about the plan, Scott asked, "How many shooters will we have here after you leave?"

"You, David, Nate, and Peyton," Stuart said.

"Four. Angel?" Scott asked.

"Charo, Mom, Cal, Blanche, Tom, Lela, Judge, and Jennie at the Websters'. Peyton and Doc will stay with their patients."

"Eleven shooters, Stuart," Scott said.

Stuart sighed. "I was thinking with blinders, wasn't I? If Blanche and Mom stay home with the kids, and two people drive the truck, there are seven available shooters who can guard the truck while it travels from the Smith farm to the Cabello driveway, or six guards, depending on Jennie's mood."

Scott nodded. "I got the feeling when I said Tom made the third man to defend the house that Angel and Red didn't agree with me from the way Red looked at me. It's the first time I've seen so clearly how in tune you and Red are, Angel."

"It's so subtle that it's easy to miss, Dad," Stuart said. "I miss it all the time, don't I, honey?"

"Most of the time," Angel said.

Stuart chuckled, "Yes, most of the time."

"To expand the plan now that we've recognized the strength of our team, if we reassign two shooters to a pickup truck with a loaded trailer to follow the transport truck to the Cabellos, we'll still have at least four guards and could take along the little girls in the vehicles," Scott said.

Stuart nodded. "Two to clear the way and two to protect the rear."

"I'll call a meeting tomorrow after breakfast and reopen the discussion by saying that I still agree with Sandra and Angel that we needed a little time for heads to cool and think things through because accidents happen when people act in haste, but I don't see any reason to wait to make the move to the Cabello house if we can come up with a plan."

"You're right, Dad; you may hear new ideas tomorrow after everyone's rested," Stuart said.

When Sandra and Peyton joined them in the kitchen, Sandra motioned for them to leave. "Beds are ready; y'all shoo; we saw Blanche and her posse headed this way for a snack, and we need to start working on supper."

Blanche and the boys trooped inside followed by Brody, Tracker, and Ethel.

"Snack time for the boys, and the dogs need a drink," Blanche said. "Cal and David are going to gather the supplies for us that we'll need to build our raised bed garden tomorrow. They told us about the sleepover; I don't suppose we can have a campfire in the living room."

"No, but we can have a small fire in the back and roast marshmallows after we eat supper, and the girls are here. I may have a little leftover graham flour," Sandra said.

"If you'll make graham crackers, the boys and I can make marshmallows after their snack, right boys?" Blanche asked.

"If you teach us, Cook Blanche," Brandon said.

Blanche nodded. "We have ourselves a plan."

"We have crackers and the wild blackberries you picked yesterday for your snack," Sandra said, and the boys rushed to the table and took their seats.

While Sandra served the crackers and berries, Peyton poured water into three large glasses to go with the snack, and Scott, Stuart, and Angel went outside to the front porch.

"What can I do for you?" Scott asked.

"Check the trucks to be sure we haven't forgotten anything critical," Stuart said.

On the way to the Smith barn, Angel said, "I want to check with Leo after we're sure we have what we need in the trucks."

"We split our supplies between the two trucks, so if we suddenly have to abandon one truck, we'll still have resources," Stuart said.

When they reached the truck, Stuart showed Scott what they had loaded.

"I can't think of anything to add or leave behind," Scott said. "If you two want to go to the Websters', I wouldn't mind taking some time to look at the barn. David and I are still mulling over some ideas for how to make it useful."

"Don't leave me," Stuart said.

"I'll run with you," Angel said.

They ran in silence to the Websters; when they reached the driveway, Angel slowed her pace to a walk. Stuart put his arm around her shoulders, and she wrapped her arm around his waist as they walked in step to the house.

Angel giggled when he shortened his stride to match hers. "You're going to fall down walking like that."

He stopped and kissed her. "I love your laugh. Ready to go inside?"

"Yes."

Before they reached the house, Nate, Tom, and the three girls were on their way to the barn.

Nate waved then joined them. "We're going to visit the cows; Scott told me the barn is a great place to hide. Red and Andy are in the radio room with Leo, and the rest of the house is a circus with no ringmaster. Good luck."

"We'll go straight to the radio room," Stuart said. "Thanks."

Nate saluted then strode to the barn.

When they went inside, Jennie was in the kitchen.

"We're here to check on the radio news," Stuart said, and Jennie glared.

As Stuart and Angel continued to the radio room, Charo yelled something in Spanish from her room, and Lela replied in Spanish from her room.

"I didn't know Lela knew Spanish," Stuart whispered.

When Angel nodded, Stuart furrowed his brow. *Does that mean she knew I didn't know or was she agreeing that she didn't know either? Did she know? I'll have to ask her later.*

CHAPTER EIGHT

Andy met them at the doorway. Leo sat in front of the radio with his headset on and Holly at his feet; Red sat next to him.

"We're still not getting a decent signal from Florida," Andy said. "Red talked to a ham in north Georgia about the weather a few minutes ago; she'll catch us up. We decided we'd leave after you got here, then we'll come back after supper."

"Stuart," Charo called out from her room.

"Coming," Stuart said as Angel went into the radio room.

"I'll go with you." Andy followed Stuart down the hallway.

Charo stood in the middle of her bedroom with her hands on her hips.

"What's up?" Stuart asked.

"I have a large duffel bag packed with clothes for our overnight. Lela has one too. Could you take them back with you? We can bring our backpacks. We finished packing, and Nate and Tom are hauling our boxes to the transport truck. We won't be too far behind you."

Stuart lifted the duffel bag. "Sure. We'll check with Lela before we leave."

"Thank you, we'll see you soon," Charo said.

Andy went to talk to Lela while Stuart carried the duffel bag to the radio room.

Red rose from her seat and tapped Leo on the shoulder. "We're going; we'll be back later."

Leo nodded as Red and Angel left, and Andy joined them on their way to the back door.

After they left the house, Angel said, "Jennie is very ill."

"You mean physically ill?" Red asked.

"Yes."

As the four of them strolled to the driveway, Stuart said, "We'll see you at the house," and the two young women took off.

"Rough place," Andy said. "Uncle Leo's oblivious because he lives in a world of ham radio operators, but I didn't notice that Aunt Jennie was sick. Maybe that's why she's so out of sorts."

"I don't know why I didn't know Lela spoke Spanish," Stuart said.

"Pretty cool, isn't it? Lela told Red that her grandmother was from Puerto Rico and spoke only Spanish in the home. Lela and Charo decided all three girls will be bilingual and plan to speak mostly Spanish in their new household."

"I would like for Henry to learn Spanish too. Maybe we can work out a schedule for some playdates for common lessons for the kids," Stuart said.

"I'll talk to Blanche about it," Andy said.

Stuart told Andy about Scott's plan to reopen the discussion about the move to the Cabello house.

"Charo and Lela are really excited about the sleepover," Andy said. "When Tom said he wanted to go too, the judge said he wouldn't mind tagging along. Can your mother make room for that many people?"

"It didn't take much of a shuffle for everyone to have a place to sleep. The plan is for the boys to camp in the living room with Peyton, David, Blanche, Cal, and all the dogs," Stuart said.

"Funny that you mentioned dogs. I have a feeling that Pixie will be wherever the girls are, and Fire Dog will be with Nate." Andy smiled.

"I'm sure you're right. Ethel stays with Doc Larkin at night too."

"Farm Dogs have been sticking close to Sam and Cami Sue. I asked Leo if he was going to let them go with the girls, and he told me it was up to the dogs and girls, not him," Andy said. "I'll bet the girls have named them, but I haven't heard anyone mention any names; Uncle Leo told me he helps the girls sneak them into the house at night by distracting Aunt Jennie."

"There won't be a shortage of guard dogs at the Cabellos if all three girls and Nate have their dogs," Stuart said.

"I'm catching the excitement from being around the chatter between Charo and Lela, and it might be hard, but I like the idea of getting some rest before we leave."

"I thought we might go to bed early but close to our usual bedtime makes more sense, so we aren't trying to force sleep."

Angel and Red greeted them when they went into the kitchen. "What's in the duffle bags?" Red asked.

"Charo and Lela sent us back with their sleepover bags," Stuart said. "Nate and Tom are loading their transport truck, and it won't be long until they're here."

"Put Charo's in my room and Lela's in Blanche's room," Peyton said.

"Did you hear that?" Angel asked as she grabbed her rifle and raced out the back door.

"Gunshots near the state highway." Red grabbed her rifle then dashed to the door and shouted out in her command voice, "Inside," before she raced after Angel. Stuart and Andy grabbed their rifles and followed Red.

The children dashed into the house with the dogs and were followed by Scott, Blanche, and Cal. David raced with his rifle in his hand to catch up with Stuart and Andy.

Red waited midway up the driveway for them. She whispered, "Angel went to check; wait."

At the sound of more gunshots, Stuart and David slipped into the tall grass; Stuart signaled that he was moving forward, and David stayed parallel to him and within Stuart's sight. When the gunfire stopped, they were close to the crossing point to the Cabello driveway.

Before they reached the road, Stuart paused at the roar of a car engine from the state highway as the car sped north then crawled to the road; David dropped to a kneeling shooting position. When Stuart whistled the cardinal call, David crawled to join him.

Stuart whispered, "Angel's about a hundred yards down the road; she's crouched behind a large fallen tree. She saw me and waved. Stay with me but out of sight."

David nodded.

Before Stuart reached Angel, she called out, "We're here to help."

"She's hurt," a man shouted.

When Stuart reached Angel, she said, "One car in the ditch with four people: a dark-skinned family with two children. They were ambushed by three light-skinned men. The woman is wounded. I shot one man, and the second man raced away in the car. I'm not sure where the third man is. I'm going back to Red. We'll bring help."

Angel darted into the grass and disappeared. Stuart and David cautiously made their way to Angel's tree.

"We've sent for help," Stuart shouted. "Can we come closer?"

"Yes." The man said.

David peered through his scope. "The man is light-skinned, Stuart; he's one of the bad guys."

After Stuart and David were closer, David kept his rifle aimed at the man while Stuart stepped out where he could be seen.

Stuart held his rifle in the air. "I'm going to walk toward you. My wife has gone for help."

David remained hidden in the tall grass as he kept pace with Stuart.

As Stuart slowly approached the car, two children stood at the back of the car on the driver's side. Their dark skin almost hid them in the shadow of the dusty, black car. The boy, about six years old, stared at Stuart with piercing, dark-brown eyes and shook his head vigorously. The older child, a girl about ten, stared wide-eyed at the woman lying on the pavement and the man standing next to her. When she shifted her attention in the same direction as her brother, she frowned at Stuart and shook her head. She tugged at the young boy's shirt and when he looked at her, she put her finger to her lips, then the two of them slowly stepped away from the car to the other side of the road. When they reached the ditch, they crouched down out of sight.

"Did you see the kids?" Stuart whispered.

"Yes, there's a man lying in front of the car; he must be the man Angel shot. The man is holding his rifle with his finger on the trigger. Is he pointing it at the woman, or is it just my angle?"

Stuart whispered, "At her. Watch his eyes and hands. He hasn't looked at her once. If he aims his rifle at her or raises it toward me, drop him."

When Stuart was ten yards from the road, the woman tried to rise, and man growled, "Be still."

"Everything okay?" Stuart asked.

"I'm afraid for her to move," the man said.

The woman screamed, "Help!"

The man raised his rifle toward Stuart, and David shot him. The man reeled, and the woman snatched away his rifle as he fell to the ground.

As Stuart approached her, he asked, "Are you okay?"

"Where are my children? Where's my husband?" she cried out in anguish.

"Mommy, we're okay," the girl shouted as she and the young boy rose from their hiding place and hurried to their mother.

"I saw Daddy move his fingers," the boy said.

Is the father on the other side of the car? Stuart crouched down and peered at a man on the ground near the driver's door.

The mother sobbed. "I thought they…" she bit her lip and tried to sit up. "Noel, can you hear me?"

The man's fingers twitched, and Stuart said, "He's alive, ma'am. I'm going to check him."

Stuart smiled at the sound of 48-4, as Red had dubbed their utility vehicle. The increasing roar of the familiar engine headed toward them from the farm as he knelt next to the man and felt the man's neck for a pulse.

"Angel is on the road in her utility four-seater." David joined Stuart at the car.

"He has a weak pulse," Stuart said. "We'll load the parents into 48-4. The kids and I will walk to the farmhouse unless I can start the car and get it out of the ditch."

Aimee Louise parked 48-4 close to Stuart after she turned the vehicle to be in position to return to the farmhouse. Stuart and David gently loaded the man onto the backseat, and David knelt on the floor next to the man.

Stuart knelt next to the woman. "My name is Stuart. Angel is my wife, and David is with your husband. I'll help you to the front seat, then Angel and David will take you and your husband to our farmhouse. A surgeon is there, and he'll look after both of you. The kids and I will try to get your car out of the ditch. If we do, we'll be not far behind you. If we can't, we'll walk. Is that okay with you?"

"Yes, thank you," the woman said.

After Stuart helped the woman to the front seat and buckled her seatbelt, the woman turned to Angel. "You're Angel?"

"Yes."

The woman smiled. "Thank you, I recognize your voice; you shot the man who said he was going to hurt our children. I'm Louisa Wheatley. Mandy, you and Jimmy will be fine with Mr. Stuart. Help him as much as you can," the mother said, and the two children nodded.

After Angel headed to the farm, Stuart quickly checked the two men on the ground then picked up all the rifles and guns he could find to put them in the back of the car. His eyes widened at the four cases of canned food that were already on the floorboard, and the two suitcases on the back seat. He shrugged and put the rifles on top of the canned food and stuffed the pistols into the voids. After Stuart slid into the driver's seat, the two kids climbed into the passenger's seat.

"Ready?" he asked. "Mandy and Jimmy, right?"

Mandy nodded. "You have to get into the back seat, Jimmy. I can't click the seatbelt with you crowding me."

Jimmy grumbled as he climbed over the seat and dropped onto the back seat. "Why do I always have to ride in the back seat?"

"Because you have to be nine to ride in the front seat," Mandy said with a sniff.

Stuart snorted then held his breath as he turned the key and exhaled when the engine started.

"Hold on; this is going to be bumpy," he said then rocked the car back and forth until the car surged, and the back wheels were on the shoulder. Stuart backed out then turned the car around and headed toward the farm.

On their way to the Newtons', Mandy said, "That other car bumped us, then we went into the ditch. When Daddy got out to check our car, the men parked across the road from us and shot at him. He shot back, and so did Mommy. She told us to stay low, so we did, but after they shot Daddy and he couldn't move, Mommy told us to run. We hid behind the car because we were scared the man was going to hurt Mommy, and we didn't know which way to run."

"It was great that you hid in the ditch," Stuart said.

"We saw you and knew you would help Mommy, so we didn't have to watch her anymore," Jimmy said.

"Where were you going?" Stuart asked.

"We left our house in Port St. Lucie; do you know where that is?" Mandy asked.

"It's on the Atlantic side of Florida," he said.

Mandy nodded. "We went to Grandma's in Tallahassee, but the neighbors who lived next door said she was gone, and Mommy cried."

"Daddy said we'd find something in the mountains, like a shack or something," Jimmy said.

"Mommy said it sounded like pioneer days, but she didn't sound happy. Daddy checked Grandma's house, and we helped carry out cans of food and stuff that's in the back with us," Mandy added.

"Mommy wanted to drive Grandma's car and follow Daddy, so she could take some old things to remember Grandma, but she didn't because Daddy got really mad," Jimmy said. "Mommy told me to put my hands over my ears because Daddy said words I'm not allowed to say."

Stuart nodded. *I completely understand.*

"We left home four days ago. Daddy said driving on the backroads was safer than going on the interstate, but Mommy wanted to get to the mountains faster," Mandy said. "Daddy got off the interstate because he said it made him uneasy, but when he saw that the bad men followed us, he drove really fast."

"They drove faster," Jimmy said.

"Are Daddy and Mommy going to be okay?" Mandy asked.

"Angel took them to a doctor who is really smart and will take great care of them," Stuart said. "We'll pray that they'll be okay."

"Amen," Mandy said, and Jimmy whispered, "Amen."

"I'm going to drive the car into a field then behind some trees, so no one can see it from the road. We'll walk from there," Stuart said as they passed the driveway to the Cabello house. "Do you have clothes and things that are packed?"

"We have our backpacks, and Mommy packed a big suitcase for us and one for her and Daddy," Mandy said. "Daddy was going to put our suitcases in the trunk, but there was already a lot of stuff there, so he put them on the backseat. Mommy said it was crowded, but we could pretend we were sardines because they're packed really tight in their can."

"Angel and I can come get your things later," Stuart said.

"Is Angel a real angel?" Mandy asked quietly. "She's really pretty like an angel."

Stuart smiled. "She's a real person; Angel is her name, and she's my wife; I think she's pretty too."

After Stuart maneuvered the car through the field and into the woods, the kids jumped out with their backpacks.

"Which suitcase is yours?" Stuart asked.

"This one." Jimmy pointed.

"Are any of your things in the trunk?" Stuart asked.

"No, just Daddy's pawn shop stuff."

After Stuart lifted out the large suitcase, he locked the car. "Angel and I are going on a trip tomorrow. We'll be back late tomorrow night or the next day. We'll empty the car after we get back."

As they walked toward the farm, Jimmy asked, "How much longer do we have to walk?"

"Not long. After we reach the road, we can walk down the driveway to the farmhouse. When was the last time you had anything to eat or drink?"

"We ate crackers for breakfast," Mandy said.

"We ran out of water before we got to Grandma's. Daddy said there wasn't any at her house, but he found a small bottle of pineapple juice, and we shared it," Jimmy said.

When they reached the driveway, Mandy asked, "Where's the house?"

"Not much farther," Stuart said.

"I see the house," Mandy said. "Is that where Mommy and Daddy are? I'm glad we didn't have to walk the whole way."

"We almost did," Jimmy said.

Angel and Red raced out of the house, and Andy strolled along behind them.

"Wow," Jimmy said. "Your hair is really red."

Mandy's eyes were wide. "You are as pretty as Angel. Are you an angel too?"

Andy laughed, and Red narrowed her eyes at him then smiled at the children. "Angel is my sister; my name is Red."

Andy waved. "I'm Andy."

Mandy narrowed her eyes. "Are you Red's boyfriend?"

"Good guess, Mandy," Red said. "You could say that because we're married."

Mandy nodded then whispered. "I thought so, Red, because he thinks you're pretty too."

As they walked toward the back door, Mandy walked with Red, and Andy walked next to Jimmy.

"A whole bunch of people are staying at the house, and a bunch of dogs too; it's a big crowd, but they are all nice," Andy said. "You won't know everyone's name right away, and that's okay."

Mandy swallowed hard. "Thanks. I'm kind of shy in crowds, but I like dogs."

Jimmy hid behind Andy as they went in. "And I'm worse shy except I like dogs too."

"We're right here with you." Red offered her hand to Mandy, who tightly clutched it.

When they walked inside, Stuart said, "We have two hungry people here."

Sandra smiled. "You are in luck. We're about to put supper on the table."

"You have to wash your hands and face before supper," Dolly said.

"Why?" Jimmy looked at his hands. "They aren't dirty."

"Of course, they aren't, but you can't see germs." Dolly looked at her hands. "I can't see germs either."

"We'll go with you," Andy said.

"I need to wash off germs too," Henry said.

"I do too," Brandon said.

"While everyone is washing, let's figure out seating arrangements. We can seat eight, and we have seven children, so they will be our first to eat."

"I'll be child number eight," Blanche said.

Cal chuckled. "Same age group."

"Where will everyone sleep?" Charo asked.

Stuart set down the large suitcase. "This has the children's things. I don't think Mandy and Jimmy are ready to be split up," Stuart said.

"Mandy can join the camping crowd unless she'd rather stay in the girls' room," Blanche said. "It would be nice to have another cowgirl around the campfire."

"We can ask her after everyone eats," Red said.

"That's good; I'll take all the cowboys and cowgirls to the campground living room for an Old West story while you all eat," Blanche said.

"I'd like to check on the Wheatleys. Where are they?" Angel asked.

"Charo's new room, or Peyton's old room," David said. "I'll go with you."

"So will I," Stuart said.

"Ask Doc Larkin and Peyton if they want to eat their supper in here, or if they want us to bring them plates when we bring a plate for Louisa," Sandra said.

When they reached the doorway, Louisa sat in a chair next to the bed as she held Noel's hand.

"Hi, Angel. We're worried about Noel, aren't we, Doc?" Louisa said.

Doc Larkin nodded. "I removed the bullet from his upper chest, and I think I've stopped the bleeding."

"He was unconscious, which made it less of an ordeal for him," Peyton said. "I may have to visit Jennie tomorrow to see if she has any pain killers and antibiotics."

"I'll go now," David said.

"I'll go with you," Angel said. "We won't be long."

Stuart furrowed his brow. "Before we leave, Doc and Peyton, Mom is fixing a plate for Louisa, do you want to eat supper in here or at the kitchen table?"

"If it isn't too much trouble, Doc and I would like to eat in here to keep an eye on Noel," Peyton said, and Doc nodded.

When they returned to the kitchen, the children were sitting at the table with their food, and Sandra hovered.

Nobody's allowed to leave Mom's kitchen hungry. Stuart smiled. "Mom, three plates for the sick room."

"I'm on it," Lela said.

"I'll help carry," Cal added.

Angel said, "David and I are going to the Websters' to ask Jennie if she has any pain killers or antibiotics. I want to check with Leo; I need to know whether he's heard anything more from Florida."

"I need more information about the weather." Red grabbed her rifle, and Andy picked up his.

"Wait a second," Stuart said. "We're about to empty the house. Red, David, and Andy, you three go. Angel, you need to be here for our new family and to make sure I don't decide to go too."

Andy snickered, and Red said, "Let's go."

"Let David talk to Jennie," Stuart said. "My gut tells me she does better with strangers."

"We'll be in the radio room with Leo, so we won't be in your way, David," Andy said as the three of them hurried to the door.

After they left, Angel kissed Stuart. "Well done."

Stuart glanced at his dad, who winked at him.

"What are the overall sleeping arrangements?" Stuart asked.

"Right after supper, everyone's going to race for a bed," Lela said. "Whoever doesn't get one will sleep in the chicken coop."

Lela smiled while all the adults, except Angel, laughed.

"I had a plan," Sandra said after she wiped away her tears of laughter, "but I'll toss it out because there's no way I could top Lela's plan."

Jimmy tugged on Stuart's sleeve and whispered, "Mama Sandra is a good cook; I was hungry. These people are weird. I like them."

Stuart smiled as he leaned down. "Yes, they are, and I do too, Jimmy."

"Can I see Daddy and Mommy?" Jimmy asked.

"I'll check with the doctor," Stuart said.

Stuart left the kitchen; when he reached the bedroom, he asked, "When can the children see their parents?"

"Noel's condition is still critical, but Louisa, you know your children. What do you think?" Doc Larkin asked.

Louisa bit her lip and reached for Peyton's hand. When Peyton nodded and squeezed her hand, Louisa said, "Might do everyone good."

"Be best if they don't stay too long," Doc said.

Stuart strode to the kitchen. "Angel, Mandy, and Jimmy, come with me."

As they walked down the hallway, Stuart said, "Your mommy wants to see you, and she thought you might like to talk to your daddy. He was hurt very badly and won't be able to talk to you, but you can talk to him because we think he will hear you."

"Is he going to be okay?" Tears filled Mandy's eyes.

"He's got the best doctor in the world taking care of him, so he's got a good chance to be okay, but we'll just have to wait and see," Stuart said.

"I don't like waiting," Jimmy pouted.

"I don't either," Stuart said.

When Mandy and Jimmy reached the doorway, Louisa held out her arms and smiled, and the children ran to her. She hugged and kissed them.

"You two were so brave. I heard you guarded me until you saw Mr. Stuart," Louisa said.

"Mr. Stuart is nice. Did you know a whole bunch of people live here, and they are all nice?" Jimmy asked.

Mandy nodded. "Mama Sandra gave us supper. Somebody's going to bring you some supper too, but I forgot her name. Mr. Stuart said it was okay that we don't remember everybody's name."

Mandy moved close to her father. "Daddy, we had a great supper; it was as good as grandma's. When you can sit up, you'll see how good it was."

Jimmy crowded his sister. "My friends told me they are having a campout tonight in the house, not outside, and maybe I could camp with them, if I want to. I think it would be fun."

Mandy patted her dad's hand. "That man wanted to hurt Mommy, and you stopped him." She leaned close. "Mr. Stuart said a prayer for you to get better."

"Me and Mandy said, 'Amen,'" Jimmy added.

Louisa's eyes welled up, and Peyton sniffled.

"Might be time to let your mom and dad rest," Stuart said.

CHAPTER NINE

Stuart, Angel, Mandy, and Jimmy passed Lela and Cal as they carried three plates of food for Doc, Peyton, and Louisa.

"How's everybody doing?" Lela asked.

Jimmy's downturned mouth quivered into a small smile, and he held up a thumb.

Cal smiled. "Good news."

Before they returned to the kitchen, Angel asked, "Mandy, it sounds like Jimmy would like to sleep at the campout in the living room. Would you like to join him, or would you rather sleep upstairs in the girls' room with Dolly, Cami Sue, and Sam?"

"Would you be okay without me, Jimmy?" Mandy asked.

"If you want to camp out, you can, but I'll be with my friends, if that's okay," Jimmy said.

"It might be fun to be with the girls. One of the twins told me they read books in the kitchen with Grandma Lela before bed."

When they went into the kitchen, Charo and Dolly rose from the table. "We were waiting for you," Dolly said. "Storyteller

Blanche is waiting for us at the campsite. Henry said she tells good stories."

Dolly skipped to the living room, and Mandy and Jimmy followed her.

"If you'll excuse me," Charo said, "I need a good story tonight too."

Angel cocked her head. "I've been thinking about where everyone will sleep. Charo and Nate could take our room; they'd be close to Dolly and the other girls. Lela and Tom could take Red and Andy's room."

"Where will you sleep?" Sandra asked.

"The boys will be camping out; the four of us could take over their bedroom until we leave."

"That might just work because when you return with the Florida family, Charo, Nate, Judge, Lela, and Tom will be moving into the Cabello house."

Scott came into the kitchen. "Do we want to bring Noel and Louisa's car here? I have an idea."

"I'd like to bring it closer because it could lead bad guys to us, but it's too far away for us to know that someone found it. What did you have in mind?" Stuart asked.

"We've been worried that if we drive the car through the grass, it would be easy to track. That's true for a few days, but after the grass recovers, there won't be anything that anyone would notice other than someone with a very discerning eye," Scott said.

"Henry," Angel and Stuart said in unison.

Scott chuckled. "Right. That Henry sees on a different plane, doesn't he? Not much daylight left. Let's get to it."

While Stuart led Angel and his dad to the Wheatleys' car, he told them what he'd found in the backseat of the car.

After they reached the car, Scott scanned the area. "This spot is actually well-hidden from the road. It will be a risk to take it out of the trees and into the field, but that's the quickest way to the driveway."

"We'll go to the road to watch for cars. I'll whistle if I see anything, and if you don't hear it, Angel will still run to the car and warn you."

"I like it," Scott said, "otherwise I'd be stopping every few feet to listen. Knowing how you two work, I'll just drive."

Stuart handed his dad the key to the car, and Scott climbed into the driver's seat.

"Give us one minute to get in place," Stuart said.

After Stuart and Angel reached the road, she slipped back into the field, and Stuart stepped onto the shoulder for a good view of the road both ways.

She's always thinking; she can watch me and be closer to Dad if I whistle.

When Scott started the engine, Stuart narrowed his eyes as he scanned the road to his right and listened before he quickly scanned the road to his left then back to the right.

As the sound of the car engine grew fainter, Stuart tensed. *Should I move closer to the driveway?* He exhaled. *No, the interstate is our worst threat.*

He remained in place until he heard the familiar who-cooks-for-you call of a barred owl. He smiled as he slipped back to the field and hurried to the driveway. *We didn't talk about an all-clear, but Angel knew I'd recognize her call.*

When he reached Angel at the driveway, he hugged her. "You're brilliant."

"Dad drove the car to the house," she said.

When they reached the car, Scott waited for them with the small suitcase. "We'll take it inside; the food can stay. We'll leave the car as is until the Wheatleys decide what they want to do."

When Angel picked up the small suitcase, Stuart said, "That one goes to the sick room."

She nodded. "I'll let Mom know that's it."

After she left with the suitcase, Scott asked, "Is she always thinking?"

"Always."

Nate met Stuart at the end of the driveway.

"I'm the bellboy." Nate grinned. "What do I do?"

"Angel took in the suitcase. Dad told me to leave the canned food in the car for now."

"My goal is to overload Sandra." Nate said. "So far, we're unsuccessful."

"There are only five of us against a mom; we're outnumbered." Stuart grinned.

Before they were inside, Red, Andy, and David returned from the Websters'.

"Is that the Wheatleys car?" Red asked.

"Sure is," Stuart said. "We'll tell you how we got it here while you have supper."

"We've got antibiotics and news; I'll take the antibiotics to Doc and share our news before we eat," Red said. "The best news is that Leo talked to Mr. Young, and the Florida family will be ready when we get there."

Stuart went inside to talk to his mom. "This is all we needed to bring inside for now. I'll take it to the sick room."

After Stuart returned to the kitchen, Sandra asked, "Where are the four of you sleeping, Angel?"

Stuart smiled. *Mom knows Angel has a plan.*

"In the back of our transport trucks."

"The Smith barn campground," Lela said, and Sandra chuckled.

Stuart furrowed his brow. *Smith farm.*

When Scott came into the house, Stuart asked, "Dad, do you know where the Smith farm well is?"

Scott stared at Stuart. "Whatever made you think of that?"

"Angel said we're spending the night in the transport trucks, and Lela joked about the Smith barn campground."

"I didn't even think about where we'd sleep," Andy said. "That's a really good idea; it'll be quiet, and we won't disturb anyone when we get up."

"I think the well was closer to the house; that's all grown over, so that's why we never see it when we take the shortcut to the Websters'."

"I'd like to find it after we get back from Florida then see what it would take to get it into operation. If we decide to build a rough cabin for temporary housing when we have an overflow, a nearby water source would be critical."

Scott nodded. "I've been wondering how functional the chimney is. That might be an option on location for the cabin, or if it's not usable as a fireplace chimney, we could take it apart and build an outdoor wood-fired oven."

"Really opens up a lot of possibilities, doesn't it?" Andy asked.

Red said, "Supper's on the table, honey."

"I'll be right there after I wash," Andy said.

"Wash fast; David's hungry." Red giggled.

While Red, Andy, and David ate, Angel, Stuart, Cal, and Judge sat with them.

"Angel, Lela, and I talked. We'll take their breakfast, snacks, and lunch out to them in the morning. Nate wants to close up the driveway behind them, but he can do that any time after they leave. There's no sense in waking up the entire household," Sandra said.

"We live with geniuses," Cal said.

"Of course, you do," Charo said as she brought the dishes back from the sick room. "Mama Sandra, I have no scraps for the dogs; Louisa thought she wasn't hungry, but she ate everything on her plate."

Sandra chuckled. "Poor dogs never get scraps around here."

After everyone finished eating, Red said, "Speaking of geniuses, David and Jennie strolled outside and chatted. Jennie gave David all the antibiotics she could find."

"We talked about the chicken coop and what she could do to make it more varmint proof. She'd like for someone to take the cows," David said. "I told her we'd make her a deal: we'd take the cows and her antibiotics for Doc Larkin to have on hand, and she laughed then agreed."

"Why did she laugh?" Angel asked.

Red smiled. "It was a goofy, one-sided trade. We'd take the antibiotics that we wanted and the cows she didn't want. What we gave her was the opportunity to be rid of the cows."

Angel shook her head, and Stuart put his arm around her. "It was goofy and genius."

Angel nodded. "Still not funny. What about the weather?"

"We may run into bad weather on the trip back. The storm hasn't dissipated at all; in fact, it seems to be strengthening. Our best bet is to get there as early as we can, load up, and get back here before the storm hits," Red said.

"That sounds risky," Sandra said. "Shouldn't you wait until after the storm passes to leave?"

"No," Angel said. "They aren't safe."

"The farm family will have everything done tonight," Stuart said, "so we can get a few hours' sleep then get there before daylight if we're okay with driving there with headlights."

"When do you expect the storm to be here?" Nate asked.

"It's hard to say, but my guess is late afternoon," Red said. "If you're going to move tomorrow, I'd suggest doing it in the morning, so you'll have time to unload the truck before lunch."

"I want to make one more trip back to the house to make sure we loaded everything," Nate said.

"I'll go with you," David said.

"I'd like to tag along to talk to Leo, if I won't slow you down," Judge said.

"You won't slow us down, but we might use you as an excuse not to run," David said. "Let's go."

After the three men left, Sandra said, "Lela and I will fix your meals for tomorrow before we go to bed, Stuart. You can slip in to pick them up before you leave."

"We need to relax now," Angel said.

"Camp Counselor Blanche and the boys made marshmallows earlier, and I made graham crackers for them. Check with Blanche because it might be time to light the campfire in the back," Sandra said.

Andy and Red hurried to the living room then returned as quickly as they left.

"Counselor Blanche and the boys are ready for the campfire," Andy said.

After the camping crowd went outside, Brandon and Henry started the fire with Blanche's guidance.

"We laid the fire right after supper," Henry said.

"You did a good job," Stuart said. "Your kindling caught right away."

"Grandpa Scott helped us pick out branches to roast our marshmallows," Cami Sue said.

"Mr. David put points on all the sticks, so everybody can cook their own marshmallows," Sam added.

"We need campfire music while we wait for the fire to be perfect for roasting," Red said.

"I'll grab our guitars and be right back," Stuart said. "It's been a long time since we've taken the time to have fun."

When Stuart returned with the guitars, Red tuned hers, then Stuart tuned his to hers.

"Big advantage in having a guitar partner with perfect pitch." Stuart grinned.

While Stuart and Red strummed and sang, Angel hummed, the rest sang along, and the children danced.

"Any requests?" Red asked after five songs.

"Do you know 'Five Little Speckled Frogs'?" Blanche asked.

Red and Stuart glanced at each other, and when Stuart shrugged, Red said, "Sing a verse, and we'll pick it up."

"Okay, y'all, listen up; this is an old nursery rhyme; pay attention and when I sing, 'Eating some most delicious bugs,' you say, 'Yum, yum.'"

Everyone laughed.

After Blanche belted out the first verse, Red nodded. "Got it. You?" She glanced at Stuart.

He grinned. "Let's get pickin'."

Red, Stuart, and Blanche sang the first verse, and everyone joined in and shouted, "Yum, yum!"

Blanche led the rest of the verses while Red and Stuart sang with her, and everyone jumped in with, "Yum, yum."

After the song was over, Sandra asked, "Ready to roast marshmallows?"

The children shouted, "Yum, yum!"

After the fire died down, and everyone had their fill of marshmallows and graham crackers, Blanche said, "Time to clean up, cowboys and cowgirls. We got the stickiest faces and fingers in the state right around this campfire. After everyone is clean and ready for bed, I'll tell you a story."

As the children filed away, Charo joined Stuart at the dying fire. "It was heartwarming to see the children having so much fun, and it was a great time for all the adults to forget their worries for a bit, but weren't we making a lot of noise? Weren't you afraid we might draw attention and be ambushed?"

"Not at all; tell me, who was missing from the campfire?" Stuart asked.

Charo furrowed her brow and glanced around. "Judge, your dad, Mr. Cal, Mr. Tom, and Ms. Lela."

"That's right; they were only a few yards away and were hidden in the dark. We were circled by a protection of guards."

Charo's eyes widened. "Did you coordinate that?"

Stuart shook his head. "I just watched it happen; it was awesome."

"Next time, you tell me to open my eyes; I would have loved to have seen it." Charo smiled as she headed into the house.

Stuart and David spread out the coals and doused them before they stirred the ash and embers until they were certain the site was cold.

While they worked on the fire, David said, "If you don't get to Florida on your timetable, I'd strongly suggest you stay an extra day. If the storm is moving as fast as Red thinks it might be, the next day will be safer."

"You're probably right, but I'm worried about the escalation of highway robbers who are increasingly vicious, and the vulnerability of the Florida family is my biggest concern."

"I know them well and understand what you mean," David said. "I'd like to go along; you need an additional strong shooter with you."

"I hadn't thought of taking another shooter, but you're right: Major's end is weak in terms of fire power. You need to know, though, Dad has an idea on how to move the Cabellos while we're gone and will discuss his plan with everyone in the morning." Stuart summarized his dad's plan.

David frowned. "It makes sense."

"Let's pull in Angel, Red, and Andy, so the five of us can talk it over," Stuart said.

David nodded. "It'll take me two minutes to pack and two hours to convince Peyton or make her so mad that she tosses me out."

Stuart snorted. "Meet us at Dad's barn."

Stuart strolled toward the house and found Angel waiting outside for him. "Meeting at the barn."

He smiled and headed toward the barn as she dashed away. *Fastest way to get everyone together.*

After all five of them were in the barn, Stuart said, "David brought up an interesting point. I'll ask a question similar to what Dad asked me earlier. How many shooters does Major have?"

"Pops, Sheriff, and Annie are the strong shooters," Red said.

"Annie?" David asked.

Red smiled. "She's a fairly new shooter, but she dropped her first deer a few weeks ago."

"Good for her," David said. "Molly is a possible shooter, but I never knew her to practice. Mr. Young's eyesight is failing."

"Aunt Vanessa would be willing, but I don't think she's had any training," Red said. "The other limitation they have is drivers; as far as I know, Pops and the sheriff are the only ones experienced enough to pull a trailer."

"Sounds like they could drive one vehicle and pull a trailer, but not two," Andy said.

Stuart nodded. "We can only guess because we don't know how many vehicles they plan to drive, but even if they bring two, we'll be in the lead and guarding the rear. It wouldn't be ideal, but they could tow two trailers."

"If David leaves with us, any plans to move to the Cabello house while we're gone will be less feasible," Angel said.

David shook his head. "Angel, I didn't think of that. It's really important to Charo to move tomorrow, and I don't think that's going to change." He exhaled. "I should stay."

As he left the barn, David smiled. "The good news is that I didn't say anything to Peyton yet."

"We need to take our guitars inside, and we'll want to tell Henry and the rest of the children good night," Stuart said.

When they went into the kitchen, Peyton and Doc Larkin sat at the table with Scott.

"Lela and Tom told us we had to take a break and replaced us in the sick room," Peyton said. "I told Blanche, but I thought you'd like to know how much Louisa enjoyed hearing the campfire songs, and I'm certain that Noel's color improved when the kids shouted, 'Yum, yum.'"

Doc Larkin nodded. "I thought so too. I'm going to see if I can get a few hours' sleep because Noel is currently stable and not restless at all. Lela promised to come get me if there was any change in his condition. Louisa told us he hasn't slept more than an hour at a time since they left home, so I suspect that in addition to his gunshot wound, he's exhausted. She probably didn't sleep very well, either, because she fell asleep right after their children came inside and told them good night. I'm hoping Noel will rest easy, and we'll see a big improvement by morning."

"The children already had their snack. I gave each one a cracker even though I'm sure they were all full, but I knew better than to try to skip snack. Can you imagine breaking the bath, snack, bed rule?" Sandra smiled. "They're getting the treat of a Cowgirl Blanche story, though, and not one of them mentioned that was outside the rule."

Scott snorted. "It wouldn't surprise me a bit if a Blanche story was added to the rule."

The children trooped into the kitchen for goodnight hugs and kisses. When Stuart hugged Henry, Henry said, "Dad, you are a good singer. When I get older, would you teach me to play the guitar?"

"I sure will," Stuart said. "I heard you singing, and you were great."

Henry beamed and hugged Angel. She returned his hug and kissed his cheek. "Mama Angel, are you sure I can't go with you?"

"I'm positive. You have important things to do here. You and Brandon have the job of making sure Jimmy feels welcome, and no one can do it except you and Brandon."

Henry nodded. "All the new stuff might be scary, even if Jimmy is a big kid like Brandon. Aunt Charo is going to sing a bedtime song to us in Spanish when we're all in our sleeping pallets. Dolly said her mama's songs always help her go to sleep."

Angel gave Henry an extra hug. "Sleep tight."

Henry nodded, then he, Brandon, and Jimmy went to the darkened living room. The children giggled and whispered until Blanche settled them down, and Charo began singing.

"We'll leave for our campsite, so the house will be quiet," Stuart said.

After hugs, Sandra gave Stuart the lunches and snack food then gave Andy a basket with more food.

"Just a few things to eat in case you get stuck anywhere. There's enough for everyone," she said.

On the way to the truck, Stuart said, "I was thinking I couldn't go to sleep right away, but if I lie down and relax, I have a feeling it won't take long for me to fall asleep."

"I'm the same," Andy said. "This was a full day."

"Wake us when you wake up, Angel," Red said.

After Stuart and Angel settled down in their sleeping bags, Stuart rolled to his stomach then pulled back the flap of their transport truck. "It's peaceful lying here under the stars. How are you doing, sweetheart?"

Angel peered at his cloud then snuggled closer to him. "Why are you so concerned? What is bothering you?"

He put his arm around her. "I was trying to be subtle. I want to know how you're feeling about killing that man."

"He wanted to hurt the children and couldn't have been stopped any other way. His cloud was more than danger; he wanted to hurt them in front of their mother to torture her. Does that answer your question?"

Stuart kissed her lightly. "Sometimes I forget how much depth there is in your clouds; thank you."

Stuart rolled to his side and wrapped Angel in his arms. "Good night, honey."

Angel yawned. "Good night."

"Good night y'all," Red called out from the truck next to them then giggled.

* * *

"Honey," Angel whispered, "Red and I are going to the house. Be right back."

Stuart rolled to his back. "What?"

He patted Angel's sleeping bag, but it was empty. He pulled back the flap and stared out. *No stars; it's getting cloudy. To the house? Why?*

After he quickly dressed, he jumped out of the back of the truck at the same time that Andy hopped out of the other truck.

"What's going on?" Andy asked.

"I don't know, but I have a feeling we better be ready to hit the road in about two minutes. All I need to do is roll up our sleeping bags."

"Got it." Andy climbed back into the truck.

The two young women appeared when Stuart and Andy climbed out of their trucks.

"Mom made coffee before she went to bed and poured it into two thermoses. Let's go," Angel said as she and Red headed toward the cabs of their trucks.

"How did you know?" Stuart asked as he headed toward the passenger's seat where he'd left his rifle.

"Mom told me when she hugged me good night. Ready?"

"I'm ready; I'll pour coffee after we're on the road."

"Yes."

Angel maneuvered the driveway using her parking lights; when they reached the hard surface road, she turned on the headlights.

Stuart glanced in his side mirror; Andy turned on the headlights when his truck reached the road too.

Stuart reached into their supply backpack for cups. "Do you want any coffee?"

"I'm good," Angel said.

Stuart smiled as he poured a cup for himself. *Yes, you are, sweetheart.*

When they reached the interstate ramp, Angel sped down the ramp and picked up speed, and Andy stayed within a car's length behind her.

"What time do you think it is?" Stuart scanned the road ahead and the passing landscape. *Only a light fog; that's good.*

"Morning."

He smiled. *I had to ask.*

He narrowed his eyes as he scanned the dark sky. *I can't tell, but the clouds seem heavier. Maybe it's just the fog.*

Angel pushed the truck to an even faster speed, and Stuart shook his head when he checked the road behind them in his side mirror. *Andy's still right there. My wife is a speed demon and a bad influence on a nice teacher, but it's all good because I am not a deputy sheriff.*

When Angel switched the headlights to bright, Stuart asked, "Why did you turn the headlights to high beam?"

"Buzzard."

Stuart furrowed his brow. "Did you say buzzard?"

"Yes; although technically, I should have said turkey vulture, but I like how the word buzzard sounds; it's more ominous."

"You want the truck to appear more ominous?"

"Yes."

"So if anyone sees us speeding down the road with high beams, they'll assume we're the bad guys."

Angel nodded as she scanned the road ahead.

Stuart smiled. "Drive it like you stole it."

"I don't get it," Angel said.

"Buzzard." Stuart grinned, and Angel giggled.

"You got my joke," Stuart said. "I don't think I've ever heard you laugh at a joke before."

"It was an excellent twist, and it tickled me," she said.

"I'll have to work on that. I loved the sound of your laugh."

"Hold on; I see something at the overpass." Angel pressed the accelerator to the floor then just before she reached it, she swerved to the far-left lane.

As they whizzed under the overpass, Andy maintained the narrow gap between the two trucks and made the same lane shift as Angel; Stuart narrowed his eyes as he peered into his side mirror and watched as a fifty-five-gallon barrel bounced several times on the highway on their previous travel lane next to Andy's truck then rolled into the ditch.

"Wow. I wouldn't have thought that was possible," Stuart said.

Angel eased up on the accelerator. "It was simply a rapid change in our velocity that they didn't anticipate."

Stuart nodded. *Sure, I knew that.*

CHAPTER TEN

Sandra smiled when she hurried into the kitchen, lit a kerosene lantern then started a pot of coffee.

Scott was behind her. "Why were you smiling?"

"I told Angel last night I would fill two thermoses with coffee before I went to bed, and they're gone. They're on the road."

Scott opened the back door to let the dogs out. The puppies led the way, but Fire Dog and the Farm Dogs raced past them, then Ethel lumbered to the door, and Scott smiled. "We've got the best dogs in the world. Did you ever expect to be overrun with dogs?"

"Dogs and grandkids," she said. "I'm living the life."

Scott kissed her cheek. "We are, aren't we? Not exactly like we expected, but I don't think either one of us has been this happy in a long time."

Before the coffee had finished perking, Blanche and Lela came into the kitchen.

"What's today's schedule?" Blanche asked.

"We need a meeting right after breakfast," Scott said. "We have options."

"Yes, but we have priorities, and I smell coffee," Lela said. "Doc and Peyton are in the sick room; I'll take them coffee. When they relieved Tom and me early this morning, Noel was holding his own, and Louisa was sleeping comfortably. I'm anxious to see how they're doing now."

After Lela left with two cups of coffee, Blanche asked, "How can I help with breakfast?"

"I was thinking eggs, biscuits, and gravy."

"You're the gravy guru; I'll do the biscuits." Blanche tied on an apron and pulled out the flour.

When Lela returned, she said, "Louisa wants to clean up a bit and put on fresh clothes. I told her I'd help her after breakfast. Her face is still badly swollen, and the bruises are starting to show all over her body. Doc told her she's lucky that she doesn't have any broken bones or internal injuries, but she's having a very difficult time moving because of the pain. She's refused any medication to take the edge off because she wants to save the medicine for Noel. Peyton convinced her she should take one pain pill after breakfast, so she can make it on her own to the bathroom to wash without squealing like a stuck pig." Lela grinned. "Peyton's words."

David came into the kitchen. "My wife has always had a way with words."

Nate handed him a cup of coffee and chuckled. "She never had a subtle bone in her body when she was my partner in the FBI."

When the girls ran down the stairs, and the boys rushed to the table, Blanche said, "Breakfast is ready; form a line in alphabetical order by your first name, and I'll give you a plate."

"I don't know everybody's name." Jimmy furrowed his brow and bit his lip.

"It's okay," Brandon whispered. "Just get in line behind Henry, and you'll be right."

"That's not fair," Sam said. "I'm last."

"Best for last," Blanche said, "but we'll shake it up next time, so you might end up in the muddled middle."

"What's the muddled middle?" Sandra asked.

"The magical part," Blanche said.

After Henry stepped behind Dolly, Jimmy scanned the line. "Henry, you're in the exact middle; you must be extra magical."

Henry nodded. "I can see really good."

David downed a cup of coffee then grabbed his jacket and rifle. "I want to check with Leo to see if he's heard any more news about the weather."

"I'll go with you." Nate put on his coat and picked up his rifle on the way out.

"We'll feed the dogs when we get back," David said.

"Too late," Sandra said. "I fed them earlier."

"Good because if Nate's going, Fire Dog's going for sure, and the Farm Dogs might follow along."

* * *

On the way to the Websters', David said, "It's dark with the extra cloud cover. Glad we've traipsed this path between the two houses often enough that we can do it blindfolded because that's exactly what it feels like."

"I'd be concerned about something lurking in the dark if we didn't have Fire Dog and the Farm Dogs along with us," Nate said. "You sure called that one."

When they reached the Websters' driveway, Leo was coming out of the house.

"Leo, it's David and Nate," David called out.

"Glad you warned me; I can't see a thing," Leo said. "I'm glad you're here because I was on my way to Scott's house. Let's go to the barn to talk."

After they were inside the barn, Leo said, "I've been on the radio, and the storms hit Alabama, Tennessee, and north Georgia hard. There were three operators from Alabama who are regulars that weren't on this morning, and everybody's worried. The storms are strengthening, and as near as I can tell, we can expect to be slammed before lunch."

"We'll have to move fast," Nate said, "but that shouldn't be a problem."

"I've got a wrinkle for you," Leo said. "Jennie's frantic. She told me the cows and chickens have to be gone from our farm this morning because she can't take care of them. She is so anxious that she wanted me to turn the chickens loose, so they wouldn't be stuck in their coop when the storm hits."

"They'd be safer in their coop than free," David said.

Leo sighed. "It doesn't make any sense to me either, but she's insistent to the point of being hysterical."

"Doesn't sound like Jennie," David said.

"She's not herself. She didn't want me to tell anyone, so you're stuck with helping me keep her secret. She has advanced breast cancer, and Doc thinks it has probably spread to other organs. Doc Larkin wanted her to go to Atlanta several months ago for treatment, but she refused because she said it wouldn't be safe to go to a city, and I couldn't disagree because she was right."

"Is that why she wanted everyone out of the house?" Nate asked.

"I think so," Leo said. "She won't admit to any pain, but Doc told me it was bad."

"It must be unbearable. We're really sorry," Nate said.

"We couldn't wait until tomorrow to move the cows?" David asked.

"No, she's obsessed with having them gone; she told me it would be kinder to shoot them because she doesn't have the strength to make sure they're safe before the storm."

"I can't imagine what she's going through to get her to this point," David said.

"We've got the trailer that Cal used when he brought them here, and you can use my truck to haul them to Scott's. If you'll give me a half hour or so, I'll clear my driveway with the big tractor."

"We'll go check with Scott," Nate said, "but I'm sure we can load them up and move them."

"Can I go inside and talk to Jennie?" David asked.

"I'd rather you didn't. She's in tears and hysterical over the cows and needs a little time to calm herself."

"We'll be back as quick as we can," David said.

As the overcast sky lightened, David and Nate jogged through the woods to Scott's house and were out of breath when they arrived.

"How do Angel and Red do that run at full speed?" Nate asked as he caught his breath.

"Muddled middle," David said as they went inside.

"Just in time for breakfast," Sandra said. "Blanche and the kids went to the living room to plan their day."

I'll refill coffee," David said as Sandra dished up breakfast, and Peyton handed everyone their plates.

After David and Peyton joined the rest at the table, David said, "We need to talk."

"Can't it wait until after breakfast?" Peyton raised an eyebrow.

"No," Nate said. "Tell them, David."

"First thing, the storms are getting worse, and Leo thinks we'll see them before lunch," David said. "We need to make sure that we have everything put away before then."

"Does that mean we'll have to move fast?" Charo asked.

"There's more news than just the storm, honey. It's a long story, but the short version is that we have to move the chickens and the cows from the Websters' farm immediately," Nate said.

"That's absolutely crazy," Sandra said. "Why?"

"That's the long story part that we'll have to save until later," David said.

Scott rubbed his forehead with his fingertips. "I don't know where we could put the cows before lunch. It would take us a full day to clear out enough room in the barn for them, and they wouldn't be safe in the trailer. The chickens are easy; Jennie doesn't have a rooster, so we could put the chickens in our coop. There might be a few scuffles, but they'd be too busy sheltering from the storm to pull too many tail feathers."

"We could put the cows in the Smith barn," David said.

Scott frowned. "How would we secure them?"

"It wouldn't take long to put a fence across the doorway, then we could make a gate after the storm." David said.

"You're our builder, so if it can be done quickly, I'm sure you'll do it," Tom said. "I could help."

"What about moving this morning?" Judge raised his eyebrows at Charo.

"The cows are a priority because we can always move tomorrow. I certainly don't want to try to move today after we move the cows to safety; it would be too risky," Charo said.

"Is the Smith barn safe enough for the cows?" Cal asked.

David nodded. "It's sturdier than the Webster barn. Tom and I can build a couple of stalls for them before we move the animals."

"The Smith barn is a good idea because we cleared the driveway to the road," Nate said. "We'd have a little work to do here at the driveway entrance, and while it might not take long, time's not a luxury for us right now."

"Nate, why don't you and I get the cows and chickens, and David and Tom, you two can get the barn ready. Another option we have is to back the trailer into the barn, but if you build stalls, the cows will be more comfortable."

"Judge, Peyton, and I can take care of the security here while you're gone," Tom said.

"Clean those plates before you leave," Sandra said as Scott and Nate started to rise from the table.

Scott shoved the rest of his food into his mouth, and Nate did the same then grabbed a second biscuit and his rifle on his way out the door.

"We won't be too far behind you," David said. "We'll put some tools into a wagon and pull it to the barn."

"Grab 48-4; right now, working quickly is more important than trying to save gas for later," Scott said.

* * *

When Scott and Nate reached the Webster driveway, Leo drove past them on his way to put away the tractor. Leo waved, and they followed him to the barn.

"I've already hooked up my truck to the trailer. While you're transporting the cows, I'll put the chickens in dog crates and stack their feed to go. I don't have much left, but it will tide them over a day or so."

"We're taking the cows to the Smith barn because the barn is empty, and the driveway's already been cleared. David's going to build a couple of stalls for us while we're on our way."

"Let's load up," Leo said.

When they reached the barn, Scott's eyes widened. "I'd forgotten one of the cows had a calf."

"I knew, but we've always referred to them as the cows. Do we need to let David know?" Nate asked.

"Let's just load up and go. I need you with me to ride shotgun. David's stalls will be fine; he can always expand one later if he likes or even build a third one."

Before they reached the end of Leo's driveway, Nate said, "Stop here; I need to check the road."

After Nate whistled, Scott continued to the road. Nate jumped in the truck, and Scott headed toward the Smith barn.

"I've gotten so used to walking, I didn't realize what a short drive it would be," Nate said as Scott turned then crept along the circuitous driveway to the barn.

When they neared the barn, Scott backed the trailer closer to the door. "I didn't realize I was holding my breath the entire time; let's see how David and Tom are doing."

Scott and Nate strolled into the barn, and Scott's eyes widened at the stalls.

"How did you know to build three?" he asked.

"Tom told me. He and Nate took their girls to see the cows not long ago, so I built the largest stall for the mama cow and her calf and the third stall for the calf after its weaned."

"I have to get into the loop." Scott shook his head. "We need to get back to Leo's and pick up the chickens."

"We're almost finished, but why don't you take 48-4 to pick up the chickens?" David asked.

Scott nodded. "Makes it quicker than waiting for the cows to be unloaded. If you want to wait for us to help unload the cows, we shouldn't be gone very long at all."

When Scott and Nate pulled up near the tractor, Leo came out of the barn.

"I have the chickens and their feed in the barn. I have a couple of extra waterers for you too," Leo said.

Nate carried one crate of chickens to 48-4 and set it on the back seat; Scott set the second one next to the first then put the waterers and small bag of feed on the back floorboard.

"The trailer is Cal's; I'm sure he'd say it goes with the cows," Leo said. "You can unhook my truck and bring it back tomorrow or when the driveways have had a chance to dry out. I'm getting everything tightened down. The latest is that the storm will hit mid-morning."

When Scott and Nate reached the Smith barn, David and Tom were attaching the bottom of a Dutch door to the barn.

Scott peered inside the barn. "You've already put the cows into their stalls and built a door?"

"Tom's a cow whisperer. He coaxed them into their stalls then milked the cow that doesn't have a calf. I had hinges and wood that looked like a Dutch door to me," David said. "I'm almost done."

"Stuart asked me about the Smith well, and I think it may be near the house. I'm going to take a quick walk around the house. It would be great to have a water source near the barn," Scott said. "We don't have much time, though, because Leo expects the storm to hit us mid-morning."

"I'll go with you," Nate said.

As they strolled around the charred remains of the house, Nate pointed. "Doesn't that look like an oversized doghouse?"

"Bingo." Scott strode to the shabby structure. When he found the door and pulled, it came off in his hands, and he set it on the ground.

"We'll turn our builder loose and have a new well house in five minutes." Scott smiled.

Nate peered inside. "Needs work too."

"Hopefully, the tank can hold its pressure. We'll more than likely have to repair the pump, then if we install a hand pump, it will be operational."

"Sounds good to me," Nate said.

Scott sighed. "I'm itching to get my hands on it; sure would be nice if the storms fizzled."

Nate nodded as they headed back to the barn. "More ways than one."

When they returned, David had installed a latch to hold the two door pieces together and was slipping a bar through brackets to secure the door.

"I made a trough for their water, but we need to fill it. Tom told me Leo had a hand pump for his well. I'd like to borrow some buckets and fill them, so the cows will have water the next couple of days. What do you think?" David asked.

"I know where everything is, and Leo will come out of the house when he hears the engine unless he's on the radio," Nate said. "Let's go."

David and Nate lifted the crates off the back seat and set them on the ground then jumped into 48-4 and left with Fire Dog running along behind.

"I'll give you the tour." Tom slid the bar back, then the two men went inside.

Scott examined the stalls and the trough. "This is nice work, and that door is amazing."

After Scott closed up the barn, he said, "The crates are bulky and heavy. We can leave them for David and Nate to bring when they return."

"What's our plan when we get back to the house?" Tom asked.

"After I take the bucket of milk inside, I need to do a good walk-around and pick up any tools or equipment, especially around the garden and the coop. I'd like to make room in the barn to pull in my truck, and I want 48-4 inside the barn too," Scott said.

"If you want to start on the barn, I'll pick up the area," Tom said.

When they arrived at the house, Blanche met them at the back door. "I want to take the children outside; they'll probably be cooped up until tomorrow."

"Go right ahead. Tom's policing the yard, so he'll be out here with you."

"Charo's coming too; she's as anxious as the kids are, and the fresh air will do her good." Blanche opened the door, and Scott and Tom went inside; all the children and Charo trooped out to join Blanche.

"Is that milk? Did you get the cows?" Sandra asked.

"The cows are safe in the Smith barn, and Tom milked the cow that doesn't have a calf. David and Nate went to Leo's for water. Did you know about the calf?" Scott asked.

"Of course; Charo told me."

Of course. Scott rolled his eyes. "Leo said the storms may arrive earlier than lunch. It would be nice if they weakened, but Leo didn't think that was likely."

"We'll just need to keep everyone busy until we have to hunker down," Sandra said.

"I agree; I can't think of anything worse than sitting around and waiting for a storm. Anybody you need out of the house?"

"Peyton, Lela, Cal, Judge, Doc, and it wouldn't hurt to give Louisa a little fresh air too, but I'm not sure she can walk," Sandra said.

"Tell Lela to open a window, so Louisa can hear the kids outside," Scott said.

"That sounded exactly like something I would say. I must need a little fresh air too. I'll go open that window and bark a few orders. What are you going to be doing?" Sandra asked.

"I want to make room in the barn for the truck; Tom is picking up stray tools and equipment. Jump in anywhere."

"I might help Tom. I'd get in your way in the barn."

"Never," Scott said.

Sandra stared at him with her mouth open, and he leaned in and kissed her thoroughly. When he stood back, he grinned as her face reddened.

"What if someone had walked in on us?" she asked.

Scott winked. "We'd never live it down, would we?"

Sandra giggled. "Probably not. Go clean your barn; I've got a window to open."

CHAPTER ELEVEN

Molly stood at the stove waiting for the coffee pot to finish perking as Mr. Young yawned when he strolled into the candle-lit kitchen.

"Nice ambiance," he said.

Molly slammed a pot on the stove. "It wasn't meant to be nice; I couldn't see in the dark."

She poured two cups of coffee and set one on the table at Mr. Young's place.

"Why didn't you stop that whole antenna shenanigans last night?" she asked.

Mr. Young sat in his chair and sipped his coffee. "I'll have a coherent answer soon."

Molly slammed the pot onto a different burner. "You men are just hopeless; you always stick together."

"Let's go stand on the back porch for old time's sake," Mr. Young said. "We can't rock because we loaded up the chairs, but we could sway."

Molly snickered as she refilled both of their cups then carried them out back while Mr. Young opened the door for her.

"I just remembered I restricted you to one cup. Why didn't you remind me?"

Mr. Young shrugged and tried to cover his smirk.

"I'm more distracted and stressed than I realized." She sighed. "I completely support leaving here, but it's become my home, and I hate to leave it. Can you believe that?"

She handed Mr. Young his coffee. "Careful now, it's hot."

Mr. Young nodded. "I lived in my old farmhouse for years, but when it was time to leave, I loaded up my trailer and hauled my sorry tail feathers here. This house has become my real home, but it's not the house, is it? It's the people."

"You can't tell Jack I'm not mad anymore," Molly said. "I haven't had a good cranky spell in ages. It's been kind of fun."

Mr. Young chuckled. "You did it justice."

Molly glanced up at the starry sky. "Do you think they'll be here by lunchtime?"

"It would have been a three-hour drive in the old days, so if they left after breakfast, they'd certain be here for lunch, but I'll bet they got an early start. Our Dead Eye Red, the weather girl, would be pushing for us to be in Georgia before lunchtime because of the big storm headed their way."

"It will be nice to have everyone back together, won't it? I've really missed the girls, except they're young women now, aren't they? I'm worried about them, the storm, and us."

Mr. Young sipped his coffee. "Annie and I will find some kind soul to help us string up a temporary antenna, so we can check on the weather. The last I heard, there was more than one storm, and they were all strengthening and moving east at a faster clip than they had been before now."

"Are we going to end up spending tonight here?" Molly asked. "I think everyone's geared up to leave today and would be disappointed to wait until tomorrow."

"I hope not. I'll rest easier when we get Major away from the area," Mr. Young said.

"He's a target just like Jack, isn't he?" Molly shook her head. "I hear stirring in the house. Time for me to rattle those pots and pans again."

As Mr. Young followed her into the house, he asked, "Do I cower or smile? I've forgotten my lines."

Molly snorted.

The children rushed into the kitchen. "Do we eat breakfast then load up the chickens?" Sara asked.

"After breakfast, we'll do all our normal chores and put our backpacks on the front porch, so we'll be ready to pack the second Aimee Louise and Rosalie pull into the driveway."

When Jack came into the kitchen, Mr. Young said, "Annie and I could get onto the radio if we had a little help stringing some wire in a tree for an antenna."

"You want to do that now?" Major limped into the room and used his stick to take the weight off his left knee.

Molly narrowed her eyes. "You're moving a little better, at least, Major."

"Dressed myself too." Major grinned, and Molly rolled her eyes.

Mr. Young cleared his throat. "I'd like to get on the radio right away. We won't have our usual range, but I'm sure whoever we can hear will be talking about the storm."

"Josh and I can do that for you. Just show us where and tell us what to do," Jack said.

"We've got wire in the radio room. I'll grab the transceiver," Mr. Young said.

"I'll get the rest," Annie added.

"I'll supervise." Major hobbled along behind them.

When the five of them left the kitchen, Vanessa met them in the hallway then continued to the stove and poured a cup of coffee. "What's going on?"

"Jack and Josh are going to set up an antenna for Mr. Young and Annie, and Major is security. Mr. Young thinks they'll be able to hear news about the weather in Georgia."

"That would be good, wouldn't it? What do we have left to do?"

"Make sure we've got everything packed and ready to load," Molly said.

"No lollygagging," Sara added.

Molly chuckled. "Exactly; where did you hear that word?"

"It was in one of the books I read last week. I've been waiting for a chance to use it." Sara beamed.

"I learned a new word from a book too," Brett said, "but I can't remember what it was."

Sara whispered so quietly that not even Molly heard her.

"That's it," Brett giggled. "Trousers. Isn't that the funniest word you've ever heard?" Brett lowered his voice, furrowed his brow, and held his fork over his upper lip to serve as a mustache. "I'm wearing my best trousers."

Brett and Sara laughed, and Vanessa smiled as Molly rolled her eyes.

Sara wiped her eyes. "It's so funny when you say it like that, Brett."

"It's a perfectly normal word," Molly said.

"I don't know about that." Vanessa cleared her throat then spoke in a high-pitched voice while she made a sweeping motion. "How do you like my fancy, new trousers?"

Molly laughed along with Brett and Sara.

After Brett and Sara finished eating, they dashed to their rooms for their last-minute items and their backpacks then dropped off their backpacks on the front porch.

"We'll feed and water the chickens and give the goats water," Sara said as they raced through the house to go out the back door.

Molly set two plates on the table. "We might as well eat. Just don't drop anything on your trousers."

Vanessa choked on her coffee.

"Sorry," Molly said. "I had to get it out of my system."

Vanessa coughed. "Sure you did, and don't think your timing went unnoticed either."

After they ate, Molly said, "I'm going to check on the radio antenna people. I'm certain they are..." Her eyes twinkled as she paused for effect, "dawdling."

"You're terrible." Vanessa chuckled. "I'll help you with the dishes after the radio crowd eats breakfast. I'm going to see if I can help with the chickens and goats."

* * *

Major and Shadow stood on the porch while Josh and Jack strung the wire in the trees. Major scanned the road that led toward town then turned north to peer at the sky. "The road and the sky are clear, Shadow, but it still feels like a storm is brewing somewhere, and I'm not sure if I'm sensing more than just the weather."

Shadow dashed to the gate then stayed there until Major joined Mr. Young and Annie who had set up the transceiver with the charged battery. Major gave Shadow a nod, and the German shepherd raced to him then trotted to where Penny guarded Jack and Josh.

Annie wore the headset, and when she glanced at Major, she shook her head.

"Are there any adjustments we can make?" Jack asked as he and Josh joined them.

"No, nothing to do now except scan and listen," Mr. Young said.

"Josh and I are going in," Jack said. "No sense in all of us staring at the radio."

"We might make it nervous," Josh said.

After they went into the house, Annie handed the headset to Mr. Young. "I hear some static. Josh may have been right."

Mr. Young adjusted the dials then frowned and held up his index finger.

Annie eyes brightened, and she whispered, "He hears a ham."

When he held up two fingers, she said, "A second one; they're talking."

She grabbed her notebook and pencil, and Mr. Young handed her the headset. She listened and took notes.

Major squinted at what she had jotted on the paper. "Orl attack. Tmp & Tally riot. 75 blocked."

She shook her head and handed the headset back to Mr. Young.

"The two hams are just north of Orlando," Annie said. "All they talked about was how bad it is in Florida. They said that Orlando is under attack, and people in Tampa and Tallahassee are rioting over food and water. Interstate 75 is blocked, but they didn't say where. Their voices were shrill, which isn't normal for ham operators; I don't know if they were repeating rumors or facts, but I'm guessing they were in the middle of it and scared. Mr. Young will try to pick up someone from Georgia or Alabama because we need to hear about the weather north of us."

"The problem with rumors is that they're such a waste of time because we don't get a report of where the hams are and what it's like at their location," Major said. "We already know the cities are having problems."

Mr. Young keyed the microphone. "Maybe around lunchtime. What do you think?"

He listened then nodded. "Thanks, we will if we have to. We'll check in as often as we can."

After he signed off, Mr. Young said, "We can disconnect everything now, Annie, and pack it up. When we go inside, we'll ask your dad and Josh to bring down the wire. The storms may be slowing. That's bad news because the hams in Alabama are still reporting catastrophic tornados, and the Georgia hams are worried the storms will strengthen then new tornados will plow across the state. Phil was on, and he thinks our travel will be iffy if we aren't sheltered before late morning."

"Mr. Phil is kind of halfway between us and the Newtons' farm, isn't he?" Annie asked.

"That's right. He suggested we might want to stop at his place for the night or at least until after the threat has passed. He's going to try to get in touch with Leo. I've got my handheld, so I'm hoping we can contact him when we're closer."

Mr. Young and Annie walked slowly on either side of Major, and Shadow followed them.

"I'd rather go straight to the Newtons' from here, but the option to stop at Phil's takes off a lot of pressure," Major said.

When the three of them strolled into the kitchen, Molly said, "Your breakfast is ready."

While Mr. Young sipped his coffee, he reported what the Alabama radio operators said. "Phil came on and told me to stay in touch with him, and he'll try to contact Leo. He thinks the question is not if the storms, and possibly tornados, will hit the Newtons' farm, but when. He offered for us to stop at his place if it's not safe to continue."

Major added, "We'll load up as quickly as we can after Aimee Louise and Stuart arrive then head north. It's a big advantage to have Phil located where he is; he'll watch the weather for us."

"Come on, Josh," Jack said. "Let's get the wire down and rolled up then we can put the chickens and the goats in the horse trailer. That will be one less thing to do after the transport trucks arrive."

Vanessa cleared Major's plate the second he finished his last bite.

"Let's take everything that goes outside and separated into two groups: supply truck and passenger truck, so we won't have to take the time to decide where a box goes," Major said.

Annie quickly finished her breakfast, then she and Vanessa began carrying out boxes from the kitchen.

"All the kitchen boxes go in the transport truck after the large items are in," Molly said. "I'll check the upstairs one more time, but I think all that's left are the mattresses."

"I'll get those now," Major said.

"No, you won't," Molly said. "Jack and Josh can take care of the mattresses. I'll carry out a chair to the front porch, and you can let everyone know where to set the boxes. You're probably the only one that has a good overview of what we have and where things should be anyway, and I'm not trying to be nice."

"I would never, ever accuse you of that, Molly," Major said with a deadpan face.

Molly narrowed her eyes. "Good."

Major sat in the chair on the porch with Shadow at his side.

When Jack and Josh came outside with the first mattress, Major said, "I'm thinking we can put half of the mattresses in the supply truck, but we'll have to see how that works out. For now, put the twin mattresses on the passenger truck side, and the queen mattresses on the supply truck side."

Jack nodded. "Makes sense to me."

"Sorry you're stuck, Pops." Josh held out his fist.

"Thanks, Josh; so am I." Major fist-bumped Josh.

CHAPTER TWELVE

Angel sped down the interstate then slightly lifted her foot and eased off the accelerator as Stuart's handheld crackled then broke up.

"Hang on; we're getting off the interstate," she said.

"Why?"

"Red heard something."

Stuart shook his head. *How could Angel know what Red heard?*

He glanced in his side mirror, and the right turn signal on the truck behind them was blinking.

Angel changed her headlights to parking lights, and Andy did the same.

Stuart peered at the road and the upcoming ramp. *I wish it was light enough to see the road.*

Angel took the ramp and sped west away from the interstate until she came to the state road. She turned south and continued on the road until she found an abandoned gas station and pulled behind the building. Andy parked behind her.

"We need a quick break," Angel said. "We can eat breakfast then go."

Stuart exhaled, but he didn't relax his vigilance as he climbed out of the truck with his rifle and scanned the area. *Every muscle I have is on alert.*

Red handed out breakfast, and Stuart and Andy drank coffee while Angel and Red drank water.

"I was scanning. There are shooters at the next overpass, according to the locals," Red said.

"I didn't hear that," Stuart said.

"We're using simplex, you know, a channel that doesn't hit a repeater, so it has a limited range but is fine for handheld to handheld when they aren't too far apart. Angel set your radio so it wouldn't scan because we don't need both radios to scan."

"I don't get it," Stuart said.

"Neither do I. Do we stay on the state road?" Andy asked.

"Yes."

"It goes straight to Plainview and Major's farm," Red said.

"How much longer?" Andy asked.

"We're about an hour away," Stuart said.

Angel headed toward her truck, and Stuart rushed to follow her and climbed into the passenger's seat. When she started the engine then pulled away from the gas station, Andy followed.

After they passed the state line, the pale, first light of dawn glowed in the east on the horizon. Stuart narrowed his eyes. "There's a man hiding in the trees ahead."

Angel nodded. "Not dangerous."

She slowed then stopped. Stuart lowered his window and glanced into his side mirror. His eyes widened as Red jumped out of her truck, then he scrambled to open his door when he realized Angel's door slammed.

"Hey!" Red shouted. "It's Angel and Red."

The man stepped out of the woods. "Of course, it is, who else would be driving two gangster transport trucks?" He chuckled as he strode to meet them. "I've got some news for you."

"Stay with the trucks," Stuart said, and Andy nodded.

"I won't keep you. The storms slowed in Alabama, but tornados are as strong as ever; there's still no indication of when the storms will reach your Georgia farm," Phil said. "I haven't heard of any problems on the road between here and Major's. I'll be listening and watch for you on the return trip. I talked to Mr. Young earlier, and he knows if it's unsafe for you to continue, you can shelter at my place."

Angel and Red hugged him and raced to their trucks while Stuart shook Phil's hand. "Thanks."

Stuart ran to the truck and jumped in just as Angel put the truck into gear then pulled away. He waved as Phil disappeared into the trees.

Angel picked up her speed. Stuart glanced at her speedometer and shook his head. *Faster than I like.*

When they passed a roadside sign that said, Town Limits, Stuart said, "There's a town coming up."

"Yes." Angel maintained her speed, and Andy stayed with her.

As they roared into town, Stuart's eyes widened, and he bit his lip. *We could never stop if someone pulled in front of us.*

When they blew through downtown, Stuart noticed a group of men as they ran out of a building and to their cars. Stuart lowered his window and raised his rifle, and the men dashed back into the building.

"I think we just passed a group of small-time thugs that decided against taking us on."

"I expected that."

That's why she's driving so aggressively.

When they reached Plainview, Stuart shook his head as the sunbeams streaked through the clouds onto the abandoned buildings. *Feels like a ghost town.*

Angel slowed, but before they reached the middle of town to turn toward Major's farm, a car pulled out and blocked the road.

"Hang on," Angel said.

Angel aimed straight for the car then veered toward its nearest front fender and caused the car to spin out of the way when she slammed into it. The truck lurched slightly from the blow, but she maintained control; Andy stayed behind her.

"That was amazing," Stuart said. *Wonder if Andy was as scared as I was.*

"Thanks."

She slowed then made the left turn to leave town. After she turned onto the dirt road to Major's farm, she slowed only slightly.

"Aren't you worried about stirring up dust behind us?"

"No."

After they passed the Gastons' house, Stuart said, "The Gaston house looked abandoned with everyone gone. We knew Major needed help, but I'm not sure I realized how vulnerable Major's farm is."

When Angel pulled through the gate then began her wide swing to back in at the house, Stuart smiled. "Everybody's on the porch."

Andy backed in next to Angel, then the four of them jumped out of their trucks.

"Everybody grab a hug, then we're going to get busy loading these trucks," Molly said. "Major's in charge."

"This is Andy," Red shouted.

"Hi, Andy!" the children shouted as they mobbed Angel and Red for hugs.

While everyone else hugged Angel and Red, Stuart and Andy hurried to talk to Major.

"What's our plan?" Stuart asked.

"One truck is for passengers, and the second one is for equipment and boxes. We'll put the twin mattresses in the passenger truck."

Stuart nodded. "Angel drives the lead, so her truck is for passengers. Andy and Red will bring up the rear, so their truck will carry equipment and boxes."

"Mr. Young is going to drive his white truck and pull his camper; I'll be his lookout. Sheriff, except we're calling him Jack now, will drive my truck with the horse trailer; we've already loaded the goats, chickens, and supplies into the horse trailer. Annie will be his guard."

"Got it. What equipment do we load first?"

"The generators. One of them has wheels. The other one is already on my heavy-duty dolly. Do you have ramps on the trucks? If you don't, we have ramps. After the generators, we'll load the large mattresses then boxes."

"We have ramps. We'll pull them out then start loading the generators," Stuart said, then he and Andy headed toward the generators.

When they reached the generators, Sara joined them. "Excuse me, are we going to be close to anybody? Josh said we aren't safe here because nobody is close, so now the boys are worried where all the farms are in Georgia. Could you draw a map I could show them?"

Andy said, "I could draw a rough map for you."

Sara handed him a torn slip of paper and a pencil.

Andy roughed out a quick sketch. "It's rough; tell the boys it isn't to scale." Andy pointed as he explained his map. "All the driveways go straight to the road, except the Smith barn kind of winds. The Newton and Webster houses are on the south side of the road with a big barn in between them; the Cabello and Mitchell houses are on the north side and are close together."

He gave the pencil and the map to Sara, who furrowed her brow as she studied it. "Do you have to go to the road to go from one farm to another?"

"No, the houses on the same side of the road have shortcuts." Andy pointed to the shortcuts from the Mitchell farm to the Cabello farm and from the Newton farm to the Smith barn then to the Webster farm.

"Like this?" Sara asked as she added dotted lines for the shortcuts.

Andy and Stuart peered at the map; Andy smiled. "Exactly."

"I'll show the boys while we're riding." Sara stuffed the pencil and map into her pocket and scampered away.

"I think you have a friend," Stuart said. "Let's get this generator to the truck."

After Stuart and Andy loaded the generators and the queen-sized mattresses, Jack, Molly, and Vanessa carried the largest boxes to Red's truck while Stuart and Andy placed them inside. After Josh and Annie handed the antenna to Stuart, they helped carry boxes to the truck. The children and Mr. Young carried the backpacks, extra clothing, and the food for the day to Angel's truck, and Angel and Red organized the items for travel. In less than an hour, the trucks were loaded.

"I need to do a walk around before I leave the farm," Major said.

"Want some company?" Stuart asked.

Major nodded.

"We'll get everyone in place, so we'll be ready to roll," Jack said.

"Vanessa and I will check the house to be sure we didn't miss anything," Molly said.

As Major limped slowly to the barn, Stuart walked alongside him.

"What happened?" Stuart asked.

"I twisted my knee yesterday. Terrible timing, but it's a little better today," Major said.

"Phil met us on the road coming here and said he talked to Mr. Young about staying with him and Deana if there was a chance we couldn't make it to dad's farm. Angel drove fast to get here, but we're not going to be able to keep up that pace going back. If Phil isn't waiting for us near the road, I think we should go straight to his place for news about the weather."

"I've been thinking about that too. Unless the storms dissipate or divert, we can't get to your farm before the rain and wind starts." Major headed back to the house. "Thanks for coming with me; I was hoping we'd have a few minutes to talk."

Angel and Stuart rolled through the gate to the road with their passengers in the back of the truck.

Jack drove Major's truck and towed the horse trailer as he and Annie followed Angel and Stuart.

Mr. Young followed them to the gate then stopped and exhaled. "Major, I've had second thoughts. Can you take over? I could drive in an emergency, but I don't think I can manage a long trip after all."

"That's fine; let's switch now." Major limped around to the driver's door and climbed inside while Mr. Young walked to the passenger's side.

"Are you going to be okay?" Mr. Young frowned.

"I'll be fine; I can stretch out my left leg to take off the pressure that's on my knee when I bend it."

Major drove through the gate, and Andy and Red followed him.

As they drove through town, Stuart lowered his window and put his rifle out the window. Mr. Young and Annie then Red did the same.

Major narrowed his eyes then chuckled.

"What's funny?" Mr. Young asked.

"Josh must have seen you. There's a shotgun poking out one side of the back canvas cover of Angel's truck, and a rifle is peeking out the other side."

"We're a dangerous caravan of bad dudes." Mr. Young smiled.

Major nodded. "That we are."

As they traveled through town, Mr. Young said, "There's a car crashed against a light pole up ahead. The front end is really messed up too. What do you suppose happened?"

As Angel picked up speed, Major said, "No telling, but I think Angel might have had something to do with it. Did you see the fresh ding on her front bumper?"

* * *

As Angel increased her speed, she said, "Let me know if anyone is having trouble keeping up. I'm going to push."

Stuart nodded. "If Mr. Young's truck can keep up, everyone else can. I'm glad Major's driving."

"Yes."

When they were five miles north of town, Angel accelerated. "Let me know how Pops is doing."

Stuart peered out his side window. "Still with us."

Before they reached the state line, Stuart said, "I'll watch for Phil. So far, the sky to the west is clear."

Stuart scanned both sides of the road ahead then glanced in his side mirror. "They're staying with us," Stuart said. He turned his attention to the roadside ahead.

When they approached the side road that led to Phil's, Stuart said, "I think I see someone not too far from the road. Is it Phil?"

"Yes." Angel slowed then pulled to the shoulder, and the trucks behind her did the same.

Phil hurried to Angel's truck, and she lowered her window. "I'm hearing that the storm is still stalled, so it's not likely to hit until late this afternoon. I have a feeling, though, that it will turn into a monster storm when it gets going and may even spawn a twin. You have time to get to Scott's if you keep up your pace, or you can stay here until tomorrow. One more thing, not long after you came through this morning, one of the neighbors up the road told me he heard a couple of guys were asking in a nearby town if folks had seen any army officers, like a colonel or a major."

Angel glanced at Stuart then said, "We'll go. Thank you, Phil."

"God speed, darlin'." Phil stepped away from the truck and rushed into the trees as Angel pulled onto the road and accelerated north with the trucks behind her.

"I agree completely, but you knew that because you checked my cloud," Stuart said.

"Yes."

Stuart picked up his handheld and clicked the mic. "Storm is still moving slow. We aren't making any stops."

Stuart watched the trucks behind them as Jack flashed his lights, and Major flashed his, then the radio crackled; Red said, "Got it."

Stuart exhaled. "Somebody's hunting Major."

"I don't like it."

Stuart side-glanced her. *Not a usual Angel answer. She's worried too.*

"Do you know what Phil meant when he said, 'twin'?" Stuart asked.

"Sometimes a large tornado splits and a second tornado that is frequently just as large travels next to it or behind it."

She glanced at Stuart. "Red has always talked about weather a lot."

He chuckled. "I should have guessed."

Angel sped up then glanced in her side mirror. "Pops is still keeping up."

Stuart chuckled. "I'd love to hear the conversation between Sheriff and Annie."

"Jack," Angel said. "Pops said they call him Jack."

"Thanks for the reminder. I'm certain it's for security." Stuart frowned. "What about Major?"

"Pops."

Stuart nodded. "Makes sense to me."

"Ask him."

Stuart laughed. "Great idea."

After they traveled a few more miles, Stuart asked, "Don't we have a town coming up that has a traffic circle around the county courthouse in the middle of town?"

Angel nodded.

Stuart glanced at Angel when she slowed then turned at a residential street two blocks before the main section of town. He turned his attention to their surroundings and scanned each house as they crept for two blocks then turned north. He shook his head at the deterioration from neglect and vandalism. After their white-knuckle crawling drive through the once family-friendly neighborhoods, Angel turned back to the state road on the north side of town. She sat at the intersection for a few moments then crept onto the state road.

"Now." Red's voice came through clearly on the radio, and Angel punched her accelerator.

Stuart checked his side mirror. "Pops and Mr. Young got the message, and so did Jack and Annie. You knew they would, didn't you?"

"Sure."

Stuart laughed. "You're awesome."

"Be ready to shoot; the canvas doesn't protect our passengers, but the mattresses will help."

"Which side?" Stuart peered down the road.

"Your side. I'll stay on the left to avoid any driver's side threats."

Stuart picked up the mic. "Shooters be ready."

He narrowed his eyes at the Jersey barrier across their lane on the road ahead, and the two men who stood behind a car in the left lane. *Can't tell how many are behind that barrier; is she going to use the car to knock the barrier away?*

After Stuart lowered his window, he shouted toward the back of their truck, "Get down!"

I hope they heard me.

Stuart exhaled in relief at the sound of two bangs on the back of the cab. *Somebody did.*

"Tell the drivers to stay farther left than I do," Angel said.

Stuart keyed the mic and passed on the message then watched the trucks; Major flashed his lights, Jack flashed his lights, then Red keyed the mic. "Got it."

Before they reached the roadblock, Angel veered into an abandoned strip mall parking lot and drove on the sidewalk as she barreled past the car on the road. Stuart aimed, and while he shot repeatedly at the car and behind the barrier, the ambushers scrambled to take cover. The constant barrage from the speeding trucks continued as Mr. Young, Annie, and Red fired at the car and the rear of the barrier.

After she was clear of the car and barrier, Angel took the first break in the curb for an exit to the road and accelerated.

Stuart twisted in his seat and leaned out his window to examine the side of their truck then shouted, "Everybody okay?"

He grinned as one of their passengers pounded twice, then he keyed the mic. "Everyone here is okay."

"We're fine," Mr. Young said.

"Okay," Annie said.

"Awesome," Red said, and Stuart chuckled as he raised his window.

"I was so focused on the Jersey barrier and car that I didn't even see the strip mall; I don't think the ambushers considered it either."

"It was a risk, but I considered it a low risk."

"Why did you want them to stay to the left of your path?"

"To make the distance from the attackers to the trucks different. Pops moved the farthest to the left, and Jack drove a few feet to the right of the camper. Andy drove on the sidewalk like I did."

Stuart added, "Because Red told him to."

"Yes."

"How did Pops and Jack know what you had in mind?"

"It was logical."

I didn't understand because I was in charge of shooting. Stuart rolled his eyes. *I'll call that a reason not an excuse.*

As they traveled north, Stuart narrowed his eyes at the sky in the northwest. "The clouds are dark to the northwest of us. I'm guessing we're thirty-five or so minutes away."

Angel sped up; the closer they got to the farms, the darker the sky became, and Angel and the rest of the drivers turned on their high beams.

"Our turn is coming up," Stuart said.

Stuart lowered his window to listen for traffic from the interstate. "It's eerie; I don't hear any traffic or birds."

"Birds are bracing for the storm." Angel slowed for the turn.

When she reached the Mitchell driveway and pulled in, Stuart said, "I can smell the rain. We don't have long to unload the mattresses. Stop before you park, so I can find a spot for the trailer. I think I saw a spot behind the house near that old shed."

Angel stopped midway up the driveway, and Stuart raced to the back of the house. His eyes widened when he saw the cleared slab, and he chuckled. "David's hand."

He ran to the front and met Major as Angel backed her truck close to the front door.

Major lowered his window, and Stuart said, "There's a pad for the camping trailer in back. I'll guide you."

Major crept along as he followed Stuart then smiled when he saw the pad for the camper. "Mr. Young can back me onto the slab."

Stuart ran to the front of the house and motioned to Jack to pull around back with the horse trailer. Stuart led Jack to the barn.

Jack lowered his window. "Do you think we'll have time to put the goats and chickens in the barn?"

"I think so, if you leave the chickens in the crates until after the storm passes us. There's a small stall in the barn that is secure enough for the goats."

When Stuart returned to the front, Andy and Vanessa were carrying in a queen-sized mattress, and Molly was behind them with a twin mattress.

"We're dropping all the mattresses in the living room. They can sort them later," Angel said as she and Molly carried in another queen-sized mattress. Sara followed them with two pillows in her arms.

When Stuart reached the truck, Josh was inside the truck sliding mattresses closer to the rear for unloading.

"We're trying to unload Angel's truck, so you'll have a way to get to your farm faster," Josh said.

Stuart took the mattress that Josh slid to him and carried it into the house.

Red stood watch near the driveway with her rifle.

As the group scrambled to unload the rest of the truck, the sky became darker, and the rolling rumbles of thunder became louder. The wind picked up, and rain pelted them.

Major drove Mr. Young's truck around to the front then waved when Stuart came out of the house. "We unloaded the back of Mr. Young's truck onto the back porch. We thought you could take his truck while we finish unloading what we can."

"Thanks." Before he ran into the house, Stuart shouted, "Red, put your stuff into Mr. Young's truck. We're leaving."

Angel was on her way out of the house; Stuart said, "Angel, let's get our backpacks and take Mr. Young's truck."

Stuart followed Angel as she raced to the truck and grabbed their backpacks. Stuart picked up the extra rifles and ammo. Andy had started the truck; after Stuart and Angel threw their items into the truck and jumped into the back, Stuart said, "Go to the Smith barn unless Dad's driveway is cleared."

The thunder became deafening; after Andy turned onto the paved road, he turned the windshield wipers to high and lowered his window to watch for the Newton driveway.

"It's cleared." Andy sped down the Newton driveway then stopped at the house.

As the thunder became ear-splitting booms and the crack and sizzle of lightning left the smell of ozone in the air, the wind blew with a fierceness that threatened to knock them down; they grabbed everything they could carry and rushed toward the house. The wind knocked Red off balance, but Andy snatched her close to his chest before she slammed to the ground; her feet dangled inches above the ground as he carried her to the house.

When the four of them were inside the house, Andy leaned against the door while Red leaned against him, dropped what she had carried, and hugged him.

Sandra met them in the kitchen. "We're in the hallway," she yelled over the roar of the storm. "Blanche has the children and the puppies in the closet under the stairs. We moved Noel's bed into the hall outside the bedroom. Doc, Judge, and Ethel are with him and Louisa."

"Y'all are soaked," Lela said after they sat in the hallway with everyone else. "Did you run from the house to get here?"

Stuart put his arm around Angel as she covered her ears and huddled against him. "We drove Mr. Young's truck. Andy parked as close as he could to the house, but we got soaked getting to the back door. If we'd gone to the Smith property, we would have had to stay in the barn with the cows. Thanks for clearing the driveway."

"I cleared it as soon as it was light," Scott said. "David, Brandon, and Henry were my watch guards. The boys wanted to help."

"Did everyone get here safe?" Charo asked, and Stuart nodded.

"Will we hear details later?" Peyton asked.

Stuart glanced at Red and nodded at her weak smile. "I think we can manage that."

The roar of wind and rain intensified, and no one attempted to talk. When the house darkened, Nate ushered Charo into the closet with the children then sat against the door. Fire Dog leaned against one side of Nate, and the two Farm Dogs snugged tightly together on his other side.

CHAPTER THIRTEEN

The windows rattled, and the house shook as the roar escalated. Stuart held onto Angel as she shuddered. *We're going to be hit.* He glanced at Andy who had Red wrapped with his arms to protect her head.

The classic rumble of an approaching, old-time freight train grew louder as it relentlessly drew closer, the house moaned, and the hallway was as black as a cloud-covered night. Stuart winced at the earth-shaking thuds of falling trees, then Angel cringed at the deafening sound of a crash from the living room. When Stuart rose to check, Angel held onto him, and he pulled her close as the freight train rumbled past them.

After the noise subsided and the hallway lightened, Stuart and Scott went to the living room.

Stuart's eyes widened at the sight of the roof from the porch against the living room windows.

"I'll run check upstairs, Dad." When Stuart turned, he bumped into Angel who stood behind him. He hugged her to keep from knocking her down, then the two of them dashed upstairs.

They went to their bedroom and looked down at the tree leaning against the house. "The porch roof couldn't hold it, but I don't see any signs of the tree breaching the house. While we're up here, let's check all around the house."

Before she left the bedroom window, Angel said, "A twin."

Stuart stared out the window at the whirling, giant, black cloud that barreled toward them then grabbed her, and they ran downstairs.

"We have a second storm almost on top of us. It looks like a second tornado," Stuart said.

"Oh no, not again," Sandra's voice trembled.

Scott took his seat next to her and wrapped his arms around her. "Just more snuggle time, honey."

Sandra sighed. "Okay, snuggle bunny; let's do this."

Peyton giggled and whispered to David, and he pulled her closer to his side.

Red pulled Andy by the hand as she hurried to sit across from Angel.

"You doing okay, Angel?" Red asked.

"No."

"Me neither."

When the two young women giggled, Stuart glanced at Andy who rolled his eyes then hugged Red.

Stuart smiled. *I never understand their jokes, but I love to hear them laugh.*

Nate opened the door and whispered to Charo.

"Thanks, honey. We'll be okay; Storyteller Blanche has to finish this story, anyway, and she hinted there's a second story to follow." She closed the door.

Nate sighed as he leaned against the door. "We need a bigger safe room for Storyteller Blanche."

Peyton cleared her throat and elbowed David who chuckled.

The wind and rain picked up, and the sky and hallway darkened. Scott hurried to his bedroom then returned with a headset that resembled hearing protection muffs and gave it to Angel. "I haven't listened to music in a long time, so I'd forgotten about it; the headset will help muffle the sound."

"Thank you."

Angel leaned against Stuart and relaxed.

Dad's a genius.

The hallway suddenly glowed green then turned darker, and the freight train returned with a roaring vengeance. Stuart focused on remaining relaxed for Angel, but when he not only saw but also felt the smothering dark as it rushed over them, and the sound of the freight train when it became a jet that was diving toward the house, he flinched then jumped along with Angel at the crash that sounded like it came from the utility room. Angel shook uncontrollably, but after Stuart took her into his arms and rocked her, she hummed and relaxed, and so did he. The jet was suddenly gone, and the natural light returned to the hallway. Stuart, Angel, Red, Andy, David, and Scott hurried to the utility room, but everything was intact. Stuart and Angel raced outside, and the others followed them into the light rain.

"The tornado threw the tractor against the house." Stuart stood at the corner of the house. "It's upside down."

Scott rushed to join Stuart and whistled long and low at the sight. "The tractor was behind the barn. The tornado tossed it backward? Should we expect more storms?"

Angel and Red ran into the house.

"Where are they going?" Scott asked. "Should we all rush inside?"

"They went to the second floor to get a better view of the sky in the west to answer your question."

Andy rushed to the barn, and David raced to the back of the house.

"Andy will check the barn and the equipment shed, and David's checking the coop." Scott smiled. "I guess I understand guys better than girls."

Stuart nodded. "Don't we all."

Scott walked around his tractor to examine it. "Getting the tractor upright is a priority because I'm worried it will start leaking oil. Let's take a walk around the house to see what other hazards we might have," Scott said. "Are you going to wait for the girls?"

"They'll find me; they have radar."

Scott chuckled as they headed toward the front of the house. They stopped and inspected the large oak tree that had broken through the porch roof.

"We'll have to make the front door and any use of the front yard off limits until we remove the tree."

"We can go around back to get to the other side of the house then on to the shortcut."

As they backtracked, Scott said, "Andy will want to check on Leo and Jennie, Angel will want to check on Major, and Charo will be ready to move. We need to have a plan for them. Did we tell you Tom, Lela, and the twins will move with the Cabellos? Lela and Charo wanted to keep the girls together. Tom said the tipping point was when you rescued the Wheatleys. The Mitchells didn't have much left after the home invasion when Lela was attacked, so there wasn't a lot of extra to pack and load onto the transport truck."

"If Angel and I, which also means Red and Andy, take Mr. Young's truck back, we can check on both houses to be sure the Cabello house is okay. Although Angel will say we should run, so we can use Mr. Young's truck to transport the Cabello family if their house is okay."

Scott chuckled. "Take 48-4; if you can bring a transport truck here, we can use it to right the tractor."

Stuart raised his eyebrows and nodded. "We unpacked one truck earlier, so I don't see why we couldn't bring it here and get the tractor back on its wheels. Assuming the Cabello house is okay, after we take care of the tractor, we can accompany Nate and Tom to the truck at the Smith barn to check on the cows then continue on to the Websters' to check on Leo and Jennie. Angel would say logical."

When they reached the coop, David was nailing a section of fence wire that had ripped free back onto the fence, and the chickens complained with loud squawks.

"The storm was obviously my fault: Sandra's chickens are mad; I'd set the crates with Jennifer's chickens on the coop floor, and they are madder, but everyone's fine."

After David finished and hurried toward the equipment shed, Angel and Red caught up with Stuart and Scott before they rounded the corner of the house.

"Our light rain will end soon. If Charo still wants to go to her new house, the driveway may not be too sloppy," Red said.

Red left for the barn while Scott, Angel, and Stuart continued around the house. Stuart squinted at a section of trees that were sheared off near the top.

Scott pointed to the trees. "I don't even see where those treetops landed. They would have been like spears."

"David might be interested in finding them," Stuart said. "They might be perfect to use for building. Major's farm will need a chicken coop and probably a new goat shed."

"I wouldn't mind a decent place to put the cows, so they're closer to the house," Scott said.

"David's a great teacher; he'll turn us all into carpenter helpers," Stuart said. "Annie's a whiz too."

"Really? How old is Annie?"

Stuart chuckled as they continued around the house. "She's fourteen, but she's a skilled carpenter. She can build whatever they'll need at Major's farm with David serving as her mentor."

Scott scanned the front of the house. "The porch did a great job of protecting the house, and the tree doesn't look like it's going anywhere."

"At least we have a clear path to the shortcut by going around back. We'll just have to see what we find as we go along."

When they went into the house, Angel, Red, and Andy were waiting for them. Sandra said, "Blanche is almost through with her story. I have lunch ready for you all before you take off, Stuart."

The five of them were joined by David and Nate at the table. While they ate, Stuart said, "We'll want to check on Major—"

Red interrupted, "Pops."

"Right, Pops, and we can check the Cabello house at the same time. Dad suggested that we take 48-4, so we can use Mr. Young's truck to transport the Cabello and Mitchell families while Nate and Tom take the transport truck to the farm. We can bring back the transport truck we emptied earlier and use it to get the tractor upright. When the tractor is back on its wheels, we can check the Smith barn then go to the Websters'; we'll need to know how clear the shortcut is to the Smith barn before Nate and Tom head that way anyway."

David frowned. "Nate and I would like to go along to inspect his house. How can we work that?"

"Easy; Angel and I will run ahead," Red said.

Stuart glared, and Angel said, "We can run right behind you, if that's better."

"But you'll slow us down," Red added.

"Why don't you wait for 48-4 at the end of the driveway then again at the entrance to Major's driveway?" Stuart said.

"Pops," Red said automatically.

Angel glanced over the heads of Stuart, Andy, and Red. "We can do that."

Stuart nodded.

"While you're there, ask Pops what I can call him, because I can't call him Pops," Sandra said.

"I want to grab a chainsaw from the barn," David said.

"Red will run with her rifle; I don't want to run with mine," Angel said.

"I'll take it along in 48-4 for you," Stuart said. "Andy's driving."

While Andy pulled around 48-4, and Stuart and Nate waited for David, Stuart rolled his eyes at the fidgety young women. "Just go; wait for us at the end of the driveway."

As the two raced away, Andy said, "They were so tightly wound, I wouldn't have been surprised if they had sprouted wings and flew away."

David carried two chainsaws with him. "I'm hoping we won't need these, but we'll want to make sure the Cabello driveway is cleared."

When they were within sight of the end of the driveway, Andy elbowed Stuart as Red smiled and waved before she and Angel disappeared down the road.

"Literal." Stuart shook his head.

Andy nodded. "They follow the philosophy of 'Don't shoot until you see the whites of their eyes.'"

Andy pushed 48-4 as he sped down the road to the driveway. When they reached the Cabello driveway, David tapped Andy on the shoulder. "Drop us off here; we'll walk to the house. We'll leave you a chainsaw."

Andy stopped, and Nate and David headed up the driveway.

Stuart said, "Your wife is glaring at you, Andy."

Andy smirked. "Your turn."

Stuart waved, and the young women disappeared.

Halfway up the driveway, Angel and Red stood next to a downed branch. "We tried to move it, but it was too heavy."

Stuart and Andy climbed out of 48-4 and tried to lift it, but the solid oak branch was too heavy for them too.

"It will be quicker to drag it out of the way." Stuart tossed a strap around the branch while Andy turned around 48-4. After Stuart looped the strap around the bumper hitch, Andy pulled the large branch to the side of the road. Stuart retrieved the strap then smiled when he looked at 48-4; Red had claimed his seat in the front. He climbed into the back seat with Angel and put his arm around her shoulder, and Andy continued up the driveway.

When they rolled to the front of the house, Pops followed everyone else who rushed outside to greet them.

"Was that our Georgia welcome?" Molly asked. "It certainly made us feel right at home."

"My trailer made it through just fine; I could have ridden out the storm relaxing on my little sofa in private," Mr. Young said.

Vanessa snorted. "You'd have been voted down."

"Come inside and see what we've done so far," Molly said.

While Angel and Red followed Molly, Mr. Young, Vanessa, and the children inside, Jack said, "We've got a little damage to the shed out back, but it's not much. The barn did fine; a couple of large branches hit the house, but it's cosmetic."

Stuart, Andy, and Jack strolled alongside Pops as he limped to the backyard.

Stuart snorted. "I don't remember that large tree next to the slab."

Pops nodded. "Mr. Young can't get into his trailer until we move it. Molly and Vanessa haven't seen it, so we'll cut it into sections this afternoon, then we can empty his trailer. He'll want to sleep in his own bed tonight."

Andy chuckled. "I'm looking forward to that too." He told them about sleeping in the back of the trucks. "I was excited to sleep outside at first because I thought I was still ten years old."

Jack smiled. "I know that feeling."

"Major, Phil told us about a group of men at a nearby town who were asking if anyone knew about anyone from the Army, like a colonel or a major. Angel and Red told us we shouldn't call you Major anymore," Stuart said. "If you don't mind, we'll all call you Pops, except Mom refuses. What can she call you?"

Major exhaled. "I don't know."

"I have an idea," Jack said. "What did your friends in high school call you?"

Major chuckled. "We thought we were tough dudes and called each other by our last names. I was Elliott; in fact, one of the new teachers thought that was my first name, and it wasn't long until everyone called me Elliott all through school."

Jack nodded. "I got into a lot of fights over being called Starry Night when I was in school, but I did get really good at fighting." He snorted. "The negotiation skills came later when Mom threatened to ground me permanently."

"Elliott," Stuart said. "Mom will be happy to call you Elliott."

"So will Mr. Young," Pops frowned. "I'd rather stick with Major, though; it's me."

"I get that," Stuart said, and Jack nodded.

When they reached the barn, Jack said, "The goats are happy with their new stall, but the chickens want out. Annie's priority is to scavenge wire from the old chicken house and build a new one. She and I plan to build a new one before dark."

"Everything looks good. I'm going to tackle that limb next to Mr. Young's door," Andy said. "I'll grab our chainsaw."

"I'll join you," Jack said, and the two men left to clear the branch.

As Stuart and Pops strolled to the house, Pops asked, "Everyone doing okay?"

Stuart told him about the Wheatleys.

Pops shook his head. "I don't even want to think about what might have happened to them if you hadn't found them."

Stuart exhaled. "I didn't even think about them being out in the storms."

"What's the plan?" Pops asked.

"We haven't gotten that far yet; right now, the plans are for Noel to heal and to keep the family together. The tornado flipped Dad's tractor; we need to right it before it leaks out all its oil. We thought we'd take one of the transport trucks with us."

By the time they reached the house, Andy and Jack were hard at work next to the camper.

Angel met Stuart and Pops at the back door. "We're unloading the second transport truck. Do we want to leave one truck here?"

"If you don't mind, Pops," Stuart said. "I like the idea of spreading out our resources. The Cabellos will more than likely keep their transport truck at their place."

Pops nodded. "I like the idea of having the trucks in different places."

Stuart glanced at the cases of food stacked on the floor next to the pantry. "I'll help unload the truck."

"Good timing, Stuart; we just finished." Vanessa snickered.

"I'll give you a tour of the house, then we'll go to the Cabellos' house," Angel said.

Before Angel and Stuart left the kitchen, Pops told Molly, Vanessa, and Mr. Young about the men asking about a major. "We came up with an alternative to being called Major: Elliott."

Mr. Young nodded. "Obvious and logical, Elliott."

"Did you come up with that by yourself, or did Angel tell you?" Vanessa narrowed her eyes.

"Remember who Angel is related to. I came up with it." Major puffed out his chest, hooked his thumbs into his belt, and grinned when Molly and Vanessa laughed.

"But after I thought about it, I decided I'd just stick with Major," he said.

"I'd tell you later, but it wouldn't make any sense to you or me," Stuart whispered as they headed to the front door.

"Hey, wait up," Red called and joined them as they went outside.

On their way to the shortcut to the Cabellos', Stuart said, "We'll want to leave as quickly as we can to get back and take care of the tractor."

David and Nate met them midway.

"We'll have cleanup to do, but the house is fine; are you ready to go back, or do we have more to do here?" Nate asked.

"I'd like to go back now in the transport truck. Dad wants to use it to right the tractor," Stuart said.

"We need to do that right away," David said.

"Angel and I will take the transport truck, and you can ride back to the house with Red and Andy in 48-4," Stuart said.

"I'll grab Andy." Red raced to the back of the house and returned with Andy behind her as they dashed to 48-4.

Angel and Stuart climbed into the large truck, and Angel headed down the driveway. Before they reached the road, she stopped, and Stuart jumped out and checked the road.

When he climbed back into the truck, he said, "Go."

Angel drove to the Newtons' driveway; as she headed toward the house, she asked, "Where do I park?"

"Back up close to the house."

When they reached the house, Scott had gathered together the equipment they'd need to pull over the tractor.

Andy, Red, David, and Nate rushed to join Stuart and Scott next to the tractor.

"I'm thinking the five of us can push the tractor to its side, then we'll attach the strap to the tractor and the truck's hitch, so we can use the truck to pull it over to its wheels while we push for extra control. Red can be our go-between with Angel," Scott said.

"I'll let Angel know what the plan is." Red raced to the truck.

"Everyone in place, and I'll give the count," Scott said.

"When you push, exhale, so you aren't straining your stomach muscles," David said. "We can't afford for anyone to get a hernia."

Scott nodded. "Okay then, push on exhale. One, two, exhale."

When the tractor flipped to its side, the men whistled and high-fived.

Scott shook his head while David secured the tractor with the strap. "Where'd you learn that, David?"

David moved to the truck and tightened the strap around the hitch. "From working construction in the summer to pay for college. An old, burned-out guy that no one would hire except for the best boss I ever had told me about it. He was a lot smarter than most people when he was sober, which was pretty rare."

"Okay, everybody, same positions," Scott said. This time we're trying to keep an even pressure on the tractor, so it doesn't twist or slide."

After everyone was in place, Scott said, "Red, have Angel move forward until the strap is tight, then we'll need the truck to move slowly forward with a steady pull. Angel will feel it when the tractor has righted but keep an eye on it and have her stop."

"Got it."

"We're ready," Scott said.

Red signaled for Angel to move forward; when the strap was tight, Red signaled for the pull, and Angel moved the truck with a smooth pull on the strap until the tractor slowly flipped to its wheels.

"Yes!" Red shouted, and Angel stopped then waited.

"I'll let the folks know we're ready to leave." Nate strode to the house.

After David unhooked the strap from the truck, Red signaled forward. "Park it."

Angel drove the truck to a spot near the barn then sprinted back.

"We're ready to go when you are," Red said.

"Are you okay from here, Dad?" Stuart asked as Nate returned.

"Yep, you all can go on to the Smith barn."

"David, you and Nate bring 48-4 with a couple of chain saws," Stuart said. "We'll go ahead of you and move any smaller limbs out of your way as we go, then we can take 48-4 on the Smith driveway to clear it."

Angel and Red dashed ahead, and Stuart and Andy ran after them. Angel and Red waited for them midway to the Smith barn.

"We moved a few branches along the way, but we couldn't move this one. It's a two-man branch." Red smiled.

Stuart and Andy rolled the branch off the path, and Angel and Red disappeared.

"Thank you," Angel called out.

"They may leave us in the dust," Andy said, "but at least they're polite about it."

Stuart chuckled as they ran to meet up with Angel and Red.

"See the branch over the path ahead? No girls," Andy said.

A cow bellowed. "Something's wrong with the cows," Stuart said.

While the two of them raced to the barn ahead, cows continued to raise a ruckus.

"Good, you're here," Red met them at the barn clearing. "A tree crashed into the barn, and the mama cow can't get to the water and is separated from her calf."

The cow bellowed even louder.

"I need to move that last branch for 48-4, so David can get here with the chainsaws." Red dashed to the shortcut, and Andy tore after her.

When Stuart went inside the barn, both of the cows mooed, the calf called for its mother, and his eyes widened at the size of the tree between the cow and her calf.

"The tree was a projectile as it crashed through the window," Angel said.

"Wow." Stuart scanned the splintered window and the stall. "Looks like a giant arrow, doesn't it? It's hard to believe the force of the tornado drove the tree into the wall and trapped the cow in the back of the stall and the calf in the front. We're lucky it didn't hit them. Let's move the calf to the third stall, so we can work. I'm glad David will be here in a minute; he'll know how to fix all this."

"Fuel cans are on the opposite wall under the old work bench on a pallet," Angel said.

"I was so busy looking at the cows, I didn't notice. Nate took extra time to do that; he could have just set them inside the door." Stuart shook his head. "The way our group thinks amazes me all the time."

David skidded 48-4 to a stop in front of the barn and dashed inside with a chainsaw. He scanned the tree.

Nate came into the barn. "I'm getting Tom."

"We'll go," Red said.

Nate nodded, and Red and Andy left on 48-4.

Stuart exhaled. *We're using up fuel, but we need to do this.*

"What's our plan, David?" Stuart asked.

"The stall wall is supporting the tree on the window side, but the other side went through the barn wall, and I don't know how much the wall has been weakened. Our wild card is that large, leafy, branch and all its small side branches on the underside that kept the calf from getting to the cow. I think we'll have to take out the branches first, so we have more control over when and where the tree falls. Do we have our handsaw, or did it go with Andy and Red?"

Nate strode to the barn door and picked up the handsaw. "I grabbed it but dropped it at the door when I saw the tree because I didn't think it would help."

"I'd rather have Tom here when we power up the chain saw," David said. "We need a support for the wall side and the leafy branches cut away with the handsaw."

"Show me where to cut, and I'll get on it if you'd like to work on the support," Stuart said.

While Stuart took out one of the side branches, Angel hummed one of Red's tunes; the cow quit bellowing, and the calf settled down in its stall.

"Angel, whatever that tune is, she likes it," Nate said as he dragged away the first branch.

Angel hummed as Stuart sawed branches, and Nate pulled away the branches from the stall. David brought in the support he'd made with the spare lumber from earlier repairs on the barn and set it on the side of the stall closest to the wall.

"What I'd like to do is to cut the tree on the stall side that is closest to the window, so the tree drops to the ground, and our lady steps daintily out of her cell to freedom," David said. "Do you know a tune for that?"

"Red will," Angel said.

Stuart smiled. "I'll bet one of Red's songs with you humming would do it."

David peered over Stuart's shoulder. "I'll take over; you've fatigued your muscles."

David began sawing the large branch close to the trunk of the tree. Stuart smiled as he noticed David moved the sawblade in rhythm with Angel's melody.

Before David finished sawing the branch, 48-4 pulled in front of the barn door.

Stuart strode to Tom and explained David's plan. Red hurried into the barn and stood next to Angel then began singing one of the old songs her mom taught her. Angel slipped to the barn door.

Stuart stared at the cow, and Andy elbowed him and whispered, "Is the cow swaying to the tune?"

Andy stepped back while Stuart moved into a better position to wait until the branch was free.

Tom strolled to the stall then stood near the cow and stroked her while Red sang. David finished sawing through the branch, and he and Stuart dragged it out of the stall, then Nate dragged it out of the barn. David picked up his chainsaw and went outside to rev it up. When he walked into the barn with it, Tom whispered as he stroked the cow, and Red continued singing.

When David was ready to make the final cut, he said, "Step behind the support, Tom."

CHAPTER FOURTEEN

The cow ignored David and watched Tom as he stepped behind the support then moved closer to Tom and the barn wall. Tom smiled and whispered to the cow.

The tree dropped, David shut down the chainsaw and left the barn with it, and Tom coaxed the cow to step over the fallen tree then led her to the smaller stall where her calf waited.

Red finished her song, and the cow mooed.

"You're welcome," Red said.

Andy was out of breath when he came into the barn. "Angel and I ran the driveway to the road and back. The driveway's clear. I need to remember that I wouldn't survive another run with Angel." He leaned against the barn wall and grinned.

"If you ran with Angel, she ran at your pace, honey," Red said. "Don't try to run as fast as you can."

"Are we ready to check on Uncle Leo?" Andy said.

"We'll walk from here," Stuart said.

"I'm ready if you are, David," Nate said. "Are you going with us, Tom, or do you want to stay with the cows?"

"The cows are fine; I wouldn't mind seeing Leo while I'm out this way," Tom said.

After Fire Dog and the Farm Dogs jumped into the back of the transport truck, and David and Nate climbed into the truck cab, David started the engine, then the truck lumbered to the driveway. When Stuart, Tom, and Andy headed to the Webster farm shortcut, Angel and Red ran ahead.

"Do they always do that?" Tom asked.

"Always; it still worries me, though," Stuart said.

Stuart narrowed his eyes as Red and Angel raced back.

"The barn's demolished, but the house looks okay," Red said.

Tom said, "Go ahead. I'll catch up."

After the four of them ran to the Websters' farm, Stuart and Andy gaped at the precariously perched, intact barn roof on top of a jumbled pile of splintered boards.

Red ran to the back door and knocked then pounded on the door, and Andy rushed to join her.

"The door's locked," she said.

Andy shook his head. "There was always an extra key in the barn; that's no help. I'll check the front door."

Andy returned. "I can't get to the front door. The storm tossed pine and oak trees all over the front yard like pickup sticks."

Red glanced around then picked up a large flat rock and reached down for the key.

"How did you know?" Andy asked.

"I heard someone at school say that her mother kept a spare key under a rock near the front door. I always thought nobody would do something like that because it seemed like the first place a burglar would look."

Andy chuckled as he unlocked the door. "So, that makes you a burglar."

Red grinned. "Thanks."

When they were inside, Andy called out, "Uncle Leo?"

"In the radio room," Leo said.

"The door was locked," Andy said as he and Red strolled into the radio room. Holly stretched then greeted them.

"Must have locked it out of habit; did you see the barn?"

"Sure did. How's Aunt Jennie?"

"She's fine, but she was shaken up by the whole thing; she's sleeping, finally. I've been on the radio all day. It was a double tornado, as far as I could tell, and the hams I've been talking with agreed. We lost siding on the west side of the house, and a tree shattered one of the windows in your old room upstairs. One of the supports for the front porch roof was knocked out, so I'm not sure how stable it is. I hated to lose my kennel that was attached to the barn, but I realized my dog raising days are over. I haven't checked the equipment shed, so I don't know how my tractors fared."

"We'll check the equipment shed. Tom came with us; he was hoping to see you."

"Send him on in." Leo turned back to his radio.

When Andy and Red went outside, Andy said, "Tom, Uncle Leo's in his radio room; he said for you to come on in."

After Tom headed to the house, Andy and Red joined Angel and Stuart.

"Uncle Leo is ignoring everything except his radio; he hasn't checked his equipment shed."

As they strolled to the shed, Red said, "He told us the storm made Aunt Jennie nervous, and she's sleeping. If she stayed awake in anticipation of the storm then was as tense as we were all through the storm, I can see where she would be exhausted."

"The shed's gone," Stuart said. "I don't see any parts of it including the metal roof anywhere."

Angel pointed. "Do you see the tractor in the field?"

Stuart scanned the field where Angel pointed. "I think I do."

The four of them stopped at the edge of the field.

"The field is wet, but I'll check it out." Andy strode toward the tractor.

"What do you think?" Red asked.

"We've been wet before," Angel said.

"We'll be wet again," Red added; they giggled and followed Andy.

Now I know how Angel feels when she doesn't get a joke. Stuart picked up his pace as he strode past them to catch up with Andy.

When they reached the tractor, Andy said, "Might be smart to wait until the field dries to get it out, but I'm going to see how far I can get. Where's the smaller one?"

"Over there." Stuart pointed ten yards away from them.

Andy jumped into the seat of the large tractor. "Key's still here." He turned the key, opened the choke then pushed the starter. The engine sputtered then started, and Andy grinned. "Success. I'll take it to the side yard where the barn used to be."

Stuart headed toward the small tractor, but Angel and Red raced through the field and beat him to the tractor. He chuckled as he changed direction to go back. *If Angel can't get it going, I certainly wouldn't be able to.*

He wasn't surprised when the sound of the sputtering engine behind him smoothed out.

Angel waved when she passed him; Red ran behind the tractor. "See you in a minute."

After Angel parked the smaller tractor, Andy refilled the fuel tanks of both tractors. "What do we do about the barn and the equipment shed?"

"As a neighbor, I can ask Leo what he'd like for us to do, but it's his decision," Stuart said. "As a relative, you can step in where he needs help but may not realize it."

Andy nodded. "I'll see if Tom's ready to go. If he wants a little more time, I'll stay and come back with him."

"You and I will stay." Red glared at Andy.

"Right; sorry." Andy hurried into the house.

Red smiled, and Stuart rolled his eyes.

When Andy and Tom came out of the house a few minutes later, Andy said, "Uncle Leo wasn't interested in talking about the tractors, his barn, or the equipment shed; he told me to suit myself. As far as I'm concerned, it's up to me, but the buildings aren't a priority right now."

Red said, "We're going to run straight to the Newtons' house. We'll see you there."

Stuart smiled. "I'm not surprised."

Angel and Red raced to the shortcut while Stuart, Andy, and Tom strolled along the path.

"Leo seemed odd to me; he's always been dedicated to his radio, but he seemed obsessed with it. Did you notice, Andy, that he didn't take off his headset while we talked?" Tom asked.

"He must be worried about Aunt Jennie."

"Probably," Tom said.

Stuart frowned. *Tom doesn't sound convinced.*

When they reached the Smith barn, Tom checked the cows. "Everybody's fine," he said.

Stuart motioned for Andy to take the driver's seat. After they returned, Tom went inside the house while Andy put away 48-4, and Stuart checked the barn for his father.

"How did it go?" Scott asked.

Stuart told him about the cows, the damage at Leo's farm, Leo's reaction, and Tom's assessment of Leo's behavior.

"He may be overwhelmed by the devastation to his farm and by Jennie's medical condition," Scott said.

"That makes sense."

"While you were gone, your mom and Peyton went on a rampage to shuffle bedrooms. The Cabellos and Mitchells gathered all their things that were still here and put them into backpacks. You'll be mobbed when you go inside because they are raring to go; I've already gotten my good-bye hugs. These people aren't fooling around."

"Guess I don't blame them, but thanks for the warning about Mom and Peyton."

As Stuart and Scott strolled to the house, Scott said, "I'll be interested in Lela and Charo's plan for how all those people will ride in Mr. Young's truck. I know what I'd do, but I'm an old guy. I'd have Tom drive with Charo as his passenger then put the rest of that crowd in the bed of the truck under Lela and Judge's supervision."

"That's better than anything I could come up with. Angel and Red will want to run ahead to make sure no bad guys are hiding in the weeds, which means Andy and I will be running too."

When Stuart opened the door, Lela yelled, "Time to load up."

Scott stood back as the three youngest girls rushed to hug Stuart then ran outside with their backpacks and waited by Mr. Young's truck.

Charo hurried to the back door but stopped long enough to hug Stuart. "I'm glad we'll be neighbors."

"I'll carry out your backpacks," Stuart said.

While Lela and Charo hurried out to the truck, Judge and Tom carried out their backpacks and shotguns.

When Stuart and Scott reached the truck, Charo and the judge sat in the cab, and the three little girls and Lela sat on the floor of the truck bed on a quilt. Dolly was holding onto Pixie.

"We're having an adventure," Dolly said. "We're on the back of an old wagon and need to stay very still because we're traveling across dangerous territory to our new homestead."

"Mama Sandra found us an old-time quilt to sit on," Sam said.

"Grandma is in charge because she's the trail master," Cami Sue added.

Stuart tossed the two backpacks next to the others that were in the bed of the truck.

"We're your scouts," Red said.

After Tom started the engine, Angel and Red raced to the driveway, and Lela shouted, "Head 'em out!"

Stuart and Andy sprinted up the driveway to the road. Angel and Red waited until Stuart and Andy joined them, then they raced on the shoulder to the Cabellos' and Major's driveways.

When Tom stopped the truck at the road, Stuart said, "Take the truck up your old driveway; there will be plenty of people to help carry the backpacks to the Cabello house, and no one will have to take Mr. Young's truck back to the road to return it. We'll be covering your back."

Tom saluted then turned right and continued at a slow speed on the road while Stuart ran behind the truck, and Andy watched the road behind them. Stuart stopped and turned to watch the road, and Andy ran to catch up with the truck. Stuart and Andy continued leapfrogging until the truck reached Major's driveway where Angel watched for them, and Red scanned the road that led to the state road with her rifle ready.

Tom turned the truck to go up Major's driveway as Stuart and Andy jogged along behind him.

"I know Red and Angel are fierce together, but they terrify me sometimes," Andy said before they reached the house.

Stuart snorted. "I know exactly what you're saying."

When they reached the house, Sara and Pops met them in the driveway while Nate and Tom helped the girls and Lela out of the truck bed. David handed the girls their backpacks, and Lela and the girls took the shortcut to the Cabellos.

"The little girls went to their new house with Ms. Lela," Sara said. "They will have lunch with us, then I might visit them at their house. Brett was invited too; he said he might go because it was a rule that no one goes anywhere without someone else along. He's right, but I didn't tell him that." Sara grinned.

After Sara skipped into the house, Pops said, "She's really excited about having friends. Josh told Brett being the only boy in the group was manly, so Brett's thinking about it. We cleared out all the extra items we packed in Mr. Young's trailer, and Vanessa and the kids made beds while Molly and Mr. Young organized the kitchen the way they wanted."

"My son had a fairly new tractor that he said needed maintenance. Do you think you could check it before you leave?" Tom asked.

Angel and Red dashed to the shortcut.

When the Stuart heard the starter whine, he said, "I'll bet it needs fuel."

Tom grabbed a diesel can and gave it to Andy who hurried to the shortcut to fill the tank. A few minutes later, the engine coughed then started.

"I think Angel has a plan for the tractors, but I can't imagine what it is," Stuart said.

When Angel and Red joined them, Red said, "Angel thinks we should take advantage of the storm damage and block our road both ways with trees and debris."

"That's a great idea," Pops said. "I can't think of where any of us need to go, even if we had an unlimited supply of fuel. I know we have the interstate at our end of the road; what threat is there on the other side?"

"There's a county road a few miles west of us," Andy said.

Pops nodded. "So, our priority would be to put up a barrier between us and the state road."

"We'll find a spot we can easily block with trees and debris," Angel said as she and Red took off down the driveway.

"Be right back." Stuart and Andy raced after them.

* * *

"Where'd they go?" David returned to check Mr. Young's truck for any more items to go to the Cabellos' house.

Pops explained Angel's plan to block the road.

"We need to fuel up the tractors. I used yours to clear the pad for Mr. Young's trailer, Tom," David said.

"I have a tracked skid steer too. I haven't used it in ages, but it does a good job of clearing brush," Tom said.

"I'll see if I can get to run. Do you have fuel?"

"I have farm diesel and gas for small engines in a shed just outside the barn."

"Let's see what we can do."

As David and Tom strolled to the barn, Tom said, "I just remembered I disconnected the batteries on all my equipment a while ago. Angel must have checked that first thing."

David nodded. "That would be Angel."

While Tom filled the tractor tank with diesel, David searched for the skid steer.

"Found it." David returned to the barn. "It's a decent sized skid steer. You didn't tell me it has a grapple on it; I could pick up some decent sized trees with that claw. It didn't want to start for me; I'll need to prime it."

"The twins named the skid steer 'Bear' because it growled and had a claw. I'd forgotten all about it." Tom shook his head. "There are the gas cans, and here's the diesel. Where do you want me to put the tractor?"

"Close to the driveway. If I can get the skid steer running, would you move it too? I'd like to see how big the other tractor is," David said.

Tom nodded. "You can never have too many tractors or too much coffee."

David carried the diesel can to the skid steer. When he peered into the tank, he said, "Poor girl; you're dry as a bone. Let's rehydrate you."

David poured diesel into the tank, then checked the battery and smiled. *Tom's smart. These babies love to get all corroded.*

After he coaxed the engine into starting, it growled. "Want to get to work, girl? We'll get something for you to growl at."

Tom joined him as David turned off the engine and was filling up the fuel tank.

"Anything else at your son's house besides the tractor that I should check on?"

"He had a tiller for the garden and a small riding mower, but nothing else. His tractor is newer and bigger than mine."

David nodded as he left then stopped at the front porch where Pops and Mr. Young waited.

"Tractor runs, and I found a skid steer with a grapple. We may be able to put Angel's plan into place today."

"That would be ideal."

"My goal is to get all the equipment running and ready to go before Angel, Stuart, Red, and Andy return."

"Good luck." Pops smiled.

After David reached the Cabello house, he found Nate. "Have you had much experience driving tractors?"

"None at all," Nate said, "but I'm sure I'll learn."

David nodded. "We'll need you for guard duty. Let Charo, Lela, and the judge know that you and Tom will be down the road working on a project to block the road with storm debris."

After David returned to Major's house, Nate and Lela came through the shortcut.

Pops smiled. "You won, David."

"Nate said you all were going to block the road, but he didn't have any details," Lela said as Angel, Stuart, Red, and Andy ran up the driveway, and Jack joined Pops and Mr. Young.

"What are we talking about?" Jack whispered.

"We're going to block the road leading here with storm debris," Pops said, and Jack nodded.

"Angel found the perfect spot," Stuart said. "It's about two miles away, and a half mile from the state road. The tornado took down about a hundred yards of trees on both sides of the road. There is already debris in the road it wouldn't take much effort at all to push more of it into the road from both sides. It would look totally natural."

"We have two large tractors and a tracked skid steer. I can do a lot of work fast with that compact, powerful piece of equipment that can pick up trees the tractors can't budge. Tom can drive one tractor; who do we have that's experienced enough to drive the other?"

"Andy, Angel, and me," Stuart said.

Tom glanced at his wife, and she raised her eyebrows. "And Lela. She was on my old tractor more than I was; nobody can coax that temperamental old machine into working hard like she can."

"Looks like we've got our team; Nate's our security," David said.

"And me," Pops said. "Nate and I will take Number 48 to where you're working, so he doesn't have to run there and back. I'd like to know what our barrier looks like, and we can carry extra rifles in case there's an attempted ambush."

"We're okay here with security, Mr. Young, if you want to join the judge while our work crew is gone," Jack said.

"Good idea." Mr. Young went inside then came out with his shotgun and strolled to the shortcut.

"You've got a full team for our barrier for the east end of the road. We've got three tractors and three drivers: Dad, Andy, and me," Stuart said. "For security, we've got Dead Eye and Angel."

Andy nodded. "We can block the west end."

"Let's go." Angel turned toward the driveway, then she and Red raced to the road.

"I guess that's what we're doing," Stuart said as he and Andy ran down the driveway.

* * *

When Stuart and Andy joined Angel and Red at the road, the rumbling of the heavy machines and the roaring engines sounded like tanks as they rolled down the driveway behind them. After they headed toward the Newton farm, Stuart glanced back, and Pops and Nate had turned west in Number 48.

Stuart smiled. *I had every confidence that Pops would find a way to make sure the roadblock is intimidating to any intruders.*

When they reached the house, Scott was refueling the tractor. "How did it go?"

"Couldn't have asked for better." Stuart told his dad about the location Angel found for the roadblock, the equipment David found and put into service, and the plan.

"The team is on their way to construct a natural-looking barrier across the road."

"Are you thinking about doing the same at the east end of the road?"

Stuart nodded. "We've got two tractors at the Websters' farm that we can use and your tractor."

Scott nodded. "Right. I'll bring mine when and where Angel says."

"I guess our first step is to turn Angel and Red loose. I hate that." Stuart sighed. "We'll take the shortcut to the Websters' driveway then go to the road from there; I'd like to be finished before dark."

"I'd like to take my tractor to the road and head toward the Websters', so we won't lose any time waiting for me to catch up."

Stuart nodded. "Andy or I will stay with you. We'll have to toss a coin."

"I'll get my backpack and my rifle that has a sling then meet whoever is going with me on the road."

Stuart furrowed his brow in thought as he strolled to Angel, Andy, Red, and Peyton. Andy finished explaining the natural barrier plan to Peyton.

"I can just see David drooling over that skid steer," Peyton said as Stuart joined them. "Make sure he doesn't try to bring it home and claim it followed him."

Andy snorted. "I'll bet he's working on his story now."

When Scott rolled past them on his tractor as he headed to the driveway, Stuart said, "Dad's taking his tractor to the road, then one of us will stay with him while he travels to Leo's driveway."

"We can run ahead and find a good location then return by the time the three tractors are at Uncle Leo's," Red said.

"Yes."

"I'll stay with Scott until the three tractors are together," Peyton said.

"It's logical," Angel said. "Let's go."

Angel and Red disappeared around the back of the house, and Peyton rushed inside and grabbed her backpack then raced up the driveway.

"I'd like to have a head start just one time. Is that too much to ask?" Andy asked as he and Stuart ran around back to go to the shortcut.

"Yes," Stuart said, and Andy laughed.

When they reached the tractors, Stuart asked, "Which one do you want me to take?"

"Take the larger one; I've driven the smaller one a lot and have become an expert at getting it out of a ditch. I'm jealous of David and that tracked skid steer. I thought Uncle Leo had one too, but I haven't seen it since I've been here. I wonder if it's back in the woods somewhere, or maybe he sold it. I'll ask him later."

When they reached the end of the driveway, Scott and Peyton were waiting.

"Guess I'm going along as your guard on the road," Peyton said. "I'd get in trouble with Brandon if I went back alone."

Scott pointed ahead. "The girls are almost here."

"There are trees all over the road about fifty yards from the intersection. It wouldn't take long at all to block it completely," Red said.

"Are you going to stay with us while we go there?" Stuart asked.

"No."

Angel and Red raced away.

Stuart shrugged. "It was worth a shot. Dad, take the lead."

"I'm not going to try to keep up with you," Peyton said. "I want to be far enough away to be a surprise if anyone attacks."

Stuart nodded, and Scott accelerated his tractor to full speed; Stuart and Andy stayed with him, and Peyton trailed behind on the shoulder.

Stuart's eyes widened at the trees scattered on the road. *We could almost leave it as is. It would take a huge effort to clear away a path for a vehicle, but it wouldn't slow foot traffic all that much.*

Scott put his tractor on idle and pulled his brake then stepped down from the seat. Stuart and Andy joined him, and they walked around the obstruction.

"Andy, if you hop the ditch and push some of those small trees over the ditch on both sides, we can tighten up what's in the road into a decent barricade," Scott said.

Andy scanned the ditch. "There's culvert behind us on this side. Stuart, if you go across the culvert then push trees toward the road across it, you'll get twice the trees. I'll attack the other side."

"Two against one." Scott smirked. "I'm going to have to hustle."

CHAPTER FIFTEEN

Andy jumped on his tractor seat and scanned the other side then crossed the ditch at a shallow point while Stuart went across the culvert and pushed a stand of fallen trees toward the culvert then onto the road. While Scott moved the trees to the large pile, Stuart pushed more trees to the culvert then continued across to push the trees Andy was pushing out of the ditch.

When almost all the trees were in place, Angel and Red raced to the woods, around the barrier.

Something's up. Stuart slowed his engine to idle.

When they returned, Red said, "We need to leave now."

Stuart signaled to Scott and Andy, and the three drivers followed Angel while Peyton and Red stayed in the rear. When they were well out of sight of the blockade, Red raced to join Angel then motioned for the drivers to pull their tractors in front of trees that had fallen on the shoulder and that were partially blocking one lane. Peyton ran to join Angel. After the three tractors were in place, Red made a cutting motion across her neck, and the men shut off their engines.

Stuart jumped off his tractor and ran to Angel. "What's wrong?"

"A truck is heading north on the county road."

"Did you hear it?"

"It's burning oil; I smelled it with that last gust of wind from the south, then I heard it. It's moving slow."

"I'm going back to make sure it keeps on going," Stuart said.

"Let's go," Angel said.

Angel led Stuart, Red, and Andy through the woods at a fast pace. After they passed the barrier, Angel stopped them near the intersection.

Stuart listened, then he heard the engine as it headed north toward them. *Transport truck.*

He belly-crawled closer with Angel staying parallel to him. The truck belched oil as it slowed then stopped a few yards north of the intersection, and Stuart realized Angel was no longer next to him. *I wish she wouldn't do that.*

He crawled toward the ditch then aimed his rifle at the passenger who climbed out of the truck and scanned the area before he rushed to the back.

The passenger growled, "Break time: make it quick. We ain't the only bounty hunters looking for that major guy. We gotta get to Atlanta before anybody else does."

Three men jumped out of the back and hurried to the ditch on the other side of the truck. After they returned, two of the men climbed back in.

The last man squared off with the passenger and grumbled, "We ain't had nothing to eat all day."

"Quit yer bellyachin'," the passenger said. "We gotta go; you can stay here on the side of the road."

The last man scrambled into the back of the truck, the passenger hopped into his seat, and the truck rumbled north.

Stuart exhaled and lowered his rifle. Angel returned to his side, and they crawled back to join Red and Andy.

After they returned to the tractors through the woods, Stuart asked, "Angel you had a good look at the men, what did you see?"

"The driver and the passenger in the cab and the three men in the back were dirty and smelled bad."

"Do you think they stole the truck?"

"I think they found it," she said. "They were sick, and their clouds still showed danger, but it was more like desperation."

"Peyton, you'll go with Angel and me through the woods," Red said.

Angel, Red, and Peyton disappeared into the trees as Scott accelerated his tractor.

After they reached the Webster driveway, Scott said, "I'll meet you at home."

When Stuart and Andy reached the end of the Websters' driveway, Stuart exhaled at the sight of Angel, Red, and Peyton.

"I want to check in with Uncle Leo," Andy said.

"We'll stay a bit to hear what the hams have to say," Red said.

"Are we staying too, Angel?" Stuart asked.

"No."

As the three of them walked along the shortcut to the Newtons' farmhouse, Peyton said, "I'm going to have a nice cup of hot tea and pretend I'm soaking in a hot bath. Remind me how grueling it is to keep up with you all next time."

Stuart smirked and nodded.

When they reached the Newton barn, Scott was waiting for them.

"I'm going inside," Peyton said. "Let me know what my next assignment is."

After Peyton left, Scott asked, "What else?"

"The truck stopped, and the men took a break." Stuart reported what the men said. "Is that how you heard it?"

"Yes, and I told Red and Peyton," Angel said.

"When are you going to talk to Major?" Scott asked.

"I don't see where waiting until tomorrow will make a difference. Everyone's already on high alert, and we've done what we can for defense for the day. Pops and Jack will set up a security detail for the night," Stuart said.

Scott nodded. "It'll be dark soon."

"We'll go at first light," Stuart said.

"Sure would like to know what the bounty is and who's paying it," Scott said as they walked to the house.

When they went into the house, Henry and Brody were waiting by the door; Henry hugged Angel then Stuart. "We learned about cows today. Farmer Blanche is smart."

Angel and Stuart returned his hugs.

"It's great that you're learning so much about farming," Stuart said, and Henry beamed.

"You all have your bedrooms back; the three boys are in their bedroom, and Mandy has the girls' bedroom to herself," Sandra said. "Peyton and I moved her and David into the sick room, left Blanche and Cal in their bedroom close to the kitchen, and moved the Wheatleys into the middle bedroom; Doc has his bedroom. Louisa wants to eat with us at the table, and Noel is doing better. He's talking, and Doc wants him to sit up to eat. Doc's talking about getting Noel up in a chair tomorrow. That's about it for our news," Sandra said. "Where are Red and Andy?"

"Red wanted to listen to the radio with Leo; I don't think they'll be long."

"Are we ready for the buckaroos to come to the table?" Blanche asked.

"Two minutes," Sandra said. "There will be enough room for you, Cal, Louisa, and Doc to eat first shift too."

"I'll help Louisa to the table," Peyton said.

While Blanche and Peyton were gathering up folks to eat supper, Scott and Sandra served the children's plates while Angel set the table, and Stuart fed the dogs then took them outside.

Louisa leaned on Peyton as they came down the hallway then sat at the table.

"That was a workout," Louisa said as Peyton helped her sit at the chair that was between Mandy and Jimmy.

"Mama Sandra is the best cook ever, except for you, Mama," Jimmy said.

"I consider that quite a compliment." Sandra smiled.

Angel narrowed her eyes at Red and Andy when they came into the house while the first shift was in the middle of eating.

"Meeting in the living room," Angel said, and Andy nodded.

Stuart, Scott, Peyton, and David followed Angel, Red, and Andy to the living room.

"There's a bounty on Major." Red glanced at David. "You know about that, right?"

David nodded. "Peyton told me."

"No one seemed to know whether it was a specific major," Andy continued, "and one of the hams said that he heard someone was trying to annihilate the US military leadership. Phil was on and asked who was offering the bounty, and that sparked the speculation that it was just a rumor."

"Phil's trying to get us a name," Stuart said.

"Any thugs who can walk are roaming Florida and Georgia, so they can collect the bounty," Red said.

Scott frowned. "Do we even know how much the bounty is?"

Andy shook his head. "One of the hams asked, and no one knows."

Scott exhaled in exasperation. "This is all so vague; I don't understand why anyone would go out to find some unknown person to collect an undisclosed bounty from an anonymous criminal."

"It would be easy to dismiss except for what Angel and I heard today," Stuart said.

"We have to take it seriously because the bad guys are," Red said.

"Yes."

"Mr. Young wasn't on the radio, so they didn't have time to set up their antenna," Andy said.

Stuart strolled to the window. "No clouds, and the moon's not full, but there's enough light to see; we could go after supper."

David frowned. "Peyton and I will go. We won't be as fast as you would, but you all have been up over sixteen hours as it is. As sharp as you are, you're still tired."

"Agreed." Peyton crossed her arms and glared.

"No, four is better," Angel said.

"Blanche and I will go with David and Peyton," Scott said.

Stuart opened his mouth to protest, and Angel said, "Yes."

Scott grinned. "Logical, right?"

"We'll go with you to the end of the driveway," Stuart said.

"One of you that's going has to tell Mama Sandra," Red said as she and Angel left the living room.

"Dang, they're good," Scott said. "I didn't see that coming. David?"

"All on you, Scott." David grinned as he and Peyton followed Angel and Red.

As he left the living room, Scott said, "I'll tell Blanche, and she can tell Sandra."

Scott sauntered into the kitchen as Blanche and the children were clearing their plates.

"Ready to go back to your bedroom?" Peyton asked.

Louisa nodded. "I guess I wore myself out more than I expected."

"Got a minute, Blanche?" Scott asked then headed to the living room.

Blanche, Cal, and Stuart followed him.

Scott filled them in on the major and bounty. "I volunteered to go to Major's place after our supper. David and Peyton are going along too. We need a fourth."

Cal and Blanche exchanged glances. "I'm your sidekick," Blanche said, and Cal nodded.

"She's a better shot than I am and can run like the dickens if she needs to," Cal said. "I'd like to go too, but we can't empty the house, can we?"

"We'll go to the end of the driveway, but we'll be defense here along with you, so you won't be completely alone," Stuart said.

"Got yourself fired?" Blanche asked.

"Something like that," Stuart said.

"Good, let's eat," Scott said. "Blanche, will you tell Sandra our plan?"

Cal chuckled. "Glad you're going, honey, not me."

Blanche linked her arm in his. "Typical gang tactic: push the dirty work off on the new kid."

"Pretty slick, Dad," Stuart whispered as they walked together to the kitchen.

While they were eating, David said, "While you all were away, Cal and I took a stroll to the south end of the property and walked as near to the road as we could get. It's blocked by trees and debris from the state road almost to the county road. My guess is that the storm plowed down the south side of the road then turned and came back on the north side before it swerved and took out Leo's barn."

"I guess I'm officially tired because I hadn't thought about the road to the south." Andy sopped up the rest of his soup with his bread. "I should have because that's where we got our transport trucks, and I got to see the tremendous duo in action."

After everyone had finished eating and cleared their places, Blanche said, "Scott volunteered to take care of the dishes, Sandra; I need to talk to you about baths and bedtime."

Blanche whispered as she and Sandra strolled to the bathroom together.

While Scott and Stuart tackled the dishes, Scott snorted. "Too much laughing coming from the bathroom."

"Definitely at your expense, I'm sure," Cal chuckled.

After Blanche returned, she said, "Sandra's got the kids until I get back. Louisa had already asked to tell their story tonight. Cal will help her to the living room."

Scott's eyes widened. "Dishes are done, and you're a genius."

"I knew you'd handle it," Cal said.

"When do we leave?" Blanche asked.

"As soon as we can gather our rifles and backpacks," David said. "We'll go over our game plan on the way up the driveway."

Blanche and Peyton hurried to their bedrooms. Blanche returned wearing a black cowgirl hat, a black neckerchief around her neck, a dark camo coat, and carrying her rifle and backpack.

"I need a black hat too," Peyton said.

Blanche left the kitchen then returned with a black ballcap. "Best I could do."

"Perfect," Peyton said. "We're ready."

David mumbled as they left the house, "Be very afraid, bad guys."

When Stuart, Red, and Andy headed to the door, Angel said, "Honey, Red and Andy at the end of the driveway."

Stuart nodded, and Red and Andy left.

"What are we doing?" Stuart asked.

"Checking south of the house like David did."

Before they got as far as the trees, Angel turned and gazed at the house. "See the lanterns in the kitchen and the Wheatleys' bedroom?"

Stuart nodded. *This is the same check we did for the front of the house.*

After they walked a hundred yards into the trees, they scanned the house again.

"I can't see the house, but I can see the lights," Stuart said. "We would be a beacon for anyone walking; we'll need to talk to Mom about heavy curtains on all the windows to block the lights at night."

"We may want to limit our use of light too. Not all rooms need to be lit up at night either; we've become a little lax with that," Angel said.

"The kitchen and the kids' bedrooms have priority," Stuart said.

"Maybe a light in the hallway at the bottom of the stairs for safety," Angel added.

After they turned back to the house, Stuart asked, "How long have you been thinking about this?"

"I thought about it last night then noticed the lights on our way to Florida. There were more lights than I expected because I thought there weren't many occupied houses along the way."

"I'll mention it to Mom to give her a heads up; maybe she'd like to bring it up tomorrow morning at breakfast."

As they reached the house, Stuart said, "Henry would have seen the lights."

"Yes."

"Don't tell him; we would be in trouble for years for not taking him," Stuart said.

"I don't think we have the stamina for that."

When Stuart chuckled, Angel giggled, and he stopped and kissed her.

"You are amazing," he said as they resumed their walk to the house.

"So are you. I thought it might be a good joke, and you laughed."

When they reached the house, Cal and Doc Larkin were outside near the back door.

"Louisa told me she's still achy, but she's walking much better; she wants to give Noel a sponge bath tomorrow when he moves from his bed to his chair," Doc said. "Do we expect their family to stay here?"

"Their car runs just fine, but I don't think they have anywhere to go," Stuart said. "They're certainly welcome to stay. Why?"

"Louisa's stressing about where they would go after Noel is well."

"I'll talk to Mom; she'll settle both of them down," Stuart said.

Cal smacked his hand. "I need to go inside; the mosquitos have found me."

Sandra met them in the kitchen. "The kids are in the living room with Louisa. She's a natural born storyteller. I came in here for some hot tea and to get off my feet. Are you all as tired as I am?"

"I'll heat the water, Mom," Angel said.

"That means you're supposed to sit, Mom," Stuart said, and Sandra smiled as she sat at her place.

"I need to hear the stories." Doc headed toward the living room.

While Sandra sipped her tea, Stuart said, "Angel and I went for a perimeter walk toward the road south of us. Angel noticed lights from houses this morning when we drove to Florida and realized those houses were occupied. We could see the lights in the kitchen and the Wheatleys' bedroom even after we were in the woods."

"That far away?" Sandra furrowed her brow. "We need to cover the windows with blackout curtains. I can make those tomorrow. Do we need to cover all the windows?"

"Maybe; we might also need to talk about how many lights we need on at night," Stuart said.

Sandra nodded. "After we eat supper, we don't need to leave on the kerosene lantern in the kitchen. A candle on the stove is all we'd need, so the children can sit at the table with their snacks. We don't need a bright kerosene lantern to gather around the table with hot tea or coffee and socialize."

"I'm not sure we need lights in all bedrooms at bedtime either," Cal said. "Maybe one light in each hallway would be good enough. Seems like we're hanging onto our old habits when we had electricity, and a flip of a switch turned on a light, then we'd just leave it on."

"Might be a good topic for our breakfast discussion," Sandra said.

"What's our candle supply like?" Cal asked.

"We have a ton of candles; we have enough kerosene, but it wouldn't hurt to conserve it, and I certainly don't like the idea of calling attention to the house," Sandra said.

"Did Doc mention Louisa to you?" Call asked.

"He sure did. I'm going to talk to Peyton in the morning; she and Louisa are becoming good friends. I think the three of us can chat. I assumed the Wheatleys would stay here with us, but I can see how Louisa could feel unsettled because I haven't extended an invitation for them to stay. I think I'm used to this crowd; we just juggle around and fit everybody in."

"I think you're right; have you noticed that Mandy and Jimmie call you Mamma Sandra?" Cal asked.

"No, but I guess I wouldn't notice, would I? It's my name, after all." Sandra smiled.

"I'd like to check on Red and Andy," Stuart said. "Will you be okay, Cal?"

"We'll be fine," Cal said.

When Stuart and Angel reached the driveway, Red asked, "What?"

"Angel was worried about how far the lights broadcast an occupied house, so we went into the woods south of the house. It was easy to see the lights in the kitchen and in the Wheatleys' bedroom."

"In the trees? That far away?" Andy asked.

"Mom's going to make some blackout curtains and will bring up the discussion in the morning about how many bright lights we really need at night."

"We need to tell Pops," Red said.

"Red and I should go now," Angel said.

Stuart sighed. "Okay."

They disappeared down the road.

"You told them okay?" Andy growled.

"They're fast. We're two shooters. We can split up; they can't, and I hate it as much as you do."

"You've been hanging around that Angel person too much; that's logical." Andy smiled.

"Guilty." Stuart chuckled. "I told Cal we were just checking on you; I need to let him know we'll be a little longer than planned. If I'm fast enough, I'll be back before my logical wife shows up."

Stuart jogged down to Cal, who stood outside near the house.

"Where's your better half?" Cal asked.

Stuart told him what happened.

"Those girls are smart, aren't they?"

"Unfortunately, yes. It makes sense to let Pops know right away, and he'll alert the Cabellos. They're closer to the state road and the interstate and more vulnerable in that sense than we are, but I sure didn't like telling them it was okay to go, and Andy was unhappy about it too."

"But they're the fastest," Cal said.

"Right, and I suppose it was the right thing to do, but I don't have to like it. Andy and I will stay at the driveway entrance to the road. We answer to bird calls."

"That's what I heard. I do a pretty good turkey call."

Stuart furrowed his brow. "I thought turkeys called during the day or early evening."

"Spoken like a true country-raised fella. How many city slickers know that?"

Stuart snorted. "Turkey it is."

When Stuart rejoined Andy, he told him about Cal's turkey call, and Andy chuckled. "I taught at an exclusive prep school, and they were all city boys. They may have recognized a turkey call at night, but they wouldn't have questioned it."

The two of them peered down the road.

"I don't see them yet; we need Henry." Stuart paced on the road in front of the driveway.

"Maybe one of us should run to Pops' to see what's wrong," Andy said. "I'll go."

"No, stay here because I'd want to go too, and we can't abandon Cal and Mom."

"Again with the logical," Andy said.

"Somebody's coming, but they aren't running; I think it's Dad and Blanche. I don't get it," Stuart said.

When Scott and Blanche reached them, Scott said, "We know about the lights; Red told us. David and Peyton relieved us while Angel and Red talk to Major. All of them will be here soon."

Scott and Blanche strolled down the driveway.

"Shall we run when we get close to the house?" Blanche asked.

"Sounds great to me; we can claim we ran the whole way," Scott said.

"Uphill, barefoot, and through the snow," Blanche said.

Stuart snorted. "Do you think they can pull it off?"

Andy chuckled. "Probably. Nobody will believe them, but only Mama Sandra would call them on it, and she might not blow their cover."

"I'll breathe easier when I see Angel and Red," Stuart said.

Stuart and Andy froze at the sound of a distant crash.

"Interstate?" Andy asked.

"Sounded like it to me. If we don't see Angel and Red in five minutes, we're taking off because that means they went to check on the crash."

"Agreed. Tell me again how we measure five minutes," Andy asked.

"Five minutes is when we can't take waiting anymore."

A few seconds later, Andy said, "Okay, go."

"Wait, I see them."

Angel and Red raced to the driveway.

"We passed Peyton and David; they'll be here in a couple of minutes. We talked to Pops, and he's going to talk to Tom, Lila, Nate, Charo, and the judge. He said that was something he discovered at the Florida farm too, so it made sense to him. He knew it was Angel's idea. Are we too late for a snack?" Red asked.

"No, honey; I'm sure Mama Sandra saved you a snack." Andy hugged Red.

"Did you hear the crash?" Angel asked. "A transport truck crashed into a large branch that was in one of the northbound lanes of the interstate; the truck is really messed up. A second transport truck stopped and picked up the two men who were in the truck. We should check the abandoned vehicle tomorrow to see what they were carrying because they didn't unload anything from the back."

Stuart shook his head. *I knew it.*

Andy elbowed him. "You were right."

CHAPTER SIXTEEN

"Are we waiting for Peyton and David?" Red asked.

"Angel and I will wait for them," Stuart said. "You can go to the house but leave us some snacks."

Red began her run to the house then turned back. "We'll run at your pace, honey."

"Okay if I don't run as fast as I can?" Andy asked.

Red hugged him. "I'll run alongside you."

Andy picked up one foot then the other and pumped his arms in an exaggerated slow-motion run, and Red laughed. "Okay, let's walk; hold my hand."

"Love to." Andy raised his arms in triumph then grabbed onto Red's hand.

"You are so funny." Red giggled as they strolled down the driveway.

"Are we that strange?" Angel asked.

"Yes." Stuart smiled, and Angel giggled.

Stuart hugged her and kept his hold on her. "I love when you answer questions with 'Yes' because I know that your mind has run through all the possibilities, and you come to the same conclusion for all of them, and there's no need to go into an in-depth explanation."

Angel wrapped her arms around his waist, laid her head on his shoulder, and sighed. "Peyton and David are almost here."

She released him, and he kissed her forehead then brushed back her hair as he gazed at her face. "You are really special."

When Peyton and David joined them, Peyton said, "Thanks, David and I have never been partners before. It was a great opportunity for us."

"Team Griffin." David grinned.

Peyton snickered. "Let's go, teammate; I'm ready to see Brandon."

"Guess what?" Stuart put his arm around Angel and whispered while they strolled down the driveway. "We don't have to sleep in the back of a truck tonight."

After the children were in bed, Stuart, Angel, and Scott walked around the house for their final perimeter check.

"Your mom is hand-stitching the curtains for the kitchen. She said that was her first priority for blackout curtains.

After Stuart told his dad about the crash, Stuart said, "We'll go to the interstate before breakfast. We'll stash whatever we find in the woods then haul the items to the house later."

"I assume Red and Andy will go with you; I'll go too."

Stuart nodded.

When they went into the house, everyone had gone to bed except Sandra.

"Finish that in the morning, honey," Scott said. "The light will be better."

Stuart put his arm around Angel, and Sandra waited to douse the lantern until they reached the top of the stairs.

* * *

When Stuart woke the next morning, he raised his eyebrows and smirked. *I've completely abandoned my side of the bed.* Angel was asleep on her side with her head on his shoulder and her arm around his chest with his arm on top of her arm. One of his legs was across her thighs, and the lower part of her legs trapped his other leg.

He smiled. *There's no way out of this tangle without waking her.*

He felt the flutter of her eyelashes on his shoulder. "I'm awake too," he whispered.

"I smell coffee. Mom's already up," Angel said.

Stuart rolled back to his side of the bed to climb out then hurried to dress while Angel peered out the window. "It's still dark."

"I'll meet you downstairs; maybe I can get a few sips of coffee before we leave. I don't hear Red or Andy stirring, do you?"

"They'll get up when they hear us go down the stairs." Angel quickly dressed. Before she reached the bottom of the stairs, Red and Andy tiptoed down behind her. When they went into the kitchen, Scott said quietly, "Ready when you are," and Sandra pointed to Andy's cup on the table.

Andy downed his coffee, then after everyone put on their jackets and grabbed their rifles, the five of them left.

Angel headed toward the barn.

"We're getting the utility carts. We'll be right back." Red hurried to catch up with Angel.

"Did Angel say anything about carts?" Scott asked.

Stuart shook his head. "I've given up trying to understand how those two operate."

Scott shrugged. "It's a good idea. Are we traveling down the road?"

"We'll stay on the road until we reach the barrier, then we'll cut into the woods; Angel will lead. Here they come."

"If you'll bring the wagons, honey, Angel and I will run to the road, then we'll meet you at the Cabello driveway." Red stood on her tiptoes and gave Andy a quick kiss, then she and Angel raced up the driveway.

"I guess we're pulling the carts." Andy grabbed a handle, and he and Stuart started up the driveway.

"I don't like this." Scott turned back to the barn.

"Did he quit on us?" Andy asked as he and Stuart continued up the road.

"I don't know what he has in mind, but he didn't quit. Have you noticed that we're out of the loop on everything this morning?"

"Couldn't happen to a nicer couple of guys." Andy stopped at the road. "Do we wait for your—"

Andy was interrupted by the hum of 48-4.

Stuart furrowed his brow. "Dad's bringing 48-4. He definitely has something in mind; wonder what it is?"

Scott grinned when he reached them. "Got to have the right tools. I decided the benefit of moving quickly outweighed the low risk of the engine noise attracting any attention. Let's put one cart on top of the other; I brought straps to keep the top one in place, then we can attach the cart to the hitch on 48-4. We can use the carts to haul whatever we find in the trucks to the woods and empty them later."

While Stuart and Andy strapped one cart on top of the other, Andy asked, "How did you come up with such a brilliant idea?"

"I think he channeled his inner Angel," Stuart said.

Scott attached the cart to the hitch. "I'll take that as a compliment."

"Dad, you drive; Andy, take the front passenger's seat; I'm going to sit backwards, so I can watch behind us and keep an eye on the carts."

When they reached the Cabello driveway, Red said, "I didn't hear you until right before I saw you; Angel heard you earlier than I did. What's the plan?"

"Dad will take 48-4 to the blockade, then after we unhook the carts, he'll position it, so it won't be easily seen. We'll pull the carts into the woods and as close to the state road as we can, then we can take both carts with us to check the transport truck on the other side of the interstate and load anything useful we find then return," Stuart said.

"We're definitely better off to minimize our time on the interstate," Andy said.

Angel and Red raced toward the barrier and disappeared.

"I suppose that's our signal to go." Scott chuckled as he accelerated to follow them.

When the three men reached the blockade, Stuart and Andy quickly unhooked the cart then removed the straps from the top cart while Scott parked 48-4 in the ditch.

Stuart and Andy pulled the carts into the woods, and Scott joined them.

"It's getting a little lighter in the east; we'll need to move fast," Scott said.

"Let's stay in the tall grass and go to the state road," Stuart said.

"I'll keep you in sight, but I want to hike closer to the road now that we're past the barrier," Scott said.

Angel and Red rejoined them before the men reached the state road.

"The back of the truck is filled with boxes, but they weren't marked, and we didn't take the time to open any of them. Angel found a small group of oak trees in the grassy area between the state road and the interstate; it's a perfect spot to stage the carts. A car with a family passed us while we were in the trees, and it was pulling a small, enclosed rental trailer," Red said. "We didn't hear or see any other vehicles going either way."

"We'll pull the carts through the woods until we get to the stand of trees to minimize our exposure," Angel said.

"Angel will show you the best path," Red said as Angel headed south into the woods and disappeared.

When Stuart started pulling his cart in the same direction that Angel went, Andy followed him with the second cart.

"How will we know which way to go?" Andy asked as he and Red followed Stuart.

"She'll be right back," Stuart said.

Before they reached the brush where Angel disappeared, she joined them then led them through a growth of young pine trees until they reached the state road.

After she stopped near the edge of the pine trees, Stuart and Scott joined her.

"The ditch isn't very deep on either side of the state road," Stuart said.

"I'll go to that group of oak trees and brush on the other side of the state road. If I hear or see anything, I'll alert you," Scott said.

"I'll go with you," Angel said.

After Angel and Scott were hidden in the oak trees, Red scanned the road while Stuart and Andy sprinted across with their carts. When the two men reached the trees, Red joined them.

"Can we go?" Stuart asked.

"Yes," Red whispered.

Andy sprinted across the interstate while Red ran ahead of him, and Stuart pulled the second cart while Angel ran behind him.

Andy had jumped into the back of the truck and pulled out his knife to slice open a box. "New shirts? That's crazy. Should I open any more of the boxes?"

"No, let's just move as fast as we can; we'll figure out all this later," Stuart said.

Andy shrugged, but when he attempted to lift a box, he groaned. "This is awful heavy for shirts."

He slid the boxes to the edge of the truck, then Stuart loaded them into the first cart two boxes high.

When the cart was full, Stuart pulled and Red pushed the loaded cart across the interstate.

Angel replaced Andy in the back of the truck and slid the heavy boxes to Andy who loaded them into the second cart.

Scott met Stuart at the oak trees and took over pulling the cart to the pine trees while Red continued to push.

"This is heavy," Scott said, and Stuart nodded then raced back to the truck.

Angel said, "This last box is light."

"That's the one that I opened; it can go on top because it's lighter than the others," Andy said.

After Angel jumped out of back of the truck, she paused. "Car!"

After Angel grabbed the light box, Stuart pulled, and Andy pushed while they ran across the interstate. Angel raced ahead of them then waited near the oaks.

"Now!" Angel shouted; Stuart and Andy hurried to move the cart into hiding.

Stuart scanned the pine trees on the other side of the state road while a pickup truck roared north on the interstate.

"Clear," Angel said.

"Let's go," Stuart said.

Stuart and Andy pulled the carts across the state road and into the pine trees. Stuart dropped the handle, but before he could turn to find Angel, she hugged him.

He held onto her. "If we can pull these carts past the barrier, we can continue to the barn."

"And breakfast," Scott added. "I'm starving."

Stuart chuckled and picked up the handle to pull it farther into the woods.

Angel froze, and Red hissed, "Wait."

They all stood in silence until Red whispered, "Truck."

Stuart peered through the pines and brush, and a truck stopped at the broken-down transport truck.

Two men hopped out of the truck and hurried to the back.

"It's empty. Those fools don't have any idea of what they left behind," one man growled as he pulled back the canvas flap. "They crashed into a little limb and abandoned cargo worth more than they are. If they'd let us know right away, we could have picked up everything yesterday before some jerk stole it."

"They sealed their coffins, didn't they?" The driver snarled.

"We need to go after those thieves, so nobody can say we didn't try."

The driver nervously glanced around them. "I heard there's a militia in north Georgia. I don't want to be the one to find out there might be one here too."

"Let's go."

While the driver rushed back to their truck, the first man scanned the roadside. After the driver started the engine and put the truck into gear, the man raced to jump into his seat. When the driver stomped on the accelerator, the truck roared and belched black smoke from its exhaust as it lurched forward then lumbered north on the interstate.

"Whatever we got, it's valuable to them; let's move," Andy said.

After they pulled the wagons through the woods then to the field and past the barrier, they reached the road to the farms.

"We can hook up only one," Scott said. "How do we do this?"

"Tandem," Stuart said.

"Double towing?" Andy asked. "I thought that was illegal."

"When a deputy sheriff says, tandem, we tandem." Scott smiled as he attached the first cart to the hitch on 48-4 then sat in the driver's seat.

Stuart used the straps to secure the handle of the second cart to the back axle of the first cart.

Angel and Red raced down the road toward the Newton farm; Stuart and Andy took their seats in 48-4, and Stuart said, "Ready, Dad; let's roll."

Scott slowly accelerated until the straps tightened then increased his speed.

Stuart watched the two carts and the road behind them. "Slow down, Dad; the second cart is wobbling off track."

Scott eased up on the accelerator.

"Better," Stuart said. Scott maintained the steady, slow speed as 48-4 passed Major's and the Cabellos' driveways.

"I thought Red and Angel would be here," Andy said.

"They probably were until Angel heard 48-4," Stuart said.

Scott nodded and continued his constant speed until he reached his driveway and stopped. "I'm not sure I wouldn't tip over the carts."

"I'll unhook them; we can pull them down the driveway. Thanks for your help, Dad," Stuart said.

After the wagons were unhooked, Scott saluted as he drove 48-4 to the equipment shed.

While Stuart and Andy pulled the carts on the driveway, Andy said, "Finally, we can walk like sane people on the relatively level ground. Big change after tearing across six lanes of interstate, through the median with oak trees, across the state road, and up the embankment then through the brush and high grass."

After they rolled the carts into the barn, they hurried to the house.

When they were inside, Red said, "About time you got here. We've eaten, and we're ready to go."

Red picked up her rifle, and Stuart said, "Wait for us."

Red and Angel were poised for flight near the back door.

"Chef Blanche made tortillas this morning; give me two seconds to put together your breakfast taco," Sandra said.

"We love you, Mom and Chef Blanche," Stuart said without diverting his gaze as he glared at Angel and Red.

When Sandra handed Stuart and Andy their breakfast tacos, Red opened the door, and Stuart and Andy dashed outside.

"We'll walk with you, so you can eat," Angel said.

"We had a chance to rest," Red said.

"You're all heart, honey," Andy said.

As they strolled to the shortcut, Red said, "Mama Sandra mentioned that we go to Uncle Leo's every day to listen to the radio, and Blanche asked why we weren't using Cal's radio and antenna."

Stuart narrowed his eyes at Red. "Cal has a radio at his house?"

"Nope, better than that. Cal said he'd forgotten, but he has a transceiver and an antenna on his truck," Red said.

"It's already set up to run off a twelve-volt battery. I've been thinking about setting up a solar power-charging station for batteries, anyway, so the battery will stay charged," Angel said.

"After we get back from Uncle Leo's, Cal and David will go to the Websters' and remove the radio, battery, and antenna," Red added.

"Couldn't we do that while we're there?" Andy asked.

"I could very easily," Angel said, "but it's his radio."

Stuart nodded as they reached the barn. "I don't understand radios, but I do understand why a man would want to dismantle his equipment himself."

Andy sighed. "Okay, go."

Angel and Red raced to the shortcut to the Websters'.

When Stuart smirked, Andy shrugged. "What can I say? They were about to bust, and it might have been my turn."

Stuart and Andy ran at a fast pace to Leo's.

"Good run," Andy said as they went inside the house and headed to the radio room. "We need to do that more often."

Leo stopped them in the hallway. "Angel's talking to Mr. Young. Andy, I was on my way upstairs to check on Jennie; she wanted to be in the guest bedroom; she said the sun shines brighter in there. I know she'd like to see you."

Andy nodded, then he and Leo went up the stairs as Stuart went into the radio room.

* * *

Andy bit his lip when they went into the guest bedroom. *She's so pale.*

Jennie's voice was weak. "How's everybody doing?"

"We're fine. Red is downstairs with Angel; Angel's on Uncle Leo's radio."

Jennie nodded. "She must be a whiz for Leo to voluntarily relinquish the headset. Right, honey?"

"She is a genius; if ham radio was a competition, she'd beat me hands-down," Leo said.

"I'm tired; thanks for coming to say hello, Andy." Jennie closed her eyes, and Leo and Andy left the room.

After they were downstairs, Leo said, "She gets weaker every day."

"I'm so sorry," Andy said. "Is there any way I can help? Red and I can stay here for a few days and clean house or prepare meals."

"Thanks for the offer, Andy, but she's hypersensitive and can't deal with any extra noise."

Andy nodded.

"Red told me about Cal's radio. After Cal and Angel get it set up, I'll be able to contact you if I need any help, and you won't have to come here every day. Jennie gets really upset every time someone comes in the house," Leo said.

"I'm really sorry; we didn't realize that."

"If there's any equipment or tools in the shed that you need, help yourself. You're the only family we have left, so it's as much yours as mine."

When Leo went into the radio room, Stuart joined Andy in the hallway, and Andy pointed to the back door.

"How is she?" Stuart asked after they were outside.

"Really weak."

"Is there anything we can do to help?"

Andy shook his head. "I offered to cook meals or clean the house, and Uncle Leo said any noise at all upsets her, including our visits. I wished I'd known because we could have waited for Angel outside. She moves with the stealth of a hungry tiger."

Stuart furrowed his brow. "I don't understand isolating from friends and family, but if it's what they want, we'll certainly respect it."

Andy nodded. "Uncle Leo is really happy about Cal's radio, and he told me the equipment and tools on the farm are mine as much as his. I felt like he wanted to give me permission to take whatever we needed without feeling like I had to check with him first."

Andy furrowed his brow. "I don't know whether to say anything to Red and Angel about how sensitive Jennifer is to the sound of people."

"I think we'll feel better if you do because we won't be hiding anything from them."

When Angel and Red joined them outside, Andy told them about his visit with Jennie and how sensitive she was to any types of sound.

"That's too bad," Red said. "If anyone understands being sensitive to sound, it's Angel. If we don't get Cal's radio in place at the Newton farm by the time of this evening's call, Angel can go to the radio room by herself. She glides like a mist."

"Did you hear anything else on the radio?" Stuart asked as they strolled along the shortcut to the Smith barn.

"One of the hams south of us said that there was a large group gathering on the abandoned farm next to his. He heard one man say they would join the rest of the troops that were going to sweep north to find the major. Another man bragged they'd be like Sherman, burning as they went. The ham said that was when he got scared. After he and his wife packed everything they could into their pickup and trailer, they loaded their kids and hit the road. He was driving east, then when he gets closer to the coast, he plans to travel north to his brother's farm outside of Charleston, South Carolina," Red said.

"Another ham said he heard something similar outside Atlanta, except the gangs were gathering to travel west and south. He said one of the men said their orders were to find the major if they had to scorch the entire state of Georgia," Angel said.

"One of the hams said he had planned to stay put, but after today's news, he has changed his mind and will leave in the morning for his son's place in Mississippi," Red said.

Cal and David met them at the Smith barn.

"Do you need any help?" Stuart asked.

"I have a rule never to turn down help," Cal said, "but in this case, it isn't necessary because it's nothing fancy that the two of us can't handle. If we don't take too long disconnecting my radio and antenna, I'd like to spend a little time with Leo."

"Leo will probably come outside when you knock at the door," Stuart said.

"Don't take it personally if Uncle Leo doesn't invite you in. Aunt Jennie is very ill, and the slightest noise bothers her," Andy said.

Cal nodded. "I'll see if he'll talk to me. We gotta get going."

CHAPTER SEVENTEEN

After Mr. Young turned off the ham radio, he peered at Major. "What do you think?"

"We've done a good job with our barriers to the east and west, and the Newton and Webster farms protect our south, but we don't know what our exposure to the north is."

"Tom would know." Mr. Young rose from his seat.

"Let's check with Jack then go talk to him," Major said.

"Where's Jack?" Major asked Molly as he strolled into the kitchen with his stick and his determination to have only a minor limp.

"You're walking pretty good today but don't overdo it. Jack's out back with Annie. Annie wants her new coop and run ready for the chickens before the end of the day. She's put Josh, Brett, and Sara to work too. Be careful and don't get too close, or she'll rope you in too." Molly chuckled. "I think Vanessa's hiding somewhere."

"I'll meet you out front," Mr. Young said.

Mr. Young's another expert at hiding. Major snorted as he slowly made his way across the uneven ground to the old chicken pen.

"We're rescuing nails and lumber for Annie," Brett said as Sara carefully tapped a crooked nail straight.

"Brett takes the nails out of the wood, then I make them straight. I'm pretty good at it." Sara kept working.

"You are; good work, you two," Major said.

Major motioned for Jack to join him. "Need a few minutes of your time. We need to catch you up on the latest news from the hams. Mr. Young's around front waiting for us."

Jack walked alongside Major to the front; Shadow and Penny stayed with the children.

"I can't be long," Jack said. "Annie's got us on a tight schedule."

"That's what I hear. Mr. Young and I are going to the Cabello house to talk to Tom."

"What's up?" Jack asked after they joined Mr. Young.

Major and Mr. Young explained what they heard on the radio, then Major said, "We want to talk to Tom about our north side."

Jack nodded. "We're very well covered on the south, and not bad on the east and west. Let me know what Tom says. We may want to pull in Stuart and Scott for us to come up with a decent plan."

"And the girls," Mr. Young added.

"Angel and Red: perfect names for those two, aren't they?" Jack turned to go to the back.

"Wait, Jack," Major said, "Do you and Annie have your rifles with you?"

Jack narrowed his eyes. "I'll get them now, thanks."

"You too, Mr. Young."

Mr. Young nodded. "I'll remind Molly and Vanessa."

When Mr. Young returned with his shotgun, he said, "All of us were so relieved to be here that we relaxed and dropped our guard. Rookie mistake."

"I started out last night for my perimeter check without my rifle. Shadow wouldn't let me past him, then I figured it out."

When they reached the shortcut, Shadow bounded to them then followed them to the Cabello house.

Major knocked on the front door.

"It's Pops, Mama," Dolly said as she opened the door.

"Pops, you don't knock on my door. You're family," Charo called out from the kitchen.

"Do you know where Tom is?" Major asked.

"Grandpa Tom and Daddy are out back," Dolly said. "I can run fast and get him for you."

"We'll find them, thanks."

"Come through the kitchen, so you don't have to maneuver that uneven ground," Charo said.

Major raised his eyebrows. "You have to come through the house too, Mr. Young."

Mr. Young followed Major as the two men made their way through the kitchen.

"Not doing too bad on that leg today, are you? Don't overdo." Charo shook her wooden spoon at Major.

After they were out back, Mr. Young chuckled. "I like the way Charo told us straight up to walk inside the house from now on. I never understood hints and innuendos."

"You don't know how bad I wanted to say, yes, ma'am, when she shook that spoon at me. Can you imagine the tirade I would have gotten if I had?" Major rolled his eyes.

Tom and Nate were laying out boards for a new raised garden over the black cloth they had placed on the ground.

Major held out his hand, and Tom brushed his hands on his pants. "My hands are pretty dirty, Major; not sure you want to shake them."

Major reached his hand closer to Tom. "If our hands aren't dirty, we're not working." The two men shook, then Major shook hands with Nate.

"We're here on a mission. Is there a place we can sit and talk for a bit?" Major asked.

"We found an old picnic table and dragged it under the trees. Let's try it out." Tom and Nate led the way, and Major and Mr. Young followed them.

Major sighed. "I'll tell you like I told Jack, but first, where are your rifles?"

Tom and Nate rose from the table and returned from the house with their rifles.

"I did the same thing last night," Major said. "We all needed the reminder."

He told them about the news on the ham radio.

Tom narrowed his eyes. "We're the defense on the north."

"Right, and that's not what we want. What's north of us?" Major asked.

"Immediately north of us is woods then a small community of vacant houses on a dirt road, a lane that's not quite wide enough for two cars to pass each other. It goes through to the county road, just like ours does. One difference is that it dead ends about where we are and doesn't extend to the state road."

"What's north of the community?"

"Bureau of Land Management Property. It's fenced, but there are no houses and no roads."

"That's our first real buffer then," Major said.

"Are there any houses west of the community?" Mr. Young asked.

"No, in fact if the tornado closed off that road at the county road, it wouldn't look any different than the rest of the property around it."

"That's good news. Are the mailboxes close to the community?" Major asked.

Tom rubbed his chin. "You know, I don't know, but I'd suspect they would be in a cluster at the county road."

Major nodded. "That's what I would have expected."

"We'd need to pull up mailboxes," Mr. Young said.

"The name of the lane is Meadows Lane; I think there was a sign at one time. We might want to pull it down and drag it into the brush at the same time," Tom said.

"I'm going to see if we can get with Stuart and Scott before lunch. I'll sleep better if we have that little lane blocked today. Can you think of anything we haven't addressed?"

"David, Angel, Red, Stuart, and Andy already know about the road south of the Newton, Smith, and Webster farms. That's another road that goes from the state road to the county road," Nate said.

Tom nodded. "It wouldn't hurt to remind them."

Major rose. "We've got our work cut out for us today, and so do you. We'll keep you posted."

On the way back to their house, Mr. Young asked, "Anyway you and I could take a little ride on Number 48 to check out that lane behind us?"

"Crazy idea." Major snorted. "Who would tell us we couldn't?"

"Everybody." Mr. Young rolled his eyes.

"Too bad we can't just check in with Josh and go," Major said. "Let's talk to Jack, but if we were taking Number 48 out for a spin, seems to me the place to go would be the Newton farm to talk about that lane behind us."

Mr. Young nodded. "Leo was on the radio this morning as usual, which means so were Angel and Red, so they would know about the gathering of gangs looking for a major."

"How do we figure out who is behind all this?" Major narrowed his eyes. "I need to think this through; I definitely need to talk to Jack."

"Why don't we make that a priority? I can help Annie. She just needs somebody taller than she is. As far as building questions, I have some DIY experience, so I could understand what she's talking about, but since she's the expert, I'd be smart enough to agree with her."

"We could pull in Vanessa," Major said. "In spite of what she might like for others to think, she loves helping."

"I didn't know that. I'll ask her for help with Annie's project, then I'll pull out my old man card."

Major snorted. "Never knew that card existed; I'll have to sign up for mine."

"You could do that, but you'll have to wait a few years before it's approved."

When they reached the house, Major said, "I'll talk to Jack if you'll corral Vanessa and take her with you to help Annie."

After Mr. Young went inside, Major leaned on his stick and listened to the sound of hammering that came from the back of the house; when the back door slammed, and Vanessa said something he couldn't quite understand, the children laughed.

Annie's in her environment: building, and the rest of them are happy to help.

When he shifted his weight, his knee almost buckled, and he grunted as the pain reminded him that he had no business putting any weight on his knee.

Before Major straightened up, Jack came around the corner behind him.

"Pain's pretty bad?" Jack asked.

Major sighed. "Didn't expect to get caught; I'm trying to push past it."

"Stressing that knee has to be delaying any healing. Why don't you take it easy the rest of the day?"

"There's too much to do; no way can I spend the rest of the day sitting around," Major grumbled.

"Let's sit while you tell me what all you need to do today," Jack said.

After Major made his way to the chair on the front porch, he told Jack what Tom said about the north side.

"I agree that we need to discuss this with Stuart and his family. They've got the experience here that we don't. We can't empty the house of all our shooters, though. There's no reason you can't stand guard on the front porch for the day, and by stand, I mean sit. While you watch the front, Annie, Mr. Young, and Vanessa are in the back yard, and Molly is in the kitchen that oversees the back yard. I'll tell you what I understand so far, and you can tell me where I'm wrong before I go see Stuart and Scott."

"I'm not wired to hand off my responsibilities," Major growled.

"No, but you don't want to have a permanent limp, either, and it's not like you don't know how to delegate. You've always been a stellar leader, so lead and heal while you're at it. I'll check with Molly to see if we have any anti-inflammatory meds somewhere."

Major exhaled. "Dang it, you're right. Before you go talk to Molly, I need to talk to you about something else. Mr. Young has finally convinced me that someone has me in his crosshairs. I have a strong feeling that I must know who it is and don't realize it."

"I agree that we've gone from the random, amateur gangs to a more disciplined assembly of killers with the order to attack you," Jack said. "What are you thinking? Is it someone like Cliff Roybal that you sent to prison?"

Major frowned. "I suppose, but it seems more personal, like I did something singlehandedly. Being the leader of a team that arrests a man who is convicted and goes to prison doesn't seem all that personal to me. Roybal wasn't the only man I knew before he was arrested that later went to prison. It has to be something more to it."

Jack nodded. "Could it be an old friend or family?"

"I didn't have any siblings, and I don't even know of any cousins; they would have all been quite a bit younger than me."

"A friend of Trish's or someone in her family?" Jack asked.

Major shook his head. "They were all fine people." He stared at the sky as vultures circled overhead.

"Except one," he muttered.

"Who?"

"Dan Benson, Trish's brother."

Jack shook his head then sat on the front step. "I don't know him."

"Trish and I moved to Plainview as my first assignment with the Florida Highway Patrol. I was a rookie with the state police." Major chuckled from the memory. "Make that a gung-ho, wet-behind-the-ears rookie. Her family wasn't happy because we were so far away from them."

"Where were you from originally?"

"Jacksonville. Her folks lived in a nice neighborhood in a new house. They were horrified when we bought the farm. Her parents sent us food packages after we were married because they were sure she'd starve because she married a cop. They kept her bedroom ready for her because all their friends told them she'd be a widow in a year. Trish told her mom that she made me promise to run off with a floozy, so she could shoot me herself."

Jack guffawed. "I always liked Trish. She could make the worst day into the best just by walking into a room."

Major sighed. "That she could; anyway, the food packages stopped."

"No, really? So, tell me about her brother."

"Trish told me he had a mean streak and was always in trouble when they were growing up; he was two years older than she was. After she found a copperhead snake in her closet when she was six, she installed a lock on her bedroom door to keep him out of her room, so she could sleep at night."

"She installed a lock when she was six years old? It's awful that she had to do that, but what a remarkable young girl she must have been."

"She was definitely self-sufficient," Major smiled. "She read a book then asked her dad to buy her a power drill and a screwdriver, and he did. Trish was delighted when she realized that Aimee Louise had her skills." Major sighed.

"I can imagine they really bonded the short time they were together."

Major nodded and swallowed hard. "Trish told her parents not to tell Dan where we were after we moved away from Jacksonville. She was pregnant and worried about our baby. They must have been afraid of Dan because they never crossed him, so he knew exactly where we were. He joined a notorious drug gang in Orlando, then six months later after a bloody battle, he took over the gang and added extortion to his drug business. He was known as 'General,' and his tactics were brutal. When he moved his headquarters to Plainview, it was supposed to be a slap in my face, but I was young and would have done anything to protect Trish and our baby. I took it as a challenge, and I intended to win."

"Did you send Trish away to safety? Never mind, Trish wouldn't have left you; she needed to stick around for that floozy," Jack smiled.

"Exactly." Major nodded. "Remember the old beauty shop? Dan offered the owner 'protection,' and Ms. Dorothy asked Trish what to do. Trish recognized her brother right away; we didn't know whether he recognized her because her folks didn't know she was pregnant. Anyway, I managed to get a warrant, and put a microphone in Ms. Dorothy's shop near her cash register. The point was to catch Dan strong-arming Ms. Dorothy for protection money. She'd been resisting threats, but this time, she was supposed to give him the money. It was a crude audio system, but it was the old days. She gave him the money he'd asked for, but when he demanded more, she got scared and told him that was all she had in the shop, and he knocked her to the ground. When I heard her scream, 'Knife!' I disobeyed my order to record and listen; I burst into the shop as Dan slit her throat."

Major swallowed hard, clenched his fists, and stared at the sky. "Vultures again."

Jack said gently, "Are you okay? Should I give you a little time?"

'No, it's just been so long since I thought about it; I didn't realize how raw it still is for me. He cut so deep, he nearly decapitated her. I jerked him off her, but it was too late. I would have beat him to a pulp if your predecessor hadn't burst in the front door. I didn't realize I had a backup, but like I said, I was a rookie and wasn't necessarily in on all the planning. The sheriff pulled me off Dan, but he gave Dan a solid kick to the kidneys with his pointed toe cowboy boot when Dan reached for the knife."

"What happened to Dan?"

"He was charged with murder and extortion. He tried to claim I blinded him in one eye when I hit him in the face, but then one of his old rivals testified in court that Dan was blind in that eye when he first showed up in Orlando. I don't know if it was true or if the rival was getting revenge for something Dan did to him. The judge sentenced Dan to life without parole, but I'm sure no one's in prison anymore."

Jack nodded. "A lot of prisons just opened the doors when their guards walked away after the grid went down."

"I'm sure that rival of his is either dead or well-hidden because he would be first on Dan's list; I have no doubt that I'm at the top of his list now."

"He would have known when you were promoted to Major and that you've been called Major all these years, even after you retired."

Major nodded. "He's smart. The purpose of that first wave of blundering amateurs was to give us a false sense that whoever was after me would be incompetent too; he knew I'd hear about them. Dan is not incompetent. He's cunning. The only one who ever outsmarted him was his sister."

"What do we do?" Jack asked.

"First we need to make sure we're safe from the inept raiders; the next step is to divert his army away from us, so we can lure him into an ambush."

"I suppose you're the bait." Jack frowned.

"Of course."

"Maybe you and I should go to the Newtons'; this is more than I want to carry by myself."

"Judge can replace me on the porch. He's skilled and has proven himself in the field," Major said.

"I'll go get him; Josh can go with me. I'll let Mr. Young know what's going on. He'll want to go too, but we need him to stay here to back up Annie." Jack sprinted around the corner, then a few minutes later, he came out the front door with Josh. Molly followed him with a glass of water and a small bottle.

"We won't be too long," Jack said as he and Josh raced to the shortcut.

"You know those two are training to run with Angel and Red, don't you? I'm not supposed to know, but I see their elbow nudges and can smell their competitive spirits across the room. I'm glad we thought about anti-inflammatory medicine for your knee." Molly handed him the glass of water and poured two pills out of the bottle before she read the bottle. "We've had this for ages, but it's only a year out of date."

He took the medicine and downed the water then gave the glass back to Molly. "Thanks."

After Molly went inside, Major's shoulders slumped. *I think I'm doing fine then the pain of losing Trish returns.*

When Jack, the judge, and Josh appeared out of the shortcut, Major shook off his melancholy and exhaled. *Been a while since I've been this down. It's got to be the knee.*

"We'll take Number 48," Jack said.

"Thanks for trusting me with your station, Major," Judge said.

"Do I go too, Dad?" Josh asked.

Jack glanced at Major, who nodded.

"Yes, get your rifle; you need to start carrying it regularly."

After Jack brought Number 48 around to the front porch, Major used his stick to help him to his feet while he kept his weight off his left knee. Josh hopped into the cargo bed and sat facing the rear.

Jack pressed the accelerator, and they traveled down the driveway to the road then turned right to the Newtons' driveway.

On the way, Major said, "I felt funny about not being called Major; it's what Trish called me, and it was like I was abandoning Trish. I know the idea was to make the family safer, but does it really?"

"I personally think whatever you want is what we'll call you."

"I'll think about it."

As Jack drove down the Newton driveway, Major said, "I want to stick with Major and set up an ambush for Dan Benson. I'm not interested in hiding."

"I've thought about it too, and Elliott doesn't sound right to me either," Jack said.

When they reached the end of the driveway, Angel and Red were waiting for them.

"Angel heard Number 48, so we ran out to wait for you. You're here because of the talk on the radio this morning, aren't you?" Red asked as they jogged alongside them.

"Sure are. We should have known we couldn't sneak up on you two unannounced," Major said.

Jack parked, Stuart and Andy came out of the house to greet Jack and Major, and Scott waited at the barn for them.

"It's great to see you, but I know this is business, not pleasure because you would have heard the hams on the radio this morning too," Scott said.

Major nodded. "Where's the best place to get everyone together for a discussion?"

"Without involving the children, the best place is my barn. Shall I gather the troops, and we'll meet you there?" Scott asked.

"We'll do it, Dad." Stuart and Andy jogged to the house.

As the five of them strolled together at Major's pace, "You have a plan," Angel said.

Major grinned. "I do, but it's up for discussion."

"Can we have a hint?" Red asked.

"Of course not," Scott said. "You'd run off and implement the entire plan before the rest of us knew what was happening."

Major chuckled. "You definitely know these two well."

"Doesn't take long," Scott sighed. "Were they always like this?"

"Yes," Angel said, and Red giggled.

Peyton, David, and Cal came into the barn.

"Doc Larkin is staying with his patient. Sandra will be here in a few minutes; she's waiting for Blanche. Blanche and Louisa had started the children on an assignment earlier, but Louisa is taking over, so Blanche and Sandra won't be long," Peyton said.

After Blanche and Sandra arrived and everyone was comfortable, Major said, "Does everyone know what the hams were talking about his morning on the radio?"

"The gangs looking for a major," Sandra said. "We assumed that was you, Major."

"This is my interpretation," Cal said, "The unorganized groups that have been invading homes and stealing food are shills to give people, and specifically us, a false sense of security. It would be natural to think if we successfully defend our homes from any attacks or successfully fought them off, then we are safe."

"We came to the same conclusion; we're here to discuss Major's plan. May I kick it off?" Jack asked, and Major nodded.

"We know a bad guy is looking for a major, but we also know it's personal because he's really looking for our Major. Our initial thought was to hide Major behind the name of Elliott, but that's only a temporary defense. We need to stop the guy because other people are losing or abandoning their homes in fear."

"You know who this guy is, don't you?" Peyton narrowed her eyes.

"Yes, the details aren't important right now, but he's my deceased wife's brother. When I was a rookie trooper, I caught him in a brutal murder that he committed while trying to extort additional money from a shop owner; I was the main witness against him at his trial that resulted in a murder conviction. He was sent to prison for life with no parole, but all the prisons emptied after the grid went down. He took over a drug gang near Orlando in a ruthless battle for power then developed them into a savage army," Major said.

"We suspect his army is following the freelancing thugs north from Orlando. While their orders are to find Major, their method is to annihilate whatever is in their way," Jack said.

"What's his name?" Sandra asked.

"Dan. Uncle Dan," Angel said.

"How did you know?" Major's eyes widened.

"Gram told me when I was three. She said Uncle Dan was dangerous, and I should never let him get anywhere close to me. She told me to remember Uncle Dan was Dan-ger. We played a game: she'd whisper, 'Uncle Dan,' and I'd whisper, 'Danger.' She said it wasn't a secret because it was a good code to share."

"What's your plan, Major?" David asked.

"We need to divert the army. There was a coalition of militia along the Georgia, Tennessee, North Carolina border. If they're still in operation and can be ready, we can send the army to them."

"After you confirm they could handle the army, it would be simple to drop a few hints on the ham radio, right?" Blanche asked.

"That's right," Stuart said.

"We divert the army then set a trap for Uncle Dan," Angel said. "Every trap has bait. Is that you, Pops?"

"In a way, yes," he said.

"Well, now we know why Ms. Vanessa's not here, don't we?" Sandra asked. "Fine. I'll be her proxy. What kind of fool idea is that, Major?"

"Actually, a pretty good one," Andy said. "Uncle Dan is hunting for Major. We give him a decoy."

David stared at Andy. "How do we do that?"

CHAPTER EIGHTEEN

"There are some old houses on the dirt road north of the Cabello and Mitchell properties, and the road is a dead end. Major, is Dan a hiker or a woodsman?" Andy asked

Major snorted. "Not at all. When he came to Plainview, he walked into Pete's Diner, said it was a dump, and left. He complained at the gas station that there was too much noise at night. Evidently the crickets kept him awake. He only came to Plainview to harass his sister by setting up a protection racket to fleece the town's small businesses."

"That's good," David said. "That means the only exit he would see is the road. Does the dirt road have a dead-end sign?"

"Used to when I was a kid; I don't know if it's there anymore."

"It is," Cal said. "I know that little lane. Andy's idea has real possibilities."

"We can't just stick Major in one of those houses and let him wait to be shot," Blanche said.

"Nope. What's our best decoy for Major?"

"A state police cruiser," Peyton said.

David stared at her. "That's genius."

"I don't mean to be negative because I know we're all just offering good ideas for discussion, but where on earth are we going to find a Florida State Police car?" Sandra asked.

"An unmarked car," Angel said.

Peyton smirked. "Exactly. A Florida State Police unmarked car."

"We put our unmarked car at one of the houses with one of Major's old trooper hats on the dash," Blanche said, "and before you ask, I've got a trooper hat if we need it, but you can't ask how I got it because that's a story."

"After we lure Dan to the dirt road, and he parks near Major's unmarked car, we expect him to what?" Jack asked.

"He'll either break into the house or make noise to lure Major outside. Either way, I think he'll want to see the look on Major's face when he recognizes Dan, so Dan can gloat then shoot Major," Stuart said.

"We've got ourselves a plan that's starting to shape up. We'll probably refine it later; meanwhile, where do we start?" Scott asked.

"Making sure the militia north of Atlanta could take on Dan's army," Red said.

"I'll have our radio operational by this evening. I'll do that," Angel said.

"How?" Stuart asked.

"Easy," Red said. "She'll just tell Phil that we've got company to send north, and she'll ask if the family is ready for a rowdy crowd."

"Phil would understand that," Peyton said.

"Is Phil in north Georgia?" Blanche asked.

"No, but he has the contacts. He'll take care of it," Red said.

"After we confirm the militia can handle Dan's army, how do we divert the army?" Blanche asked.

"Counter-intelligence," Andy said. "Mr. Young can report the sighting of a major at the state line north of Atlanta."

"Where do you come up with this stuff?" Peyton asked.

"He minored in military history, honey. This man is in his element." David smiled.

"Dan's army won't be spending much time on side trips to rob anyone if they've got a definite target. So far, I don't see any downside to moving forward with the diversion after we verify the coalition of militia can handle a potential invasion," Major said.

"I'm going inside. If you assign anything to me, give me the deadline, and I'll get it done." Blanche rose and saluted Major, then she and Sandra left.

Cal chuckled. "Please don't tell her she has to capture Dan before morning. I'll be up all night setting traps."

"Cal's right; we need more than one trap," Andy said.

Jack frowned. "Right. I need a little time to think about that."

"Are we done?" Red asked.

"Yes, thank you," Major said.

Angel and Red hugged him, then they raced out the door.

"I've got a radio to set up," Stuart said. "It's great to have you back, Major." He and Andy rushed out of the barn to catch up with Angel and Red.

"Meeting adjourned," Major said, and Jack, Scott, and Cal chuckled.

"Glad to see you kept our feral group of thinkers under control, Major." Peyton snickered as she and David hurried to the house.

"Where'd the radio come from?" Major asked.

"I remembered I had one in my truck along with a decent antenna. I'm not going to be driving around, so I removed it and gave it to Angel. I could have offered to help, but she knows more than I do; I'd just slow her down," Cal said.

"We should talk about setting up a simplex," Major said.

"I'll mention it to Angel. She's probably already got it planned, though." Cal left the barn.

Major rose to leave, and Scott walked along with him to Number 48.

"I wanted to tell you, Major, how much we've come to love those beautiful, talented granddaughters of yours," Scott said.

"Thanks, Scott. It's a shock to see how they've grown into young women since the last time I saw them, but at the same time, they're still the same awesome, unpredictable girls they always were."

Scott shook his head. "They scare me all the time."

Major smiled. "I understand what you're saying. Welcome to my world."

* * *

"Where should we set up the radio?" Stuart asked. "You'll need to be away from the bustle and noise of the family."

"Our bedroom," Angel said.

"I'll ask Mama Sandra if she has a table you can use," Red said.

"What about power?" Andy asked.

"Cal ran his truck for a bit to make sure his battery was charged. We've got his truck battery. We'll need to charge it regularly. We've talked about a solar charging station for batteries; guess we better get busy on that," Stuart said.

"Ask Blanche," Red and Andy said in unison then laughed.

"You're right; we've got people." Stuart grinned as he put his arm around Angel.

Cal came inside. "Where are you going to set up?"

"Our bedroom," Stuart said.

"Good idea. It's hard to hear with commotion going on around you, especially in the evening. I packed everything from my truck into a box and put it in the utility room. Let me know if you need any help. What about the antenna? Are you going to put it in the attic?"

"Yes."

Cal nodded. "How are you going to charge the battery?"

"I'd like to have one battery in service while a second or even third battery charges at a charging system for twelve-volt batteries. We may want to check the roads regularly for abandoned vehicles, so we'll have some extra automotive batteries," Angel said.

"Good idea. I've been thinking about handhelds. We could set up a charging station in the utility room. I'll talk to David and Blanche about solar charging systems. Next time I see Leo, I'll ask if he has any extra twelve-volt batteries or extra handhelds that we can use to stay in touch with our four different farms."

"Is setting up the charging stations something you'd like to take on?" Stuart asked.

"Wouldn't mind at all. I'll make the charging stations a priority. I'll talk to my consultant, Blanche, and her assistant, David. I'll mosey into the bunkhouse known by city slickers as the living room to join Cowgirl Blanche and her buckaroos, as she calls them. Have you noticed the kids have started calling her Grandma

Blanche? She told them they could if they wanted to because Grandmas wear many hats." Cal chuckled as he left the kitchen.

"I'll carry the box," Stuart said as they went to the utility room.

Angel removed the antenna from the box. "Okay."

On the way to their bedroom, Stuart asked, "Why did Cal ask about putting the antenna for his mobile transceiver in the attic?"

"We have two choices: the roof or the attic. The roof would have better reception, but the attic provides protection for the antenna from high winds."

Stuart nodded. "I can see a security advantage too. A house with an antenna on the roof might have other resources. Of course, there are lots of houses in rural areas with old TV antennas, but a savvy person would know the difference between the two. It won't take me long to install the antenna in the attic then drop the antenna wire down to our room. Dad's got a hand drill in the barn. I'll grab it then get to work."

After Stuart returned to the house with the hand drill, Peyton was supervising Brandon and Henry as they carried a small table up the stairs.

"Want to help me install an antenna in the attic?" Stuart asked.

"Heck, yeah," Brandon said, "Right, Henry?"

"Heck, yeah," Henry said.

Stuart chuckled and handed the antenna to Peyton as he pulled down the attic stairs. "It might help orient me if you all tap on the ceiling. After the boys get a broom or mop from the kitchen, ask Angel where she wants the wire to come down into the room while I carry the antenna and my drill up to the attic."

When Stuart stepped into the attic, he waited until his eyes adjusted to the limited light. He moved toward the outer wall and his bedroom then knocked on the attic floor.

"Can you hear me, honey?"

"Sure can," Angel said. "You sound like you're behind me about five feet. I'm closer to the wall. Can you tell where the window is?"

Stuart squinted toward the roof line. "Not really."

"Peyton and the boys are here."

"Dad can hear you?" Henry asked.

"Angel, where do you want the antenna wire to come through the ceiling?" Peyton asked.

Angel pointed above the radio.

"I'll tap on the ceiling, Stuart," Peyton said. When she tapped, Stuart moved to the sound and knocked on the floor.

"Here?" Stuart asked.

"Yes," Angel said.

After Stuart drilled the hole into the floor he said, "Bring the antenna wire to the attic, Peyton. Angel will show you which wire."

"I'll do it, Dad," Henry said. "Can I do it, Aunt Peyton?"

"I'll watch his back," Brandon said.

"I don't know," Peyton said.

"You can spot them while they go up the ladder," Stuart said. "Boys, it's important to remember to have three points holding on to the ladder at any one time; so if you're stepping up with one foot, your other foot and both hands have to be on the ladder."

"I didn't know that," Brandon said. "Grandma Blanche said it's good to know safety things. We'll have to tell her about three points touching the ladder."

"Yes," Henry said, and Stuart chuckled. *He's definitely Angel's boy.*

"How do we keep our three points while we carry the wire, Mom?" Brandon asked.

"Very good question; I'll show you," Peyton said.

Before the boys came up with the wire, Stuart heard Red shout, "Inside."

"Coming down the ladder," Stuart said.

While Peyton and the boys ran downstairs, Angel waited at the bottom of the ladder for Stuart.

After Stuart raised the attic ladder, he and Angel raced down the stairs. She waited for him at the bottom, and he grabbed her into a hug and swung her around. "You cheated; you blinded me with your cuteness."

Angel giggled, and Stuart said, "You got my joke!"

"Yes because if I wanted to cheat, I would have gone downstairs before you were down the ladder, so it was a joke."

Stuart rolled his eyes. *Logical.*

"You're still cute," he whispered as they joined everyone else in the kitchen.

Stuart glanced around the kitchen. *Everyone is here except for Andy and David.*

"I'll tell you why I called Inside, but Andy and David will have more details after they get here," Red said.

"Should the buckaroos and I hit the trail?" Blanche asked.

"No," Angel said.

"Everyone ran for the house when I called for Inside, so everyone should hear why," Red said. "Andy, David, and I were checking the road south of us to see how accessible it was and what we might need to do to block it. When we heard a pickup truck that was having engine trouble as it headed east on the road toward us and the interstate, we hid in the trees. The engine sounded awful as it passed us, then it quit not far from us, and the driver was unsuccessful in starting it." Red shook her head. "The truck looked like an antique to me. I was surprised it was running at all. When the passenger and the three men who were riding in the truck bed jumped out and started cussing, I ran to the house and called Inside. Andy and David will be here later to tell us what happened after I left."

"Will my dad be okay?" Brandon asked.

"He most certainly will," Red said. "He's smart, and so is Andy, and they will take good care of each other."

Brandon nodded, and Blanche said, "It's time for our bug study, buckaroos."

The three boys cheered as they scrambled to the living room, and Mandy asked, "Grandma Blanche, we'll talk about beneficial insects, right?"

Blanche smiled. "We sure will, but don't tell the boys it's educational."

Mandy nodded as the two of them strolled to the living room.

"How long do you expect David and Andy to be?" Peyton asked.

"I wouldn't think too long," Red said.

"Peyton explained Inside to me earlier," Louisa said, "but I was shocked at how quickly all the children, including mine, ran into the house."

Sandra nodded. "Kids are the quickest to catch on."

"It's comforting to know that they're safe here, especially when they're outside," Louisa said. "I've worried about that, but I seem to be worrying more than usual lately."

"You're entitled. How is Noel doing?" Sandra asked.

"Ask him yourself." Doc Larkin strolled into the kitchen. "Sandra, we put that old walker you gave me earlier to good use."

Louisa's eyes widened as Noel shuffled down the hall with his head down to watch his steps as he held onto the walker.

"Oh my gosh, you're doing great, honey," she said. "Where did you get those stylish pants?"

Noel raised his head and grinned. "Doc had an old pair of scrub pants that he helped me put on, then he bribed me with a cup of Sandra's coffee if I made it to the kitchen without falling on my face."

"I've got a fresh pot right here with your name on it." Sandra's eyes misted.

When Noel reached the kitchen table, Stuart helped him to sit.

"Nice to see you up and around," Scott said.

"Glad to be here; is this a meeting?" Noel asked as Sandra put his cup in front of him.

Peyton gave him a quick recap.

"I'm not sure I understand everything that's going on, but I'll catch up," Noel said as Andy burst into the house.

"Hey, Noel, you're looking great," Andy said then turned to Stuart. "We need some help. After Red left, there was a big fight, and the passenger pulled out the driver from the truck and knifed him. The passenger and the rest of the men grabbed up their small backpacks from the truck bed then headed toward the interstate. After we were sure they weren't returning, David checked the man; his shoulder was bleeding pretty badly. David stopped the bleeding, but we're not sure yet if the man is strong enough to walk. Angel would know if he's a bad guy or a good guy."

Angel and Red raced out the door.

"David's waiting for Angel," Andy continued. "If he's a bad guy, we'll patch him up the best we can then make him a temporary shelter near the road if he isn't strong enough to walk today. If he's a good guy, David wants to move him a little farther from the road, but not close enough to see the house, and make him a temporary shelter he can use until he's stronger."

"I'll pull together a snack for the man," Sandra said.

"We'll get it later, Mom." Stuart grabbed the first aid box from the utility room, then he and Andy left.

As they ran through the field then into the woods, Stuart said, "You didn't even flinch when Angel and Red ran out of the house."

"It was so mild compared to some of the other stuff they do, it didn't faze me at all."

Stuart snorted. "Exactly."

Before they reached the road, Angel and Red met them.

"We decided to stop before he saw us. I stayed out of his sight earlier, and Angel agreed that he doesn't need to know how many of us there are," Red whispered.

"He doesn't have a danger cloud; he's hurt and a little angry," Angel added.

Stuart nodded. "Andy, take the first aid box to David. He'll understand that we're not all coming close to the man unless David thinks it's important. We'll move closer."

Andy nodded then crashed through the woods to announce his presence.

Red smiled. "He plays his part of the crashing bull well, doesn't he?"

The three of them moved closer. When Stuart heard the men talking, he stopped, and Angel stopped alongside him while Red stopped next to her.

"Now that we've got that bleeding slowed, Juan, it doesn't look so bad," David said.

"Thanks; I was desperate. I hoped they didn't know anything about old trucks," Juan said.

"What do you mean?" Andy asked.

David chuckled. "Let me guess. Your old truck has a choke, doesn't it?"

"Sure does. I popped the truck into neutral then revved the engine before I cut the ignition and pulled the choke to flood the carburetor. After the truck stopped, I pretended to try to start the engine while it was still flooded. I held my breath, but they didn't catch on."

"Your truck smelled like a fuel spill in a gas station; I'm surprised they didn't recognize it. Little risky, but it paid off," David said. "When did they kidnap you and your truck?"

"The men broke into my house early this morning. My wife and I had planned if anyone ever tried to break in the front door and the back door was clear, she'd grab her rifle and the kids and hide in our barn. Maybe it wasn't the best plan, but I was glad we had one. The thugs beat me then took my truck keys. I was just getting to my knees when they came back inside for me because none of them could drive a stick shift. I decided to wait until I was close to the interstate before I stalled the truck, so they wouldn't go back to my house. I'd put the truck into fourth gear and ease off the accelerator until the truck sputtered, then I'd drop into second or third gear and speed up. I played with the gears and gave the guys in the back a rough ride. I wanted to set the expectation that it took a lot of shifting to operate the truck."

"If you can stand up, think you can drive home?" David asked.

"Oh, yeah. In fact, if I can't stand up, if you'll just put me behind the wheel, I'll turn that truck around, and it'll go home on its own." Juan chuckled.

"How can you drive? You have to use your right arm to shift. How can you steer?" Andy asked.

Juan chuckled. "Same way I drink a cup of coffee, shift, and drive; I steer with my knees."

David smiled when Andy raised his eyebrows, and so did Stuart.

"Did the men talk about anything around you?" David asked.

"Quite a bit; that's why I knew they planned to murder me after I got them to where they wanted to go. I didn't understand most of it, but I'll tell you what I heard. The guy in the front seat with me was the leader. He told the men not to bother taking anything from my house because they couldn't be slowed down with stuff since the bounty was rescinded, and the army would catch up with them in two days. I have no idea what that means. One of the men asked where they were going, and the leader pulled his gun on him and told him it was none of his business. I fully expected the leader to shoot the man just for asking, and I think the man did too because he became so gray that I thought he was going to pass out. I heard the men talk about how scared the leader was of the army, but they were careful to be sure he didn't hear them. They never really explained what or who the army was, but from the way they talked and acted, I wondered it if was someone who was going to clear the area of bad guys."

When Angel kissed Stuart on the cheek, he nodded as Angel and Red disappeared into the trees on their way back to the house. *They'll get the radio set up, so Angel can get the word about the army to Phil.*

"I'm not sure who the army is either, but I'm pretty sure they're worse than the thugs. Do you have anywhere you could take your family?" Stuart asked.

"My sister lives in Mississippi, but she's not used to children, and I worry about invading her with my kids; maybe we'll go there if things look bad," Juan said.

"I wouldn't wait past today, if I had a family," David said. "The two of us are taking off as soon as it's dark."

"Really? The leader did tell them two days. Help me up; I have to get home, and thanks."

After Stuart heard the sound of the engine hum when Juan started it, David and Andy joined him in the brush.

"What do you think?" David asked.

"As soon as Juan mentioned the army in two days, Angel and Red ran to the house," Stuart said.

"They'll have the radio in operation before we get back," Andy said.

"Stuart, we didn't get a chance to check both ends of the road, but now we know the west end is clear. We're not that far from the interstate, and while we can assume it's clear because the men didn't come back, we don't know that. I'll rest easier if it's clear and they're on their way north," David said.

The three men ran through the woods then stopped when they neared the state road and slipped closer to the road south of the Newton property to listen.

"I don't hear any voices," Andy whispered.

When they stepped close to the intersection, they scanned the road then turned back toward the Newton farm.

"No debris," Stuart said, and the three men turned back.

After they went through the woods and reached the field behind the Newton house, David said, "The clear road was good news and bad news. The good news was that it was clear, but that was also the bad news because it means more work for us to block it."

"Our time's short. If we're going to block it, we'll need to move fast, but we can't do everything," Stuart said. "What else do we have to do? We're going to have to prioritize."

"We have work to do at the Smith barn for the cows; for starters, we need to get the well operational, so we have a ready source of water for them. Nate told me he left the hand pump and the parts to install it in the barn. I still have to go with Cal, so he can ask about handheld radios, and I want him to ask about solar panels. I'll bet Leo has some put back," David said.

"The blackout curtains Mom is making are a priority, but she's got her team working on that."

"Your dad has a couple of tree stands in the barn. We could put them in the woods as watch towers if we have handheld radios for our watchers. I could help Scott with the tree stands," Andy said. "Red will be our guard."

"Peyton could go with Cal to Leo's, and you and I could work on the well and whatever additional work you want to do in the Smith barn," Stuart said.

"I wish I could borrow Annie," David said.

"We need to find another Annie here. I'll check with Blanche before we leave for Leo's," Stuart said.

David smacked his forehead. "I'm an idiot; we don't have to check with Blanche because I've got Brandon. He and I have been working on projects all along."

"Brandon, it is," Stuart chuckled. "Will you be able to separate him from Henry?"

"To quote my son, 'Heck, no.'" David snorted. "They're a package deal kind of like Angel and Red."

"What about Jimmy?" Andy asked.

"The boys have taken him under their wing, haven't they? If he wants to and can convince his mom it's okay, why not? I've worked with a greener crew," David said.

"If Cal and Peyton come back with any solar panels, Cal and Blanche can set up the charging stations we've been asking for."

"I don't know about priority," Andy said, "but it wouldn't take us long to open those boxes from the transport truck for a quick inventory. Red and I can do that, and you'll have a list."

"That's true. Andy, get Red and Dad going on your projects. David, while you gather Peyton, Cal, and the rest of your crew, I'll check with Angel and Mom then go with you to the Smith barn," Stuart said.

"Okay, and I'll let Blanche know we're hoping for more solar panels. We'll meet you by the chickens," David said.

When Stuart went into the house, Sandra and Louisa were stitching curtains at the table. "Mom, we've got a crew going to the Smith barn to set up the well for the cows while Cal and Peyton see Leo. Dad, Red, and Andy are going to set up two tree stands behind us as watch towers. Can you and Blanche take care of security for the house?"

"We'll handle it. Louisa's part of the security team too. You tell him, Louisa."

"I didn't think about mentioning that I taught firearms classes for women at our gun range next to Noel's pawn shop until Sandra told me about Dead Eye Red. Mandy has done well in junior competitions with her .22 too," Louisa said.

Stuart smiled. "Add Mandy to your team, Mom."

"Already did."

Stuart dashed up the stairs; Angel waved when he hurried into their bedroom, then she returned her attention to the radio for a minute before she removed her headset.

CHAPTER NINETEEN

"I contacted Phil; the radio traffic has been more active than usual today for so late in the morning," Angel said. "Mr. Young has already dropped hints earlier than I expected about a militia ready in west Georgia. I listened to other hams talking about a Georgia militia, and there are some retired military and national guard people who may have picked up the idea. I heard a recruiting call go out just now."

"That's awesome," Stuart said. "I would imagine law enforcement officers would be interested too."

Angel stared over Stuart's head then turned back to her radio and put on her headset.

Stuart stared at her back and bit his lip. *She knows.*

Stuart raced down the stairs. *I'll talk to her later.*

"Angel's on the radio with her headset, Mom. You may have to go upstairs to talk to her."

"We'll manage."

"Stuart, thanks for including Jimmy. He's usually too shy to want to be with a group, but he likes his new friends," Louisa said.

"Good."

When Stuart reached the coop, David, Peyton, Cal, and the boys were wearing their backpacks, and David, Peyton, and Cal carried rifles. Brody and Tracker were on leashes.

Stuart cocked his head then shrugged. "It's not a bad idea at all to begin training the puppies to stay close."

"That's what I thought too. It might be a little tricky while we're working, but the dogs are the boys' responsibility." David smiled. "All of us have the tools we'll need in our backpacks, and the boys have water bowls and water for Tracker and Brody."

"Grandma Blanche has been working with us and our guard dogs, Dad, and Jimmy has extra water just in case," Henry said.

"I should have known that's exactly what Grandma Blanche would do. David, why don't you and Brandon lead with Tracker? Cal and Peyton, walk behind them, then Henry, Brody, Jimmy, and I will cover the rear," Stuart said.

"Is this like Aunt Red's hiking rule? No talking?" Henry asked.

"Yes," David said. "No talking unless it's important, then we'll whisper."

All three boys nodded, then David and Brandon led the way to the shortcut.

Stuart glanced at Jimmy's serious face. *Glad we planned to include him.*

After they reached the Smith barn, David said, "We can talk now if we're quiet. You can check out the barn while I talk to Stuart."

The boys and dogs investigated the property while Peyton and Cal headed to Leo's house.

"I know how I want to install the hand pump; Brandon and I can handle it," David said.

Stuart pointed. "I'm assuming patching the hole where the tree crashed through the wall is my first priority. What do we tackle next? The window or is there something you'd like for us to do to the stalls?"

"The window repair can be next; if Brandon and I have trouble installing the hand pump, we may have to wait for Cal. He's installed a lot of these for himself and for his neighbors."

"There's your challenge. Get it installed before Cal gets back, and we'll get the wall and the window repaired before you install the hand pump," Stuart said.

David smiled. "You're on."

As Stuart went into the barn, Jimmy said, "There are real cows in here. I didn't know cows are so big."

"These are farm cows, right, Dad?" Henry asked. "Farm cows get bigger."

"Never thought about that before, but you're probably right," Stuart said.

Henry asked, "Are we in a race? Do we have to work fast?"

"We're in a pretend race, so we don't have to work fast; we'll focus on doing a good job," Stuart said.

"I like to do a good job," Jimmy said.

"We can cover the hole with a pretend window," Stuart said. "We'll measure the hole then pick out boards that can help us. We'll take out any nails in the board then cover the hole. It won't take us long to make the frame for our pretend window, then we can decide how to fix the real window."

"Will we paint a picture, so the cows can see something when they look at the window?" Jimmy asked.

"That's a great idea; we'll save it for a later project," Stuart said.

"We have gloves in our backpacks," Henry said. "Mama Sandra found us gloves to use for our construction work. She said if they are too big, we can save them." Brody sniffed the cows then moved close to Henry.

The boys pulled out flower-covered gardening gloves and tried them on.

"They're a little big, but they'll be perfect for protecting your hands while you pick up boards," Stuart said.

"Yes," Henry said. "Splinters aren't fun."

After Stuart measured the window, he sketched an outline on the ground outside the barn. "This is about how long we'd like the boards to be. If we find only a few boards long enough, we can use shorter boards on the diagonal."

"That would be a nice design," Jimmy said.

"You're right." Stuart smiled as he donned his own gloves before he and the boys returned to the stack of lumber.

"We can do three piles," Stuart said. "Long enough boards, kind of short boards, and too short boards."

The boys nodded then Henry dropped Brody's leash as he and Jimmy began picking up boards and sorting.

Stuart stood back then shifted a few boards from one pile to the other and smiled. *Brody's staying close to Henry. He'll protect his boy as long as he lives.*

When there were enough boards to cover the hole and create the window, Stuart said, "Let's take a quick break, then we'll check our long enough boards for nails."

He and the boys pulled out their canteens and drank some water, and Henry pulled out Brody's bowl and gave him water too.

Stuart strode to the well, and said, "Don't forget to take a break."

"You're right; it's not that warm today, but we've still worked up a sweat," David said.

After Stuart returned to the barn, he said, "Next, you two will take the nails out of the boards after I make the nails straight. I'll show you how. We'll start with the longer boards."

Stuart selected a board with nails and turned it, so the head of the nail was down. "Some of these are crooked. My job is to straighten them, so you can take them out. You can watch how I do it because you will do it another time."

Stuart used the claw of his hammer to straighten out nails. "Now we've come to your first part of the job. We have to tap the nail to get it out of the board, but if we hit it too hard, it will bend, and we'll have to stop and straighten it out."

Stuart gently tapped the nail until it no longer protruded out of the board. "We do all the nails on the board until they're all flush on this side. After you finish all the nails on your board, let me know, and I'll take out the nails while you work on the next board."

"What if I bend a nail?" Henry asked.

"Leave it, take a breath, and go on to another nail."

"And don't hit it so hard," Henry added.

Stuart nodded as he straightened the nails on a second board, then the boys began working on their boards. Brody found a spot near the door where a sunbeam streamed inside. He flopped down and fell asleep.

Stuart raised his eyebrows. *Brody's just a puppy, but he's guarding the door.*

After Stuart straightened all the nails on the long boards, he began removing the nails from the boards the boys had finished.

When the boys finished their long boards, Stuart said, "Take a quick break while I catch up with you, then we'll prepare the short boards to help cover the hole. We have long boards for the widest part of the hole; we might use the others to build the window frame. Do we want the boards horizontal or on the diagonal?"

"We like diagonal," Henry said.

Stuart finished pulling up the rest of the nails from the boards, then he and the boys moved to the short boards.

After the three of them had the boards ready to cover the hole, the boys handed Stuart the long boards and nails until Stuart said, "I'm ready for short boards."

The boys handed boards and nails to Stuart then stood back as Stuart nailed the last board.

Stuart smiled as the boys examined the work as carefully as any discerning art critic.

"What do you think?" Stuart asked.

"We're awesome," Henry said.

"Yes," Jimmy said.

Jimmy fits right in. Stuart chuckled then peered at the covered hole. "Our best work; let's frame it."

The boys selected two long boards and two short boards then handed nails to Stuart.

While Stuart and the boys admired their work, David, Brandon, and Tracker came into the barn.

Brody and Tracker wrestled for a few minutes then returned to guard their boys.

"We're almost finished," David said. "We came inside for a break because the sun was getting hot. Wow, that looks good."

Brandon nodded. "It's fancy."

"Thanks," Stuart said. "We're thinking about another project later. The boys plan to paint a picture, so the cows will have something cheerful to look at."

While the boys and dogs took another water break, Stuart and David strolled outside with theirs.

"Tracker's staying close to Brandon; how's Brody doing?" David asked.

"The same, and I was surprised, but I should have realized Blanche would have spent time with the boys to teach them how to train their dogs."

After David and Brandon left to resume their work on the well, Stuart said, "We probably have enough boards to fix the window."

The boys handed Stuart boards and nails, and he quickly repaired the window frame.

"Let's check with David and Brandon to see if they need any help; if they don't, we can take nails out of more boards."

When they reached the well, David grinned. "Okay, show them, Brandon."

Brandon used all his weight as he pulled down on the pump handle twice, then the third time he pulled down, water gushed out of the faucet.

"I'm glad I didn't miss that; you two are awesome," Peyton said. as she and Cal strolled from the shortcut to the well

Peyton shifted the weight of the box she carried then placed it on the ground, and Cal set his box down next to it.

"It's sometimes hard to get it sealed right," Cal said. "Good work."

Brandon's cheeks reddened. "Thanks, Mom. Wait until you see what Henry and Jimmy did in the barn."

"These boys are hard workers," David said.

"Sure are," Stuart said. "What's in the boxes?"

"Handheld radios and extra batteries for the radios," Peyton said. "We hit the motherlode."

"Wow." David peered into the box that Peyton carried. "We're set."

"This isn't all. Leo gave us a dozen solar panels and apologized because he never got around to getting storage batteries to go with them." Cal shook his head. "Can you imagine? I told him we could find batteries, and he laughed, so I told him we'd have Angel find us batteries, and he agreed."

Stuart chuckled. "You got that right."

"I think you two can manage the solar panels. Leo said he has a utility trailer we can use to haul the storage panels to Scott's place. While you get the panels, Cal, the boys, puppies, and I will take our two boxes to Scott's, but I want to check the barn first," Peyton said. "I suspect the boys are ready for lunch. I know I am."

"Is it getting close to lunchtime already? We'll be there soon," David said.

As Stuart and David headed to Leo's farm, David asked, "Do you think it's odd that Leo's suddenly become very generous with all these items he's been hoarding?"

"I hadn't thought about it, but I guess it is. He has been fairly tight-fisted with his things. What's your theory?"

"I don't know because I've never known a hoarder to let loose of a collection before," David said.

"Maybe he's not a true hoarder," Stuart said.

"I certainly don't intend to ask him," David said.

When they reached Leo's house, Stuart's eyes widened at the neat stack of solar panels and two utility wagons near the back door.

"Guess we can load up our loot," David said.

As they pulled the loaded carts to the shortcut, Stuart said, "I feel like a burglar that didn't have to break into a house because all the silver was outside on the front porch with a big ole sack to tote away my haul."

"Nice." David chuckled. "We're the law enforcement officers who went to the dark side over solar panels."

Stuart laughed. "Now that's funny."

"I'm glad we took the boys and dogs along. Brandon was a big help, and it was great to see how well Tracker's training is coming along. I know Brandon enjoyed our time working together as much as I did."

Stuart nodded. "It was a good idea to take Jimmy. Those two little guys worked hard. I really expected to do everything myself with Brody along, but Brody is taking his guard assignment seriously. That Blanche is a wonder, isn't she? I couldn't have done all the work by myself as fast as the three of us did. We'll have to keep the boys in mind when we take on a task close to home."

When Stuart and David reached the house, they rolled their carts into the barn then hurried to the kitchen.

Louisa was clearing curtain fabric off the table, and Sandra stirred a large soup pot.

"Lunch is almost ready," Sandra said. "Blanche, Mandy, the boys, and Peyton are washing their hands."

"Angel has news, but she wants someone to stay with the radio," Louisa said.

"I can relieve her." Cal headed up the stairs.

"We better wash our hands." Stuart elbowed David.

Stuart and David passed the others who had already washed for lunch.

"Hurry, Dad," Henry said. "We're ready for lunch."

When Angel came down the stairs she held onto the railing when she turned to go down the hallway and crashed into Stuart while he was on his way back to the kitchen.

Stuart laughed and grabbed her into a tight hug. "Gotcha."

Angel peered over his head then touched his cheek. "Nice laugh."

"I guess I have to let go of you, so you can wash your hands." Stuart leaned down and kissed her. "It was nice bumping into you, and that's not a joke."

"Thank you."

Stuart smiled and released her then watched her walk away. *She is so pretty, and I'm so lucky.*

"What are you doing there, Stuart? Lunch is almost ready. You're going to have to take second shift if you don't hurry," Sandra said.

Stuart smiled as he hurried to the kitchen. *Guess I can't tell Mom I was admiring my bride's tight jeans.*

The children, Peyton, and Blanche finished eating before Angel came to the table.

"Hi Aunt Angel, we're going to gather eggs, then Aunt Louisa will read us a story," Brandon said.

"Aunt Peyton and Grandma Blanche will go milk the cow," Henry said. "We can learn when we're older."

After Stuart, Angel, and David sat at the table with their lunch, Scott, Red, and Andy came into the house.

"Good timing. Angel has news, and we were waiting for you," Stuart said.

The three of them washed quickly then picked up their lunch plates from the counter before they sat.

"Some hams that live east of the interstate in Florida say that the army had fanned out to the northwest, and their eastern edge was along the interstate, but they've shifted their course to straight north now," Angel said. "Other hams who are scouting the army from the rear found groups of men who had been slaughtered. The dead men don't appear to be well-fed or to have practiced good hygiene, according to one ham. Another one said all of the men's throats were cut, even the ones who had been shot."

Stuart frowned. "It sounds like someone wants to send a gruesome message."

Red cocked her head. "They're murdering the raiders? That's good, isn't it?"

"No, there is more. Mom, Louisa, please sit with us a minute," Angel said.

"I have too much to…" Sandra frowned. "Never mind."

Sandra sat next to Scott, and Louisa sat next to her. Scott pulled his chair closer to Sandra then glanced at David and raised one eyebrow as he side-glanced Louisa. David nodded then moved closer to Louisa.

Angel cleared her throat before she continued, "The men following the army also found burned homes, dead livestock, and murdered men, women, and children."

Sandra gasped, and Scott put his arm around Sandra. Louisa face became ashen, and David put his arm around her.

Angel bit her lip. "It was awful to hear. The army is not good."

"Was Mr. Young on the radio?" Stuart asked.

"Yes, the scouts are in Florida. They're moving north around the army as fast as they can to join the Georgia militia. Tennessee and North Carolina are sending men and women to help too."

"One of the hams said he'd relay the message to the growing militia that help was on the way."

"What do we do? We don't have anywhere to go." Sandra sobbed. "What about the children?"

Scott held her tighter. "We'll figure it out."

"We've got a little time; let's take an hour or so to grieve for those who've been murdered and to get our bearings before we try to decide anything," David said, "but we will keep our children safe from harm."

"This is horrible." Tears streamed down Louisa's face.

"Yes," Angel said quietly.

Stuart hugged her and whispered, "Sweetheart, I'm so sorry."

"Thank you."

Sandra said, "Major made the right decision to bring the rest of the family here."

"I'm grateful we're here with you," Louisa said.

Noel held onto Doc Larkin's arm for balance as they walked down the hall to the kitchen.

"We heard," Noel said.

"We're not the most fleet of foot here, but both of us can sit at a window and shoot." Doc Larkin winked at Sandra. "Got any lunch for two hungry cowpokes?"

Sandra snorted. "Grab yourselves a couple of seats."

"I'll relieve Cal," Angel said. "I briefed him before I came downstairs."

"I'll relieve Blanche and Peyton," Louisa said.

"I'll go with them to milk the cow and explain everything to them," David said.

Louisa's smile was weak. "Thank you, David. I don't think I could right now without breaking down."

Louisa stopped to give Noel a kiss then hurried to the living room.

David rose when Peyton and Blanche came out of the living room, then the three of them grabbed their rifles and left.

Before Stuart and Scott rose from the table, Andy said, "Stuart, we discussed our watch tower idea with Scott and decided it was interesting in theory, but our guards would be too vulnerable. Any movement they made would attract the attention of even the most unaware city slicker, and Scott reminded us that the urban gangs sent their members into the military for training before the grid and economy collapsed. We decided our best perch to watch the south was the second story windows."

Stuart nodded. "Henry would be great; his eyes see things the rest of us miss."

"It would be perfect for Henry," Red said, "and he'd be safe too."

"I don't know why we didn't think of it before. Henry at one window, and a shooter at the second window," Andy said.

Noel shook his head. "It's amazing to hear you all discuss options."

"I agree," Doc said, "I'm grateful to be part of this team. Are you ready to head back?"

"Guess I am," Noel said.

"I'll walk back with you." Scott rose from the table.

When Red furrowed her brow as the men headed down the hallway, Stuart said quietly, "Dad wants Noel to understand he and his family are welcome to stay with us after he's healed. Mom's already talked to Louisa."

Red nodded. "I almost forgot our best news of all: look at my list."

Stuart's eyes widened as he read. "Thirty-six deep cell marine batteries with power converters and battery chargers. Wow." His whistle was low and long. "This is what was in the lightweight box? Night vision goggles and coffee?"

"That's it; awesome, isn't it? No wonder that second guy was so angry. It's going to be his neck, isn't it?" Andy shook his head. "Literally."

"I'll bet the other truck traveling with them had the solar panels," Stuart said.

"Does this mean we can set up power to run the well and the washer?" Sandra asked.

"Angel can," Red said.

"We need to get with Major, so they can set up both of their houses."

"What a boon for Charo with the baby coming," Sandra said.

"Will we be able to have warm baths for the boys?" Red asked.

"Maybe. Angel could tell us what it would take. Mom, your water heater is electric, isn't it?" Stuart asked.

She nodded. "I always wanted an on-demand gas water heater, but it just never fit into the budget."

"Just as well; we're conserving our propane for cooking," Stuart said.

"That's true." Scott returned from Noel's room. "What are we talking about?"

Stuart handed the list to his dad. "The items in the boxes from the truck on the interstate."

Scott's eyes widened as he read the list. "We'll have solar power for the house. The well is first on my list."

"Ours too," Sandra said.

"It shouldn't be hard to add the washer and the water heater," Stuart said, "but we'll have to talk to Angel."

Scott nodded and smiled. "Our in-house expert."

"Setting up the well should be our priority today. Fetching water is one of our most vulnerable activities," Andy said.

"Do we know what solar equipment Major has? Hauling water from the well sounds high-risk to me, now that you've mentioned it," Sandra said.

"I charged the handheld radio you gave me earlier this week; why don't we try to get Mr. Young or Pops on simplex?" Red asked.

"The handhelds, of course," Stuart said. "I've been worried about Angel not being able to leave the radio. After David and Blanche get back, they can set up the charging station for the rest of the handheld radios that Leo gave us, then Mom or whoever is in the kitchen can listen to stay up to date."

"How do we pull Angel away from the radio to help with the solar system for the well?" Andy asked.

"Easy," Red said, "I'll replace her. Just tell me when to send her down."

"Now," Sandra said, and Stuart chuckled.

Red raced up the stairs, then Angel bounded down. "Red told me to read her list."

Angel read it. "So, what are we setting up first? The well and the hot water heater?"

Sandra grinned. "That's my girl."

"The batteries might be partially charged, but when we hook them up, the solar panels can charge them."

"I'm your helper," Stuart said.

"Both of us," Andy added.

"Let's get busy," Angel said; the two men picked up their rifles and followed her.

* * *

"Those three are determined to get those solar batteries charged as soon as possible, aren't they? Red said she charged the handheld, but did I miss it when she said where it was?" Scott asked.

Sandra blinked. "Are we going to get in touch with Major?"

"I'll ask Red where the charged handheld is and how to put it on simplex," Scott said. "I have an idea and could muddle along, but she'll be able to give me a quick lesson on using the handheld, then I'll contact Major. I'm glad they left that list for me, so I won't sound completely lost."

"Teach me what you learn from Red and call him from the kitchen, so I can learn too."

"You got it, babe." Scott kissed her. "You're sexy when you talk about learning new things; did you know that?"

Sandra giggled. "We're quite odd, aren't we?"

"Definitely," Doc Larkin called from the back bedroom, and Scott grinned as Noel laughed, and Sandra's felt her cheeks warm.

"Forgot about that," he whispered.

"You did not; you love to make me blush." Sandra rolled her eyes.

Scott took the stairs two at a time then ran back down and returned to the kitchen. "I'm going to take the handheld upstairs, so Red can show me. I didn't know they'd set up two simplex channels. Do we have any paper and a pencil I can use to take notes?"

While Scott retrieved the handheld from the utility room, Sandra pulled out paper and pen from a kitchen drawer.

"Why don't I go with you, so both of us can hear what Red says? Oh, never mind, I have the curtains to finish, and I want to be available if Louisa needs to be rescued."

"Why don't you go upstairs? I don't think we want me to work on the curtains, but I can relieve Louisa, and she can finish the curtains. It might be good for the kids to go outside, and maybe we can learn about solar."

Sandra's eyes welled up. "Really? That's wonderful, honey." She kissed him, then he watched her as she hurried up the stairs.

Scott smiled. *It's my job to make her happy and leer at her while she sways those hips when she climbs the stairs.*

CHAPTER TWENTY

When Stuart saw his dad come out of the house with the four children and the two puppies on their leashes, he grinned. *Dad will have a story.*

After they reached the barn, Scott said, "Our plan is to stay together. Mandy's mother thought it was a good idea for Mandy to carry her .22."

"My sister is a good shooter. She's won prizes," Jimmy said.

"That's great," Scott said.

"You boys are doing such a great job training Brody and Tracker to stay with you. It's easy for puppies to wander off," Andy said.

"That's what Grandma Blanche told us," Brandon said.

"We're working with a leash, so they know we're serious," Henry said.

"We have some solar panels, solar batteries, and inverters that will help us to have some things powered by solar. Angel will start with the system for the well, so we will have running water inside the house and won't have to carry buckets of water from the well anymore," Stuart said.

"You can do that, Mama Angel?" Henry asked. "My mama is very smart."

The other boys and Mandy nodded their heads.

"The solar panels capture the sunlight and turn it into energy, and the batteries store the energy, so we can have running water in the house at night too," Angel said.

"How long will it take for the system to be ready?" Scott asked.

"It won't take me long to hook it up, then later we can check it. After the system is in service, we'll have power for the well all the time," Angel said.

"While these folks work, why don't we check the chickens? I don't think anyone has collected eggs today," Scott said.

Mandy checked the nests for eggs and handed each one to Jimmy, who carefully placed them into the Easter egg basket that Sandra gave them to use for collecting eggs. Brandon and Henry stood outside the run and watched.

"Tracker and Brody want to play with the chickens, but Grandma Blanche told us we should keep them outside the run until they are a little older because they scare the chickens," Brandon said.

Sandra rushed out of the house and motioned to Scott and Stuart.

"We'll be right back," Stuart said.

When they reached Sandra, she was out of breath.

She exhaled then said, "We talked to Major and Mr. Young. They have a charging system for their transceiver, but that's all they have. Major would like to have a solar system for their two houses. Red and I thought that would be fine."

"Angel designed a system to power our well, water heater, and another circuit that we can use to charge our radios," Stuart said.

"Can you take what they will need for two houses now, so they can get set up? Major's worried that tomorrow will be too late."

"Tell them we'll be there as soon as we can load 48-4," Stuart said, and Sandra ran back into the house.

"You and I can load the solar panels and the boxes with the batteries and equipment. Who goes?" Scott said.

"You and I will go," Stuart said. "If you'll take the kids and dogs inside, I'll talk to Andy and Angel. You can tell Mom, so she can tell Red."

Stuart and Scott returned to the barn, and Scott gathered the children and took them into the house.

"Dad and I are taking two solar systems to Major, so they can set up both houses," Stuart said.

"You might need to hook up a utility cart to carry some of the boxes," Angel said. "Mr. Young has a few panels that he brought from Florida in his camper."

"Are you two okay with doing the system here by yourselves?" Stuart asked

"Yes," Andy said as he side-glanced Angel then raised his eyebrows at Stuart.

Stuart shook his head as he hurried to bring 48-4 around, so he could begin loading. *Andy was right. I was hovering, and that was a silly question.*

Scott rushed out of the house with two blankets under his arm.

"Your mother's a genius. These are to cushion the solar panels."

After Stuart and Scott covered then loaded the solar panels, they loaded boxes.

"Why don't you drive, Dad? I'll ride shotgun."

After they climbed into the vehicle, Scott headed up the driveway. When they reached the road, Stuart stepped into the road and scanned both ways then climbed back into 48-4. "Go."

As Scott neared the Cabello driveway, Stuart motioned for him to continue to Major's driveway, and Scott slowed for the turn. When they reached the house, Major, Jack, Josh, Nate, and Mr. Young waited for them.

Scott, Major, and Mr. Young stayed on the porch and chatted quietly while the younger men unloaded 48-4 and the cart.

"This is unbelievable," Jack said as they carried the boxes to the porch. "Thanks so much for bringing them to us so quickly.

Mr. Young is anxious to begin hooking up both houses as soon as we can."

Stuart chuckled. "Angel was the same."

After 48-4 and the cart were unloaded, Scott stepped into the driver's seat, and he and Stuart headed back.

"We'll talk after we get back," Scott said.

Stuart scanned the road behind them as Scott sped back to his farm. After he turned at the driveway, he said, "I figured if anyone was close enough to hear the engine, it wouldn't matter if we were going fast or slow, so I opted for fast."

Stuart snorted. "Makes sense to me."

"It would," Scott said. "You told me when you were six that you were going to learn to run faster, so you could run in between the raindrops and not get wet."

Stuart chuckled. "I still can't run fast enough, but I'm convinced Angel and Red can."

"I'll drop you off then park and check 48-4's fuel level."

"Dad, what were you, Major, and Mr. Young talking about?"

"Go check the progress on the solar, then if they don't need your help, come to the equipment shed, and we'll talk."

"How's it going?" Stuart asked when he strolled to the barn. Andy finished nailing the rack large enough for several solar panels.

"Pretty good," Andy said. "We're going to put this where the panels can get the maximum exposure to sunlight. We may want to eventually adjust the angle or the location, but we're confident this will be fine to get us started."

"Want some help?"

"You can help me carry the rack, but Angel has almost everything else done," Andy said.

"Let's do it then," Stuart said.

Angel followed them then directed an adjustment to their position. "Good, that's it," she said.

"Do you want me to help carry anything else?" Stuart asked.

Andy grinned. "I'll grab a cart; Angel already told me what she needs; all I have to do is load then pull when she tells me."

Stuart smiled. "That's my cue to get out of the way. I'll see you in the house. Dad wants some help in the equipment shed."

He hurried to join his dad and frowned at Scott's somber face.

Scott rubbed his face then exhaled. "Major, Mr. Young, and I are worried about that army coming from the south, except Major told me he refuses to call them an army because they're a gang of domestic terrorists. Mr. Young's diversion plan has had the tremendous side effect of actually creating a swell for a southwest Georgia militia, and the army may be headed more northeast than straight north to us, but we can't tell if their shift is enough to bypass us. Major and Mr. Young want us to move the children,

Louisa, Noel, and Doc Larkin to Major's house. Nate told Major that Charo and Lela want to make room too. Their point is that the army is likely to hit us first. We're the first line of defense for their houses, and the children will be safer there."

"I don't know. I don't like the idea at all. I'd rather we built trenches or bunkers to make the army shift east. We could certainly appear to be part of the militia."

"We may want to do that too; think about it. Talk to Angel, Andy, and Red. I'll talk to your mom, Peyton, and David. I'd like to get their ideas without a big uproar of a meeting, but we should decide today before nightfall."

"Mom and Peyton will want to talk to Louisa," Stuart said.

"You're probably right; I'll ask David to talk to Cal and Blanche, and I'll talk to Doc Larkin and Noel."

After his dad left, Stuart sighed then walked slowly to Angel and Andy.

"Just in time," Andy said, "We just finished."

"The four of us need to talk."

Angel stared at Stuart's cloud, and he put his arm around her. "Let's go upstairs, so we can talk with Red too." *She knows it's bad.*

When they went inside, Peyton, David, and Blanche were in the kitchen.

"Scott wants to talk to us." Sandra's face was dark. "Cal's with Louisa and the kids."

"I'll grab Cal," Blanche said.

Scott nodded, then Peyton and David sat at the kitchen table next to each other, and Sandra stood next to the stove with her arms crossed.

"Please sit with us, honey." Scott sat at the table.

Angel, Stuart, and Andy went upstairs.

"What's wrong?" Red asked when Stuart walked into the room.

Angel reads clouds; Red reads faces.

"Dad talked to Major and Mr. Young, and they are as worried as we are about the approach of the deadly army, except Major called them the domestic terrorists. Major and Mr. Young are afraid the militia coming from the north and the growing southwest Georgia militia won't be able to divert the entire army fast enough to keep the western edge from hitting us," Stuart said.

"They may be right," Andy said.

"Major and Mr. Young believe the army will hit us first if they continue their path of traveling to the north. Major thinks it would be wise for us to move the children to his place. If we don't stop the army, we may be able to scatter them, so even if they hit the two farms northeast of us, they will be much weaker, and Major, Jack, and the Cabellos will be able to fight them off to protect the children."

Angel took over the headset from Red, and Red glared at Andy with her face as red as her flaming hair.

"Hate it," Red growled. "We can't send Henry away, and we can't protect him if we're all dead."

Andy hugged Red then said softly as he stroked her hair, "Exactly. If we send Henry to Major's, he will have a fighting chance to grow up."

Red pushed away from him. "What if the terrorists miss us and go straight to Major's?"

"Major has the firepower to hold them off, and we'll attack them from the west. They'll think a militia hit them," Stuart said.

Red glanced at Angel. "We still hate it."

"So do we," Andy said.

Stuart put his hand on Angel's shoulder, and she removed the headset.

"We should tell Henry," Angel said.

Red sighed. "Right before you came upstairs, Phil contacted Major. He's on his way here. All his neighbors have abandoned their homes, and the terrorists are at the Florida-Georgia state line. Phil left last night with his wife, son, and his son's family in two pickup trucks. They're going to drive up the state road as far as they can then ditch the trucks if they have to and walk."

Andy frowned. "Is this the Phil I know? How would Phil know where Major is?"

"Phil knows Mr. Young and Leo from their years of being on the ham radio, he'd know Major is close to Leo's farm," Stuart said.

"When do we take the children to Pops?" Red asked.

"As soon as we all agree, then we'll pack them up and go."

"Today?" Andy's eyes widened.

Stuart nodded. "We'll need the time to plan and prepare for the terrorists' arrival."

"How can we get them to Pops' house today?" Red narrowed her eyes. "They can't run or even walk fast that far."

"We'll figure it out. First, we need to make sure everyone agrees this is our best way to keep the children safe."

"I'm staying with Angel until everyone is ready to talk about what we do next," Red said. "I'll be her runner if there is any more news."

When Stuart and Andy reached the first floor, the discussion was still in progress in the kitchen.

"Let's go talk to Noel and Doc Larkin," Stuart said.

"You go. I'll relieve Louisa, so she can join the discussion," Andy said.

"Grab Mom, so she can fill in Louisa before they go to the kitchen," Stuart said.

When Stuart reached Noel's bedroom, Noel said, "Doc and I were just about to head to the kitchen. We didn't catch the topic of discussion, but it sounds serious."

"The reports about the army heading our way are very disturbing. They have murdered everyone in their path, families included, and burn homes as they go. We're hoping the news of the militias from the north and from the west will push them to the east and away from us, but so far, they are headed straight toward us. Major and Mr. Young recommend moving our children to Major's new place because the army will hit us first. Major refuses to call them an army because he says they are domestic terrorists. If we can stop, or even scatter the terrorists, Major's team will have a chance to keep the children safe."

"What does Louisa say?" Noel asked.

"Andy's taking over the lessons for the kids, so she can join the discussion in the kitchen."

"What did Angel say?" Doc Larkin asked.

"She hates to send Henry to Major's, but she wants us to be the ones to tell him," Stuart said.

"She wants Henry safe; I can understand that," Noel said.

"How would we get them there?" Doc Larkin asked.

"We haven't talked about that yet; I have few vague ideas, but if we keep them here, we need to have a solid plan in place quickly to be sure the children aren't harmed," Stuart said.

"What about guns, ammo, and shooters to defend this house?" Doc asked.

"We have at least eight experienced shooters, we're in pretty good shape with ammo, and most of our rifles are deer rifles," Stuart said.

Noel frowned. "You have the guns and ammo from my car, don't you?"

"What? No, we decided to leave your things alone until you decided what you wanted to do," Stuart said.

"Scott invited us to stay here, and Louisa and I decided that it was best for our family to be part of a larger family like this one. We were pleased at how readily the other children accepted Mandy and Jimmy, and for the first time in months, our children are happy and not anxious. I'm with Angel, I hate the idea, but you need to unload everything in my trunk into the house."

Stuart cocked his head. "It's been there since you crashed. It'll be fine until we're not under such a time crunch."

Noel smiled. "I hate to ruin the surprise, but you'll find ammunition and semi-automatic rifles. I emptied my shop of all the guns and as much ammo as I could get into the trunk before we left; I didn't want to leave anything behind that could harm us or someone else later."

"What? Semi-automatics?" Doc Larkin asked.

Noel nodded. "I owned a gun shop and operated a shooting range to train new shooters and give experienced shooters a place to keep up their skills. Louisa taught most of the classes."

"I thought you owned a pawn shop," Doc said.

"Pawn shop and gun shop," Noel said. "After I was discharged from the Marines, I went from job to job. I talked about reenlisting, but my brilliant wife reminded me that I know guns, so both of us worked and skimped then bought the gun shop and gun range from an old friend who was ready to retire. We put up a sign that said pawn shop because we bought and sold more than guns."

"Once a Marine, always a Marine," Stuart said, and Noel nodded.

"It makes sense to send the children to the Mitchells' old house," Doc Larkin said. "From a professional standpoint, I'm not interested in treating any pediatric gunshot wounds, and the more barriers between terrorists and the children the better."

"I have to go to the kitchen; Louisa will need some moral support," Noel said.

Stuart helped Noel to his feet then followed Noel and Doc to the kitchen.

"I'm glad you're here, Stuart. What did Angel say?" Sandra asked.

"Angel said she hates the idea, and she wants us to be the ones to tell Henry."

Sandra's smile was weak. "That's our Angel."

"I've seen savagery firsthand that I didn't know existed, and I agree with Angel. David and I will talk to Brandon," Peyton said.

"Honey?" Louisa bit her lip as she gazed at Noel.

Noel sat next to her and took her hand. "Our decisions have always been based on what's best for the family. We'll talk to them together."

"Sounds like we're all in agreement that we don't like it, but we're ready to protect the children," Scott said. "Next up for discussion is timing."

"We need to move as quickly as possible, so the kids can get settled, and we can begin planning for an attack," Stuart said.

"I don't like that either," Louisa said, "but it makes sense. We don't have a lot of time."

"What do you have in mind, Stuart?" Scott asked.

"I would recommend that one parent accompany the children, so they don't feel like they were sent away," Blanche said.

"I wouldn't have thought of that," Sandra said, "but I remember reading about the children who were put on trains and sent to the country in England during World War II. The children didn't understand and thought they were sent away because they'd done something wrong."

"The parent can't be Angel," Stuart said.

"I'm not saying the parent has to be a mom, but not Peyton," David said. "She's a crack shot."

"David has skills we need," Blanche said, and Scott nodded.

Noel raised an eyebrow at Louisa.

She sighed. "I'll go. I can shoot, and I'm very accurate, but I've only shot my gun and rifle on a range. I don't have the field experience everyone else has, but Henry and Brandon don't know me very well."

"They know everyone at the Cabello house, and they know Major is Angel's grandfather," Sandra said. "It wouldn't be all strangers like it would for Mandy and Jimmy."

"Will Major have room for all of us?" Louisa asked.

"All the families have the magical skill of making room," Stuart said.

Louisa smiled. "Point taken. How do we get there?"

"What about driving our car?" Noel asked.

"I could do that. I'll just need to know where I'm going," Louisa said.

"Is that possible?" Cal stared at Stuart.

Stuart snorted. "Wish I'd thought of it. I was cooking up an impossibly elaborate plan in my head that didn't make sense even to me. This definitely is much simpler and makes sense; Angel, Red, Andy and I will escort your car, Louisa."

Sandra frowned. "Doc, shouldn't you and Noel go too?"

Doc narrowed his eyes. "Noel and I can sit at a window and shoot. I've never shot a semi-auto and look forward to it. If you need somebody to run after the terrorists to chase them away, I'd be the first to tell you I'm not your man. I'll leave that up to you young folks."

Sandra giggled. "Guess I better claim a window too."

"Atta girl," Blanche said.

"What do we do after we talk to our children?" Louisa asked.

"Ah, finally. My area of expertise," Blanche said. "The children can pack their own things in their backpacks. I'll make sure everyone has clothes for three days, and anything special they want to take. I'll show them how to pack efficiently. Give us fifteen minutes for all the children to have their backpacks ready. We only need ten, but I have a story to tell them before they leave. Tracker and Brody go too, right?"

"Absolutely," Peyton said.

"I'll pack for the puppies," Sandra said.

"Let's talk to our children." Peyton rose from her chair.

Louisa, Peyton, David, and Stuart went to the living room.

"Mandy and Jimmy, Daddy and I would like to talk to you. Come to the kitchen with me."

Peyton and David sat on the sofa with Brandon between them.

Stuart said, "Henry and Andy, let's go talk to Angel; she's upstairs on the radio."

"Is this sad, Dad?" Henry asked as they climbed the stairs. "Everybody looked sad."

"I'd say it's serious, not sad," Stuart said, and Andy nodded.

When they went into the room, Angel handed the headset to Red then moved to sit on the bed.

"Hop up with Mama Angel," Stuart said.

Angel put her arm around Henry when he hopped onto the bed, and he snuggled against her.

Stuart knelt next to the two of them.

"Henry, there is an army of bad men that is headed our way. We're going to stop them, and we need your help. All of the children need to go to Pops' new house that is next door to Aunt Charo. You're the only one that knows the people at Aunt Charo's house, and you know Pops. You are related to Pops because he's my grandfather."

"Dad told me it was serious. This is serious," Henry said, "but you need me to stay with you because I see good."

"You certainly do; that's another reason it's important for you to be with the other children. You see things that aren't the way they should be. Pops knows he can count on you to tell him if something isn't right for one of the children," Stuart said.

Henry nodded then gazed at Angel's face. "Will you be okay, Mama Angel?"

"Dad will be with me; I'll be okay," she said.

"Uncle Andy, are you going to take care of Aunt Red?"

Andy smiled. "I definitely will."

"You have to let Uncle Andy take care of you, Aunt Red."

Andy winked at Red, and she rolled her eyes.

"You're right, Henry, and I'll be okay," Red said.

"When am I leaving?" Henry asked.

"We'll go downstairs, and Grandma Blanche will tell you what to pack. She might make it a game or a race. You know how she is," Stuart said.

Henry snickered. "Grandma Blanche makes work fun."

He hopped off the bed. "You'll hug me and give me a kiss before I leave?"

Angel hugged and kissed him. "Just like that, Henry."

Henry nodded then took Stuart's hand. "Let's do this, Dad."

As they went down the stairs, Henry asked, "How do we get there? Do I run?"

"No, Aunt Louisa's going to drive you in her car. Mama Angel, Aunt Red, Uncle Andy, and I will show her the way to go and make sure you get there safely."

Henry nodded. "That's good."

When Stuart and Henry went into the living room, Brandon grinned. "We get to meet Brett and Josh, Henry. Did you know Brett is practically the same age as you, me, and Jimmy?"

"That makes five boys and five girls," Henry said. "We're finally even."

Brandon nodded. "Annie's old, so she doesn't count."

Stuart coughed, and Peyton glared at him.

Stuart cleared his throat. "Excuse me, had a little tickle."

Blanche followed Louisa, Mandy, and Jimmy into the living room.

"Okay, buckaroos. It's time to pack for your next adventure while the parents do their boring, grown-up things," Blanche said.

"I'm a buckaroo here for the packing lesson too," Louisa said, and Blanche nodded.

Stuart, Peyton, and David slipped out of the room.

"Let's unload the trunk," Stuart said as they went into the kitchen.

Peyton frowned at Noel. "You're not going to wear yourself out, are you?"

"Probably, but I promised Doc I would rest after I know Louisa and the children are safe at Major's," he said.

"Bring everything in here," Scott said. "We'll sort later; Andy and Cal went outside with the car keys."

"After you empty the trunk, I have extra pillows and blankets they can take in case Molly needs them," Sandra said.

Andy and Cal had the trunk open and were loading guns into a cart when Stuart, Peyton, and David reached the car.

"Noel carried some nice guns in his shop. I would have been poor if we'd lived close to them," Cal said.

"You and me both." Peyton ran her hand over the stock of one of the rifles that was still in the trunk. "These are beautiful."

"Dad always told me to marry a woman who knew her guns," David said.

Peyton giggled. "We could use another cart."

David hurried to the barn.

Stuart and Andy rolled the full cart to the house, and Peyton walked along to help carry the guns inside the house while Cal waited for David, so they could finish unloading the trunk.

When they went into the kitchen, Scott pointed to the quilt he'd laid in a corner near the back door. "That should be out of the way enough for the time being."

Scott organized the rifles and pistols as Stuart, Cal, and Peyton carried them inside.

"Wow, what a haul. All this was in your trunk?" Scott said after Peyton carried in the last two rifles.

"I have the storage skills of a packrat." Noel grinned.

CHAPTER TWENTY-ONE

After Stuart carried out the pillows and blankets to the car, he returned to the house.

When he walked inside, Sandra placed a large bag of rice into a box on the kitchen table then added four cartons of eggs. "I'm sending a few things to help feed our folks. I know they have chickens, but theirs were probably stressed by the trip." She peered into the box. "It's almost full. Give me a minute, then you can load it into the car. I wrote Molly a note to tell her about the bath, snack, bed rule. Do you think that was too much? Will I be stepping on her toes?"

"I think she'll appreciate it; I'm sure she's stressing as much as you are because she wants the children to be comfortable."

"Should I go with Louisa?" she asked.

Scott walked into the kitchen. "That's up to you, honey, but I'd rather you stayed here. The children are all packed and listening to Blanche's story. Evidently it's completely age-appropriate because they're laughing, and I didn't understand why a turtle riding an ostrich to visit his family was so hilarious."

"It does sound like a silly story." Sandra sighed. "I guess it would be smart for me to stay here. Molly doesn't need to try to find a sleeping spot for another person."

"The story's almost finished." Cal came out of the living room and headed to the stairs. "I'll relieve Angel and Red."

"Stuart, everybody's assuming you four are going to accompany Louisa and the children to Major's." Sandra frowned.

"It's logical," Scott said, and Stuart smiled.

"The box is ready to go," Sandra said.

"I'll take it out, and I'll check to be sure the car starts and has enough gas. I meant to do that earlier," Stuart said.

Stuart carried the box to the car and placed it into the trunk. After he removed the keys from the lock, he headed to the driver's seat. *I understand why Mom wanted to go with the children; I do too.*

He sighed as he started the engine and checked the gas gauge. *All good.* He turned off the engine then strode back to the house. As he walked inside, the children and Louisa had on their backpacks, and Angel and Red raced down the stairs.

"Ready for hugs?" Blanche asked.

Peyton and David hugged Brandon, and Jimmy and Mandy hurried to the table, so Noel could hug them.

"I'll wait for my hug," Henry said, and Stuart smiled.

"Makes sense to me. No sense in using up all your hugs at one time," Scott said, "but maybe everybody can hug Mama Sandra."

The children stood in line for their hugs, then Stuart said, "Time to go."

On their way to the car, Stuart said, "Louisa, Angel and Red will run ahead to make sure the way is clear. Andy and I will stay with you. Watch me for the signal to turn at the end of the driveway."

"Will do." Louisa climbed into the driver's seat, the three boys got in back, and Mandy jumped into the front passenger's seat.

Stuart nodded; Angel and Red raced up the driveway, and Louisa headed the car up the driveway. Stuart and Andy ran behind the car until Louisa slowed when she approached the road. Stuart continued.

"Clear," Red said, then she and Angel raced down the road toward Major's driveway, and Stuart signaled for Louisa to turn right.

As she slowly drove toward Major's, Stuart signaled her to speed up. When they neared the driveway, Red waved and pointed to the entrance; Louisa slowed, and Stuart signaled for her to turn. As she drove up the driveway, Angel and Red joined Stuart.

"We'll wait for you here," Andy said, and Angel ran up the driveway and passed Louisa to clear the way while Stuart ran along behind the car.

When Angel reached the house, Jack stood in the driveway, and Major was on the porch.

"Everyone else is waiting inside because otherwise there'd be too much commotion. Everybody okay?" Jack asked.

"Yes, Angel and I will get our hugs from Henry, then we'll leave," Stuart said.

Before the car arrived, Angel rushed to the porch and hugged Major.

"Thanks, Angel. I know this is hard on everyone," Major said.

"Nobody likes it, but it's the best way to protect the children."

Angel returned to the driveway before the car and Stuart arrived. After Louisa parked, the children spilled out of the car, and Molly and Annie came outside.

Henry hurried to Stuart and hugged him, then he ran to Angel and clung to her. "You're the best, Mama Angel. I love you."

"I love you too, Henry." Angel hugged him and stroked his hair then kissed him. "See you soon."

Henry and the rest of the children followed Annie into the house; Molly joined Louisa while Stuart opened the trunk.

"It's nice to meet you, Louisa. I'm glad you came," Molly said.

"We hoped it would help the children feel less like they were sent away," Louisa said. "Sandra sent a box of goodies and some pillows and blankets in case we need them."

Jack carried the box into the house then returned for the pillows and blankets.

"Thanks for everything." Stuart waved as Angel raced down the driveway.

Angel waited for Stuart halfway down.

"Everything okay?" he asked.

"Yes. I was just waiting for you." She raced away, and Stuart jogged after her.

"Still nothing," Red said when Stuart joined the three of them at the end of the driveway.

Stuart nodded, and Angel and Red dashed away. Stuart and Andy ran toward the Newton farm.

When they neared the driveway, Andy said, "I don't see them; is something wrong?"

"Not at all. Watch," Stuart said.

After they turned, Angel and Red appeared in the tall weeds next to the driveway then ran to the house.

Stuart and Andy strode after them.

"Dang, they're really scary good, aren't they?" Andy asked.

"You got the scary part right," Stuart said.

When Stuart and Andy went into the kitchen, Scott said, "We've been listening on the handheld. Just a few minutes ago, Phil said on simplex, 'Just around the corner, but might be lost, Mom.' He said something else, and I think Mr. Young said something too, but I didn't catch the rest of their conversation because they faded out."

Angel and Red tore down the stairs.

"What is it?" Stuart asked.

Red's eyes were wide. "Cal heard Phil say, 'Just around the corner, but might be lost, Mom.'"

Scott nodded. "I heard that too."

"Phil followed up with 'Where do I turn to get to Major's?' Mr. Young told him to go north a mile or so on the county road he was on then turn right at Meadows Lane," Red said.

"They were talking on the simplex channel most hams use, not the one of our two simplex channels we set up with Mr. Young," Angel said.

"Our terrorist would scan the commonly used simplex channel, wouldn't he?" Stuart asked.

"Yes."

Angel and Red ran up the stairs.

Scott frowned. "Now what?"

Stuart sighed. "I have no idea."

"I need to find David," Andy said.

"David and Peyton went out front. David wanted to look at the tree that fell on the porch roof," Sandra said. "Cal and Blanche want to bring the cows here to the barn, Scott. They went to the barn to see how it could be done."

"Come with me, Stuart," Scott said. "I might need backup on this one."

When they reached the barn, Cal said, "Good, you're here. Tell them your idea, Blanche."

"It would take me two minutes to organize your tools on your pegboard and on the shelves under your worktable. See how this side of your barn was all stalls? Looks like maybe four to me. It would take Stuart and David twenty minutes to put in two stalls: one large one for the cow and her calf, and the other one for our cow that we've been milking."

"David already built the water trough. It's heavy, but you or Andy could bring it here on your tractor, Scott," Cal said. "We hate to think that we'll lose our cows and milk, and we will if we leave them at the Smith barn. I could walk all three of them here through the shortcut."

Scott looked at Stuart. "What do you think?"

"I'll be right back." Stuart ran to the house and up the stairs. When he went into his bedroom, Red smiled.

"Mr. Young told Phil on the common simplex to avoid the west side of the interstate, or he'd run into the militia. Phil said he'd divert."

Stuart frowned. "Why is that good?"

Red grinned. "That was right after Mr. Young contacted us on our simplex channel two and told us the songbird had landed."

Stuart stared at her. "Phil's at Major's?"

"We think so; they're trying to divert the terrorists," Red said.

"Cal and Blanche want to bring the cows here. Do they have time?"

Angel put down her headset. "How much time would it take?"

"It's a twenty-minute round trip walk at their pace, and assuming they don't run into any problems, they'd be back within thirty minutes," Stuart said.

"From a timing standpoint, they would have time. I think the terrorists are a little over two hours away," Angel said.

When Stuart rose to leave, Angel put on her headset, and Red said, "We're trying to talk Leo into coming here. We're offering transportation for Jennie. So far, he's refused. He said he has to stay by his radio."

"I'll tell Andy," Stuart said.

"Thanks."

Stuart rushed to the barn. "I estimated it would take thirty minutes to bring the cows here. Angel said you'd have enough time."

"Scott told us someone had to go with Cal. I'm going along," Blanche said, then the two of them headed toward the shortcut."

Stuart stared at the pegboard and the worktable. "She said she could do that in two minutes."

Scott shook his head. "Cal pulled me out of the barn and told me I'd end up on a shelf if I didn't get out of the way. I'm going to find David and let him know he has thirty minutes to build two stalls, then I'll gather the lumber."

"I'll get David, Dad," Stuart said.

When Stuart walked out of the barn, David, Peyton, and Andy were headed his way.

"David, Cal and Blanche are on their way to bring the cows here. How fast can you build two stalls in Dad's barn?"

"Your dad's barn? It'll take us three days to clear it out before I can build any stalls."

Stuart smirked. "Blanche straightened it up."

"I want to see this," Peyton rushed to the barn, and Stuart, David, and Andy followed her.

David laughed when he saw the barn. "How's Scott doing?"

"He's in shock." Scott grinned as he came around the corner with a load of wood in a cart. "We've got thirty minutes before the cows come home," he said.

"Any way we can bring the trough here?" David asked.

"Red and I can get the large tractor from Uncle Leo's to carry it here."

"You'll have to hurry if you want to make it back before the cows are on the path," Stuart said. "We don't have people to spare to be guards for you to bring it by the road."

Andy dashed to the house, then he and Red ran to the shortcut.

"At least he can sit on the way back," Scott said.

"Scott, Andy and I discussed digging trenches for defense behind the house. We've got the tractors, what do you think?" David asked

"It's a good idea in theory, but you're used to the Florida sand and forgot about our Georgia clay. You'd need to send Angel to bring you a full-blown backhoe."

"Ouch, you're right. I won't ask her, though, because she'd do it, and I'd fold under the time pressure. Let's get those stalls built."

David examined the area for the stalls then glared at Peyton and Stuart. "You bystanders need to vacate my worksite. We're under a deadline here."

"Yes, sir," Peyton said.

As she and Stuart headed toward the house, Peyton said, "David works well under pressure except his social skills fly out the window."

"Whatever it takes," Stuart said. "Let's talk to Noel. I'd like to get his thoughts on defense."

When they reached Noel's room, he and Doc were sitting at the south window of the bedroom, and Noel was sketching a diagram of the house, the surrounding buildings, and the woods.

"Glad you're here," Noel said. "Doc was giving me a tour of the house and grounds. He wasn't positive about the windows on the second floor, though. Are there any windows on the east side of the house?"

"There are two windows upstairs on the east side. Our bedroom has one window on the east side, and the storage room has a small window on the east side near the back corner. There aren't any windows on the east side downstairs."

"If we had a barrier between the barn and the house, do we have windows that could protect it?"

"Only the storage window. What are you thinking?"

"Sandra and Blanche talked about bringing the cows here," Doc said. "Noel's been trying to figure out how to extend protection for them. Is there a window on the east side of the barn in the loft?"

"I don't remember one, but I'll have to check."

"If we had one of our experienced shooters in the barn, he or she would have a different shooting angle and could provide additional protection for the cows, but if we have a barrier for cover and the attackers become too close, our shooter could get to the house while the east window and maybe the southeast window shooters kept the attackers busy. Doc said he'd help me walk from the house to the barn and back. My theory might be good, but I'd like to check it out," Noel said.

Stuart nodded. "I'll go to the storage window to see how wide the viewing range is. You might want to use the old walker, Noel, to walk over the uneven ground."

Doc Larkin smirked. "Told you."

"Fine, let's go," Noel growled.

While Noel walked to the closet for the walker, Stuart dashed upstairs to talk to Angel before he went to the storage room.

When Stuart strode into the bedroom, Angel removed her headset and switched the radio to speaker.

"The attackers are using simplex like it's their private channel," Red said. "One said he had a message for the general: Major is on Meadows Lane, sixty miles north of the state line. Another replied he'd relay. We're waiting to hear if this general has any orders."

"Any indication who the general is?"

"No," Angel said.

"He must be behind his army and probably in a vehicle, not driving. If he's on the state highway, it would take him no more than an hour to get here, depending on his speed. Do you think Major and Mr. Young heard it too?" Stuart asked.

"Yes."

"Everything is moving so fast, I'm not sure what you've heard. Blanche and Cal left to get the cows, David and Dad are building stalls in our barn, and Noel and Doc have gone outside, so we can see if there's a way to set up a defense for the cows."

"I'm glad the cows will be here," Red said. "We've tried to contact Uncle Leo several times, but he's refusing to answer."

"I have to check the storage window to see if it works to defend someone who was in the barn but needed to escape to the house," Stuart said.

Red hurried to the east window. "I can see the north edge of the barn but only part way to the house."

"Thanks." Stuart headed to the storage room then began moving items away from the east wall. *I'm going to be in trouble for this.* He tossed items to the floor that were on the shelves of the old storage case that was against the wall then pulled the heavy case to the side.

Stuart moved to the window and peered at his clear view of the barn then struggled to open the window. *Dang. Nailed shut. I'll take care of that.* Stuart watched as Noel watched the placement of his feet on the ground while Doc stayed close to him.

Stuart smiled. *Doc's approaching ninety, but you'd think he's in his prime.*

When Noel and Doc turned to look at the window, Noel waved. Stuart returned the wave, but Noel spoke to Doc, then the two men shook their heads. *They can't see me because the window's dirty. That's not bad at all, and I can't tell Mom that.*

Stuart watched Noel as he motioned a line between the barn and the house. *I'll check the kitchen window for that section I can't see next to the house.*

The two men returned to the house, and when Stuart lost sight of them, he hurried to his bedroom. "Could you see them?"

"Not at all." Red moved away from the window to sit in the chair next to Angel.

"Thanks." He rushed downstairs before they reached the back door and watched their progress across the yard.

Sandra sat at the kitchen table. "I'm almost finished with the kitchen blackout curtain. Louisa was working on the curtain for Blanche and Cal's room, and it won't take me long to finish those, then after Blanche returns, we're going to decide which room we want to do next. Did you know Noel and Doc went outside? I'm glad Noel's getting some fresh air."

After Noel and Doc came inside, Stuart followed them to Noel's room. Noel groaned as he lowered himself to his chair.

"I could see you from the upstairs east window except when you were close to the house, then I could see you from the kitchen window," Stuart said.

"Excellent," Noel said. "Did you see me wave?"

"Yes, and I waved back. You couldn't see me, could you?"

Noel shook his head, and his eyes twinkled as he whispered, "Window glare."

"Good cover story." Doc nodded.

"When Dad and David finish the stall, I'll talk to them about the barrier between the house and barn. We have plenty of downed limbs and small trees nearby from the tornado and could take a chainsaw to the larger trees, so the tractor could manage them," Stuart said.

"Remind me how many shooters we have," Noel said.

"We have eleven; twelve, if you count Angel; she's a good shot, but I never assign her to be a shooter because of all her other skills," Stuart said. "I counted Mom, but I'm not certain she's shot anything other than her shotgun."

"We have a houseful of shooters," Noel said. "I can't remember how many semi-autos I brought."

"I can check Red's list, but I think there were eight."

"We can give one to almost everyone," Doc said. "I'd expect our sharpshooters would decline, like you and Red, Stuart."

Stuart nodded. "We would, and Peyton and David would probably decline too. Mom would be fine with one if Dad or I spend a few minutes going over the operation with her."

"I'd like to give a quick review with the entire group before we hand them out; is that possible?" Noel asked.

"Good idea," Stuart said. "We'll gather everyone in the hallway, so you can talk, and Angel and Red can hear you from the radio room."

"Excellent," Noel said. "It won't take me more than a minute or so with the experience level of this group."

Stuart smiled at the sound of a tractor coming from the shortcut. Noel peered out his window. "What's that Andy is carrying with the grapple?"

"Should be the cows' water trough, but I didn't think Leo's tractor had a grapple." Stuart hurried to the back door then headed to the barn in front of Andy and Red.

When Stuart and Red reached the barn, David and Scott were picking up boards and tools.

"We've got to put everything back in place before Blanche returns." Scott stared at the hammer in his hand and the pegboard. "I don't see where this goes."

Red held out her hand; after he gave her the hammer, she hung it on the board. Scott grinned and handed Red one tool after another as she put each one away. After she was finished, David stared at Andy when he stopped the tractor at the barn door.

Scott asked, "Where did that grapple come from?"

"Uncle Leo told us he didn't have one, but the last time Red and I went to his house, Red spotted a blue tarp in the woods. When we checked the blue tarp today to see what it was, we also found the grapple."

Scott peered around the tractor. "That's a large trailer; what's under the tarp?"

Andy grinned. "Technically, it's a hay wagon. Cal told us he'd given Leo some hay too, but he assumed it was gone and never mentioned it. Where do you want the trough?"

"Center it between the two stalls," David said, "but let's unhook the hay wagon first. After the cows are here, we can push the wagon into the barn."

After Scott and Andy unhooked the wagon, Andy carried the trough into the barn then centered it and backed out.

"Do I put the tractor by the equipment shed?" he asked.

"On the north side of the equipment shed, so it can't be seen," Scott said.

"Wait on that, Andy," Stuart said.

"Cows are here." Red dashed out of the barn and to the house.

"Where's she going?" David asked.

"To tell Sandra and Angel," Scott said.

Sandra, Peyton, and Red came out of the house while Andy and Red headed toward the shortcut to wait until Cal and Blanche cleared the path with the cows.

"We'll haul the water for them after we push the hay wagon inside the barn," David said. "Angel said we had to wait until tomorrow for the system to charge before we will have running water."

Both cows stopped at the hay wagon and refused to continue. Blanche coaxed the mama cow and her calf into their stall, then Cal handed Blanche a handful of hay, and she lured the other cow into her stall. The cows bellowed and pushed against their stalls. Stuart, Andy, Peyton, Cal, and Scott pushed the heavy hay wagon while Blanche and David steered it inside.

"I need to help Sandra with lunch," Blanche said after the wagon was in place.

"Go ahead," Cal said.

Cal and Scott pulled off a bale while Stuart, David, and Peyton hurried for buckets to fill the water trough.

The cows settled down and munched on the hay.

"What's our next task?" David asked.

Stuart explained Noel's plan for a sharpshooter in the barn loft and a barrier to protect the shooter if he needed to take cover in the house.

David looked at the loft. "I want to check the window." After he climbed the ladder, he said, "This is great."

"Where does the barrier go?" Scott asked. Stuart led his dad and Andy to the yard between the house and the barn and showed them where he had seen Noel and Doc.

"Got it," Scott said as they returned to the barn.

David scrambled down the ladder. "There is a stand of downed trees close to the firebreak. We could move them here because they would be perfect cover for the attackers to gather without being seen before they approach the house."

"I'll grab a chainsaw in case we need it," Stuart said.

The three men hurried to the tractors then rolled out to the firebreak.

When they reached the down trees, David said, "I think we'll be able to take back what we need in three or four trips, especially with Andy's large tractor and the grapple."

"Dad's got our back, but we need to stay alert. We don't know if they have advance scouts."

"Scouts? We need to talk after we get the barrier done," Andy said.

CHAPTER TWENTY-TWO

Scott stood where Noel had recommended the barrier and directed each tractor operator where to drop his load of trees. Stuart and David brought their last loads, and Scott motioned for them to turn around and dump, then he motioned for them to continue to the equipment shed. When Andy brought his last load, he turned around and dumped the trees to close the hole in the barrier then continued to the equipment shed.

Stuart, David, and Andy returned to join Scott at the barrier. "She's a beauty, isn't she?" David asked. "What's next?"

"We go inside. We need a break, and we don't want to miss a meal," Scott said.

"After lunch, Noel will give us all a quick lesson on the semi-automatic rifles then hand them out. We still need to establish everyone's positions," Stuart said as they strolled to the house.

"We'll want to be in place when the attackers hit us," Scott said.

When Stuart was inside, he dashed up the stairs two at a time and hurried to his bedroom.

"Good, you're here," Red said. "I love these guys. They're such radio neophytes."

"Sarcasm," Stuart said automatically.

"Right. Sorry, Angel; sometimes I get excited. Of course, I could be reading them all wrong, and they are cunning because they are using simplex for us to hear completely false information."

Angel shook her head. "Neophytes."

Red nodded. "According to the ones we heard, the general has ordered his army to turn east to avoid the militia. He'll join them near Savannah after he's taken care of Major. The message was relayed, so we couldn't hear the general because he must still be out of range for us, but neither can his northernmost gang. More importantly, he can't hear them either. One of the men said the message from the general was actually from the militia, and they needed to stay the course. He also claimed the general gave him orders to take over and continue north until they were at Atlanta. I think we'll be attacked."

"Noel is going to give a quick lesson on the semi-automatic rifles. I need both of you to listen. He'll be in the hallway, so you can hear what he's saying."

"Before you leave, Angel and I talked about possible positions for us at the different windows in the house. I have a sketch for you." She handed a sheet of paper to Stuart.

Stuart shook his head as he carried the paper down the stairs.

Andy met him in the hallway. "I need to talk to you and David."

"Got a minute?" Andy asked David, and the three of them went into the living room.

"When you mentioned scouts while we were working on the barrier, I realized we don't have to wait for the attackers. We can gather our own data on where they are and which direction they are heading if we send out scouts," Andy said. "Unfortunately, our best scouts are Angel and Red, and they know it. Who could we send instead of them?"

"You're right about the scouts and about Angel and Red. Where does that leave us?" Stuart asked.

"I've spent my entire career stalking poachers," David said. "I'm not as fast as Angel and Red, but I'm an experienced scout. Angel and I could get the intel we need."

"No, we won't be able to split Angel and Red," Andy said.

"What about the three of us then?" David asked.

"The only way that would work would be if Stuart and I trailed along behind as backup," Andy said.

"Wait, look at this. If the five of us get mowed down, the house has lost five key shooters," Stuart said.

David said, "The only person likely to be ambushed if we're discovered would be me. Angel and Red could get away, and the four of you could make it back to the house."

"I don't know," Stuart said.

"Let's ask Angel and Red," David said.

"You know what they'll say," Stuart grumbled. "Is there any other way?"

"You and I could go; you could decide whether to tell Angel we're leaving," David said. "Personally, I'll tell Peyton because she'd kill me when I came back to the house."

Stuart snorted. "That's a good point. What do you think, Andy? It was your idea, and we're talking about leaving you out."

"I don't have a patent on it. I'm okay as long as I don't have to guard the staircase, so Angel and Red can't follow you; I couldn't take on the two of them alone."

"I'll go talk to Peyton," David said.

"I might as well talk to Angel and Red together," Stuart said.

"Want backup?" Andy asked.

"Come on."

When Stuart went into the bedroom, Andy trailed along behind him.

"What?" Angel asked as she removed her headset and handed it to Red.

"David and I are going to see if we can find the attackers, so we know where they are, which direction they are heading, and an idea of how many there are," Stuart said.

"You know it would be better to let Red and me go, right? We're faster. I could find them, so we could gather the information we need and be back to the house before you even reached them," Angel said.

"You know she's right." Red turned and glared at Stuart without taking off her headset.

"David's experienced," Andy said.

Red rolled her eyes and turned back to the radio while Angel continued gazing over Stuart's head.

"Dang it, Angel. You're reading my cloud," Stuart said.

"So, what are we doing?" Andy asked. "I think I got a little lost somewhere."

"If David trailed us, he could be our backup," Red said.

Andy's eyes widened. "I don't think David could trail you."

"You're probably right, honey," Red tittered, and Andy's face reddened.

"I have earbuds. Red should listen to a handheld with earbuds," Angel said. "The attackers will tell us where they are."

"They complain about everything," Red added.

"Tell David he'll trail us," Angel said. "That will give you your answer."

As Stuart and Andy reached the hallway, Doc said, "Can you gather everyone for our semi-auto lesson?"

"Won't take us long," Stuart said. He strode to David and Peyton's room while Andy gathered everyone else.

"Peyton said no, but I can go," David said.

Stuart chuckled. "Sadly, that makes sense to me. David, if Angel and Red were the scouts, could you trail them as their back up?"

Peyton pursed her lips and raised her eyebrows at David as his brow furrowed.

Got my answer.

David sighed. "I'd like to say yes, but I'd have to ask them to come find me before they headed back to the house."

Peyton nodded. "That would be too embarrassing."

"If I wait for them near the fence line, I'd at least be closer if they needed back up," David said. "Do we have any earbuds? I'd like to listen to a handheld too."

"We'll get you some; Angel had the same idea for Red. Let's join the others for our rifle lesson."

After Scott joined them, Stuart said, "I'll need to step away for a few minutes after Noel explains the semi-autos. Angel and Red discussed possible positions for our shooters. Here's their sketch."

Scott grinned as he took the paper.

After everyone was in the hallway, Stuart called up the stairs, "Noel's ready."

"We hear hallway conversations clearly," Red said.

Noel smiled then quickly reviewed the operation of the semi-auto. After he finished, he asked, "Any questions?"

"Do you have enough for everyone?" Sandra asked.

Noel nodded. "Everyone that wants one. Stuart, did we want to decide on our positions?"

Stuart nodded. "Cal, would you take over the radio for Angel and Red? Tell them David will need earbuds."

"Heard you; got it," Red said.

After Cal went upstairs, Angel and Red slipped downstairs, and Stuart and David met them in the kitchen.

Noel discussed the diagram he'd drawn of the house and pointed out the windows that provided defense against the attackers then handed the diagram to Scott.

"I can draw up a list to assign each person, but I'd be happy to hear where you'd like to be," Scott said.

While the discussion continued, Stuart whispered to Angel and Red, "I'll be south of the barn with a handheld, and David will take a position near the fence to back you up with a handheld. Go with David until you see where he'll be. If you need us, call us."

Andy joined them while Stuart spoke.

Red smiled and kissed him on the cheek. "Thank you, honey, for your support," she whispered.

Andy rolled his eyes. "Like I had a choice."

When Stuart finished, Angel hugged him. "What Red said."

Stuart chuckled as he returned her hug.

Red said, "Let's go."

The girls headed out the door, and David hurried to follow them.

"What do we do now?" Andy asked.

"Join the discussion in the hall."

Scott smiled when Stuart and Andy joined them. "So far, Doc and Noel have chosen their windows. They're going to be at the two windows in Peyton and David's corner bedroom, so they'll cover the south and the west."

"David wants to be in the barn loft, and I'll take the upstairs storage window," Stuart said.

"The diagram shows me at the kitchen window," Sandra said.

"I'll join Sandra there, so we can switch off kitchen duty," Blanche added.

Stuart nodded. *Blanche wants to make sure we have a semi-auto at that window.*

"I'll be in my bedroom, so I can back up the kitchen," Cal said.

"I'll take the upstairs windows in my corner bedroom that face south and west," Andy said.

"Peyton, I'd like for you and me to cover the front and float. If we're attacked from the south, you go to the middle bedroom, but

I'll stay in the living room. If I start shooting, join me. Red will be upstairs to back up Andy or us, if we need it," Scott said.

"Any adjustments?" Stuart asked.

When no one spoke up, Noel said, "Come to my room if you want a semi-auto."

"Save one for me." Stuart headed to the kitchen then left.

He hurried to go around the barn then stopped. *The barn loft.*

After he was in position, he used their simplex two and keyed the mic. "In the barn loft."

David replied, "Got it."

Nothing from the girls; they've gone silent.

Stuart listened to the birds and settled in to wait. *I hate this worse than sending Henry to Major's.*

The squelch broke as a man spoke on the commonly used simplex. "You going east or north?"

"Haven't you seen how everything's falling apart? My buddies and I are headed south."

"Wait up; we'll go with you."

Stuart switched his handheld to the same simplex channel. "We will too."

He smiled. *Might as well stir them up while I'm sitting around.*

"You're going too? We weren't sure what to do; we'll meet you at the state line," a man said.

"Hadn't thought about it, but we'll be there," another man said.

Stuart grinned as he changed his handheld back to his simplex channel two. *The more we can turn back, the better.*

Stuart snorted at Mr. Young's voice on the common simplex. "Saw the general heading west."

"I got family in Mississippi," Cal said.

I'm glad that's all we have on the radio.

"Cut the chatter," a new voice growled. "Just show up at the state line."

Stuart's eyes widened. *That was Leo.*

Stuart exhaled when he saw Angel, Red, and David head toward the barn. He waited until they ran into the brush behind the barn and scrambled down from the loft to meet them in front of the barn.

"What's the news?" Stuart asked.

"Let's go inside," David said.

"I'll relieve Cal." Red dashed upstairs, and Cal hurried down. He grinned when he saw Stuart, Angel, and David.

When Blanche saw them, she hurried to gather the rest of the team.

"Thanks to a little extra help, some of the attackers are deserting," Cal said.

"Extra help?" Scott asked.

Cal chuckled. "They were using the main simplex that everyone has always used to check in with a neighbor and talked about heading south. Stuart came on and chimed in, and that started a chain reaction from our team of ham operators. If I hadn't recognized Stuart's voice, I would have thought it was a Colonel or something in the General's army. Mr. Young said he saw the General going west, so I said I had family in Mississippi, but the best part was when Leo came on and told everybody to cut the chatter and just go to the state line."

Scott chuckled. "What a crew."

"So, we have the army splintering into groups that are sneaking away to the south or west, and the band that the general ordered to go east. What does that mean for us?" Sandra asked.

"A man who is trying to establish himself is leading a faction north towards us, which is better than missing us and going northeast to Major's and the Cabellos'," Angel said.

"Against the general's orders?" Noel asked.

"Yes," Angel said.

"We still have a group that will attack us. When?"

"They aren't that far away. I would guess within the next thirty minutes."

Andy dashed upstairs; Angel and Stuart followed him into the radio room.

"Red, call Uncle Leo on simplex two; tell him I'll come get him and Aunt Jennie in 48-4 right away because we're going to be attacked in thirty minutes."

Red keyed her mic. "Uncle Leo. Attack in thirty minutes. We'll come get you."

"No. Tell my nephew we're okay."

Andy dropped into the chair next to Red. "What do we do?"

"We can't take enough people to drag him out, and that would be the only way to get him here," she said.

Angel put on the headset. "They'll smash all your radios."

She set down the headset. "Go. He'll have his radio disassembled by the time you get there. Take David because you'll need to carry Jennie down the stairs."

As Andy and Red tore downstairs, Red shouted, "David, you're going with us."

The three of them raced out of the house with their rifles, then Andy flew past the front of the house in 48-4 with David in the front seat, and Red in the backseat.

Angel stayed with the radio, and Stuart went downstairs to the kitchen.

"What was that all about?" Scott asked.

"Angel convinced Leo to come to our house with Jennie." Stuart shook his head.

Peyton came into the kitchen. "Why did Andy drive like a banshee to the shortcut in 48-4 with David and Red? They went in front of the house; I thought we weren't supposed to go in the front. Where are they going?"

"They're going to pick up Leo and Jennie," Sandra said.

"If they didn't knock down the tree on themselves, they're fine," Scott said.

"I thought Leo refused to leave, and Jennie was too ill," Peyton said.

"We did, too," Doc said as he and Noel came into the kitchen.

"Angel told Leo the attackers would smash all his radios. We all need to get back to our stations and be in place. The attackers will be here in twenty minutes, and we need to be ready," Stuart said.

"Of course, it was Angel," Doc said as he and Noel hurried back to Peyton's room.

Cal chuckled as he headed to his room. "The rest of us were too polite and ignored the obvious. Lord, make me smart and literal."

"I'm taking David's place in the barn, Dad. Can you cover the storage room?"

"If you'll come back as soon as you see one attacker in the trees," Scott said.

Stuart dashed to the barn and climbed into the loft and scanned the field and the trees.

After he heard the roar of 48-4, he narrowed his eyes as he scoured the land south of his dad's property. When the engine stopped, Stuart scrambled down the ladder and rushed to 48-4.

"Anything?" David asked.

"No."

David and Andy gingerly lifted Jennifer by the improvised stretcher that was an old quilt and carried her to the house. Red dashed ahead of them and opened the back door. Stuart helped Leo out of the seat.

"Wait," Leo said. "All my equipment."

"I'll bring it in, if you can go inside by yourself."

Blanche rushed outside and took Leo's arm. "Come with me, old man. Stuart will make sure all your equipment goes into the house."

Leo's smile was weak. "Okay, old woman."

Blanche chuckled as she helped him into the house, and Stuart followed them with all the boxes he could carry. Peyton rushed outside and carried in the rest of the boxes.

"I'm going to the barn." David kissed Peyton then raced to the loft.

"Places, everyone," Red announced.

Stuart, Andy, and Red raced up the stairs. "I see them in the trees," David said on simplex channel two.

Stuart joined Andy in Andy's room. "I'll shoot with you until they get close to the barrier, then I'll shift to the storage room."

Andy nodded and took his position at the west window while Stuart took the east window in Andy's room.

"Wait until they're within your comfortable shooting range," Major said on the same channel two.

Stuart grinned. *Back seat driver. Major's perfect to coach our newer shooters.*

"Don't shoot at everyone. Pick one target and shoot." Major said. "Let one of the strong shooters shoot first then take down your target and pick another one. If they're rushing, and you're scared, pick one target and shoot. You've got this."

"Hell, yeah!" Noel shouted.

Everyone in the house echoed, "Hell, yeah!"

We've got this. Stuart picked his target then shot, and his man dropped. The rest of the attackers stared at the man, and after they dropped one after another, some ran toward the house, and some ran back to the trees. The attackers kept coming, firing at the house as they ran, and the house shooters dropped one man after another.

"Doc," Sandra called out from the kitchen. "Need some bandaging in here. Blanche was shot."

"Only in the arm; it's a flesh wound. Ms. Busybody wouldn't rub dirt on it for me," Blanche growled.

Stuart shook his head. *Only Blanche would come up with that.*

"Everybody be careful," Sandra said. "Don't be like Blanche."

"I'm coming," Doc Larkin chuckled.

"What was the name of that road?" a man asked on regular simplex.

"Meadows Lane," another man answered.

Oh no. Did Angel and Red just run down the stairs?

He rose then resumed his position and kept shooting.

"Did the girls go downstairs?" Andy asked after he shot and was getting ready to aim.

"That's what I thought. I'll check. Take the storage window if anyone gets close to the barrier."

Peyton met Stuart at the bottom of the stairs. "Angel and Red ran out the front door. Red said east, and Angel said north. What does that mean?"

"Did they say where they were going?"

Peyton shook her head.

"I'm hit," David said on channel two.

Peyton raced to the door, and Stuart chased after her. "Peyton, wait. You need back up and cover fire."

Sandra grabbed for Peyton before Peyton reached the back door, but Peyton eluded her and ran toward the barn.

"Need cover!" Blanche shouted as she began shooting and Sandra rushed to the other window.

Stuart stood in the doorway and shot a man who was aiming at Peyton, but a second man shot her, and she collapsed. The man who shot her dropped, and so did another man who was next to him.

A mob ran out of the woods toward the house as the men near the barrier turned to run as semi-automatic fire peppered them from more than one window on the south side of the house. Stuart ran out and half-carried, half-dragged Peyton into the kitchen.

"Take care of her, Mom; cover me, Blanche, I'm going to get David."

"Cal, clear the men in front of the barrier," Blanche called out.

The attackers either dropped or scattered to the trees to escape from the hail of fire from the south and upper east windows while some of the men running toward the house continued, and others turned back.

Stuart found David at the bottom of the loft ladder, and his radio was across the barn under the worktable. *David must have fallen when he tried to get down from the loft.*

David's skin was gray, and when Stuart reached under David's arms to lift him; David's skin was clammy.

"Can't..." David's breathing was raspy.

"I'm going to drag you into the house."

Stuart held onto David while he keyed his mic. "Coming in."

Stuart kept his head down as he dragged David to the door.

After they were inside the house, Blanche called out, "Stuart's inside with David."

Doc hurried to the kitchen.

"Cal and Scott are moving my bed to the living room. It's a safer room." Blanche cleared her throat.

"How is he?" Doc asked.

"He has a chest wound. The bullet may have nicked a lung because he's struggling to breathe."

Scott lifted David's feet. "Blanche's bed is in the living room. Let's take him there."

After Stuart and Scott placed David on the bed, Sandra joined Doc. "I'm your nurse, Doc," Sandra said.

Doc Larkin rubbed his face. "This might be beyond me."

"Where's Peyton?" Stuart asked.

Tears welled in Sandra's eyes, then she shook her head and pointed to the sofa where a body was wrapped in a soft, old quilt. She quickly turned her attention to Doc and David, and Scott and Stuart walked into the hallway.

"Dad, I think Angel and Red went to find Major; I need to bring Phil's son here. He was an emergency department doctor in Atlanta, but that leaves you short five shooters," Stuart said.

"We'll manage," Scott said.

Andy raced down the stairs. "I'm your driver."

"Listen up," Scott called out as he stood in the hall. "Angel and Red left, and Stuart and Andy need to bring Doc some help. We're going to be down six shooters. Can we manage?"

Everyone was silent until Noel said, "We surprised them with more force than they expected; we can hold them."

"Hell, yeah!" Blanche shouted.

"Hell, yeah!" the others answered, including Scott.

"Hell, yeah." The weak voice of a woman in Blanche's room echoed the others.

"Dad?" Stuart furrowed his brow.

"Jennie's in my old soft chair next to an open window with her favorite carbine, and Leo is with Noel," Scott said. "We're on channels one and two."

Stuart grabbed a sturdy long-sleeved shirt from the hook in the utility room.

"Hit it, cowboys!" Blanche shouted, and Stuart and Andy bolted out the front door to 48-4.

The team at the house kept the attackers busy as Andy and Stuart sped up the driveway in 48-4.

"After we reach Major's, take Scooter back to the house. I'm going to back up Angel and Red," Stuart said.

"You know where they are, don't you?" Andy glanced at Stuart.

"I'm certain they went to help Major."

When they reached Major's driveway, Jack and Scooter were waiting for them next to Number 48.

"Scott called us on channel two and told us what was going on, so we thought we'd save a few minutes," Jack said.

After Scooter jumped into the passenger's seat of 48-4, Andy floored the accelerator, and they roared away toward the Newton farm.

"Are you going to find Major?" Jack asked. "Jump in."

As they rushed up the driveway, Stuart said, "I think Angel and Red are with him."

"No doubt," Jack said.

Before Jack stopped Number 48, Stuart jumped out and ran to the shortcut then toward the deer trail that was west of the Cabello house. *Angel and Red would have used the trail to go to Meadows Lane. I just hope I don't have to crash through the brush to get there.*

He trotted until he was in the brush then slowed because of the amount of noise he made as he crushed leaves and sticks underfoot in his rush. *Doesn't hurt to catch my breath and slow down my heartrate a bit too.*

Before he was close to the dilapidated group of cabins, he froze and listened. *Silence. Angel's north of the lane; Red's east.*

He keyed his mic and whispered, "Southeast corner." A single click of a squelch break answered him, and he continued to creep toward the east side of a cabin at the end of the lane. When he peered around the corner, Major leaned on his stick as he stood at the edge of the lane next to the cabin west of Stuart's position. Stuart scanned the woods and brush but didn't see any sign of Angel or Red. *No surprise.*

"Well, Major. You didn't age as well as I thought you would," a man said.

"I'm kind of surprised to see you, Cliff; I always thought you were smart enough to go straight after you ruined your brother-in-law's career in law enforcement," Major said.

Stuart's eyes widened as another man crept behind Cliff.

"My sister was an idiot for marrying a cop; they got what they deserved," Cliff said with a sneer.

"How you doing, Cliff?" the man behind him asked.

Cliff's face paled then he faked a smile as he unholstered his gun and pointed it at Major then slowly turned. "Got him for you, General."

"Right." General narrowed his eyes. "You would never go behind my back, would you?"

General raised his pistol. "You've been trying to take over my army unsuccessfully for months. You aren't stealing Major from me, either."

Before General pulled the trigger, a shot rang out from the north, and General's eyes widened, then he slumped and fell face first into the dirt. When Cliff turned to shoot Major, Major swiftly pulled his gun from the holster and fired as a second shot sounded, and Cliff collapsed.

"Thanks for the help, girls." Major lowered his gun.

Stuart said, "I'm here too, Major."

"Of course, you are." Major grinned.

Stuart keyed the common simplex and said, "General and Cliff are dead. I'm getting out of here."

Mr. Young said, "The militia got 'em. Let's go while we can."

Angel and Red hurried to Major, and Stuart hugged Angel as he joined them.

"Why did you shoot General?" Stuart asked.

"Uncle Dan," Angel said.

"Thanks for the backup, Red," Major said.

Red narrowed her eyes at Major. "Does Aunt Vanessa know you came here?"

Major grinned. "Heck, no. I needed a little fresh air. Guess I can go back now."

"I have something to tell all three of you," Stuart said.

Angel stared over Stuart's head.

"It's bad, isn't it?" she asked.

Stuart cleared his throat. "David was hit when he was in the barn, and Peyton ran to rescue him, but she was hit and didn't make it. David was shot in the chest and was critical when I left, but Andy took Doc Scooter to help Doc Larkin."

"We have to get back," Angel said, then she and Red disappeared into the brush.

"I hate to hear that," Pops said. "I'm not saying anything to anyone at the house. I'll let you all decide how best to handle that."

"What do we do with those two?" Stuart pointed to the men on the ground.

"I'd say leave them here for the coyotes and the vultures, but you and Nate can take care of them tomorrow or the next day."

Stuart nodded. "Works for me."

"Have you been abandoned?" Major asked.

"No, they'll wait for me at the road." Stuart sprinted into the woods then hurried down the deer path.

When he reached the road, he caught a flash of Red's hair as she and Angel raced toward the Newton farm, and he ran after them.

He stopped at his dad's driveway and listened. *No gunfire.* He ran down the driveway, and Angel waited for him near the end of the driveway.

When the two of them went into the house by the front door, Andy said, "Red told us Major's okay, and she'd tell us the rest later; she went to check on David."

When Red returned, she said, "David's much better. Sandra said David's lung collapsed, so Doc Larkin put in a chest tube, then Doc Scooter hooked it up to a small battery-operated pump Doc Larkin had to help pull out the blood. Doc said the bullet must have hit a rib because he can feel the bullet; the rib must have punctured David's lung. Before Doc Scooter takes out the bullet, David wants to tell Brandon about Peyton."

"I understand," Stuart said.

"Ask Louisa to return with the children," Angel said.

"Usual escorts?" Scott called from upstairs.

"Yes."

"I'll call," Cal said from the hallway near the back bedroom.

"Go," Scott said.

Angel and Red left, and Andy and Stuart rushed out behind them.

When Andy and Stuart neared the entrance to the Cabell house, they heard Louisa's car as it came down Major's driveway, then Angel and Red came to the road. Red waved as she and Angel rushed toward the Newton Farm. Andy and Stuart waited until Louisa turned onto the road, then they followed her.

Louisa sped up as she drove down the road, and Stuart and Andy ran at top speed to Scott's farm. When they reached the house, Louisa and her two children were unloading the car.

Angel and Henry were standing together in a hug; Stuart rushed to hold them as tears streamed down Henry's face, and Angel's tears overflowed and spilled onto her cheeks.

"Red took Brandon inside." Louisa furrowed her brow as Andy strode to her.

Andy whispered to Louisa, and her eyes welled up as she turned to Mandy and Jimmy. "Uncle Andy told me sad news. We'll go inside and talk with Daddy."

"I'll bring in the backpacks," Andy said as he followed them.

Henry looked up at Stuart. "Mama Angel told me Aunt Peyton died, Dad. I'm sad."

"I understand; we'll all miss Aunt Peyton," Stuart said.

Henry nodded as the tears continued to stream down his face. His lip quivered, then he wiped his nose with his sleeve and sniffled. "Aunt Peyton was fierce and smart. When she said we learned skillful negotiations, Brandon asked her what that meant, and she showed us how to look up words we didn't know in Mama Sandra's big dictionary, so we could be smart too."

"We'll go inside; we all need to be together, and everyone can hear stories about Aunt Peyton," Angel said.

As the three of them held hands and strolled to the house, Henry said, "Yes."

When they were inside, Sandra rushed to Angel and Henry and hugged them. She swiped at her tear-stained face, but the tears kept streaming down.

Henry headed toward the living room, and when Stuart moved to stop him, Scott shook his head.

Brandon met Henry in the hallway. "My mama died. My daddy is hurt bad, but Doc said he'll be okay."

"I'm sorry," Henry said.

After the boys went into the living room, Scott said, "We have to beef up our defense. We never want to have anyone in an unsupported position again, and we can't forget our two-person rule. Ever."

Stuart said, "After we have our service for Peyton, we need a meeting."

"It's exactly what Peyton would want us to do," Sandra said.

"Hell, yeah!" Jennie shouted in a voice that was strong for her, and Noel echoed, "Hell, yeah!"

ACKNOWLEDGMENTS

Huge thanks to my husband for his amazing patience, support, talented technical expertise, and guidance, to my editor for her encouragement, eagle eye for a stray comma.

Thank you for reading! *You keep reading; I'll keep writing!*

What to read next?

SEASON OF DANGER

GRID DOWN SURVIVAL SERIES, Book 6

The power grid and society collapsed years earlier, but spirits are high in the anticipation of a Christmas with snow at the four Georgia farms until impending danger looms. The powerful leader of a cartel targets all the families to die by Christmas Eve.

Subscribe to the newsletter!

Look for the Subscribe button on www.judithabarrett.com

ABOUT THE AUTHOR

Judith A. Barrett, award-winning author, lives in rural Georgia on a farm with her husband and two dogs. She writes post-apocalyptic science fiction, thriller, and cozy mystery novels.

When she's not busy writing, Judith is busy with farm chores, walking with her husband and dogs, or watching the beautiful sunsets from her porch.

Website   www.judithabarrett.com

Newsletter   *Subscribe* to her eNewsletter via her Website

Let's keep in touch!

www.ingramcontent.com/pod-product-compliance
Lightning Source LLC
Chambersburg PA
CBHW030749030726
47497CB00001B/207